How to Dance on the Moon

Laura Ginter

How to Dance on the Moon

Copyright 2013 by Laura Ginter
Cover Art Copyright 2013 by Laura Ginter
Inside Art Copyright 2013 by Laura Ginter

Cover Art and Inside Art by Mandy Main
Mandy Main Studios
Rancho Mirage, CA 92270

FIRST EDITION SOFT COVER

ISBN-10: 1494249200
ISBN-10: 1494249200

How to Dance on the Moon is a work of fiction. Names, characters, places and incidents are the product of the author's imagination. Any resemblance to actual persons, living or dead, events or locals is entirely coincidental.

All rights reserved. No part of this book may be used or reproduced in any manner whatsoever without written permission from the author, except in the case of brief quotations embedded in articles and reviews.

How to Dance on the Moon

For my Great-Aunt Bebe, who took in children
and raised them with love and kindness
to be exceptional people

For my Aunt Janet, who enjoyed dabbling
in the "less specific" arts and did not need a logical
explanation for everything in life

For my mother Bernice, whose spirit has
seen her through so many challenges, and has
made her an accomplished woman

For my father Warren, who still inspires me every day

For my husband Gary, who has hung in there
through this growth experience

Prologue

When Grace Summers was five years old, a lumpy, bug-eyed troll moved into her bedroom closet and built himself a nest. He was a nasty creature who liked to spit at Grace, wear her shoes on his ears, and flash his hairy bum. When she complained about the troll to her father, he gallantly went to her closet, stared at the floor and commanded the freeloader to build a home in someone else's bedroom.

Grace quickly grasped that her father did not actually see the troll, because the troll was not on the floor. He had stuffed himself into a space between two shoeboxes on the upper closet shelf, and was responding to his eviction by sticking his thumb in his eye. Rather than point this out, Grace nodded and accepted her father's proud declaration of success. She also decided to accept the creature's residency for the time being, until she could figure out what to do about it. That night she slept with her light on and a chair in front of her closet door.

Soon a second resident appeared. A snake with greasy black skin that emitted a soiled diaper odor. Grace found the snake coiled in the closet's deepest corner, staring at her with glowing red eyes and flicking a long, orange tongue. The snake was more horrifying than the troll, having the ability to push random pictures and words into Grace's head, then stop them, as though Grace were a television set the snake could turn on and off at will.

With the second closet resident's arrival, Grace decided to consult her Teen-a Doll about her growing problem. If anyone could tell her how to get rid of the troll and the snake, Teen-a Doll could. She always had practical advice.

As Grace slid a black sequined evening gown over the curves of Teen-a Doll's breasts, Teen-a Doll reassured Grace in a soothing, dulcet voice neither creature could hurt her because Grace had created them herself with a special magic. The same special magic her Aunt Bootie had. This magic had made the closet monsters invisible to others, and if she ignored the monsters, they would have no power over her.

Grace pulled black rubber pumps over Teen-a Doll's slender feet, then rubbed her thumb across the elegant face that all five-year-old girls imagined they will grow into, and thanked her doll for her advice. Teen-a glowed and asked if Grace wanted to hear a secret the troll told her. Grace nodded, and Teen-a said Grace's father was going to die, and her mother was going to abandon her, and Grace was going to grow up as Just-Grace-All-Alone.

Grace poked at the pink painted lips that made words without moving, and asked how the troll could tell Teen-a a secret when he had no tongue to speak with. When Teen-a-Doll laughed and reminded Grace dolls don't have tongues either, Grace smacked the top of her head and tossed her into to the closet with the troll and the snake.

Teen-a had revealed herself to be just another monster who belonged with the closet dwellers, but Grace correctly sensed the doll's explanation of her ability to see and hear what others could not, was accurate. Although she was too young to

How to Dance on the Moon

understand the physics of her gift, simple logic told her if she had made the monsters, she could make them go away.

Grace sat on her bed, closed her eyes and envisioned the troll and the snake and Teen-a clinging together on the floor of her brain. She imagined scraping them up with a grapefruit knife and squeezing them all into a gummy cluster in the middle of her head. Then she peeled the magic gift away from the walls of her skull like a label from a jar. She wrapped the clump of creatures inside it, and buried the whole mess deeply and surely inside a cranial graveyard in a back corner of her brain she would use to store unwanted pieces of herself forever.

When Grace finished, she rose from her bed and opened the closet door. The troll and the snake were gone, and Teen-a Doll was upside down on the floor, her head twisted backward, staring at Grace from between her shoulder blades with her dead, painted eyes.

Grace believed she had succeeded in ending her problem, but the source of her magic, her inbred gift of second sight, was as ancient as humanity itself. It originated from an extraordinary and metaphysically complicated gift she had inherited from her mother's family. At five years old, her gift was underdeveloped, and it manifested itself in a primal way. Lusty and tenacious, it was too deeply imbedded in her genes to be entombed. And it continued to live quietly inside her, its power leaking stealthily back after Grace became Just-Grace-All-Alone, and when her emotions weakened her character and made her vulnerable to harm.

Part 1

The Perils of the Pirate Princess

Bootie 1993

1.

Bootie Baxter was adept at understanding her tearoom's chatter and clatter. From the tinkling tea cups, shifting chairs and animated conversations, she could accurately interpret the wishes of her guests, sometimes before her guests themselves knew what they wanted. And halfway through lunch service, on that unusually busy Wednesday, Bootie paused from the bustle long enough to check on her servers and ensure nothing had escaped her attention.

Erline was delivering raspberry tarts to table two, and Faye was setting up tea at table four. First-time guests were sitting at table seven, the garden window, and Bootie made a note to introduce herself at her first opportunity. She stocked the dessert caddy and refilled water glasses, then loaded a bussing tray with dirty dishes and brought it to the kitchen.

Bobby, her kitchen helper, was emptying the dishwasher, and Bootie couldn't help but smile as she watched him bounce with a graceful, confident rhythm to the soft hip hop music coming from his boom box. "Bobby," she said, setting down the tray and wiping her hands on her apron, "where is Mrs.

How to Dance on the Moon 5

Wallaby?"

Bobby looked over his shoulder at Bootie. "In the garden eating the mint."

"But it's raining!" Bootie exhaled sharply. She left the kitchen through the back door and made her way down the stone path that ran along the building to the garden. Mrs. Wallaby was indeed under the spearmint, chewing off a leaf from a low stem. Bootie bent forward to grab the rabbit, but Mrs. Wallaby wriggled free and scurried behind a rosemary bush. Bootie extended her arms into the bush and as she swept Mrs. Wallaby into the crook of her arm, she fell sideways into the wet mulch.

Bootie managed to contain the fidgety rabbit as she rose awkwardly to her feet and tried to brush the mulch off her slacks and apron. A tap-tap-tap drew her attention to the garden window. From inside, her new guests at table seven were grinning at her and waving enthusiastically. Bootie shrugged and waved back, and her audience laughed. She rubbed her hand along Mrs. Wallaby's wet back and carried her into the kitchen.

"Here." Bootie held the rabbit out to Bobby. "Feed her real food, please." She released Mrs. Wallaby into Bobby's hands just as Faye bustled into the kitchen, dishes stacked on her forearm. A teacup slipped off the top and fractured on the floor. Startled, Mrs. Wallaby twisted herself free from Bobby's tenuous grip, dropped to the floor and hopped into the dining room through the open kitchen door.

Bootie swiftly followed the rabbit but stopped as all the tearoom lights turned off and the front door blew open. A wind gust whistled through the room, rattling teacups. At table six, strands of Mrs. Oglethorpe's hair came loose from her bun. Mrs. Wallaby bounded toward the open door, but to Bootie's relief, she stopped halfway to wiggle her nose at a crumb on the floor.

Bootie scrambled across the room and trapped the bunny

against the wall with her feet. The tearoom guests watched the drama with unconcealed amusement. Bootie pursed her lips and leaned forward to lift the rabbit, but jerked upright when the seat of her pants split. Cradling the rabbit to her chest with one hand, she covered her rear end with the other. The lights flashed on and the front door slammed shut, stopping the wind.

"Mrs. Baxter," said Mrs. Oglethorpe smoothing her mussed hair. I think you may have ripped your pretty red pants."

Bootie gave Mrs. Oglethorpe a quick nod, and, striding toward the kitchen, overheard one of the new guests at table seven remark, "I guess it's true what they say about all the curious things that happen at Bootie's Tea Room!"

****

Bootie handed the rabbit to Bobby. "Let's try this again."

Bobby acknowledged his boss with a grin, and Bootie retreated up the back kitchen staircase to her apartment, closing the bedroom door behind her. She removed her apron and stood in front of the full-length mirror mounted next to her closet, twisting her torso to see the tear in her slacks. She wondered dismally when her rear-end had become so bulbous. The rip running down the seam of the red slacks reminded her of an overwatered tomato that had split. She shuddered at the view she imagined providing her guests when she bent over to lift Mrs. Wallaby, even with the lights out.

Bootie straightened and gave a hard look at the petite, dark-haired woman who frowned back at her from the mirror. She examined her face the same way she would day-old teacakes, and saw the evidence of her own approaching expiration date. The sagging corners of her mouth, the wrinkles framing her cheeks, and the canyon-deep lines crossing her forehead all made it impossible to deny. She was both fat *and* old. Youth had shriveled from her body, and soon, middle-age would be a memory too. At fifty-seven years old, life was

How to Dance on the Moon 7

drying her up.

Bootie wondered if Eddie would have accepted her wrinkles, sags and generous rear end if he were alive. He had been just thirty-five years old when his Army helicopter crashed, making Bootie a childless widow at twenty-nine. Would he have aged any better? She would never know. Eddie's death would insure he would always have a young man's face.

Laughter wafted up from the tearoom. Bootie opened a dresser drawer and removed a pair of black slacks. As she slipped them on, she admonished herself for being bitter over a few lines and creases and some back seat padding. Her self-pity was even more unattractive than the wrinkles and fat. It reeked of vanity, and vanity was a luxury, suffered by women with too much free time. Instead of sulking, she should fix what bothered her. She could find a way to eat healthier, even if her guests were required to check their diet books and calorie counters along side their wet umbrellas at the tearoom's front door. She could exercise, too. Walk to the beach every day. A good skin moisturizer wasn't expensive. And maybe she could get her niece Grace to take her shopping for new clothes. It had been a long time since she had worn something with a grander purpose than hiding food stains.

Through the mirror, Bootie saw a black, cat-sized specter slide across the floor. She cursed under her breath as it nestled between the wall and her nightstand. Its features were typical of most haunts, bulky and umbral with vaguely human features. But this one was unusually animated, bouncing up and down from within itself like a sprung jack-in-the-box. Normally she would fret over a haunt appearing in her apartment. They often materialized at stressful times or as a precursor to trouble. But this one's energy most likely came from her self-indulgent fussing. She turned and flicked an indifferent wrist toward the inky blister. It seemed to understand it would receive no attention and dissolved into the floor.

Bootie retied her apron and descended the staircase back to the kitchen. Someone had swept up the broken cup. Bobby was refilling the dishwasher, and Erline was carefully arranging a finger sandwich tray. Bootie watched Erline fuss over her tray and wondered if her friend ever fretted over getting older.

Erline, too, was approaching sixty, but in her youth she had been a tomboy, the girl picked first for a sports teams and last for a dance. Although Erline's body had lost its athletic tone, it still lacked curves. But Erline had married young and her husband still fussed over her. Bootie watched Erline tuck a strand of white hair behind her ear and concluded Erline probably had a more pragmatic attitude toward old age, which had to be life's cruelest stage after puberty.

Erline turned and saw Bootie looking at her. "Where did you go?"

"I changed my slacks." Bootie glanced around the floor. "Where is Mrs. Wallaby?"

"Back outside," Erline said. "We can't have any more rodent races in the dining room today."

Bootie rolled her eyes. "Rabbits are not rodents. Did she get to eat?"

Erline glanced up from her sandwich tray. "Yes, but you shouldn't feed her, Bootie. She's a wild animal."

"She is not a wild animal." Bootie allowed annoyance to creep into her tone. "She is my pet."

Erline snorted more loudly than Bootie had thought necessary, and crossed the kitchen to the cooler, removing a chicken salad. "I heard the words ''Rabbit' and 'Health Department' coming from table three. You need to do some damage control. And Janice Oglethorpe is complaining about the coffee again."

Bootie bristled. "Remind Mrs. Oglethorpe this is a tearoom, not a coffee shop."

"She says coffee shouldn't taste burnt."

"She should go to Starbucks then. I have more important

How to Dance on the Moon 9

things to worry about."

"More important than pleasing Mrs. Oglethorpe?"

"Yes," Bootie said, adding, "I am concerned about my health."

Erline carried two bowls over to the soup crock. "Why? Are you sick?"

"No. But my rear end looks like a balloon and my face like a prune Danish. Gravity is pulling my cheeks down to my chin, and my breasts are getting awful close to my belly button."

Erline ladled soup into the bowls. "Bootie, don't be so hard on yourself. You look great for a woman your age."

"What do you mean 'for a woman my age'?" Bootie crossed the room and, for no other purpose than to annoy Erline, flipped open an egg salad finger sandwich.

"Well, you're not a kid."

"Mrs. Baxter," Bobby interjected, slapping his own rear end and grinning. "From the back you could be one of my girlfriends."

Bootie glared at Bobby. "Good grief, Bobby, is that supposed to be a compliment?"

Erline went back to her sandwich tray, repaired the egg salad fingerling and looked up at her friend. "Bootie, I'm busy. Can you whine after lunch, or call Grace?"

Bootie frowned at her niece's mention. "I should check in with Grace. She has a hard week coming up." She glanced around at the chaos in her kitchen, absorbing the consequences of a busy lunch. Bruised cabbage leaves had spilled onto the floor near the garbage can. Napkins fanned across a counter like a discarded deck of cards. A plate with a half-eaten salad balanced on a dishwasher rack.

Erline shifted her hand under the sandwich tray and lifted it. "Bootie, take those soups to table three and pacify those ladies. Should I tell Mrs. Oglethorpe she must get her coffee at Starbucks, or do you want to? And when are you getting a handyman in here? Everyone thinks you made the lights go out and the door open for their amusement. They're all still cackling over it."

"I don't care what everyone thinks." Bootie threw her hands up. "Why are we so busy today? It's a Wednesday!"

Erline lifted the salad with her free hand. "Don't ask me," she said. "You're the psychic." And with a controlled swing around, she went out the door.

Bootie watched Erline leave before yelling belatedly, "Don't call me psychic!" She rinsed her hands and dried them on her apron, and when her frustration was in check, she entered the dining room and delivered the soups.

Erline waved her over to the cash register. "I need change for a twenty," she said. "There are no ones in the till."

"Look under the tray," Bootie said.

"Aha! Thank you."

Erline counted out her change and tried to step away, but Bootie blocked her path. She spoke in a low voice. "So everyone thinks I created a commotion to entertain them?" Erline crinkled her nose and nodded. "That's great! West Seattle is too small. They'll be telling that story for a month."

"Bootie, people see you answer questions before they ask them, and address people you've never met by name. I know you don't want your guests to know your secret, but they are always going to test you. As long as you are careless and let things slip, they will talk."

Bootie brushed off a mulch chip still dangling from her apron. "Did I tell you a woman yesterday crossed the street when she saw me coming?"

Erline sighed and patted Bootie's arm. "You are having a tough day, aren't you? Let's do something fun after work. *Sleepless in Seattle* is playing at the Admiral Theater."

Bootie brightened. "I'd like to see that."

"We can have a good cry over something other than your backside and wrinkles and how your guests misunderstand you. It's a date?" Bootie nodded, and Erline stepped aside and

How to Dance on the Moon 11

bustled off with her change.

****

The tearoom was running smoothly again, the drama caused by the lights and the door and Mrs. Wallaby's dash through the dining room was forgotten. Bootie leaned against the hostess stand and glanced around the room, taking a moment to enjoy the cozy comfort radiating from the mismatched teacups, pots, and knickknacks that commingled on the tables, shelves and windowsills and defined the tearoom's ambiance.

A glint of light drew her attention to a cream-colored antique teapot perched on a high shelf near the kitchen door. With its gilded rim and fine china frailty, the teapot looked more like an antique boudoir decoration than a vessel for holding water. A peculiar glow, soft and lemony, emanated through its porcelain shell like moonlight behind a cloud. Bootie looked away before the teapot could stir her emotions. She pretended not to see Mrs. Oglethorpe waving for her attention as she worked her way back to the kitchen for some more raspberry tarts.

It pleased Bootie to see Bobby scraping food scraps into Mrs. Wallaby's bowl for her dinner, even though she hadn't asked him to do it. She was proud of the boy. He was a tough, resilient West Seattle street kid who had lived on his own since he was fourteen years old. When Bobby had applied to be Bootie's cook, Erline had insisted on giving the high school dropout a chance, and the natty-haired boy with the sharp wit and unexpectedly strong work ethic had become the favorite son of their eclectic tearoom family. "Thank you, Bobby," she said.

He glanced over his shoulder. "You're welcome. For what?"

For being you, she wanted to say. *For reminding me how*

life can still pleasantly surprise you. For caring about Mrs. Wallaby. For making me smile when you dance in my kitchen. "For complimenting my backside." Bootie patted herself on the butt before adding a slice of pecan pie to her tray of tarts to give Janice Oglethorpe as a peace offering.

2.

The entry bell jingled and Bootie looked up to see Erline's granddaughter Ashley enter with her friend Polly. Tall and slim, Ashley was a Seattle University student with long blonde-streaked hair. Polly, Ashley's roommate, was a shy girl who barely reached five feet in height and wore her brown hair short with red highlights. A stream of animated chatter flowed between them, each girl devoting her full attention to the words of the other. Their youth created an enthusiasm for every detail of their lives, and to watch them, with their unlined faces and flawless skin tone on a day when Bootie was brooding over the loss of her own bloom, was bittersweet.

Bootie was about to call out to the girls when she noticed a flurry of energy surrounding Polly. Little lights flitted within that energy, like sparks off a fire. A shadow formed around the lights and extinguished them. Bootie lowered her eyes, and when she looked back, the shadow was gone, and Polly's sunny aura had returned.

"Ashley! Polly!" Bootie called out. The girls responded with broad smiles.

"Hi, Miss Bootie!" Ashley waved as Bootie crossed the room to join them.

"What brings you here on this rainy spring day?"

"My mom wants me home tonight," said Polly. "I think my

How to Dance on the Moon 13

dad might be flying in from Guatemala. Did you know my dad's a captain in the army?"

Bootie did know this about Polly's father, but wasn't sure if she had ever been told. That happened to her a lot.

"I'm driving her to Tacoma," said Ashley. "We decided to stop first and say hi." She glanced past Bootie. "Where is Grammy?"

"Making salads, I think." Bootie led the girls to a table near the kitchen. "Take off your raincoats. Would you like menus?"

Ashley looked at Polly, who shook her head. "Thanks, but we're not staying long."

Bootie plopped into the vacant chair at the table. "It's been a crazy day." She slipped her shoes off her heels. "So, Ashley, how is Gus?"

Ashley blushed. "Really good, Miss Bootie. He graduates in two weeks."

"I know! Very exciting! And Polly? Is there a special man in your life these days?"

Polly shrugged. "Not really."

Ashley reached across and hit Polly on the arm. "Polly likes this guy Joe in her math class, but she's too afraid to find out if he likes her too."

Polly's eyes grew large. "No, Ash! I know he doesn't like me."

Ashley tilted her head coquettishly. "Hey Miss Bootie, maybe you could use your psychotic powers to find out."

"You mean psychic powers," Polly corrected her friend.

Bootie looked sternly at the girls. "What makes you think I'm psychic? Or psychotic?"

Ashley looked surprised. "Everyone knows it. Maybe you could read Polly's tea leaves."

"Ashley!" Bootie started to explain that tea leaf reading was a scam used to prey on vulnerable, troubled people, but she hesitated. Normally, using her gift to see inside someone's life was a felonious breach of her rules, and the outcome could be unpredictable. But what harm would there be in sneaking a peek into Polly? If it appeared Joe was interested, she could find a way to give Polly the confidence to talk to him.

Bootie said, "Polly, I can't read your tea leaves but you are a very pretty girl, and smart." Bootie clasped Polly's hand. Images whirled randomly and slowly came into focus. Polly and a boy with a twin brother. But not Joe. "My instincts tell me you are going to meet someone soon. And my experience tells me when it happens you won't have to wonder about his feelings toward you."

Abruptly, sharply pointed pictures flashed over the benign ones. Bootie's head filled with pictures of trees and screaming men, and she smelled burning rubber. "Your father," Bootie said, and a sharp pain shot through Bootie's chest. Her stomach clenched, and she tasted blood. Polly let out a squeal, and Bootie realized she was squeezing the girl's fingers. Polly's hand burned within Bootie's grip like hot metal, and she released it and stood.

"What were you going to say about my dad?"

A grey haunt hovered over Polly's shoulder. The haunt that had nested in her room earlier. The figure that had lurked around Polly when she had first arrived. Bootie's nightmare that never completely went away. "Nothing," Bootie said. The haunt had a face now, distorted, long, thin, and misty black, with white, empty holes for eyes. Its mouth was round, the size of an apple, contracting and expanding as though breathing. Then it was gone, but the tragic sadness in its energy filled the space for a few more seconds.

When Stella came into the dining room, Bootie called to her, and then excused herself. She fled to the kitchen and up the staircase to her apartment. Thick, angry tears blurred her way. She stumbled on the top stair and banged her knee. Closing the door to her bedroom, she pushed her abandoned red pants aside and sat on the mattress.

Bootie massaged her injured knee and replayed her vision

How to Dance on the Moon 15

in her mind. She had seen the pictures of Polly's father, on special assignment in a Guatemalan jungle, dodging gunfire, and a teenage guerilla fighter, hiding behind a tree, shooting him through the heart, killing him. Dressed in fatigues and overcome with nobility, the young soldier was not going to college or worrying about relationships. He was hiding in his mother's home from the Americans, and the vision suggested the young man would soon be killed too, resisting arrest. An army priest had notified Polly's mother of her husband's death earlier that day.

The lights dancing around Polly earlier had been a flag, a giant red stop sign in front of a precipice with no guardrail, warning something bad was ahead, and Bootie stupidly had walked past it. Why had she weakened? Nothing good ever came from using her gift. If she had learned about Polly's father later, from Ashley, it would have been sad, of course, but she wouldn't have physically experienced a family's anguish, or the intense emotion of a teenage guerilla fighter, or a bullet piercing a heart.

She hated her gift for visions. She hated when one sucked into her mind without warning as this one had with Polly. She hated the controlling energy that forced her eyes to look at ugly pictures, like a demon needing exorcism. She hated suffering through the pain and horror of violence. She hated the haunts and the lights and the auras. And mostly she hated having so little control over any of it.

The rainclouds had passed, and sunlight now illuminated the space where the haunt had appeared earlier. Kitchen noises filtered into the bedroom, reminding Bootie she was needed downstairs, but the pain that crushed her chest immobilized her.

Bootie reached up to her CD player, set on a shelf over her window, and switched it on. It had been a gift from Grace, her sister Sellie's daughter, given to Bootie the week before Grace's husband Stephen had driven his car into a tree. He had been

Laura Ginter 16

forced off the road by a drunk driver, and killed almost two years ago. Another violent, wasted death.

The melody of "Mister Me and Missus You" from an Irish classics collection filled the room, and Bootie thought about Eddie, who sang the song to her when she was Polly's age.

Mister me and Missus you, with you I will stay, to you I'll be true. Though our lives will go by our love will never die, it will always be you and me, a love song for two, Mister me, Missus you.

She forwarded the CD to the next song. Her evening was difficult enough without thinking about Eddie singing Mister Me and Missus You. Or about Stephen.

The song "Mo Mhathair's Apron Pocket" began to play, and the phantom aroma of macaroni and cheese casserole filled the room, slicing through her morose thoughts like a knife releasing puss from a blister. Bootie closed her eyes and saw her childhood home, the New Hampshire lake house. Her shoulders relaxed. Instead of gunshots, she heard her brothers splashing into the lake and from their rope swings and hollering Indian war cries as though she were standing on the beach watching them. She thought about each of her siblings, Woody and his comic books, Bernice's secret teenage romance, Sellie's perfect curls and cheeks made pink with watercolors, Scooter's sticks, Ike's little songs, and Clark's stories. Especially Clark's stories.

Her room darkened as clouds again filled the sky. Bootie rose and put on a sweater. She crossed to her window and looked down into her garden. Mrs. Wallaby was under the spearmint again, and she watched the bunny chew her late afternoon snack. Erline had said Mrs. Wallaby was a wild animal. Although Bootie had argued the point, Erline was right. No one would ever tame her rabbit. But Mrs. Wallaby was not without self awareness. She was a resilient survivor who chose freedom over human companionship. Wasn't life about choices? Or was she fooling herself about that?

The stairs to her apartment creaked, and Bootie remembered her movie date. She jumped up and reached for her lipstick tube on her dresser. As she drew the lipstick across her lips, the face of aging Bootie disappeared from the mirror, replaced by her child-self, the little girl who grew up on a bucolic New Hampshire lake. Bootie smiled.

Henry Kurz 1907

3.

The little house on the lake had sat snuggled among the farmlands and rolling hills of New Hampshire's central lakes since Otto Kurz built it in1895. Originally, it was a ten-acre farm, small, but workable for one man as long as there was capable seasonal help. Otto Kurz had four cows, a barn, chicken coops, an apple orchard and a small cornfield. He also had a bad temper and was mean to his animals. Otto's neighbors avoided him, but he did not notice their lack of hospitality. Social frivolities were wasted on him. He believed people respected him as a hardworking, honest man, devoted to God and his church, and he expected nothing else from anyone.

Otto first saw Madeline Rawson on the front steps of Saint Mark's Episcopal Church in Ashland in 1905, sitting next to a crushed felt hat, a leather suitcase, and a long white, strappy cloth for which Otto couldn't identify a purpose. She was thin and wore a feather-light cotton dress with a lace neckline. Her peach blonde hair hung loose around her shoulders. Although Otto had never seen a society woman, he did recognize she was fancy. She smelled pretty even from a distance, and looked clean and polished up, like a silver spoon.

The girl sat slumped on the church step, her head cupped in her hands, deep in thought. Something about her thin, down-turned mouth and boney wrists pushing into her strangely pink cheeks attracted him and affected his manners. After staring at her for a time, he made a gesture completely out of character. He removed his hat and said hello.

Fumbling his way through conversation, he learned the young woman was seventeen years old and from Boston. Her mother had recently died in a collision between an automobile and a horse buggy, and she had run away from home with $300 after a terrible, terrible fight with her father. She had boarded the first train leaving Boston. The train had made her stomach queasy, and she had disembarked in Ashland, and now she did not know what to do.

At her soliloquy's end, she sighed deeply and pulled on a strand of her hair. Otto nodded, as though he cared about what she had said, but all he heard was how she was seventeen years old, and had three hundred dollars. Had Madeline understood that three hundred dollars was a substantial amount of money to a New Hampshire farmer, she might have kept that information to herself, and Otto would have left her sitting on the step after awkward words of regret. Her future would have most likely involved a train ride back to Boston.

However, Otto was lonely, and the girl was at the proper age for marrying, breeding, and working a farm. She was bony and wouldn't eat much. She didn't seem afraid of him and had no moles on her face. And with three hundred dollars, he could buy a couple of bulls.

Otto offered to find Madeline bed and board while she sorted things out. Madeline was wary of accepting his help, but her circumstances left her few options, and she let Otto take her to Breyton Kennedy's farm, which bordered Otto's to the south. Otto introduced Madeline to Breyton, his wife Sylvia

How to Dance on the Moon 19

and the six Kennedy children, and she stayed with the family while Otto courted her.

Madeline didn't care much for Otto, who she saw as a crass old man. But there were things about Ashland that made her want to stay, her growing affection for Breyton Kennedy mostly. Otto provided an avenue to Breyton's company and discreet attention. After six weeks, she married Otto and moved into his farmhouse. Because Otto had no interest in his new wife's circumstances, he never learned that Madeline Rawson was the only child of Alexander Hamilton Rawson III of the Beacon Hill Rawsons, and heiress to the fortune her father had amassed in banking and investments with his brother, Wilber Burke Rawson, or he might have exploited his new bride even more. But he just took her money as a dowry and let her settle in.

Once married, Madeline quickly grew to loathe her husband, who worked her like a mule on a farm with no electricity. The chores around the house were demanding and seemingly endless. And when their son Henry was born, or Heinrich as Otto insisted on calling him, the boy did nothing to improve Madeline's spirits. She trudged through each day with the added responsibility of a child who needed food, clothing, and protection from his father's temper.

After eight years, Madeline received her retribution and her freedom when Otto Kurz died unexpectedly from a prolonged and grizzly goring by both his abused bulls. She had been reading with Henry on the porch when she heard her husband's screams and pleas for help, as the animals teamed up to inflict as much damage on the man as possible.

Madeline did not try to save Otto. She did not seek help from a neighbor, nor try to distract the animals. She allowed the slaughter to play out. But not because she hated Otto, or because he was abhorrent to her, but because after eight years of marriage, Otto had never bothered to call her by her name. She was woman or frau or hei, and that was all. She told herself she would save him if he called out for "Madeline". But she knew he wouldn't, and he didn't.

Madeline put down the book and pushed on Henry's ears and sang loudly, blocking Otto's screams and the sounds of the bulls gutting and slashing him into chunks of kibbled flesh the way one would block out a blaring alarm clock on a Saturday morning. Later, Breyton Kennedy removed the body parts and washed away the blood.

****

Although Madeline did her best to pretend to mourn, she reveled in her liberation. At twenty-five, she was still beautiful and young enough to start a new life. And she was finished with serving a foul old man who neglected her and bullied her son, treating him even worse than his animals. But she didn't want to move back to Boston. She could not imagine leaving Breyton, the one man she had ever truly loved, for fear her heart would give out, and she'd die of grief. Breyton encouraged Madeline to stay on at the lake house. She was a sweet girl who doted on him when they were together, and asked for nothing. She knew how to be discrete, and he wasn't ready to quit on her yet.

However, Madeline had to find a way to fund her life in New Hampshire. She had no savings and no way to make money outside of farming, and she vowed never to pick another ear of corn. She decided to sell all the animals and equipment and most of Otto's land. With the money from the sales, she bought several expensive dresses with matching hats and gloves from the Sears and Roebuck catalogue, and a suit and bow tie for Henry. She also purchased two train tickets to Boston, but only one return ticket. She offered Alexander Hamilton Rawson III an heir in exchange for a trust fund. She knew he would not refuse, but it cost her Henry's companionship, and she lost forever her father's love, which

How to Dance on the Moon 21

she didn't want anyway, now that she was free from Otto and had Breyton to love her.

****

Alexander exposed Henry to all the comforts and pleasures afforded to the affluent. Henry attended a private boy's school in Boston, and was accepted into Harvard, despite mediocre grades. For a short time, Boston society considered him one of their most eligible bachelors.

But Henry had inherited his father's ill temper and introverted social tendencies, and his mother's bitter spirit, and he did not exploit his opportunities. His grades slipped to poor, and he blamed his indifferent mother for not preparing him more for his future, and his arrogant grandfather for not bringing him to Boston at a younger age. He would have quit school, but there could be no quitting. His grandfather had mapped his future. He was to get his business degree, and then work at his grandfather's investment company. It was the path to the presidency. It was his destiny.

Henry graduated from Harvard, thanks to a generous financial contribution to the Alumni club, and his grandfather gave him an office next to his. However, a series of events occurred in one long, painful year that redirected Henry's future. Beulah Flynn, the quietly lovely but peculiar daughter of immigrants who were house servants for Alexander, became pregnant by Henry. She married him after disavowing her family and her Irish heritage. Her parents disappeared into the South Boston slums. Weeks later the stock market crashed. Alexander Hamilton Rawson III lost his investment business, followed by his fortune. He lost his life when he had a massive heart attack. Soon after, creditors took Henry's home, and Beulah Flynn Kurz lost her baby.

Married, with no inheritance, no money and no options, Henry approached Uncle Wilber for a job. The Savings and Loan had remained solvent through the troubled times, and Uncle Wilber had grown even more affluent. But, unfortunately for Henry, Uncle Wilber had two sons who exhibited much more aptitude for business than Henry.

Wilber considered his nephew an uninspired man of average intelligence who would never excel or make a strong name for himself, and who had married beneath his social position. But Uncle Wilber did have sympathy for Henry's personal circumstances. He gave Henry a suitable but banal account management position, and allowed Henry and Beulah to move into a home he owned in Brighton, where the couple started their family again. Bernice came first, and Clark two years later, followed by three more children in three years, Woodrow (called Woody), Beulah (little Bootie) and Selma, who they nicknamed Sellie. William 'Scooter' Kurz was the last child born in Boston, arriving three years later, when the Japanese were loading their planes with bombs to blow up U.S ships in Hawaii.

When Scooter was two years old, the three youngest Kurz children contracted poliomyelitis. For Bootie and Sellie, the virus brought on symptoms comparable to a bad cold. Scooter, however, contracted a more devastating strain, paralytic poliomyelitis, and suffered permanent nerve damage in his legs. Luckily, he didn't catch the strain that affected the respiratory system. But with Scooter's exhaustive need for care and five other children to watch over, Beulah Kurz's health suffered. She blamed the bad city air for her son's illness, and begged her husband to move the family to the country before anyone else became sick.

Henry was a proud man, and not one to have his wife's demands pressure him. However, he grieved for his little boy, who struggled with leg braces when he was barely old enough to walk, and his helplessness made him sullen and difficult. He was also in debt for the first time in his life, but after twenty years of familial slavery, Uncle Wilber had prevented him from

How to Dance on the Moon 23

having the distinguished career he believed he had earned. If anything, his uncle had deliberately held him back. By leaving his job and his uncle's house, he would be independent of anyone's control, and he could build his professional reputation. Henry quit his job at the bank and fired his great-uncle from his life as his mother had done to his grandfather thirty years earlier. The Kurz family packed and left the city behind.

Despite Henry's actions, Uncle Wilber could not let go of his sense of responsibility for his nephew and family, and he created a trust fund with a monthly stipend to provide a comfortable life for them. But Henry would not accept charity from the man who had stifled his ambitions and demeaned his character. Madeline Kurz had died from an infection two years earlier, and the New Hampshire lake house was empty. Henry moved his family to the home where he had been born and had lived through his early childhood. Henry repaired the neglected house and updated the electricity, and the family settled in. A year later Beulah delivered another baby. Henry named his new boy Ike, after General Eisenhower, who had once visited Uncle Wilber at his home.

He found a job as a bank auditor with a salary that paid the bills but provided little extra money. The job also took him away from home on business trips and required him to work evenings after the banks had closed. Sometimes Beulah would accompany her husband on his trips, leaving the children in the care of Uncle Wilber's only daughter Theodora, who the children called Aunt Theo, and who migrated to New Hampshire's Lakes Region for reasons remarkably similar to her cousin Madeline's.

The house was small for the family of nine, but everyone had a niche. Henry and Beulah shared one bedroom while Scooter and Baby Ike had the other. Bernice had scratched herself out a closet-sized space under the attic stairs. She had partitioned it with a three-paneled room-divider and had decorated with pictures from magazines. The remaining four children slept on cots on the porch cooled in the summer by the breeze from the water, and warmed in the spring and fall by a Franklin stove. Canvas flaps attached to the porch screens trapped the heat. When the temperatures dropped and the winter winds became harsh, the children moved to the attic.

The barn was still in good repair, and a small plot remained for a garden, but Henry Kurz had no interest in farming. He had no happy memories of raising animals or cultivating crops. Beulah, however, loved the two apple trees that remained on the property, and she spent her autumn months making applesauce, apple juice, and canned apple pie filling.

Despite the crowded living conditions, the little house at the lake proved to be ideal for raising a family. After Breyton Kennedy's death, his son Patrick became patriarch, and the Kennedy clan provided a passel of playmates. Aiden was Clark's best friend, Josephine was Sellie's age, and Filly Kennedy, the youngest son, was between Bootie and Woody in age. Patrick's oldest son, Mickey, was the boy Bernice was sneaking off to see at every opportunity.

Apart from some volatility between Henry and Patrick, the two families were close. Four years passed quietly and peacefully for the Kurz's in the house on the lake until that hot summer night, when an argument erupted during a tasty macaroni and cheese dinner.

Bootie 1948

4.

The last Saturday of summer vacation had been hot, muggy and pleasantly quiet for twelve-year-old Bootie Kurz, marred only by a fight with her brother Woody over a missing comic book he later found under his bed. Outside, the air was now cooling in the evening shade. Bootie washed the day's stickiness from her face in preparation for dinner. An excited twinge in her belly reminded her that her first day of junior high school was just three days away.

She sniffed the air, heavy with trapped afternoon heat, mixing with the smell of the buttery crispy cracker-topped macaroni and cheese casserole her mother was baking. Bootie skipped into the kitchen to the beat of her favorite song, "Mo Mhathair's Apron Pocket", playing on the radio. With a flick of her wrist, she dismissed the zebra only she could see lounging in the laundry basket by the porch door.

****

Young Bootie Kurz knew she saw the world differently than others, but didn't understand how. She didn't know why grownups praised her vivid imagination when she stroked a stray cat that sang songs, or why her brothers laughed at her for reaching up to snatch a fairy sparkle dancing over her bed. But one Saturday morning, while she was drying dishes for her mother, she finally gleaned insight into her unique viewpoint from a monkey-beast with yellow knickers and a red plastic clown hat.

The animal appeared with a silent *poof*. It was stretched out on its back on the kitchen table and shook in spasms, its arms and legs curling like ropes, as if they had no bones. They lashed out at her repeatedly, whipping the air and recoiling. Blood trickled from its nose to the table and evaporated with a sizzle, sounding like water droplets in a hot skillet. It grimaced and whimpered, and Bootie wondered if it was in pain.

The monkey-beast emitted no light from within itself, nor did it make a shadow on the table. It had a crisp outline, but a spongy, blurry middle. Bootie put her hand over it, wondering if it was safe to touch it. She was surprised to see its belly disappear, as though her hand was emitting a blinding light. The creature looked at her and exposed its teeth in a lipless grin. Startled, Bootie pulled her hand away, and the belly reappeared. She tried the trick again, moving her hand above the monkey's face. It, too, faded away, returning when she pulled her arm back. When she asked her mother if the bleeding monkey was going to die, Mother asked "what monkey?" And it vanished.

Bootie spent many hours trying to sort out what happened that morning in the kitchen, and concluded the monkey's body wasn't real. It was made only from light. Without a real body, it should not live. But it did. She could see it. That meant she could see what others couldn't. Invisible things. Satisfied with her logic, Bootie decided to learn how to sort the invisible things from the real things, so she could ignore them.

It was a year later, on a rainy, windy April afternoon when Bootie realized how certain pictures she saw in the middle of her head were also unique to her. These pictures weren't like the blurry, obscure images seen while reading a book or reliving a memory. Bootie's special pictures were vividly bright and colorful, and pushed inside her head independently from her will, as though they lived apart from her. If normal-thought-pictures were like shadows behind frosted glass, her living-pictures were like View-Master slides.

Her discovery came on a rainy afternoon. Father had come home grumbling about his feet, cold and wet because he had lost his rubber boots. A grumpy orange glow surrounded him.

How to Dance on the Moon 27

After Father patted her on the head, the living-pictures showed Bootie his boots were in the old barn next to the house where Father spent most of his time. He had removed them the day before to put on work shoes. Bootie could not retrieve the boots because a raccoon had moved into the barn and Father had forbidden the children to go inside. Instead, she described to him the exact spot where he could find them.

Expecting praise, Bootie was shocked when Father banished her to a chair at the top of the attic stairs to punish her for sneaking into the barn. She tried to explain how she had seen the boots in her head, but her explanation confused her father and made him angrier.

During the hour Bootie spent in that chair, she decided a living-picture, like the flailing monkey-creature, was probably something others couldn't see, and, therefore, couldn't understand. If sharing living-pictures could make Father this mad, she would never talk to him or anyone else about them again.

At nine years old, a most unfortunate event advanced Bootie's education further. Esther-Agnes Kennedy, Patrick Kennedy's seventeen-year-old daughter, was marrying a Navy man from Manchester. The wedding was supposed to be Esther-Agnes' most special day, but during the service, the light around Mr. and Mrs. Kennedy was foggy and gray. Probably, reasoned Bootie, because their daughter's new husband was leaving within the week to fight in the war in the Pacific.

While hugging the bride, Bootie had a vision she believed could change everyone's sadness into joy. She announced at the reception buffet that Esther-Agnes' baby, although still tiny as a fingernail, was going to be a girl, as Esther-Agnes hoped, and she would be named Nancy.

Upon hearing her secret exposed to the entire town, Esther-Agnes fled, sobbing. Her new husband fled too, in the opposite direction. At that moment, Bootie realized she could hurt people by sharing the living-pictures, and she decided she would never again use them to help someone. It was too unpredictable.

Through her childhood, Bootie struggled to understand the complexities of her abilities. Like a separate entity with its own heart and brain, fluid and flowing, her gift crested and ebbed like wind-whipped surf. Touch was always the catalyst for seeing visions, but it wasn't always required.

As she grew older, some aspects weakened or went away. The creatures she saw in her youth evolved into mere haunts or shadows. With practice and maturity, she learned how to touch people without pictures bombarding her, and to choose when she wanted to see something. She learned to interpret what she saw more accurately, and to hide it better, but she never fully controlled it.

****

Mother smiled as she plated dinner. The kitchen was too small to accommodate nine people for a meal. Only eight-year-old Scooter and two-year-old Baby Ike sat with the parents at the rectangular, Formica table pushed against the wall. Bernice, who was sixteen, and Sellie, who was eleven, ate at the pine table on the screen-enclosed back porch that ran the house's length. When the weather was warm, Clark and Woody, who were fourteen and thirteen, ate on the porch steps or carried their food down to the lake.

Earlier that summer, Bootie had begun eating her meals alone on a stool in the tiny kitchen pantry. She was the middle child of seven and slept in a room with three other siblings. She shared a dresser with her younger sister and had few possessions not handed down to her. But privacy alone did not make her favor a space barely wide enough to fit a stool. She could also listen to the radio during dinner, and, even better, she could eavesdrop on her parents' conversations. Bootie didn't know why, but she couldn't see pictures inside her

How to Dance on the Moon   29

mother as she could with everyone else. And Father's pictures hurt her head. Occasionally, her parents' discussions took a mature tone usually reserved for when they were alone. Mother and Father often forgot she was nearby. Baby Ike was too young to understand what they said, and they overlooked Scooter, as if his leg braces prevented him from comprehending their adult talk.

The radio music was muffling her parents' conversation as Bootie settled onto her pantry stool, but she didn't care. She was savoring her dinner. The slurpy, saucy noodles mixed with the texture and taste of the cracker crumb topping made her mother's casserole perfection on a plate. With each forkful, she let the cheese sauce coat her tongue and throat, and then she sucked on the noodles until they dissolved in her mouth. But her ritual was interrupted when abruptly the music stopped. The sudden silence made Bootie sit upright.

"You didn't need to turn off the radio," Bootie heard Father say to Mother. Her father's tone suggested her parents were arguing. "I was listening to you."

"No, you weren't, Henry." The tension in her mother's voice sat coarsely on the surface of her words. "I don't think we should go. I have a bad feeling. It's only been three weeks."

"We will lose the opportunity if we don't go tonight," Father said, sharply.

Bootie cringed. Go tonight? Were they going on a business trip?

Mother's voice shook. "You told me we were done."

Her father's chair scraped along the linoleum, and his footsteps crossed the kitchen floor. When he spoke again, he was outside the pantry door. "Beulah!" Father's shout echoed through the pantry. "You are being insolent!"

Bootie jumped up from the stool. Bootie's birth name was Beulah, like Mother's. Since she had never heard Father call Mother insolent, Bootie assumed she was the subject of his anger, maybe for listening to their quarrel. She stood to face

Laura Ginter 30

the consequences of her crime.

"Don't raise your voice," Mother said, her tone somewhere between a plea and a chastisement. "And don't call me insolent. I'm not a child."

Father's footsteps receded to the table. Bootie blew quietly through her teeth and sat back down.

Baby Ike whimpered. "Mama?" Scooter asked in a tentative voice. "Are you okay?"

"Scooter, you mind your own business," Father said. His tone mellowed, but Bootie could imagine the man waving a finger at the cringing boy. "So Beulah, you don't want to go because you have a bad feeling." His voice grew loud again. "You're sounding like your crazy mother. Touched in the head, like all the other women in your family. I thought her leaving would spare you."

A pan fell to the floor, clanging loudly. "Sorry," Mother said, not sounding sorry at all.

The noise seemed to hit a switch in Father's head, and his tone softened. "Beulah, please. You know I need you for this." His pleading was as foreign sounding to Bootie as Mother's defiance had been. "This will be the last time, I promise. But we must leave right after dinner."

Mother responded to Father's statement with a silence that filled the room like a toxic vapor, dissipating over several minutes. Bootie sucked on her last noodle.

Mother's shadow darkened the pantry wall. "Bootie?"

Bootie cringed at her mother's somber tone. "Yes, Mother?"

"You have dish duty." The shadow vanished without waiting for a response.

Bootie raised the plate to her mouth and stretched her tongue across its surface. Licking her lips clean, she rose from the stool and stepped from the pantry. Mother was refilling Father's coffee cup. and Baby Ike was singing a song of his own creation. Bootie looked at her mother for a clue as to her

How to Dance on the Moon   31

thoughts. Because Bootie's gift usually told her everything she needed to know about people, she struggled to read faces. Mother's was as expressionless as a stone slate

As far as Bootie was concerned, Beulah Kurz was the prettiest mother in all New Hampshire. Even prettier than Mrs. Kennedy who had once been Miss Weirs Beach. With a thin, straight nose and small bones, Bootie thought Mother resembled a pretty songbird from Clark's nature book. A Mourning Dove or a Nightingale. People said Bootie resembled her mother. Both had auburn hair, milk chocolate eyes and light, freckled skin. Both were also petite, unlike her sisters Sellie and Bernice, who were tall and more filled out, and growing into beauties in their own right, with the maple wood hair that was common in the Rawson bloodline.

Sometimes at night, Bootie would stroke her lucky rabbit's foot and wish she would grow up to be as pretty as her mother. Now, though, she would trade her rabbit's foot just to be able to see inside her.

Bootie stole a peek at her father. He was staring across the room, working a toothpick between his lips. His pale yellow aura implied he was distracted, and it encouraged Bootie to approach her mother. "Mother, did Father say you are going out tonight?"

"Yes, we are!" Father said behind Bootie, and she jumped, almost dropping her plate. Baby Ike was also startled into stillness, but his singing resumed with new fervor. "Take my plate to the sink, and tell Bernice to come get Ike. I want everyone in the living room in five minutes."

"Yes, sir." Bootie retrieved her father's plate, stacked it on top of her own, and placed the dishes into the sink before scurrying to the sleeping porch. Bernice, Sellie, Clark, and Woody had all overheard their parents' loud conversation, and, like Bootie, had been keeping quiet company.

"What was that all about?" whispered Sellie to Bootie.

Woody snickered. "What do you think? Bootie made

Father mad with her ugly face."

Sellie rolled her eyes. "No, stupid. What was the fight between Mother and Father about?"

Bootie shrugged and collected the empty plates from the boys. "Bernice, Father wants you to get Baby Ike, and everyone is to meet in the living room."

"I heard," said Bernice.

"And Sellie, you are supposed to help me with dish duty."

"You are a liar, Bootie!" snorted Sellie. "Mother didn't say anything about me helping you."

Baby Ike wandered onto the porch, and Bernice stood and lifted the boy to her hip. Sellie stood, too, and took the girls' dishes to the kitchen. Bootie followed them with her brothers' plates, and then brought Scooter his crutches. Together the children shuffled to the living room.

Mother had changed into trousers. A bad sign. With fading hope that she was wrong about her parents' evening agenda, Bootie slid next to her father and gently put her hand on his forearm. She was not wrong.

Father glanced sternly around the room. "I have a bank audit in Laconia tonight." When nobody spoke, he added, "Your mother is coming with me. Do you want something, Bootie?"

"No," Bootie said. She removed her hand from his arm and slipped over to the couch. She could see his lie revealing itself in his aura, no longer yellow but olive green.

While Mother was soft and delicate like a dove, Father bore the ferocity of a hawk. He was larger than life, with a giant head of pumiced red hair, and a hooked nose that pushed down his upper lip to give him a permanent scowl. He didn't waste words and rarely touched the children. When someone irked him, he would threaten to pull out the whipping stick, but he hardly ever used it.

Father was gruff, he was intimidating, he was distant and unaffectionate, and he was like most fathers she knew. In

How to Dance on the Moon   33

contrast to Mother, for whose attention Bootie competed with her six siblings, she gave Father plenty of room. She feared him. She also loved him, and knew he loved his family back. Although love was something he never expressed. Men were like that. That's what Father taught her.

"Is Aunt Theo coming over?" Woody asked.

"No," said Mother. "We'll be back tonight around midnight. Bernice?"

"Yes, ma'am?"

"Scooter and Ike should go to bed at seven-thirty. Everyone else at nine o'clock."

"I don't want to go to bed that early," protested Scooter, lifting a crutch and stamping it on the floor. "I'm not a baby!"

"Okay, Scooter, if you behave you can stay up until nine, too." Mother continued, looking around the circle into each child's eyes. "No fire in the wood stove tonight. No staying out after dark, no swimming in the lake, and absolutely no rowing to the island. You can all have Cracker Jacks if you promise to mind Bernice."

"Cracker Jacks," Echoed Baby Ike.

"Do I have to share mine with Ike?" Scooter asked, still pouting.

"There's enough for everyone to have their own box."

Father studied the children. "Bernice, I want a full report in the morning."

Bernice gave a quick nod. "Yes, sir."

Mother smiled, although to Bootie, her smile was a sad, distracted facade. No child asked where Mother and Father were going. The business trips caused a vague uneasiness for them all, but only Bootie knew what the trips were about, and she often prayed with her rabbit's foot that the others would never learn the truth.

"Mama Bear hugs all around!" Mother put her arms out and received a squeeze and kiss from all seven children. When Bootie had her turn, Bootie wrapped her arms around Mother's waist and squeezed until Mother pulled herself free.

"Bootie, I have to go," Mother said, and as though she were reading her daughter's thoughts, she added, "No need to worry." She kissed her daughter on the forehead, and turned to leave.

The children followed their parents out to the driveway. Scooter did his best to navigate the rocky path until Clark lifted him onto his hip, mimicking Bernice and Baby Ike. Together, they watched the black Chevy Suburban bounce its way down the gravel road, past Maslow's cornfield, until the car was out of sight.

Bootie ran back inside the house, passing through the kitchen to the sleeping porch. She pulled out her rabbit's foot from its hiding place under her pillow, and dropped onto the quilt her mother had made her. As she petted the soft fur with her fingertips, she made the deal with God she always made whenever her parents took these trips.

"Lord," she said, "I'll go to church every Sunday, and I'll say prayers for an hour, and I'll take dish duty every day, and you don't have to make me pretty. Just bring Mother and Father home. And make it true this is their last business trip." As an afterthought, she added, "Please take the pictures away I see in my head. And the haunts and animals and people nobody else can see, too. I hate them. I want to be like everyone else. I want to be normal."

The silver light that glowed from the rabbit's foot dimmed.

5.

Bootie's head snapped backwards. She pulled her hands from the dishwater, turned and flung water at the assailant

How to Dance on the Moon 35

who had yanked her pony tail. Woody stepped back and laughed.

"That hurt!" Bootie glared at Woody, who was exactly her height. "Go away unless you're here to help."

"We're swimming over to the island." Sweetly pungent Cracker Jack bits spit from Woody's mouth. "But I guess you can't go."

"Mother said no swimming."

"So what? If Aunt Theo was here, she'd let us go."

"Aunt Theo is not here."

"Like I said, so what? Sellie's going, and Clark too."

Bootie wavered. "Clark's going?"

"Yep."

"Will Bernice tell on us?"

"She doesn't care." Woody pulled at Bootie's sleeve. "Finish the dishes later. We still have some of Aunt Theo's gin."

Scooter's crutches thumped into the kitchen. "What's going on?" He dropped his empty Cracker Jack box into the wastebasket.

"We're swimming over to the island," said Woody.

Scooter's eyes grew wide. "Can I go too?"

"You can't swim with your sticks," Woody said dismissively, pointing to Scooter's crutches.

"I'll go in the boat," Scooter countered.

Woody shook his head. "You can't row by yourself."

Scooter stuck out his bottom lip. "Take me or I'll tell on you!"

"I'll row you over, Scooter," Bootie said.

Scooter's scowl eased. "But I can row myself."

"If I row, you can carry everyone's clothes."

"Sellie's already at the beach," said Woody. "We want to go now."

Bootie splashed her hands back in the dishwater and flicked soap on Woody's shirt. "Then help me finish the dishes."

Laura Ginter   36

Woody scowled and pushed Bootie away. "Boys don't do dishes," he snapped, and he was gone before she could punch him.

"Can I help you finish, Bootie?" asked Scooter, his blue eyes sympathetic.

"You can help me by going down to the beach and telling Clark to wait for me."

"Okay." Scooter thumped through the kitchen and out to the porch, his unruly cowlicks making his blond hair stick out in every direction. Bootie put away the plates without drying them, and went to find Bernice. Her older sister was in the living room reading a book to Baby Ike.

In Bootie's eyes, Bernice stood on a higher platform than the other children did. She was sometimes moody and aloof, but she could be sweetly sisterly, pitching balls to Clark after school and fixing Sellie's hair into bouncy curls for birthday parties. Bootie received pictures from her sister but could not always understand them. The complexities of Bernice's teenage angst made her pictures difficult to understand, but the gloomy aura surrounding her sister suggested the bank audit had derailed a secret meeting with Mickey Kennedy.

Bootie cleared her throat. "Sis?" Bernice looked up at Bootie with a questioning rise of her brow. "Are you going to tell Mother and Father if we go to the island? We're taking Scooter in the boat."

Bernice shook her head. "Just be careful with Scooter. Don't let his braces get wet." Bernice resumed reading, and Bootie slipped from the room.

   ****

The lake bordered the west side of the Kurz homestead, and a narrow, soft sand beach was accessible from the house by a planked walkway that cut through a marsh. During the warm weather, the lake was the children's playground, and

How to Dance on the Moon 37

their toys were their rope swing and rowboat. They trapped frogs and turtles, and the boys waded through the marsh looking for crawfish and bloodsuckers. Mother sometimes watched them from the porch, although Mother never watched for long.

Putnam's Island was far enough from the Kurz's beach to require a short swim or a boat ride to reach it. Nobody had ever tried to build on the rocky outcrop. Open land around the lake was plentiful. An occasional boater would come to the island to explore, but nobody ever stayed long. Raccoons swam there looking for food. Father had taught the children to stay away from the raccoons. They looked friendly enough, but they could be as bad tempered as bears, scratching with claws that could gut a dog.

By the time Bootie reached the beach, Sellie and Woody and Clark had stripped down to their underclothes, and Clark was helping Scooter into the boat. The swimmers handed their pants and shirts to Scooter who balled them up in his lap. Bootie climbed inside across from Scooter and pushed off the sand with her oar. The sun's reflection gleamed in Scooter's face and highlighted the excitement radiating from his eyes. He had left his crutches behind on the beach since they were useless on the uneven island ground.

The sun resembled a blood orange propped up by the treetops on the far side of the lake. The swimmers stroked their way across the lake. Amber light splintered off from the splashes made by their kicking feet, and turbulent crests of water bounced off the boat's bow. The water was shallow between the Kurz's beach and the island, and the cooling evening air made the lake as warm as a summer puddle.

Halfway to the island, just offshore, was a large granite boulder known by the local children as the Wailing Witch, The cracked, flat-topped rock extended three feet above the water line and was large enough for four small children to sit on the top. However, no child had ever been brave enough to approach it. The Wailing Witch had been the subject of many ghost stories and had caused sleepless nights for generations of youngsters. The Kurz children's father had been raised with the legend of the Wailing Witch and had told the children a tame version. More explicit story details passed among the kids like schoolyard gossip, with tremendous drama and hushed voices.

The name came from the cracks and bumps resembling an ugly crone's profile with slits for eyes. Her mouth stretched open as if she were about to bite down on something, or someone. According to legend, the Wailing Witch could come alive on any moonless night, but always awoke on the year's darkest. She hunted throughout the town for sleeping children. Her wails would sound like the loons' tremolo, so no one ever recognized her approach. She would snatch the prettiest and plumpest from their beds, and imprison them in caves under the water. When she was hungry, she would boil them in tubs of skunk fat and chew the cooked meat off the bones. Carving out the brain, she would eat it like spaghetti, and she would drink blood from the empty skull with a straw. The witch pickled the eyes and froze the hands and dipped them in chocolate like Klondike bars. With nothing else left to eat, she would suck marrow from the bones until the next year's blackest night, or until the mood hit her to start a new hunt for fresh meat.

As Bootie rowed past the Wailing Witch, long shadows created by the setting sun made the boulder's cracks appear cavernous, as if she could bite off your arm if you were stupid enough to put it into her mouth. But unlike the other children, Bootie shrugged off the boulder's power to frighten. She knew real demons existed in the world, more terrifying than the Wailing Witch. Demons most people couldn't see, that people didn't even know about, and from whom nobody was entirely safe. Nevertheless, Bootie shielded her eyes from the sun and glanced at the rising moon as she passed the rock. The moon was close to full. The Wailing Witch would not be prowling.

How to Dance on the Moon 39

The swimmers and boaters landed simultaneously. Clark and Sellie dressed, and Clark lifted Scooter from the boat and carried him up the short bank. He set his brother down on a flat rock within their makeshift camp. Sellie, who had dressed behind a tree, sat next to her little brother.

The children's camp had been carved out with rusty tools found in the barn. Oak trees and scruffy brush provided privacy. Three flat rocks, a fallen tree and a battered metal trunk provided seating. The children stored their more valuable loot inside the trunk, secured with a Yale lock. Besides storing Aunt Theo's pilfered gin, Woody had moved most of his comic books to the trunk. Clark also kept his baseball cards inside, encased in a yellow biscuit tin. Two old rubber boots housed firecrackers Woody had swiped from the town's previous July Fourth celebration.

A stone circle surrounded smoky, charred sticks and blackened paper bits, the remains of their last fire. Father had forbidden campfires on the island, so like Bernice's romance with Mickey Kennedy, and Bootie's gift, Clark and Woody kept their fires a secret from their father.

The children sat in their customary seats around the fire pit. Woody had chosen to stay in his wet underpants to annoy his sisters, although he shivered from the cold dampness of the cloth on his skin and had to slap at the mosquitoes sucking blood from his bare arms and legs. Clark unlocked the trunk and pulled out a small metal lockbox with the words *Franklin Savings and Loan* embossed on the cover. He pushed a pack of Doublemint gum aside and removed a box of Chesterfields and another box of stick matches. Clark lit the cigarette. He inhaled deeply and passed it to Woody.

"Thank you for the smokes and the gin, Aunt Theo," said Woody, displaying the Chesterfield to the others before inhaling with an enthusiastic twist of his wrist. In the dimming light, Woody's skin looked pasty white. Damp, pumpkin-colored hair bisected his head into a perfect part. Freckles dotted the plump, soft skin on his chest. His wet undershorts clung to his thighs. Woody's childlike physique made a ghoulish contrast to the cigarette stuck between his lips. He resembled a clown, performing in a freakish nighttime circus. A red nose and painted lips would have completed the picture. Bootie stifled an urge to snicker at his silly appearance. No one could laugh at this clown without starting a fight.

Only fifteen months separated the brothers, but Clark was huskier and had fluffy hairs on his upper lip. His eyes were the same blue as the lake on a sunny day. He preferred his hair cut short on the sides, but wore it longer on top, and he had a curl that sometimes fell onto his forehead. Although he had Father's physical traits, he had Mother's temperament. He was affectionate to his sisters and kind to his two youngest brothers.

Unlike Woody, who lived in a comic book fantasyland, Clark had a plan for his life. He was on two baseball teams, and spent time everyday hitting rocks into the lake with his bat, practicing for the day he would break Ted Williams' home run record at Fenway Park.

Woody inhaled, and passed the smoke to Sellie, who perched it in the vee of her first two fingers and took a gentle tug on the tip with her lips. "I'm going to smoke Phillip Morris cigarettes when I'm in high school," Sellie said, smoke spewing in puffs from her mouth, "That's what they smoke in the movies. When I grow up, maybe I'll sell them at a fancy club." With a swish of the wrist, she passed the butt to Bootie, imitating the teenage girls who smoked outside the school. "I can't wait until I'm in high school. Can you, Bootie? To smoke and wear jewelry and high heels and makeup. And date boys. Cute, tall boys that don't look like Woody. I'm already the prettiest girl in my class."

"The pretty ugliest," said Woody. "No boys are gonna want to date you ever."

Bootie inhaled. "I can wait. Would you like to try it,

How to Dance on the Moon   41

Scooter?" She pointed the cigarette at her little brother.

"No, thank you. Smoking stunts your growth." Scooter picked up a stick and hit his leg brace with it.

Woody snorted. "No, it doesn't, you dope!"

Clark stretched across the circle and mussed Scooter's hair, turning his cowlicks into golden spikes. "It's okay, Sport."

The cigarette went around the circle until it reached Woody again. It burned his fingertip, and he dropped it. "Ouch! Son of a bitch!"

Sellie admonished Woody. "Don't cuss."

Woody asked, "How many cigarettes do we got left?"

Clark stuck his fingers in the cigarette box and felt around. "Just four."

"What about Aunt Theo's gin?"

"I'll send it around, but just one chug each. We don't want any drunks when Mother and Father get home." They passed the bottle around the circle, skipping over Scooter again. Bootie's lips stung from the liquor, and she sucked on them until the sensation faded. The unpleasant fire in her stomach burned out quickly.

Woody wiped his mouth on his arm. "Mother and Father need to go on a longer trip next time so Aunt Theo can come back. We're running low on supplies."

"Don't be wishing for any more trips, Woody," Bootie said curtly, and she crossed her arms in front of her chest. "Mother should be home."

"Why does Mother have to go when Father does his audits?" Sellie asked. I don't like it either."

"Oh listen to you two Mama's Girls!" chided Woody.

"Shut up, Woody," snapped Sellie. "That's not an insult, you know."

Clark interrupted. "Stop it you guys. Woody, go get dressed. You look stupid sitting in your underwear, and you're getting eaten alive."

Woody bundled his clothes into his arms and, rising from

his seat, he slipped behind a tree trunk. "Here, Sellie. Smell my underpants." He poked his head around the trunk and threw his wet briefs at his sister. Before she could react, they slapped her square in the face and fell into her lap.

"Why don't you stop being stupid?" Sellie grabbed the offensive wad of fabric and threw it toward Bootie, who tossed it back on Woody's seat.

Clark stood and reached around the tree to slap Woody in the head, but Woody had disappeared into the dark.

Sellie giggled, and started kicking leaves onto Scooter's braces. Scooter pretended to be angry until Sellie tickled his belly, which made Scooter laugh. The children gossiped about friends and teachers until a screech erupted from the direction of the beach. Woody came charging from the darkness, his face contorted and wide-eyed, his shirt unbuttoned. One arm flailed while the other clutched at his unzipped pants trying to slide down his hips. He ran to the opposite end of the fire and crouched next to Clark. "There's someone in the bushes!" Woody screeched and pointed. "Back over there!"

"No, there's not," said Clark, annoyed. "Shut up and finish dressing."

"I saw him," insisted Woody.

"You saw a raccoon."

"Or a bear?" asked Scooter, his eyes wide.

"It was a man."

"Maybe it was the Wailing Witch," Sellie said nervously.

"The Wailing Witch is not real," Bootie said.

"She wouldn't take you anyway," chided Woody at Sellie, not missing the opportunity to mock his sister despite his agitation. "She just wants pretty girls, even if you are fat enough."

Before Sellie could hit Woody, Clark pulled his brother up. "Shut up, Woody. You saw a raccoon. Stop trying to scare everyone." Woody buttoned his shirt and pants and dropped back onto his seat on the log, grumbling about how no one

How to Dance on the Moon   43

believed him and how they would probably all get killed.

Sellie combed her fingers through her hair. "Should we look for the raccoon, or should we do something fun?"

Scooter's hand shot up in the air. "Can you tell us a story, Clark?"

"A story!" echoed Sellie. "Yes! A princess story!"

"Not a princess story!" said Woody, leaning his chin on his fist. "A cowboy story. It'll pass the time 'til we're murdered!"

Clark shook his head. "I don't know if I have a story tonight. Let me think about it."

Bootie knew Clark most certainly did have a story to tell. He had thought one up earlier that day. That was why he had wanted to come out to the island that night. He wanted to tell it. Clark loved to make up stories. Fairy tales, adventure stories, animal stories, all vibrant and more entertaining than any book. He radiated an angelic lavender glow when he told his stories, and Bootie was sure they came from the same place in his mind that her pictures came from. To him, his pictures were as alive and vivid as hers were.

Clark feigned indecision, and Bootie enjoyed watching the charade. "Come on, Clark!" Sellie bounced on the trunk.

Scooter joined in. "Please, Clark?"

Woody started a chant, and the others quickly joined in. "Story! Story! Story!"

"Woody, make us a fire." Clark scratched his chin dramatically. "You all be quiet and let me think."

They grew silent and sat with the straight backs of schoolchildren waiting for the recess bell while Woody scraped ashes from the fire pit. He reached over to a plastic tarp behind Clark and pulled out a handful of sticks and dry newspaper. Crunching the paper into a ball, he placed it with the kindling into the stone circle's center, mixing in dry leaves and cut stalks from Maslow's cornfield. On top, he put a larger piece of wood. Once he set a match to his creation, smoke curled into the air. Yellow and blue flames flickered to life and lapped the air with a sultry dance. The air began to smell like sweet birch and cornhusks.

Bootie relaxed her focus, her eyes mesmerized by the ballet of the fire. Clark lit one of the last four cigarettes but did not offer to share it. Nobody asked him to. A cigarette was a small price to pay for a story from Clark. He exhaled a waft of smoke and glanced around at his siblings, looking each person in the eye. The sun had fully set, and the fire's light danced across his face, and the flickering flames reflected in his eyes. Pausing long enough to add suspense to the moment, he took another drag from his cigarette. "Guess I do have a story."

"Yeah!" said Scooter and Sellie in unison.

"I will call this story *Princess Beulah and the Pirate's Booty.*"

Woody cackled at the humor. "Great name! Beulah and Bootie."

Sellie was petulant, though. "Bootie always gets to be in the story," she whined.

Scooter glared at Sellie. "Clark, just tell the story."

Clark laughed. "Okay, Scooter, you're in the story too. You're the big, brave pirate! Ready?" Scooter clapped his hands enthusiastically. Clark paused, and tilted his head. "I'm changing the name of the story to *The Perils of the Pirate Princess,*" he said. "I like that better." And with a rhythm of a gifted storyteller, Clark began to speak.

The fire flickered as the children listened without moving, without seeming to breathe.

6.

The Perils of the Pirate Princess

Once upon a time, there was a strong and handsome lad named Scooter, who lived a quiet life in a small village with his mother, father and seven sisters. Scooter spent his days making shoes in his father's shop. His shoes were sturdy and had thick soles, and they were the most desired shoes in the village.

But Scooter was not happy. He did not like making shoes. He did not like having seven sisters, who did nothing all day but lie around and argue with each other. He did not like being from a small village. But what he did not like the most were his eyes. Where other people's eyes were brown or blue or green, his were white. They looked like the one-dot side of a pair of dice. Many children in the village were afraid of him, and some people thought he was cursed.

While Scooter worked in the cobbler shop, he dreamed every day of being a pirate. If he was a pirate, he could sail the seas and find treasure and be friends with other pirates. And then one day, an old, ugly hag called him Satan's Child, and he knew it was time to leave home. So in the middle of the night he threw some clothes in a pillowcase and snuck away without saying goodbye to even one of his sisters.

The first thing Scooter did once he was on his own, was buy a sword, and create a noble pirate name for himself, He decided on "Pirate Devil". He also learned how to growl, and snarl the sound "Arrrgh," and call people "Matey." He invented daredevil stories about his fierce courage and told them to the sailors he met. Soon, his efforts were rewarded. He was hired onto the biggest, meanest ship in the main, The Lord Woodrow, *better known by its pirate name,* The Sunken Skull.

The captain of the Sunken Skull *was Salty Sam Scurvy. He wore an eye patch and had a black beard that went all the way to the floor. His beard had thousands of lice running its length.*

He had only three teeth and smelled like burning tar. When Scooter was introduced to Salty Sam, the captain spit on a cat trying to sleep on his desk, and told Scooter he already knew six other pirates with the name Devil. He lifted his eye patch and scratched at the bloody socket where his eye used to be and asked Scooter what his real name was.

"William, but everyone calls me Scooter."

"Arrrgh. Me lad, in all of Davey Jones' locker a pirate called Scooter wouldn't make anyone shiver his timbers.. I'm thinkin' ye be havin' the name White-eye. White-eye William Shipburner." And Scooter agreed. White-eye was the perfect name. And that's how Pirate Devil became White-eye William Shipburner.

"Scooter is a stupid name for a pirate," agreed Scooter. The children shushed him.

On the far side of a hill near the bay where the Sunken Skull *moored was a castle and a small village. In the castle lived a king and his only daughter, Beulah. Her mother the queen had died when she was born. As a baby, Beulah had very long toes, and every woman in the kingdom knitted seven pairs of booties with extra long toes for the barefoot baby princess. She became known as the Bootie Princess, which became Princess Bootie.*

Scooter interrupted again. "Is that how our Bootie got her name? From baby booties?" Clark looked annoyed, and Scooter covered his mouth.

Princess Bootie, now a young maiden, raised the most beautiful rabbits with the softest fur in the kingdom, and the young princess gave the villagers rabbit pelt muffs and mittens to keep their hands warm in winter, and her kindness made her beloved.

One day, as Princess Bootie was tending to her rabbits, the Sunken Skull *pirates snuck into the castle and captured her father the king. The pirates didn't know the town was too poor for even an army. Salty Sam Scurvy sent a ransom note to the castle, demanding all the village's gold, silver, and jewels. "Ye'*

How to Dance on the Moon
47

scalawags must be havin' some spoils," the pirates wrote. "Give us all yer booty, or yer king will be swimmin in chains."

When the town received the ransom note, they were confused. "Why do the pirates want socks?" they asked.

"They don't want socks," said the king's royal advisors. "They want Princess Bootie!"

"If it will save my father's life, then I will go," said Princess Bootie.

The villagers loved Princess Bootie more than all their possessions combined, and offered to give up everything they had to stop her from going, but early the next morning, before anyone was awake, she left the castle and walked alone to the bay to find the pirate ship.

When Princess Bootie arrived at the water's edge, she saw a ship with a skull and swords on its flag anchored not far from shore. The ragged, dirty men on the deck were singing loud songs with dirty words. Terrified, she started to flee, but a pirate grabbed her from behind, threw her into a small boat and rowed her out to the ship. Another pirate walked down a rope ladder, clutched her by the waist and pulled her up onto the ship. The pirate who hoisted her up frightened her because his eyes had no color. Princess Bootie screamed.

Clark threw his head back and let out a loud, high-pitched shrill. Startled, Sellie also hollered out.

"Hush, me heartie," whispered the pirate. "I am White-eye William Shipburner. I will keep you safe. Do ye be from the king's village? Do ye bring the booty?"

"Yes," she said.

"Then to Salty Sam Scurvy I be takin' ye to be spied on by the captain," said White-eye. "Or he'll string me bones from the crows nest. But be not scared, because you are as beautiful as a mermaid, and I won't let me scum-ridden mates cast eyes on ye." White-eye pulled her into the captain's quarters.

Salty Sam stuck a wad of tobacco into his mouth, sucked it through his three teeth and chewed on it until black drool collected around the corner of his mouth "Who ye be bringing here?" he asked White-eye.

"She says she has the booty from the village."

"Whar is the booty?"

"I am Princess Bootie."

"You be a mere wench. You cannot be booty. Booty is treasure."

"We are a poor kingdom and have no treasure. Please," the princess pleaded. "You captured my father, and I am begging you to set him free."

Salty Sam waved his arms over his head and yelled loudly. "I BE DEMANDING BOOTY AND THEY SEND ME A WENCH!"

"But I am Bootie. And my only treasure is my rabbits. I'd be happy to sew you and your crew as many rabbit coats as you want, if you would be so kind as to free my father."

Salty Sam's eyes grew large with rage, and White-eye quickly stepped forward. "Captain, pay ye no mind to her words. She doesn't know ar she says."

Salty Sam pushed White-eye back and leaned so close to Bootie she could see the lice crawling in the whiskers in his chin. "Did you use the word for the long-ear on my boat?"

Princess Bootie was confused. "Long ear? You mean rabbit?"

Black spit flew out of Salty Sam's screaming mouth and spotted Bootie's cheek. "YOU HAVE BROUGHT BAD LUCK TO ME VESSEL BY TALKING OF THE LONG EAR! TO THE BRIG YE GO!"

Scooter asked, "The brig is the jail, right?"

"Yes," said Clark.

"Why is Salty Sam afraid of rabbits?" asked Sellie.

"Rabbits are bad luck on a boat, you idiot," said Woody.

"TO THE BRIG YE GO!" Salty Sam roared like a lion with a thorn in its foot.

White-eye grabbed the princess around the arm and tugged her out of the room. She was very scared, but he whispered to her, "Ye be safe. I be what takes care of you."

How to Dance on the Moon 49

When they were in the brig, White-eye said, "Are you all right? I am worried for you."

Princess Bootie stared into White-eye's white eyes. "You are not talking like a pirate anymore."

"My name is Scooter. I was a shoemaker's son before I was a pirate. The captain sent your father off on his own brother's ship, *Neptune's Servant* to an island far from here. If we don't get silver and gold from your people, the captain will go to the island, find your father and kill him, and probably kill you too."

"We have nothing." Princess Bootie started to cry. "What shall I do? I must save my father's life."

Scooter stood tall. "Many pirates hate the captain and would welcome his head on a platter. We will wait for him to take us to the island where he is hiding your father, and then we will have a mutiny. We will overthrow Salty Sam Scurvy, find your father and set you both free." Scooter looked away from the princess. "You aren't afraid of me, because of my eyes, are you?"

"I think you are the most handsome pirate I have ever seen," Princess Bootie said.

Scooter beamed, and at that moment, knew he would love the princess forever. He led her to a cell with just a bed and a chair. "You must stay in the brig for now, but I will protect you, as White-eye William Shipburner." Princess Bootie nodded and entered the cell, and White-eye locked her in.

Meanwhile, true to what White-eye William said, Salty Sam Scurvy grew tired of the Princess Bootie's kingdom and its stupid people. He set sail to the island where he had imprisoned the king so he could cut him into one hundred pieces and drain his blood for the sharks. After that, he was going to make the princess walk the plank and fall into those sharks who would be hungry for more flesh.

During the voyage, all the pirates fell in love with Princess Bootie. They would fight over who could bring her meals or take her on her daily walk around the ship. A pirate named Blue

Tooth Billy, known as the ugliest pirate ever to sail the seas, was especially smitten. Blue Tooth Billy had a scraggly brown beard the same color as his skin. He had warts on his face in the shape of a sea bird and scars crisscrossing his bald scalp.

Princess Bootie grew fond of the pirates, especially Blue Tooth Billy. But she fell in love with White-eye William Shipburner. She did not care if he had no color in his eyes or if some people thought he was the fiercest pirate on the seas. He was her hero. She avoided Salty Sam who growled at her whenever he saw her and showed her his bloody eye socket and spit on the deck and pointed at the plank, like he might make her walk it right then and there if he felt an itch in his drawers.

After many weeks, the pirate in the crow's nest yelled, "Land ho!" White-eye was in the brig with Princess Bootie, and they heard it together.

"We're at the island!" said White-eye, excitedly. He kissed the princess on the hand and announced, "It's time for the mutiny. We are going to take the ship from Salty Sam Scurvy."

White-eye let out a mighty scream "ARRRRGHHHHHH!" He brandished his sword from its holder and swung it around over his head, before leaving her alone in her cell. Soon, all the pirates were yelling and whooping and hollering. Shaking with fright, Princess Bootie hid under her cot and listened to the battle.

When the sounds become fearsome and she thought she might faint, two people ran down the stairs to the brig, Salty Sam and White-eye by their voices. The door to her cell clanged open, and she could see their feet moving from under the cot.

"Ye be the one who did this," yelled Salty Sam. "Ye started the mutiny over a wretched, penniless wench, you scum ridden weevil eater! I will cut out her heart, and she be watching ye eat it as she dies. Then it's the plank for ye."

"I won't let you kill her!" screamed White-eye.

Swords clanged and clashed until, thud! She peered out from under the bed, and Salty Sam stared back at her. She froze

How to Dance on the Moon

with terror. Surely, she was about to be pulled out from under the bed to be killed. But Sam's eyes did not flicker. He was dead.

The battle sounds ceased. She pushed Salty Sam's face away with her hand and came out from under the cot. White-eye was sitting in the chair across the room. The door to her cell was open. She ran out and said, "Oh Scooter!" She threw her arms around him, and kissed him, but when she pulled away, her hands were sticky and red. She jumped back, and White-eye fell over onto the floor. He had a knife sticking out of his back.

"You killed me!" said Scooter.

"Oh my gosh!" said Sellie. "That is so sad!"

Yes. With blood on her hands and grief in her heart, Princess Bootie climbed from the brig and went out onto the main deck. Some other pirates were killed as well, and one, Salty Sam's first mate, was walking the plank. "If ye be lucky you can make it to shore afore the sharks git ye," yelled a survivor who had a gash on his face. "If the cannon ball on yer ankles doesn't drag ye down," The others laughed.

"Don't be laughing or you be next," said Blue Tooth Billy. He saw Princess Bootie and approached her. "Don't you be worrying, wench," said Blue Tooth. "We won't be doin no harm to ye."

"White-eyed William Shipburner and Salty Sam are dead," said Princess Bootie."

"Arrrgh," said Blue Tooth Billy. "Then I be the captain of this ship now, and the crew be mine, too."

"Will you take me to my father now?" Princess Beulah asked.

"Sadly, wench, there are a thousand islands here, and only Salty Sam knew which one the king yer father be at, and, well, he aren't be talkin now."

Princess Bootie's eyes filled with tears. "It's not this island?"

"Could be, but most like nay. But we will search for him

and not stop what ye cast yer eyes upon 'im agin!"

The pirates gave Salty Sam and White-eye burials at sea. Then they began to search the islands for the king. Blue Tooth Billy made Princess Beulah into Pirate Bootie Longtoes and taught her how to be fierce. Pirate Bootie grew even fonder of Blue Tooth. She saw his kindness and not the warts and scars. Blue Tooth loved her more each day. Then one night he disappeared from the boat. No one knew how it happened, or why, but he was gone. Because they all loved Pirate Bootie, the crew made her the captain of the Sunken Skull.

Captain Bootie Longtoes became as rich and famous as Grace O'Malley, the first woman pirate ever to sail the seas. Captain Bootie was also the first pirate captain who never killed a sailor or a passenger on any ship because she discovered she had a gift for finding treasure already buried by other pirates. But she never did find her father the king, and all the treasure in the world meant nothing to her, without him. To this day, the Sunken Skull still roams the seas as a ghost ship with Captain Bootie Longtoes searching for her father, and for her friend Blue Tooth Billy. And even now, if you climb a palm tree on a beach in Jamaica, and listen to the wind blowing, you can hear her wail, still calling to her father and mourning the death of her true love, White-eye William Shipburner.

Scooter crinkled his brow. "What happened to Blue Tooth Billy?"

"Blue Tooth Billy believed the deepness of his love for Princess Bootie came from a sorcerer's spell, and that he was too ugly for her to ever love him back. So one day, with great heaviness in his heart, he jumped into the sea after an old hag told him only the kiss of a mermaid would break the spell. But a current swept him off to a large island. Today, he hides in the palm trees so people can't see his ugliness. He blends in with the coconuts, and when he is spotted by his tooth and warts, people think he is a blue parrot."

How to Dance on the Moon 53

7.

When Clark finished, no one spoke right away. Bootie sighed, wistfully. "That was a beautiful story, Clark. I almost cried."

Scooter fidgeted in his seat. "Why did you kill William White-eye Shipburner?

"He was a hero for saving the woman he loved," said Clark. "It's noble to die a hero."

Woody shrugged passively. "It was a pretty good story, except the lovey part."

Sellie pouted. "It was so sad. Everyone died. Can we do something else, now?"

Scooter's hand shot up in the air. "Let's play Truth or Lie!

Sellie clapped her hands. "Yes!"

"I'll play!" said Woody. "But just if I get to go first."

Sellie slapped her thigh. "I want to go first."

"But I'm older than you," said Woody. "That's the rule, crybaby!"

"I'm the oldest," Clark said. "I get to start." He adjusted himself in his seat. "Truth or lie? I saw Woody kiss Marlena Margolis after school Friday when she gave him that Captain Marvel comic he's been hiding under his bed."

Even in the dark, Bootie could see Woody's face turn to flames. "You did not," he protested, almost screaming. "Take that back! You have the face of a big fat liar!"

Bootie cringed at Woody's angry words, but Clark laughed and turned toward Bootie. "What do you think? Truth or lie?"

Bootie knew it was true. She'd had a vision of Woody kissing Marlena Margolis, and, in response, Marlena had socked him in the stomach. But why make trouble? "I think it's a lie. Sellie?"

"I think it's a lie, but I know Woody loves Marlena."

"Shut up! I do not."

Sellie stuck her chin out. "Shut up yourself, Bratman!"

Scooter giggled. "That was a good one, Sellie."

Sellie turned to her younger brother. "What do you think, Scooter?"

Scooter answered, "I think it's a lie. Clark?"

Clark grinned and pointed at his younger brother. "It is a. . . . LIE!"

Woody let out a deep breath. "That wasn't funny."

"Yes it was." Clark snickered. "Now, it's your turn. Sellie."

"Hey!" Woody complained, but before he could say more, Sellie spoke.

"Father let another raccoon family move into the barn."

Everyone hollered "Truth!"

Clark grinned. "That was too easy. Father always lets raccoons live in the barn."

Sellie grimaced. "But it's awful that Mr. Kennedy fights with Father over them."

"You got to see it from Mr. Kennedy's side," said Clark. "They spook his horses, kill his chickens, and mess up his barn with their sneakiness and thieving. He wants to get a coon dog to get rid of them."

"But he makes Father so mad he says we can't play over there. They hate each other."

"They hate each other over lots of stuff. And Father *says* we can't play over there, but he doesn't mean it. You know that."

Woody scratched his chin. "He means it when he says Bernice can't be romantic with Mickey Kennedy. She has to be sneaky, too. Like the raccoons."

Bootie flushed. "I know the real reason why we can't go in the barn, and it's not the raccoons. Truth or lie? There is a secret treasure inside."

"No there isn't, Bootie!" said Woody.

Bootie pursed her lips. "Truth or Lie?"

"Lie," said Clark.

"Lie," said Sellie.

How to Dance on the Moon

"Truth," said Scooter. "Bootie never lies."

Bootie glanced around the circle. "It's truth."

"It is NOT truth," said Woody, his face turning red again. "You have the face of a big fat liar, too!"

"I'm not lying!" Bootie bounced in her chair, unable to contain her excitement.

"So where is it? How come I don't know about it? Where did it come from? Maybe you're talking about raccoon shit. Do you think raccoon shit is treasure?"

Scooter covered his ears. "Woody, don't cuss."

Woody threw a stick into the fire. "Bootie is cheating, and everyone is picking on me. I don't want to play this game anymore."

Clark shook his head. "Then what do you want to do?"

Woody turned toward Bootie, and his face brightened, as though he had been waiting to be asked. "I want Bootie to do a séance."

Bootie shook her head. "No. It might scare Scooter."

Scooter squared his shoulders. "No, it won't."

Sellie lifted onto her knees and twisted toward her sister. She clasped her hands together. "Please, Bootie? Let's have a séance."

Everyone joined in. "Please, Bootie! Please? Please!"

Bootie rolled her eyes. "Okay. I guess so." The children cheered, and Woody put another piece of wood into the fire.

Bootie had become interested in séances when she had seen one illustrated in Woody's comic book. Always trying to find ways to better understand and control her gift, the idea of directly communicating with dead people intrigued her. She had studied a picture that had portrayed people sitting around a candle-lit table, holding hands with bowed heads. A transparent figure with long, white, windblown hair hovered above them. What she gleaned from that one picture helped her create a séance game that allowed her to experiment with the concept. The game had become popular.

To play the game, Bootie would have everyone sit in a circle, hold hands, and shut their eyes. Bootie would then call into the darkness and summon the light. Usually she could smell the sweet, smoky light before she could see it. The aroma reminded her of Mr. Maslow's pipe tobacco, and it swam in her head more than in her nose. After the smell came the sparkles, one or two to start, then hundreds, flitting around like lightning bugs. The longer Bootie stared, the brighter they would flicker until they blended into one large, luminous mass.

A séance-induced haunt shined so brilliantly it cast light from inside itself, like a reverse shadow, and was similar to the colored lights that radiated from people. Bootie would tell the others to open their eyes, and they would see the light, but not the haunt. She would divert her gaze to make it disappear, and the children would scream in frightened delight, begging Bootie to share what the spirits had told her.

Bootie was unenthused by the idea of a séance. To her brothers and sisters, her ability to call out spirits was just another one of her peculiarities. But in truth, Bootie was sorry she had ever started the game. The haunts from séances weren't like the other haunts she saw. They were creepy, rubbery creatures, pasty and dead-looking, and they emitted strong, unpleasant emotions the way rotten meat sent out a wretched smell. Tonight, she would do the séance, but without using her gift. The lights didn't have to appear every time, she rationalized. Despite Scooter's brave face, an encounter with a spirit haunt would scare him, especially after Clark had killed his character in his pirate story.

Bootie glanced around at all the faces surrounding her, smiling with anticipation, as they had been for Clark earlier. With a resigned sigh, she began. "Okay, believers! Make a circle and hold hands." The children obliged, and Bootie paused for dramatic effect. "Close your eyes and draw out the power of the dead." Everyone complied except Scooter, who squeezed his eyelids into a squint so he could still see. Bootie

How to Dance on the Moon   57

lowered her voice to a baritone. "Oh ghosts and spirits, we want to see you. We want to hear you. We want to. . ."

Bootie stopped. Something rustled in the bush behind Sellie. It was too large to be a raccoon. Bootie hollered out, "Who's there?"

The other children opened their eyes at Bootie's nervous shout.

"What is it?" Clark asked.

Bootie pointed, and a hulking shadow rose slowly from behind the bush. The man circled around and took a tentative step toward the children. He wore a loose, white shirt with brown trousers tucked into tall boots. The campfire illuminated only one side of the stranger's face. The man put his hands forward, palms out. Sellie looked behind her and screamed as she leaped away and latched onto Scooter. Woody fell off the trunk and scooted backwards toward Clark.

"See! I told you!" Woody yelled. "I told you I saw a man!"

"Clark, what's wrong with his face?" Sellie asked. Her voice quivered.

The man stepped into the light and pointed to his head with one of his raised hands. "I have an eye patch,"

"Don't move again," Clark bellowed, sounding more angry than scared.

"Are you a pirate?" asked Scooter.

"No, son," the man said. "I was just looking around. Didn't know you were here."

Bootie stared at the man, trying to see inside him without the help of touch. A picture of her parents with their feet and hands missing pushed its way through,

"You're lying," said Clark. "Why were you spying on us?" Woody lifted himself from the ground and balled his hands into fists. When the man didn't answer, Clark's voice grew deeper. "Why are you here?"

The man stopped abruptly and bent into a protective crouch, stretching his arms even more. His eyes focused on

Clark. Bootie pulled her gaze away from the man and looked over at her older brother. Clark was pointing a gun Bootie had never seen at the crouching man. She gasped, and Sellie huddled beside her.

"Please put that down," the man said. "I wasn't spying on you. I don't see well as you can probably tell." Again, he pointed to his eye patch.

"People don't hide at night on an island and spy on kids," Clark waved the gun. "What happened to your eye?"

"Lost it in the war. See. I'm a good guy. A veteran. I'm not here to hurt you." The man took a step backward. "I just want to go back to my boat."

"Where is it?" Clark asked.

The intruder straightened a bit and pointed over his shoulder.

"You stay there." Clark studied the man. "We're leaving. Sellie, Bootie, get down to the beach and start swimming. Woody, help Scooter into *our* boat."

The man took another half step backward. Clark thrust the gun out further. "Keep your hands up." The words sounded silly, like something from a Lone Ranger radio show, but the stranger stretched his arms higher above his head. "I'll shoot you if you follow us," Clark said.

"I'm not going to follow you."

Bootie turned and ran to the beach. The others followed her. On her way, she tripped over a tree root, but managed to keep from falling. She and Sellie splashed into the water, and she kicked her legs, sweeping the water with her arms.

Ribbons of black waves circled Bootie. With every fourth stroke, she twisted to peer over her shoulder, looking for her brothers. She lost her bearings and began to tread water to gauge the distance to the shore. She shrieked when she saw the Wailing Witch's cracked face leering at her from inches away. The undulating water, streaked by the moonlight, made the rock woman's neck seem to stretch and recoil, as if she was

How to Dance on the Moon
59

trying to suck the swimming girls into her mouth. The breeze whistled across the water, like a siren's song of temptation. Bootie turned her body and kicked, propelling herself away from the rock. She didn't look back until her knees scraped sand.

Panting and light-headed, Bootie stood and trudged through the water to the beach. Moments later, Sellie pulled herself up, and together they strained to see across the lake as the water lapped their feet. A chilling breeze had come up, and the air smelled like stale ice cubes. Bootie shivered violently. She tracked the sound of oars banging against oarlocks. In the moonlight, she saw Woody rowing and Clark sitting backward, pointing his gun at the island with Scooter squeezed down between them.

Bootie stepped back into the water when the boat wedged itself onto the beach, and she helped the boys pull it to shore. The girls worked together to free Scooter from the boat. His pants were wet, and he grinned wildly when Bootie poked him for signs of injury.

"That was scary," said Sellie, retrieving Scooter's crutches and handing them to him. "Who was that man?"

Bootie remembered her vision of her parents without their hands and feet, and wondered if Mother and Father knew the stranger. Was he going to get the children in trouble? Maybe he had something to do with their business trip. Were her parents in danger from him? The answers eluded her. "I don't know," she said, "but we must tell Mother and Father about him."

"We can't," said Clark. "We'll get a stick whipping for going to the island, and Bernice will be in trouble, too."

Woody gave his older brother a proud slap on the back. "But you really fooled him with that cap gun."

Sellie folded her arms into her stomach to control her shivering. "So, what do we do?"

Clark glanced around at the children's faces. "Woody, help

Laura Ginter   60

Scooter up the path, then bring me back a jacket. Bootie, get Scooter dried off and to bed. I'll wait here 'til that man leaves. Then I'll go clean up the fire. Don't say anything to Bernice."

Bootie and Sellie raced up over the wooden planks ahead of Woody and Scooter. Once inside the sleeping porch, Bootie retrieved the nightshirt she kept under her pillow and hastily changed, throwing the wet clothes under her bed. She raced to the coat rack by the front door and gathered jackets for both boys, knowing Woody would want to wait with Clark on the beach. Back on the porch, she met Woody and exchanged the jackets for Scooter. Woody bolted down the wooden path. Bootie helped Scooter to his room, stopping by the bathroom for a towel. Quietly, to avoid waking Baby Ike in his crib, she leaned Scooter's crutches against the wall, removed his braces and helped him change into his night clothes. His leg braces glistened with water droplets. Bootie dried them with the towel after tucking her brother into his bed under his quilt, and kissed him goodnight. On her way back to the porch, she waved to Bernice, who was sitting on her bed in her nook under the stairs, listening to the radio and knitting.

Back on the sleeping porch, Bootie tossed Scooter's wet pants under the bed with hers. She crawled under her covers and glanced at the other three beds. Sellie had her blanket pulled over her head. The boys' beds were empty. She watched the moon rise above the porch's roofline, determined to stay awake until the boys were also safely in bed and her parents were home. But despite her effort, she fell into a dreamless sleep.

****

The next morning, Bootie awoke to a tap on the shoulder. She opened her eyes to see Clark peering down at her, his brow bent with concern. Startled, she sat up straight and grabbed his shirt, tugging it down off his shoulder. "What's wrong?"

How to Dance on the Moon 61

His grin looked forced. "Nothing. Don't worry."

"Did that pirate man leave?" she asked.

"Yes. Woody and I saw him go."

Clark was dressed. He often went to bed in his clothes, but Bootie knew he had not slept.

"I'm going over there this morning to look around in the daylight," Clark said. "And I'm bringing back the cigarettes and gin, and my baseball cards and the firecrackers and Woody's comics, in case the man comes back. If Mother asks, tell her I went to the Kennedys to help Aiden feed the horses. I already talked to Scooter about keeping our pirate a secret, until I figure out what's best to do."

Bootie could see from her hold on Clark's shirt, he was conflicted over whether or not to tell his parents about the eye-patch man. In Clark's way, he was sorting it out, but Bootie knew he would choose to say nothing. He would not want to see his brothers and sisters punished over who he hoped was a harmless vagrant, maybe more scared than they were. Although, why anyone would be on the island alone at night was a mystery that reeked of dishonest intentions. Bootie relaxed her grip on her brother's shirt. "Are Mother and Father home?"

"Mother is in the kitchen."

Mother was home! At least that worry was over. She put her arms around her brother's waist and hugged him. His muscles relaxed. He squeezed her back before slipping free from her grasp. "I have to tell you. Last night, that man scared me." Clark spoke in a thin, quiet voice. He nervously scratched a lumpy red welt on the back of his hand. Gone was the commanding protector from the evening before. "I can't explain it, but it felt like he was trouble. But he was probably just liquored up or lost. I mean, he did leave. Bootie, you understand these things. What do you think? Was he a bad man? Did he want to hurt us? Will he come back?"

Bootie shuddered with an icy chill. Clark had asked the

troubling questions she did not want her gift to explore. Unlike last night, she wanted to know nothing about the eye-patch man. Mother was home, and everyone was safe, and the man didn't matter anymore. But Clark had spoken the words, and she was unable to prevent a vision from showing her stinging images that sprouted and spread within her like poison ivy. She grimaced at a pain that stabbed her head for the slightest instance. When she finally shook off the vision, Bootie looked up into her brother's eyes. They were moist and enlarged with hope, waiting for the reassurance she could not give him. "I don't think he was just a drunk or lost. I think he was there to do something bad."

"Do you think he'll come back?"

"Yes."

Clark slumped. Bootie had just flicked away this last chance for the peace of mind he had been tenuously balancing like ashes hanging from one of their pilfered cigarette. "Let's hope you're wrong," he said. Clark walked away, surrounded by a deep blue light, shoulders bowed from the weight of his responsibility.

Bootie ran to the kitchen and hugged her mother so tightly they both lost their breath. Later that afternoon, she sat on her bed, knowing what she was supposed to do, but not wanting to. Her vision that morning made it clear she needed to tell her parents about the eye-patch man and stop the business trips. But the situation was complicated. Instead, Bootie did the next best thing. She said a prayer of thanks she had not talked more about the secret treasure during the game of Truth or Lie, and she prayed with her rabbit's foot she was wrong. That the eye-patch man would never come back.

Bootie 1993

8.

Time and transience had made *Bootie's Tea Room* one of the oldest established businesses in the Alki Beach neighborhood of West Seattle. The building that housed the tearoom had been part of Luna Park, a beachfront amusement park built in 1906. It had survived the decline and dismantling of the park, and was left unscathed during the destruction of many quaint and equally historical waterfront homes, removed to make room for high-rise condominiums. To Bootie, the building was a monument to tenacity, tattered from tough times, but fearlessly strong. A survivor.

Bootie had been a young widow who had taken a wrong turn in a rainstorm when a whimsical burst of entrepreneurial insight and enthusiasm spurred her to buy both the building and the business. She would never neglect it or do anything to undermine its character. It was her only child. At the same time, she never allowed the tearoom to swallow her up as most restaurants did to their owners, and this management style allowed her to consider closing the tearoom on the day of the funeral for Polly's father.

Ashley had been nervous about attending the service alone, and when her mother could not take her, she had asked her grandmother to go. When Erline requested the day off, Bootie told Erline she was going to the funeral with her.

Erline patted Bootie on the arm. "That's sweet, but you don't need to."

Bootie bristled. "Stop it, Erline. I want to go." Erline pulled away, and Bootie regretted snapping at her friend. Erline wanted to protect her, not exclude her. "I'm sorry. I don't mean to be short, but I owe this to Polly." Bootie's heart swelled, and she struggled to speak. "I must," was all she could add.

Erline pinched a white thread off Bootie's blouse. "Listen to yourself. First, I have told you before never say you're sorry. It makes you look weak. Second, you don't owe Polly anything. What were you supposed to do? Tell Polly her father had been killed? Of course not!"

"Of course not," echoed Bootie.

"Don't be so hard on yourself." Erline said. "And think about it some more before you decide. You know the funeral will bring back memories. I'm going to boil water for tea. Would you like some?"

"Yes, please."

As Erline walked away, Bootie reflected on her friend's advice. It wasn't the first time Erline had told her not to be so hard on herself. Erline understood Bootie's gift better than anybody outside the family. But as much as Bootie adored Erline and admired her common sense approach to life, Erline had no idea how hard on herself Bootie had to be. Erline could not understand the gift's burdens and responsibilities any more than she could understand how it felt to be a hard-boiled egg. To have people's secrets and sins and fetishes forced on you, and have their dramas and traumas suck away at tissue-thin emotional reserves, already depleted from years of violent and heartbreaking visions.

Bootie tried to remember why she had thought no harm would come of using the gift to help Polly. Going against all her own rules and ignoring blatant warnings, she had intruded into the young woman's personal life. Because of that, she had felt a bullet pierce her chest, and she shared a family's loss. The same old futile questions began cycling through her head whenever she saw something tragic. Why had she been shown the pictures? Was she obligated to share what she saw, despite how painful it could be?

In this case, clearly, nothing would have been gained sharing her vision with Polly. In fact, it would have been highly

How to Dance on the Moon 65

inappropriate. But most visions were not black and white, and it was impossible to predict the consequences of sharing what may or may not be an accurate interpretation. Not knowing what was right and what was wrong, or even if there was a right and wrong to pick from, forced her to judge people and decide what was best for them to know about themselves. This responsibility was her gift's ultimate curse, and arguably, the main reason she hated it.

Bootie's thoughts switched to the memory to which Erline had referred. An event uncomfortably similar to Polly's. Two military men knocking on her front door when Bootie was only ten years older than Polly was. A uniformed Army chaplain, young and nervous, and another uniformed man who did not introduce himself.

The chaplain had hiccupped as he had handed her a telegram and, between spasms and apologies, had relayed the Army's regrets that her husband Eddie had died in a helicopter crash. The chaplain had offered her a handkerchief, but Bootie had refused it. Instead, she had brought him a glass of water. After the men had left, Bootie suffered through a mind-numbing despair that only began to subside when she didn't think she could live with it anymore.

Because of her gift Bootie received few surprises, but the news of Eddie' death had shocked her. Even more surprising was a vision that came to her two weeks later, and had challenged everything the military had told her about his accident.

Bootie heard dishes rattling in the kitchen, and flinched at the sound of glass crashing to the floor. "Stop breaking my dishes!" Bootie called out.

"Put more mats on the floor and they won't break," Erline yelled back, making Bootie smile in spite of herself. The kitchen quieted, and Bootie peered out the garden window hoping to spot Mrs. Wallaby among the plants. She didn't.

"Knock knock!" said a tediously cheerful voice.

Laura Ginter 66

Bootie turned to see a woman and man standing in her open doorway. "We're closed," Bootie said, forcing a smile. "There are some other places to eat closer to the beach."

"I'm sorry," the woman said, stepping inside. She was tall, thirtyish, and wore her blonde hair in a sixties style flip. Her crisp white blouse and blue suit were tailored and fresh, reminding Bootie of a Pan Am flight attendant. Gloves and a pill hat would have completed the look, but the bible she was clutching destroyed it. Her companion wore a black sport coat and green tie, and had a satchel strapped across his chest. He seemed more timid, hanging back in the doorway. "We aren't here to eat." The woman glanced around the room. "Although this is a charming place."

Bootie eyed the bible. "Then what can I do for you?"

The woman smiled broadly. "I am Gloria and this is Scotty." She gestured to her companion who wiggled his fingers in a hesitant wave. "We would like to ask you a few questions about your relationship with the Lord."

Bootie gestured toward the kitchen. "I'm pretty busy right now."

"I can see that," said the woman. She put her hand out to the man who reached into a satchel and pulled out booklets. As he handed them to her she said, "Can I leave these with you, to look at later?"

Bootie pointed to a table. "Right there is good."

Gloria stepped deeper into the room. "They explain how you must accept Jesus as your Lord and Savior to enjoy the riches of the afterlife. Have you done that, Mrs. . .? What is your name?"

"Yes, I have, Gloria."

"Do you have just five minutes?"

"I wish I could help you."

"I understand. We'll leave. I'm happy you have accepted that Jesus Christ died for your sins, and that His spirit lives in all of us, because all God asks is that we accept his Son into our

How to Dance on the Moon

lives."

Bootie felt her face flush. "Really? That's all God asks?"

Gloria approached Bootie and extended the booklets for Bootie to take. "Do you know about Jesus' miracles?"

Bootie took the booklets and dropped them on the table next to her. "Yes, I do. Stories about the unexplainable, told to make people believe in something they can't see. What about when regular people do something unexplainable? Are they performing miracles? Are they like Jesus?"

"Some believe saints have performed miracles in Jesus' name. But Jesus says in Matthew 4:10, 'It is the Lord your God alone you should worship'."

"I don't mean saints, Gloria. Regular people. What if a regular person can read minds, or have psychic visions?"

"But a regular person can't."

Bootie smirked. "So, are people who claim to be mind readers tricksters looking for attention? Or trying to con people? Or do they belong in mental hospitals, to be cared for by those same people who worship Jesus' miracles?"

"Please ma'am. I don't mean to upset you. I just want to encourage you to accept Jesus' love and allow yourself to absorb the Holy Spirit. That's all."

"You can't decide to absorb the Holy Spirit into your life any more than you can decide to absorb a newborn back into your womb. Spirituality will never be anything more than an illusion for people like you, because your world is completely physical." Bootie's voice was shaking, now. "You eat, you breathe, you touch things, and you make babies. And you look to religion to make it all not hurt too much. And unless you can see more than just the physical, your spiritualism is just emotional fluff."

"But that's not true. Spirituality comes from the heart. We see it in our friends and family. Is there someone special you love with all your heart?"

Bootie reached out and grabbed the woman's arm. "You

can already taste that shot of Southern Comfort you will have tonight, like you have had every night since your prayer buddy left for South Africa. You miss him, but at least you aren't pregnant."

Gloria pulled her arm free of Bootie's grasp. "You are busy. We'll go now."

With her eyes downcast Gloria retrieved her pamphlets from the table, and Bootie's anger dissolved into shame for the way she had just chewed up the woman now trying to flee. "I'm sorry, Gloria. I didn't mean to do that."

"We'll come back at a better time." Gloria and Scotty scurried out the door.

Bootie felt a hand on her back and turned, relieved to see Erline standing behind her, and not a shadowy haunt coming to torment her while her emotions were in chaos. From the look on Erline's face, Bootie realized her friend had asked her a question. Bootie shook her head. "I'm sorry?"

"Why were you so hard on that poor girl? It's not like you to tear into someone like that. And it doesn't help your cause."

"I know. I feel bad now, but Gloria said the wrong thing on the wrong day."

"Should I put up the 'closed' sign?" Erline held out a cup for Bootie.

"Yes, but I'm going to Bellevue to see Grace and little Jennie instead of the funeral. That chatter about family reminded me the city is cutting down Stephen's tree. The one he hit when the drunk driver forced him off the road. I think it's today."

"That will be hard for Grace, but it may be a relief, too."

Bootie rubbed her forehead. "I had a puzzling vision about Grace the last time I saw her. I didn't tell her. She has enough going on. It was too vague to decipher, so it might have been about something coming up for her. A struggle of some sort. Maybe about the tree. But whatever it is, I need to check in with her."

How to Dance on the Moon 69

"How old is Jennie now?"

"She's six, and Grace is doing a great job with her." Bootie smiled sadly at her friend. "Erline, I know I've asked you this before, but please, tell me the truth. Do you think I'm truly psychotic? Or schizophrenic? Is that why I see things nobody else does?"

"That's a tough one. Ask me a simple question, like do I think you are fat. And for the record, your rear end looks the same as it did five days ago. Obviously, you have not started walking. As for whether or not you are crazy, I would say, no more or less than anyone else. Just because you can see something others cannot, doesn't mean it's not there. I can't see my car outside, but I know it's parked in its usual spot. I can't touch Tom Selleck when he's on television, but I'm pretty sure it's him."

"You want to touch Tom Selleck?"

"In the most improper way."

Bootie pursed her lips. Erline, I am fifty-seven years old, and I haven't figured out anything about my life. I am as confused today as I was when I was twelve. And I'm not talking about my gift."

"They say the most brilliant and talented are the most troubled."

"Except I am not brilliant."

"You are talented, and I'm not talking about your visions." Erline flattened a wayward strand of hair on Bootie's head. "You are a good person, Beulah Baxter. You always try to do the right thing, and that's more important than always being right."

"Thank you, Erline."

Erline raised her eyebrow. "Have you ever had a vision about me?"

Bootie chuckled. "What would I see I don't already know?"

"Are you saying I'm boring?" Erline asked.

"You don't know how lucky you are," Bootie answered.

Bootie - 1948

9.

In New England, it is no coincidence the word crisp can describe both the edgy chill of a sunny October day, and the juicy crunch of a freshly picked Macintosh apple. Crisp was certainly the perfect word to describe the morning young Bootie awoke to a sky fat with wooly cumulus clouds. Clouds that would dim the sun's heat, and lay fleeting shadows over the town, the lake, and the Kurz household.

A brisk, gusting wind whistled through drying leaves on craggy branches of elderly trees and carried the sound of whinnying horses from the Kennedy ranch. Polka-dotted apple trees infused the air with the spicy-sweet aromas of their fruit, blending with the pungent smell of the burning farm and garden waste. Yellow and brown speckled oak leaves crunched underfoot, and the maple trees, in red and orange flames, spread to the horizon like an endless forest fire, and enhanced the sensuality of the crisp and glorious day.

On that October morning, Bootie was more than content. She was jubilant. Mother had decided to put up apples, and she had assigned the children various jobs to help her with the process. She needed only one kitchen assistant, and that morning she had chosen Bootie for the chore. Bootie and her mother would be working alone together in the kitchen, and any time alone with Mother was precious.

Mother had the radio playing, and she sparkled silvery-white as she tapped her foot to the music of Glen Miller. Bootie watched as she poured simple syrup into empty canning jars.

Bootie leaned over the stove. "Are these jars done yet?"

Mother glanced at the timer on the kitchen table. "Two more minutes. Sellie and Bernice will be bringing the last

How to Dance on the Moon 71

apples any time now.

As if on cue, Sellie and Bernice entered the kitchen with a large tub filled with peeled and sliced apples and set it on the floor. "It's hot in here!" Sellie complained. "Can't we be done?" She waved her hand in front of her face. "My fingers are all sticky and swollen, and Josephine Kennedy's birthday party starts in half an hour. Clark and Woody are already there, riding Aiden's new horse."

"Sellie just wants to go to the party because there will be boys there," Bootie said to her mother.

Sellie put her hands on her hips and stuck out her chin. "Well, Bernice is going so she can kiss Mickey."

"Girls, stop that talk." Mother pointed to the tub of apples. "Sellie, you can be done after you mix some salt and cinnamon in that bucket."

Sellie moaned.

"I'll do it," said Bernice.

Beulah Kurz stretched up to her eldest daughter, who was three inches taller than she was, and kissed her on the forehead. "Sellie, thank your sister before you leave the kitchen." Sellie batted her lashes at Bernice and rushed off.

Bernice stirred the salt and spice into the bucket. "Bootie, do you want me to fix your hair for the party?"

"I don't even want to go to the party," Bootie said.

The timer pinged. "Bernice, that's good," Mother said. "You can go on. I need Bootie for a little longer." Bernice left the kitchen, and Bootie resumed stuffing apples into jars. The timer pinged, and Mother lifted the cooked jars from the boiling water with her tongs and placed them in a rack next to the burner. She added water into the large pot and adjusted the heat.

"So, tell me, Bootie," Mother began. "Do you know what I am thinking right now?"

"That I need a haircut?" Bootie guessed, brushing her bangs from her eyes.

Mother laughed. "Well that's true. But if you tried, could you figure out what I was thinking?"

"How could I?"

"Do you ever know other people's thoughts?"

Bootie eyed her mother suspiciously at the unexpected and uncomfortable question. She had an uneasy feeling Mother was setting her up for trouble, like when she had asked Woody who had crumbs all over his face what happened to a missing cookie. Bootie stuffed her jars faster. "I know when you are happy and when you aren't."

"Stop working for a minute." Mother latched onto Bootie's right hand and squeezed it. "Try to figure out what I am thinking right now."

Closing her eyes, Bootie tried to think of something to say to get her mother to change the subject, but instead, she blurted, "I think you don't want to take any more business trips with Father."

Mother dropped Bootie's hand and her expression hardened. "Do you know where Father and I go on those trips?"

This was another dangerous question. Bootie bit at a cinnamon-tipped fingernail and struggled to find a safe answer that was not a lie, but not the truth either.

Accepting no response as an answer, Mother said, "You do know. That's part of the reason we're having this chat. Do you get worried?" Bootie shrugged. The kitchen was steaming with aromatic vapor. Sweat had started to trickle down Bootie's back and, like Sellie, apple juice had made her hands swell. "Sit down," Mother said. She gestured for Bootie to take Father's chair.

"Am I in trouble, Mother?"

"No, sweetheart." After checking her pot, Mother sat next to Bootie, close enough for a wispy lavender scent to cut through the aroma of cooked apples. "But tell the truth. Can you hear people's thoughts? Please stop pretending you don't

How to Dance on the Moon

understand my question."

Bootie turned her head, avoiding her mother's gaze. "I don't hear people's thoughts. But, sometimes, when someone touches me, I know things about them. Things they may not even know about themselves." Bootie hesitated. "Sometimes they don't even have to touch me. I just know. And I can see colors around people."

"Have you ever seen things about me? Do you see colors around me?"

"All I can see is your light. I don't know why, but you're the only person I can't see things about."

"How do the colors work?"

"When I relax my eyes and look at someone, I see light around them. The longer I look, the brighter the light becomes, until the color shines, too. Sometimes the light is so bright it makes shadows, and I can't imagine how no one else sees it."

"What colors do you see?"

"Blue is the easiest. Then yellow and green. Red, brown and black are the bad colors. I always avoid Father when he is red."

"What color is Father, usually?"

Bootie studied her mother's face before answering. "Yellow. He is always dark yellow, unless he leaves on a trip, or he's angry. Then he's green or grey or red."

Mother put her hand to her forehead. "I knew it," she said, more to herself than to Bootie.

Bootie studied her mother's expression. "How did you know I could see things?"

Mother crinkled her brow. "Because I have a similar gift."

It took a moment for Bootie to grasp her mother's meaning. "You see things too?"

"Differently than you, but yes."

Bootie stared at her mother, bewildered, until the power of her words overwhelmed her. She jumped from her chair and hugged her mother's waist. "You know my secret! You know!

Laura Ginter 74

You have what I have!"

"Sit back down and lower your voice. We don't know who's around to hear us. I can't see into people or see colors. I can only touch objects to get pictures of other objects. But my mother was just like you."

"Did she see invisible things?"

"Do you?"

"I see things made just of light that nobody else sees. Like animal haunts or sparkles."

"Do they scare you?"

Bootie looked into her mother's eyes. "When they appear out of nowhere they do. It's like someone coming up behind you and yelling boo. I hate it."

"Why haven't you ever tried to talk to me about it?"

"I didn't want you to think there was something wrong with me. I've heard people who see things that aren't there get sent to a mental hospital."

"A mental hospital?" Mother looked sad. "I'm sorry you felt like that, Bootie."

"The boys and Sellie think I make things up. They make fun of me."

Mother smoothed Bootie's hair. "Let me try to make you feel better. Some people can hit baseballs pretty far. Some people can walk a mile on their hands. I can see pictures of things by touching things. You see pictures about people by touching people. It's a gift."

"It's not a gift. It's a curse. I hate it. I don't want to tell anyone about it, and I will never use it."

"You will, Bootie. As you get older, you will figure out who you can tell, and what you can and cannot do. Then you will decide how to use it." Mother stood. "Sounds like the water is boiling. We must still discuss the business trips, but let's get these jars going first."

Bootie savored the joyous moment. She wasn't a freak! The burden of keeping her secret was over. She didn't have to

How to Dance on the Moon 75

figure it out by herself anymore. Her mother could help her stop the unwanted visions. Help her not be afraid. Help her find answers to the scariest questions. And she had so many questions!

Bootie handed jars to her mother to place in the boiling water. "Mother, why did Father say you were crazy like your mother? Does the gift make us all crazy? Is that why we never see our Flynn grandparents? Did they try to send Grandmother Flynn to a mental hospital?"

Mother set the timer. "Nobody has gone to a mental hospital, and nobody ever will." She filled a second pot with the remaining apple slices and set it on a separate burner on the stove. She handed a wooden spoon to Bootie. "Stir these for me, please. I'll be right back."

Mother left the kitchen and returned a couple minutes later with a dusty, buttery-yellow teapot Bootie had never seen before. "Turn off the heat under the apples and come over here," Mother said. Bootie flipped the knob on the stove and moved to her mother's side. Mother used a towel to wipe the teapot before holding it out for Bootie to take.

"Use two hands," Mother instructed. "This teapot was given to my mother by my grandmother, Kiera. One of the few things she brought here from Ireland. It's old and special to me, but I want you to have it."

Bootie took her gift and held it gingerly. The teapot was warm and appeared to glow from within itself. The yellow belly served as a background to pink and blue flowers and white butterflies. Antique silver adorned the tip, and both the knob and the lid's rim were gilded. The porcelain was delicate and felt fragile.

"The ability to see visions goes a long way back in our family," Mother said. "My grandmother Kiera, your great-grandmother, called it the second sight."

"Who else has had the second sight?"

"Many. All women. Fiona Flower for one. This was her

teapot, given to her around 1740 we think. Fiona was a midwife. Back then, country doctors were few, and women used midwives to deliver their babies. They had nothing to ease the labor pains unless they knew a midwife like Fiona who had a recipe for something called Groaning Ale. Women believed Groaning Ale had the power to make childbirth hurt less, and midwives used it to wash the infant after birth. People also believed Fiona could reduce the pain with the touch of her hand.

"As the story goes, Fiona Flower assisted with the difficult birth of a woman's second son, and the grateful family gave this teapot to her. However, the mother died two days later, and the gossip spread that Fiona had poisoned the Groaning Ale to kill the mother to steal the husband's heart. The townspeople called Fiona a witch who used her hands to do evil magic, and it didn't help that she was a beautiful woman. Not long before that time, they hung witches or drowned them or burned them at the stake, but, luckily for Fiona, those times had passed.

"Then the baby boy died. Again, the villagers blamed Fiona. One night, they tied Fiona to a tree and burned down her house, right in front of her eyes. Afterward, a kind, old woman untied Fiona, and when Fiona sifted through her home's ashes, she found the one thing the fire did not destroy. This teapot."

"What happened to Fiona Flower?"

"Her story is lost at this point, but we can learn a lesson from her. A responsibility comes with the second sight. Your gift gives you more than just visions. It gives you information, and you can be tempted to use it to help people, or change people, or make people behave differently. And people who want your special insights can victimize you if you let them. But don't ever let anyone use you to get to your gift."

Bootie didn't understand what Mother was telling her, but she could think about it later. "How come you don't talk about our Flynn family? How come we never see them? Does it have

How to Dance on the Moon 77

to do with your mother having the gift?"

"No. My parents were immigrants and house servants. They moved away when I married your father."

"Do you miss them?"

"Very much. But that's another story for another day." Mother pointed to the dish cupboard. "I will make a spot on the top shelf. If you ever want to hold your teapot, I will take it down for you."

"Where was it before now?"

"In a special place in the barn."

Near the secret treasure, Bootie imagined. She followed her Mother over to the dish cupboard and watched her stretch up to the highest shelf she could reach and take down a gravy boat. Bootie handed her the teapot, and she set it in the empty spot. "Perfect!" said Mother. "There's an old Irish saying. Life is like a cup of tea. It's all in how you make it."

"I like that," Bootie said, then touched her mother's hand. "Why didn't you tell me all this sooner?"

"Having seven children keeps a person busy. Can you see the timer?"

"It says five more minutes."

"It's hard to see the gift in other people, especially if you have it yourself. And you have done an excellent job hiding it from me, Bootie. But last night I found your rabbit's foot under your bed, and when I picked it up, I felt its magic, and I knew the truth."

"So why do you go on those business trips with Father?"

Mother's shoulders fell forward. "I'm sorry you know the truth about that. What your father and I have done is wrong, and I should never have let it all start."

"Why did you? What about Fiona Flower, and living your own life?"

"It's complicated grownup business. It's best we don't go into that right now. But you can never, ever, tell anyone the truth about those trips. And I promise there won't be any more."

Sellie was back in the kitchen before Bootie could respond. "Come on, Bootie," Sellie said. "It's time to go to the party. I have Josie's present."

"Put a coat on Sellie!" Mother said. "It's going to get much colder." Sellie ran out, leaving Bootie in the kitchen. Mother tapped Bootie's nose. "Go to the party. I can finish the apples."

"I don't want to. I want to talk to you more."

Mother ruffled Bootie's hair. "You do need a haircut. You should go to the party. You'll have fun. And they said they wanted everyone there for a big surprise."

Sellie called to her from outside. "Hurry up, Bootie! Bernice and I are waiting."

Bootie thought about it. "Maybe I can ride the horse with Clark and Woody, and watch Bernice make whoopee-eyes at Mickey." Bootie fluttered her eyelashes.

"Get your coat. That's a good girl. Tell Mrs. Kennedy that Scooter and Ike won't be there. Scooter's new braces need adjustments, and Ike needs a nap. I'll cut your hair when you get back, and we'll talk more."

"Thank you, Mother." Bootie found her coat, and on her way out the front door she paused, suddenly filled with an overwhelming urge to run back into the kitchen, to give her mother the biggest hug she could squeeze from herself, and to thank her and tell her how much she loved her. She turned and looked at her mother swaying contentedly to the big band music still playing on the radio.

"Hurry up, Bootie!" Sellie yelled out from the top of the driveway. Bootie watched her mother dance for a moment longer before turning away and joining her sisters.

10.

After eating a hotdog, Bootie passed on the checkerboard cake and coffee ice cream, and slipped off to the stables to watch the boys take turns riding the new horse. Only Bootie noticed when Mickey and Bernice disappeared into the barn. When the party ended, the children gathered to walk home. The cottony clouds from earlier in the day had filled in and darkened, hinting at snow. Sellie blew imaginary cigarette puffs with her cold breath and picked a clump of dried grass off Bernice's coat.

"I fell in the hay," Bernice said, slapping her sister's hand away.

"Why are you telling us when nobody asked?" Woody retorted. Bernice blushed and glared at her brothers when they started making kissing noises.

As they walked, Sellie gossiped about the more entertaining events at the party. The boys pretended the smoke from the leaf fires still burning in town was the school burning down. Bernice complained the boys smelled like manure, but the boys either didn't hear her or didn't care. The jostling and playing continued until they approached their house and a knot began to grow in Bootie's stomach.

"Something's wrong," Bootie said, searching the road in front of her.

Bernice tried to see what her sister was looking at. "What are you talking about?"

"Something's wrong," Bootie repeated. "We must get home."

Sellie hit Bootie's arm. "Stop it. You are always trying to scare us."

"No, I mean it." Bootie started running. She ran until she reached the driveway, and slipped on the gravel, falling and skinning the palms of her hands. Father's Chevy Suburban sat in its usual spot, but beside it were two Grafton County Sheriff

Laura Ginter   80

cars. Four more state police cars and official vehicles were parked throughout the yard and between the trees. Uniformed men were rummaging through Father's car, and Bootie saw Mr. and Mrs. Maslow peering at the scene from behind a bush at the property line. Bootie raced down the driveway to the house. She caught Sheriff O'Brien's eye, and when he started to approach her, she turned away.

A swarm of law enforcement people buzzed throughout the property. A policeman held Baby Ike. Scooter sat on the stoop with his face buried in his folded arms. Looking down at him was a man in a gray fedora. Bootie couldn't see him clearly, until he looked up. He had a patch covering one eye.

Bootie ran to her little brother. His chest heaved with sobs. "Scooter, what's going on?"

Scooter looked up. "That pirate took Mama and Father to jail."

"What?"

The eye-patch man stepped toward her, but Bootie moved away. "Don't come near me!"

"You're Bootie?" the man asked.

Bootie clenched her fists to control her trembling hands. "You're that bad man from the island who spied on us."

"I'm not a bad man, Bootie. Please don't be afraid. Come here. Let's talk."

Bootie hesitated. An undercurrent of danger emanated from the man. She looked at his colors. Blue. Sadness. She tried to sense his thoughts without touching him. No anger, no intention to hurt her. She took three steps toward him and stopped, pulling her coat closed. "Talk to me from here."

"Fair enough. My name is Agent Chandler. I work for the FBI. Do you want to see my badge?"

Bootie lifted her chin. "Yes, sir."

Agent Chandler straightened, pulled a leather case from his jacket pocket, and flipped it open. "Do you want to see it closer?"

How to Dance on the Moon   81

"No, sir." Chandler placed the badge back in his pocket. "Did you arrest my parents?"

"Yes, I did."

Bootie glanced over her shoulder to see other uniformed men speaking with her brothers and sisters. Sellie was sobbing, and Bernice was comforting her.

"Why?" Bootie asked, although she already knew why.

"They are accused of stealing money from banks."

"When will they come home? Mother needs to help Scooter with his exercises."

"Not tonight."

Bootie's brave facade collapsed. She rushed forward and began beating on Agent Chandler's arm. "You can't take my mother! I need her! I need my mother!" Bootie's tears flung from her face as she flailed.

Agent Chandler grasped Bootie's arms, but she pulled herself free. "I know this is hard for you," he said.

"You don't know anything." Bootie swiped at her tears. I need my mother. This is all my fault! My fault! Take me to jail too!"

Chandler offered Bootie a handkerchief, but she shook her head. "And why would this be your fault?" he prodded. Bootie slumped, and Chandler put his hand on her shoulder. "The best way you can help your mother is by talking to me."

Bootie squirmed away from his touch. It made her stomach sour to see that he pitied her. "Leave me alone!" she screeched and ran into the house, looking for her mother. This all had to be a joke, she thought. Punishment for sneaking off to the island the night of the last business trip. Mother would be standing by the stove, crossing her arms the way she did when she was angry. Bootie would hug her as hard as she could and promise never to lie to her again and beg her never to pull such a mean trick again.

Inside the kitchen, a cinnamon scent swirled in the air with wafts of steam emitting from the canning pot. Police officers

Laura Ginter   82

were busy opening drawers and reaching into cupboards. The yellow teapot still rested on the shelf where she had placed it less than three hours earlier.

Bootie sat at the table, waiting to see if her insides were going to explode. Agent Chandler entered the kitchen, rinsed a washrag and handed it to Bootie. "For your hands." He sat in her father's chair, and Bootie pressed the cloth between her skinned palms. She closed her eyes to make everything go away. The policemen, Agent Chandler, the pot of steaming water.

"Do you want to take off your coat?" Bootie shook her head. "We have contacted your Aunt Theodora, and she is coming to stay with you while this is sorted out."

Bootie flung the wet rag to the floor. "I don't want to talk to you."

"Don't you want to know what will happen to your parents?" Bootie opened her eyes and saw an officer removing dishes from the cupboard shelves. "The police are taking them to Laconia, and then to Concord where they will be held at the jail. They will go before a judge who will determine if they should be charged with a crime."

"Will the judge let them come home after that?"

"If you help us, the Court will help you."

"Why were you hiding in the bushes on the island?"

The eye-patch man furrowed his brows. "I'll tell you the truth, Bootie. My men and I were watching your parents that night to see if they left the house. The island provided an opportunity to observe them without being seen."

"And what did you see?"

Agent Chandler took a long breath. "We saw them leave. And someone robbed a bank in Laconia that same night. We found enough evidence to arrest them. I'm sorry. You shouldn't have to be a part this. I know how much this must hurt."

"How would you know how I feel? You are the one who

How to Dance on the Moon 83

puts people in jail."

Although he didn't say it, his thought came through distinctly: I *put criminals in jail.* Bootie shuddered. "You think my parents are bad people."

"I didn't say that."

"You thought it."

He shook his head. "I was honest with you, now you must be honest with me. Did you ever see them bring anything home and hide it? Like suitcases or bags or boxes?"

"Or money?"

"Or money?"

"No. Never." A policeman had started clearing the top shelf of the cupboard. "Tell that man to be careful with my teapot."

"Milton, bring that kettle over here." The policeman complied, and Bootie scooped it up and cuddled it like an injured kitten.

"Where is that gun your brother waved at me?" asked the detective.

"The cap gun?"

"It was a cap gun?" Agent Chandler smirked. "Okay, where is the cap gun?"

"I think it's at the fort. In the trunk."

"Milton, ask the team on that island if they found a cap gun hidden in a trunk." Agent Chandler turned back to Bootie. "That night on the island, you said there was a secret treasure in the barn. Where in the barn?"

"We were playing a game. Truth or lie. It was a lie."

"You said it was the truth."

"Nobody believed me, remember?"

"There is no treasure?"

"No, sir. If my mother can't come home, when can I go see her?"

"That's up to the Court." Chandler forced an unconvincing smile. "Bootie, it's interesting you haven't defended your

Laura Ginter   84

parents. You haven't once said you believe they are innocent. You know more than you are telling me." He studied her with his one eye. "You know the difference between right and wrong. Do the right thing. Tell me where they hid the money. You will be helping your parents if you do."

Bootie looked away. The eye-patch man stood and fished a card from his pocket, handing it to Bootie. "Here is my phone number if you have anything you want to tell me after I leave. You're a strong girl, Bootie. You'll get through this."

Sheriff O'Brien entered the kitchen. "Hello, Bootie," he said, stiffly. Bootie hugged the teapot and looked at the floor. Sheriff O'Brien patted Bootie on the shoulder, and Bootie jumped at his touch. Her stomach again twisted and knotted into sour spasms.

"There's raccoons in the barn and the big one is hissing at anyone who gets near it." Sheriff O'Brien swept a hand over his shoulder. "We could shoot it, but Henry Kurz thinks of those raccoons as pets."

"I'll be right there." Agent Chandler turned his attention back to Bootie. "Go to your brothers and sisters. Your aunt should be here soon."

Bootie stood and, clutching the teapot, bolted out the front door. She almost stumbled over Scooter still sitting on the stoop. She glanced at the activity around her. Sellie and Bernice were still with a police officer. Bernice was now holding Baby Ike.

"Why are there so many people in the barn?" Bootie asked Scooter, although she knew the answer.

"They are looking for stolen money, but they won't find any because Momma and Father didn't steal any." He looked up at Bootie, his eyes red and swollen, his lips stretched tight. "That pirate sent Mother and Father away, and he won't let them come back unless we give him money. White-eye William Shipburner should have protected us from the bad pirate, but I didn't. I couldn't. This is all my fault."

How to Dance on the Moon

At the sound of crunching gravel, Bootie turned to see Aunt Theo's gray Cadillac pull into the driveway. When Aunt Theo climbed from her car, she dropped her cigarette and crushed it with her red high-heeled shoe. She was wearing a red polka dot party dress with a white pearl necklace and a wide-brimmed red hat. Even from the stoop, the mismatched bulges around her chest and waist showed she had buttoned her dress wrong. She wore no coat, although the temperature had dropped to freezing.

Aunt Theo flung open her arms, her white gloves flittering like two giant moths. "Oh sweet mother! Children!" she cried.

Bootie put the teapot gently on the soft ground beside the stoop where the policemen couldn't step on it, and she helped Scooter navigate with his crutches to her Aunt Theo's side. Bootie latched onto her aunt's waist. Pushing into her soft bosom, she breathed in her smoke-infused rose cologne. A slushy raindrop pelted Bootie on the head, and she began to cry again. The mascara streaks on Aunt Theo's face showed she had been crying, too. Bootie didn't care that her aunt's face was a mess, or that her dress was on wrong, or that she reeked of soured perfume and Chesterfields. Aunt Theo was here, and she would fix everything.

A shotgun blast exploded from the barn.

Bootie 1993

11.

Erline clutched the hair color bottle in one gloved hand and the top of Bootie's head with the other. "Hold still or you'll end up with zebra stripes."

"I have an itch," Bootie complained. She scratched her forehead and wiped dark purple dye from her finger onto her shirt, stained from years of hair color drips.

"So, go on with your story," Erline said. "What happened after Aunt Theo got there?"

"She moved in the night the police arrested my parents, and never left until she went to the retirement home, thirty years later."

"Didn't your parents go home before their trials?"

Bootie shook her head. "No one found the stolen money, so the judge considered them flight risks and denied bail." Bootie felt the tip of the dye bottle streak across her scalp. She tilted her head up to look at her friend. "How about cutting me some bangs tonight?"

"Stop moving!" Erline pushed Bootie's head back down. "Do you want this to drip into your eyes? You don't want bangs. They always need trimming. That would annoy you." Erline rubbed additional solution on Bootie's temples, before placing the coloring bottle on the table. She peeled the gloves from her hands. "Done. Now we wait. Would you like wine?" Without waiting for a reply, Erline disappeared into the tearoom kitchen.

Bootie's damp hair chilled her, and she shivered. The ammonia smell wafting about her head caused her to wrinkle her nose. "Why does this stuff have to stink?" she called out. "You would think someone would have figured out how to make hair dye smell better."

How to Dance on the Moon 87

"If men colored their hair as much as women did," Erline yelled back from the kitchen, "it would smell like beer. There's not much wine left. Do you have another box somewhere?"

"There's plenty left. Rip the carton open and pull out the liner. Do you need help?"

"No, I have it." Erline returned with two water glasses filled within an inch of the top with yellow wine. "Only the finest Chablis for us. Take a whiff." She handed a glass to Bootie, who swirled it under her nose.

"Ah. A June vintage, I believe. It has that late spring bouquet."

"It has that dirty refrigerator bouquet. It's a good thing you don't serve this to your guests." Erline clinked her glass against Bootie's. "Cheers." Erline sat across from Bootie and sipped her wine. "I set the timer for forty minutes."

The lights framing her outdoor sign twinkled through the rain-streaked window, illuminating the fat raindrops thumping on the ground. An Alvin Armstrong melody filtered down from the mounted tearoom speakers, and she allowed the music to wash over her, soothing her like a hot shower, softening the edginess creeping over her from reliving her parents' arrest. The two women sipped with an easy relaxed rhythm that mirrored their friendship.

"Go on," Bootie encouraged her friend. "Ask more questions if you'd like."

Erline pursed her lips. "What started your parents' crime spree? Were there money problems?"

"There shouldn't have been. My uncle had created a trust fund for us, but Father refused the money. I think he felt robbed of his birthright when his grandfather died, and was angry when his uncle failed to promote him through the ranks at the savings and loan. I suspect the first bank my father stole from was his uncle's. Father found a way to exploit Mother's gift, and at first, he used it to punish his uncle. But it worked so well he branched out to other banks. The FBI thought he brought my mother to watch for the police. I think she was the actual safecracker."

"She could use her gift to pick locks but couldn't foresee her arrest?"

"I don't think she had visions the way I do. And you never see things about yourself."

"Why do you think your mother went along with it?"

"Because either she loved him, or feared him, or some combination of that."

"Do you know how they got caught?"

"When Sheriff O'Brien patted my shoulder, I learned the police had discovered many of the burglaries coincided with Father's bank audits. The last bank they hit was a setup. That was when we caught Agent Chandler sniffing around the island. What's sad is if I had told my parents about Agent Chandler I might have prevented their arrest."

"Bootie, it wasn't your responsibility to stop them."

"That's an arguable statement."

Erline reached across the table and tapped Bootie on the arm. "You are being too hard on yourself."

Bootie sipped her wine. "The court found my father guilty of two counts of burglary and sentenced him to fifteen years in prison. The FBI suspected him in almost every bank burglary that happened for five years throughout four states, including his uncle's banks. Father died a convict."

"What about your mother?"

"In jail, Mother stopped speaking. When she stopped eating, too, the authorities sent her to Bridgewater State Hospital near Boston for a psychological evaluation. At the time, the hospital in Concord couldn't take her. Bridgeport State was, and still is I think, a hospital for the criminally insane. Aunt Theo said my mother died there of a broken heart before the trial. Aunt Theo's brothers brought her body back to New Hampshire, and we held a small funeral."

Bootie tapped her fingernail on the edge of her glass. "It's

How to Dance on the Moon 89

ironic her life ended in a mental hospital. My father had just accused her of going crazy like the rest of her family. And on the day she was arrested, she had reassured me having the gift did not mean we were crazy. But for a long time, I took it as proof that the gift did make you crazy. How much longer must this hair color set?"

Erline looked at her watch. "Less than ten minutes."

"Good." Bootie cleared her throat

Erline gave Bootie a comforting pat on the hand. "At least you children stayed together."

"Yes, thanks to Aunt Theo. She was a terrible guardian but she kept the welfare people from splitting us up into foster homes." Bootie put her glass to her lips and finished her wine. "All my brothers and sisters, except Bernice and Clark, have lived at the lake house at some point in their adult life. Ike is there now, I think you know. I wish I could get back there more often." She wiped an unexpected tear from the corner of her eye. "Our little lake has been blessed. It has escaped most of the development in that area. From the Kennedy's beach you still can't see a single house on the lake."

Erline finished her wine and picked up Bootie's empty glass, along with the bottle of hair color and her gloves. On her way to the kitchen she paused by the yellow teapot with the gilded knob sitting on the shelf near the bathrooms. The teapot Beulah Flynn Kurz had given her daughter the day she went to jail. "I've always marveled at how it glows from the inside," Erline said.

"Did I ever tell you I have a lock of Clark's hair in there?"

"Seriously?"

"My mother was cutting his hair, and I took some. For years, I kept it in a coin purse with my rabbit's foot."

Erline studied the teapot a bit longer before entering the kitchen. She reemerged with two fresh, half-filled glasses of the boxed Chablis. "The wine is really gone now." Erline sat back in her chair facing Bootie and raised her glass. "Here's to

Beulah and Henry Kurz. May their memories always live in Bootie's Tea Room."

They clinked their glasses together, and Bootie put her hand to her chest. "The scar I have from losing my parents sometimes rips open unexpectedly and my heart feels so heavy, like it all happened yesterday. But telling this story has made me realize I'm sadder for the seven children who lost their parents tragically and unexpectedly more than for my fifty-seven-year-old self. The difference is subtle, but I may be starting to face my issues."

"Like your need to forgive yourself?"

Bootie pushed a sticky strand of hair from her cheek. She knew she had a lot of dirty laundry, but sometimes things had to soak for a long time before the stains come out. "Not quite there yet, Erline." The timer for Bootie's hair buzzed, and she stood. "Time to rinse."

Bootie placed her head deep into the kitchen basin, where the hair dye mixed with tap water and spiraled down the drain.

Erline handed Bootie a towel. "Bootie, did the police get the money back?"

"Father never confessed to his crimes, and nobody could get him to talk about money. They never found any."

"Did your father spend it, or is it lost?"

Bootie allowed herself a droll smirk. "He never spent a penny of it, and it was never lost. I know where they hid it. Almost thirty years ago, to the day. . ." Bootie paused. "Erline, what is the date?"

"July 12th."

Bootie jumped from her chair. "It's Grace's birthday! I have to call her right now!"

Erline laughed and reached for her coat. "Do you think Grace is sitting at home waiting for your birthday call?"

Bootie reached for the phone. "Where else would she be?" As she dialed the phone, she saw a pig-shaped haunt in front of the door to the kitchen.

Part 2

Just-Grace-All-Alone

Grace 1971

12.

The wind blew at eighteen knots. Intrepid US 20, the 1967 America's Cup winner was entering Newport Harbor for the summer jazz festival celebration. As the news of Intrepid's arrival traveled through the crowd, Grace and Stephen, ten and eleven years old, jumped and waved their arms, their fists clenched in good cheer, knowing the collective high spirits meant a profitable day for them. They dashed down to the docks to join the throngs waiting to greet the wooden hometown hero.

The children positioned themselves in front of the marine supply store on the wharf, and Stephen removed a white, sweat-stained sailor's hat from his head and set it on the ground. Pulling out four white balls from a bag hanging around his neck, he tossed them up one at a time until they all were circling in the air. Grace tapped her feet and sang notes from a circus song she knew. "Dah da Dah Dah da Dah da Dah." People on their way to see the sailing boats paused, chuckled and commented on the children's precociousness, before dropping their spare change into the hat.

After ten minutes, the marine store manager came out, scolded the children and told them to leave. Stephen dumped the coins from the hat into his bag along with his juggling balls and grabbed Grace's hand. Together they raced farther down the dock until they were out of the cranky store manager's sight. Again, Stephen set up for his juggling show. This time, no one interrupted the performance, and when the coins filled the hat, Stephen dumped them and his juggling balls in his bag, and the children raced to the farthest pier where no one could watch them.

The breeze smelled like a briny concoction of seaweed, diesel, old fish and fried food. The sound of children's feet pounding on the wooden pier competed with the pinging of cables hitting sailboat masts and screeching seagulls. They ran until they reached a sailing yacht named *Booby Trap*. The children glanced around the boat's deck, and seeing no one on deck, they totaled up their windfall. "Five dollars and forty cents," Stephen announced. "I'm buying me some ice cream."

"I'm getting a lobster roll," said Grace.

Stephen put his head down and furrowed his brow. "You're kidding."

"You know my friend Shorty who has the lobster boat? Remember when he found me on his boat hiding from my mom? He gave me a lobster claw, and I liked it." Grace lifted her chin. "I'm buying a lobster roll with my part of the money."

"Hey, you two!" A short, slender man wearing blue creased pants and a white shirt with epaulets stood on *Booby Trap*'s deck with his hands on his hips and glared at the children. "Get over here now." Stephen and Grace stashed their coins back in the bag and approached the boat. "What are you doing?" the man bellowed.

"Just playing, Mr. McHenry," Stephen said.

"Get back on this boat and get some food. The cook is trying to shut down the galley.

"Yes, sir."

Grace and Stephen approached the gangplank and scurried onboard. They took seats at the dining table. Mr. McHenry

How to Dance on the Moon 93

brought out two plates of baked chicken with mashed potatoes and asparagus. The children looked at each other and wrinkled their noses.

"Don't give me any problems young man, or I'll tell your father," Mr. McHenry said.

"He's probably not even here," Stephen whispered to Grace.

"I hope not," Grace said, and she took a swipe at the potatoes, the only thing she planned to eat. Someone entered the galley behind her, and she turned to see who was there. "Hi, Mom."

"Grace, where have you been?" Sellie wore tight white jeans and a tie-dyed tee shirt, with large hoop earrings. The black eyeliner drawn under her false eyelashes reminded Grace of a raccoon. Then Grace saw the bruise on her mother's cheek. Sellie put her hand to her face.

"Grace and I were just hanging out," Stephen said, and he kicked Grace under the table.

"Stephen, your father wants to head back to Marblehead. The crew's been waiting for you two."

Grace pouted. "But I thought Gil had friends coming, and we were going to the Vineyard."

"Not anymore."

Grace looked at her mother, suspicious about the change in plans. "Is everything okay?"

"Yes, Grace. Everything is fine." Sellie turned and disappeared back down into the passageway toward the staterooms.

"Did you see it?" Grace asked.

"Yes," said Stephen. He hung his head for a moment before saying. "Let's go topside." He pulled on Grace's arm enthusiastically. "Maybe we can help with the lines."

The children brought their dishes to the galley mate, and scampered through the hatch to the top deck where a deckhand was freeing the sailboat from the pier. They approached him, but he shooed them off. They moved to the forward deck and watched the sailboat push away and make way toward the Newport Bridge. The sailboat did not put out sail, powering forward with its engines instead.

"Let's play pirate hide and seek!" Grace said."

Stephen shook his head. "That's a baby game."

"If I'm a baby, you're a baby," Grace said.

"I am older than you, Baby! But I'll play if you want."

Grace clapped her hands gleefully. The two went back through the hatch to the stateroom they were sharing. Stephen went under the bottom bunk and pulled out two plastic swords and five gold colored disks from a cigar box. He handed Grace a sword, and they returned to the top deck and scampered forward to the bow.

"I'll hide first," said Grace. Stephen handed Grace the disks and stared off into the distance. Small islands passed on the starboard side as Grace made her way to the stern to hide each disk in its own spot. She returned to the bow and approached Stephen from the back. "Aye, mate. You may search for the pirate's treasure."

Stephen sprung across the deck to the stern and searched until he had found all five disks. Grace turned and looked away as Stephen took the disks back to the bow and hid them again.

Stephen and Grace played the game until the sun was low in the sky. "I'm tired of this game," said Grace. "Let's feed the gulls."

"They won't come," Stephen said, but he went to the galley and brought back bread. They went to the stern, and threw chunks of the bread off the back, but they were moving too fast for the gulls to stay with the boat. They dumped the rest of the loaf overboard, and sat in deck chairs. The evening grew chilly, and the sky darkened. Stephen suggested going below deck.

"I just want to sit here," Grace said.

"Aren't you cold?" asked Stephen.

"Not if you sit with me," answered Grace.

How to Dance on the Moon 95

Stephen scooted over to Grace's chair and squeezed in next to her. "You don't want to go in and see your mother."

"I don't want to see Gil, either. Where do you think they've been all night?"

"If Dad's been drinking, he's asleep, and Sellie's probably playing solitaire."

A long pause passed between them. "Why do you think Gil hits people?" asked Grace.

"He gets mad, I guess."

"I'm afraid someday he's going to hit me."

Stephen looked at her. "I'll never let him hit you, Grace. I'll never let anyone hit you."

Grace took his hand. "Not even you? You'll never hit me? Or yell at me? Or make me mad? Or sad?"

"Never," said Stephen.

"What about kiss me?" she asked, tilting her head. "Will you ever kiss me?"

"Never," said Stephen.

"Never?" Grace asked. "Have you ever kissed a girl?"

Even in the dark, she could see Stephen blush. "No, but I don't think I ever want to."

"You should try it before you say never."

"Have you ever kissed a boy?"

"Just my father, when he was alive, on the cheek."

Silence passed between them again. "Do you want to try it?" Stephen asked. "I mean, not like we're boyfriend and girlfriend. Just to see what it's like."

Grace's stomach did little flutters. "I don't know. It's scary to kiss, don't you think?"

"Yes. But I'd try it with you. Then we'd know."

"Okay, just to see. On the lips, right?"

"Okay. On the lips." The flutters in Grace's stomach grew stronger. Stephen bent forward until their lips touched, and quickly pulled back.

"Don't ever tell anyone," Stephen said.

Laura Ginter

"I won't," said Grace. She turned away from Stephen so he couldn't see how her smile lit the night sky.

Grace 1975

13.

"Mom!" squealed Grace. "The mailman is here!"

"I hope you aren't disappointed," said Sellie, lighting a cigarette.

"Stephen wouldn't forget my birthday just because you and Gil broke up again."

"I don't want you to get hurt," said Sellie.

Grace could still see the outline of a bruise on her mother's upper arm. "Like you?"

Sellie covered the bruise with her hand. "Grace, you must get past that."

"We've never even talked about what Gil did to you."

"Gil is not a bad man. He is under pressure, with his business and legal problems. Men get worked up, and sometimes women get caught in the crossfire."

Grace threw her hands up. "That's bullshit, Mom!"

"Grace! Watch your mouth!"

"You can still talk nice about him after everything he's done?"

"I can't talk about him with you at all."

"Gee. Sorry."

Grace turned from her mother and raced through the front door, to the top of the driveway. She reached inside the

How to Dance on the Moon 97

mailbox and removed several letters and a coupon flyer. She scanned each envelope. When she reached the bottom one, she shrieked.

Running back to the house, her mother intercepted her at the front door. "Did it come?"

"Yes, Mother, despite your prediction of disappointment."

As Grace pushed passed her mother, Sellie repeated her disparaging wish. "I don't want you to get hurt."

Grace went to the sleeping porch and ripped open the envelope, removing the card. The front showed a cat sitting on a barrel. *Sometimes I sits and thinks and sometimes I just sits.* She giggled and opened the card. *Today, I thinks about you. Happy birthday!*

Grace ran back to the kitchen and picked up the phone. "I'm going to call him."

Sellie walked up behind Grace, took the phone receiver from her hand and replaced it in the base. "No, you are not. It's too expensive."

"I'll pay for it."

"No. You must let Stephen go."

Grace rolled her eyes. "I'm calling." She took back the receiver and dialed the number to the house that had been her home off and on since she had been nine years old. A gruff voice answered. Grace hung up.

"Was it Gil?" Sellie asked. Grace nodded. "How did he sound?"

"Like he was beating up some woman."

"Grace. Becoming a teenager doesn't give you permission to talk to me that way. I'm still your mother."

Grace bit back several responses and slipped outside through the porch door. She heard her mother demand her return but ignored her as she trotted down the wooden walkway to the beach. The old rowboat was up on the sand. Grace climbed inside and cradled her head in her arms and fought back tears. She wondered if all the heartbreak had made her mother heartless.

A voice whispered her name from a bush behind her. Grace lurched upright, turned and shrieked. Stephen put his finger to his lips. She jumped from the boat and scampered over to him. They hugged, and Stephen gave her a quick kiss. "What are you doing here?" she asked.

"I couldn't let my best friend have her birthday without me."

"But how did you get here?"

"I hitched. It didn't take that long."

"What about your father?"

"He won't even notice. Mrs. Gritch is off today so she can't tell on me."

"You mean Mrs. Grinch."

"What are you doing for your birthday?"

"Mom made me a cake. It will just be Mom, Aunt Theo and Uncle Ike at my party. Unless you stay!" She pulled on his arm.

"No, I have to get back home. Besides, your mom would not be happy to see me."

A voice bellowed behind them. "That is very true."

Grace turned to see Sellie coming down the path. "Mom!" She stepped in front of Stephen as if to shield him from her mother's anger.

"You two get out of those bushes." Stephen pushed in front of Grace and they approached Sellie. "Stephen, what are you doing here?"

"He came for my birthday," Grace said. "I want him to stay for my party."

Sellie glared at Stephen. "Does your father know?" Stephen looked down at his feet. "I thought not. I am calling him."

"Please Sellie, don't," Stephen said. "He'll be furious."

Sellie rubbed her temple. "Come up to the house with me. Now. Both of you."

"Can we have a minute, Mother? Please?"

How to Dance on the Moon 99

Sellie looked as though she was going to say more, but instead, turned and climbed the path to the house.

Grace stomped her foot. "I hate when they break up in the summer."

"He'll bring her back, you know that."

"What if he doesn't this time?"

"He will. My father loves beautiful women."

"But he doesn't love her. He won't marry her."

"He won't marry anyone, ever again, after my mom. You know how much they hate each other. But he does love Sellie in his way. He's not going to let her go."

"Then why does he hit her?"

"Because she lets him."

Grace shook her fist at Stephen. "I'll hit YOU if you ever say that again."

Stephen put his hands up defensively. "Okay, I'm sorry. He hits her because he's mean. They'll be back together before school starts."

"But then you'll be back at Exeter, and I won't see you until Thanksgiving. Do you think Gil would ever send you to Israel? To live with your mother?"

Stephen laughed and put on a Boston accent. "Ya mean with da fockin hippie on da fockin commune? Never. But you know what? I hate when they break up in the summer, too." Stephen looked up toward the house. "Maybe I should hitch back."

"No. Stay. It's my birthday. I want you here." Grace took his hand and led him up the path to the house.

Sellie greeted them at the porch door. "I called your father, Stephen. He's sending someone up to get you."

Grace shook her head in disbelief. "Why would you do that? You know he will punish Stephen. And you know how, too."

"As a parent, it's the only thing I could do."

"You were hoping Gil would come up himself to get

Stephen. But he's not, is he?"

"Stop it, Grace. You got your wish. Stephen will be at your party now. Enjoy your time together while you can." Sellie lit a cigarette and sat at the porch table, turning her back to them. Grace heard her sniffling, and she turned and looked at Stephen. Stephen nodded and left the room. Grace put her hand on her mother's shoulder. "Mom, I'm sorry I said mean things to you about Gil. Stephen and I both agree. He'll be calling for you to go back before school starts. He loves you. And he knows I love my school in Marblehead."

Sellie glared at Grace. Her mascara had run down below her eyes. "What do you know about love?"

Grace shrugged. "Nothing, I guess. I just hate seeing you so sad. Can I do something for the party to help you? Do you want some coffee?"

Sellie tapped her cigarette on the ashtray's edge and was quiet for a long time. When she finally spoke, the sadness came from so deep inside her Grace questioned how hollow her mother had become. "My birthday wish for you, Grace," she said. "Don't grow up to be me."

Grace 1993

14.

The server cleared the empty beer mugs from the table and replaced them with two fresh Rainier Lights. "I shouldn't have ordered another beer," Grace said to Violet, fingering her mug with one hand and her car keys with the other.

"But Biscuit's not here yet." Violet countered. "And I'm

How to Dance on the Moon 101

cheating on my diet for you."

"He may not come if he's golfing, and I need to pick up Jennie from her friend's house."

"It's your birthday, Grace!" Violet pulled her long red hair free from her ponytail holder. Relax! Let's lose these boring beers and get some lemon drop martinis."

Grace rolled her eyes. "You're wicked! No martinis for me with a six-year-old at home."

"Can't you make a phone call and see if Jennie can spend the night at her friend's house?"

"No. And besides, if I showed up at work tomorrow with a self-inflicted head injury, Loretta would know and give me extra work."

"Forget Loretta. She's a shrew."

Grace took a sip from her mug. "They cut down the tree, you know."

Violet seemed confused. "What tree? Stephen's tree?"

Grace nodded. "My aunt Bootie came over and we watched it get hauled away. Now it won't remind me of the accident every day. Next Friday is the anniversary."

Violet shook her head. "Aw, Grace. What happened sucks, but thinking about something sad when you are drinking can turn alcohol into emotional snake venom. Think happy."

Grace tossed her keys back onto the table with a flourish. "You're right. Forget Loretta and babysitting curfews and trees. Bring me a shot of vodka!"

"Seriously?"

"No!"

Violet raised her mug. "Well, happy birthday anyway. And here's to 1993! To dead-end careers, single parenting, and thirty hour days. What all us women-libbers fought so hard for."

Grace giggled as Violet took an enthusiastic gulp of her beer. Violet set down her mug with a flourish, and Grace lifted her chin and pushed her honey-beige hair behind her ear.

Laura Ginter

"Thank you again for my present. I love these hoops."

"They screamed your name to me when I saw them. Ah, here comes Biscuit. I knew he wouldn't miss your birthday."

Grace turned and spotted Biscuit making his way to their table. She couldn't help but notice how his confident swagger and strapping physique set him apart from all the other pasty, fleshy men around her. And with his sexy, silver hair, edgy humor, and charming, thick-lipped grin that he flashed generously, she wondered how her sometimes snarly boss Loretta ever hooked such a prize catch.

Biscuit put his hand on Grace's shoulder. "Happy birthday, kid. I left the course after sixteen holes to say that to you."

"Thank you. What an honor." Grace stood and gave Biscuit a hug. A man was standing quietly next to Biscuit with his hands clasped behind his back. "You brought a friend."

Biscuit gestured toward his companion. "This is Blake Morton. He claims to have a zero handicap, and I have yet to prove him wrong. Seemed nicer to bring him to the party than leave him to finish the round alone."

The man flashed an engaging smile. He could be in the movies, thought Grace. He had black, combed-back hair. His green eyes were oval and wide set, like a wildcat. He was taller than Biscuit, and had broader shoulders. His muscles rippled underneath his shirt. Fresh cologne enveloped him. MadCrush for Men, a musky cologne she had once bought for Stephen. Her chest tightened as it always did when she smelled MadCrush.

"Can your ego handle playing with a scratch golfer?" Violet chirped.

Biscuit's eyes twinkled. "Yes, Violet. My ego is fine." He gestured toward Grace. "Blake, this is Grace Abram, Assistant Director of BATSS, that non-profit my girlfriend runs. Grace is the prettiest woman there, and if Loretta hears I said that, I'll deny it and insist she fire Grace, which would be tragic because I'm secretly in love with this gal." He turned toward Violet.

How to Dance on the Moon 103

"And this is Violet Bean, volunteer coordinator and overall nice person."

Violet's smile wavered. "Translation, I'm the office mutt with the good personality."

Biscuit chuckled. "You do have an exceptionally good personality."

"Oh Biscuit, that's mean," Grace said, slapping him on the arm.

"It's okay," said Violet. "He's jealous because Loretta likes me better than him."

Grace turned back toward Blake, who had been silent through the introductions. "Ignore what Biscuit says. He loves us both."

"Yes." Violet pouted. "He loves me because I let him make fun of me."

Biscuit mussed Violet's hair. "Oh, don't be that way. I was just kidding about your personality."

Violet swished her arm over her head to push Biscuit's arm away, and retied her hair with her hair band. "You are making things worse, Biscuit. I'm not having fun anymore. Tomorrow is a work day, and Grace is getting ready to leave anyway, so I'm out of here." Violet downed the rest of her beer, stood and reached over to give Grace a hug. "Happy birthday, Grace. I'll see you in the morning."

After Violet left the table, Grace turned to Biscuit. He was grinning. "Biscuit! That was horrible! You don't tell a woman she has a great personality and then pat her on the head like a pet dog."

Biscuit straightened at Grace's chastisement. "Did I screw up? I was just teasing her. We joke like that all the time."

"Not in front of men she doesn't know. And she's lost twenty pounds. Did you even notice?"

Biscuit looked distressed. "Maybe I should go talk to her."

"Yes. You hurt her feelings. Go to her and apologize. Tell her how pretty she looks. See if she'll come back."

"I will. I feel bad now." He stood and gestured to Blake. "You behave yourself around my girl, here. I saw how you looked at her."

Grace's face grew warm. Her visual response to Biscuit's words embarrassed her, but thankfully, no one seemed to notice.

Blake sat in Violet's vacated seat. "Thanks for letting me crash your party. It's been a while since I've spent an evening with someone without facial hair." He picked up Grace's car keys and studied the attached acrylic picture frame. "Is this your daughter?"

Grace took the keys from Blake and dropped them in her purse. "Yes."

"What's her name?"

"Jennifer. We call her Jennie."

"She's pretty. She looks like you. How old is she?"

"She just turned six. Would you like a drink? I can call over a server."

Blake leaned back in his chair. "I'll wait for Biscuit. I like how you stuck up for your friend just now."

"Biscuit can be obtuse, but he means well."

"Obtuse? I heard you were smart. Biscuit likes you a lot."

"I like him, too," Grace said and quickly added, "Biscuit is a good friend."

"Why does everyone call him Biscuit when his name is John?" Blake asked.

"His last name is Biscott. Biscott, Biscuit. Easy to make the jump.

"And you know him through BATSS?"

"He is a department chief for the fire department and once served on our Board of Directors. He still helps with the maintenance for our office."

Blake flicked her a quick grin. "And he dates your boss." He leaned back in his chair and studied her. An awkward silence fell between them, and Grace flipped through her

How to Dance on the Moon

mental Rolodex of social questions. "Do you live close by?"

"About a mile from the golf club," he replied. "I haven't lived here long. What is BATSS?"

"Bringing Athletics and Team Sports to Schools. My boss calls it BRATSS when the Board of Directors isn't around. We are funded by donations and grants and have about one hundred volunteers."

Blake shrugged. "Think I could volunteer? I've coached soccer."

Pleased, Grace pulled a business card from her purse. "We look for people with related experience. Violet handles the volunteers. You could talk to her." Blake thanked Grace and put the card in his pocket.

"Did you grow up around here?" Grace asked.

"I'm from Eugene, Oregon. My mother still lives there. I joined the Navy when I was eighteen and retired last year. Now I'm going to the University of Washington." He smirked. "I'm the old man on campus."

"What are you studying?"

"Communication. Tell me about you. Did you grow up here?"

"I'm a New England girl. I moved here when I married my husband. I lost him nearly two years ago. Car accident. Jennie is my only child."

"A single parent. That's tough. Do you have family to help you?"

"My mother is back east. My father died when I was young. My aunt is close by. She has a tearoom in West Seattle."

"West Seattle is nice." Blake said. "Love the beach. Is that where you live?"

"No, I own a house here in Bellevue."

"I bet it's a great neighborhood for kids."

Grace shook her head. "The neighborhood is new. Just three houses so far. We live in the cul-de-sac. Jennie just has one friend in the neighborhood so far, Lucy, who lives at the other end of the street." Grace lifted her mug. "Jeez, if you want to know my life story, serve me a little beer."

Blake laughed. "You're just sipping it."

Grace felt an uneasiness rumbling in her stomach. Blake was sexy. No, she corrected herself. He was handsome. And he seemed to like her. And Biscuit trusted him. But that was no reason to spew her life story. She scratched the back of her neck. "How do you know Biscuit?"

"Through the club. He's a good guy. I like golfing with him."

"He seems to like golfing with you, too."

Blake's eyes darted around the bar. "I don't go out much. School and golf. I'm not married." He grinned, shyly. "Never have been, and I don't know may people here, yet. That's why working with kids might be good for me." He looked back at Grace. She reached again for her mug, but it slipped from her fingers, and her beer spilled across the table. She watched in dismay as it dripped over the edge and onto Blake's pants. Blake grabbed a napkin and dabbed at his trousers. "I'm so sorry!" Grace said. "I've had one beer and look at me! Do you need another napkin?"

"I'm fine," Blake said. "It was only a couple of drops."

A server came and cleaned the table. Blake ordered three beers before Grace could tell him she didn't want another.

"As pretty as you are, I imagine you're spoken for," Blake said when the server had left.

Grace shook her head. "I went on a blind date with a buddy of Violet's cousin a couple of weeks ago. His name was George. It was a disaster."

Blake nodded. "Blind dates can be pretty awful."

Grace smirked. "It seemed harmless at the time. A good way to break into dating. George had a good pedigree. A Gonzaga graduate who worked for the state. But he liked me a lot, and it was too much too fast. When he asked me out again,

How to Dance on the Moon

I said no. About a week later, I got a couple harassing phone calls. I'm sure they were from him."

"Scary?"

"The first one was your standard heavy breathing. And let's say the second was more creative. I recognized his voice, though, and told him if he ever phoned me again I would call the police." Grace shook her head. "I'm not ready to date, yet. And it's too hard with a six year old."

Blake looked at her sympathetically. "It must be hard to be a single woman these days. How do you weed out the creeps?"

Grace didn't respond. Her mood was rapidly deteriorating. What was she thinking? Drinking in a bar and talking about her dead husband, her mother, her daughter, and her obscene phone caller with a stranger who smelled like Stephen? And, how had Blake gotten her to open up so easily? She was not usually this chatty. She wished Biscuit would come back so she could say goodbye and go home.

"You seem sad." Blake reached across the table and patted her hand. A shock passed between them. Grace started and pulled away. "I'm sorry," Blake said. "That might have been inappropriate. My social skills are rusty." He picked up a fresh napkin, "I want to give you a present."

Blake opened the napkin, smoothed it out on the table, and began to refold it. When he was done, the napkin resembled a rose. He borrowed a pen from Grace and wrote something on the bottom. "I'm one of the good guys, Grace," Blake said, handing her the rose. "Biscuit can vouch for me. With this crazy phone caller, you may need someone to watch out for you. Someone with no expectations. I wrote my phone number on there."

Grace took the rose from Blake, and she raised her eyes to meet his. He smiled, and she couldn't help but be impressed by how he had picked up on her feelings, and had cared enough to try to lift her spirits. Her face grew warm.

Someone kicked her chair leg from behind, and she turned

to see Biscuit carrying three beer mugs. "Here you go. I intercepted the waiter. Rainier Light, right?"

Grace accepted the mug but set it down without drinking any. "You couldn't talk Violet into coming back?"

"No, but we kissed and made up. Hey, the baseball game is on at the bar. Let's go over there and watch it. Then I can have a smoke."

"I'd love to, but I can't." Grace stood and reached for her purse. "I have to pick up Jennie." She took Blake's rose from the table, and smiled at him.

Biscuit looked hard at Grace. "You can't leave. I just got here, and you haven't touched your beer."

"I'm sorry Biscuit, but I already stayed longer than I planned." Grace dropped the rose into her purse and pulled out her wallet. She set a ten-dollar bill on the table. "You can have my beer."

Biscuit stood, picked up the bill and put it back in her hand. "At least I can walk you to your car."

Grace tilted her head at him flirtatiously. "I see two seats available right now at the bar. You should go grab them."

Biscuit looked over his shoulder. "You're right. You're okay with that?"

"Of course!" Grace kissed Biscuit on the cheek.

Blake rose and extended his hand. "I enjoyed meeting you."

Grace tilted her head, surprised at her sudden shyness, and accepted his hand. Another shock passed between them. She gasped and stepped back. Blake clasped her hand again, tenderly. He stared at her longer than she found comfortable and averted her eyes.

Biscuit tugged on Blake's arm, and Grace pulled away. "Get your beer," Biscuit said to Blake, then turned to Grace. "Happy birthday, kid. I'm fixing a bookcase at your office tomorrow. See you then?"

Grace nodded and turned toward the exit. When she

How to Dance on the Moon   109

reached the door, she looked back to see that the men had assimilated into the bar. She located her car, slid into the driver's seat, and sat for a moment, pulling the paper rose from her purse and putting it to her nose. She picked up the faint scent of Blake's MadCrush cologne. Reliving their conversation, her thoughts drifted to how sexy she had found him. No. How handsome. Grace placed the rose on the seat next to her, and started her car, scratching at the itchy spot on her palm where Blake's handshake had shocked her.

    ****

The next morning Grace found Biscuit working on the broken bookcase in the conference room. She shut the door behind her and cleared her throat.

"Good morning, Grace!" Biscuit tapped her lightly on the shoulder with his hammer. "You missed a great game last night. Mariners beat the Yankees in the ninth."

Grace lowered her lashes. "What can you tell me about Blake Morton?"

Biscuit looked at her quizzically. "Why?"

Grace pulled at a strand of her hair. "He seems sweet. He made me a paper rose, and he said I was pretty."

Biscuit looked hurt. "I say you're pretty all the time and you don't get all excited."

Grace gave Biscuit a playful punch on the arm. "Yes, I do. But Loretta would fire me if she thought I was after you. Blake is lonely, though. I know how loneliness can eat you up from the inside."

"What makes you think he's lonely?"

"I know the symptoms."

Biscuit's eyebrows dropped. "Are you allowing yourself to be flattered by him?"

"No. I think he needs a friend."

Biscuit turned back to the bookcase. "Don't you have

Laura Ginter 110

enough friends, Grace?"

****

Grace struggled to focus on the work on her desk. It was the anniversary of Stephen's death, and although the tree was gone, its roots still coiled around her heart as though the accident had happened yesterday. But she found comfort knowing tomorrow the wound would begin to scab over, as it had the year before. All day her feelings were raw, her energy sapped, and her coping skills pushed to the limit. But somehow she survived, and at five o'clock, she went home.

The phone rang as Grace came down the stairs from putting Jennie to bed. The caller ID said the call location was blocked. She placed her hand on the handset but did not lift it. It was probably George again. He had left three heavy breathing messages on her answering machine in the last week, and she was too drained to deal with him. But wouldn't Stephen be angry if she allowed some jerk to control her? Especially on this day? If it was George, she could hang up. Grace put the handset to her ear.

"Hello, Grace." The voice was unfamiliar. His whisper was breathy and soft and had a masculine twang that made her think of Shorty, the lobsterman from her childhood who she had loved like an uncle. But Shorty was dead.

"Who's this?' she asked.

"This is Stan Bean. I'm Violet's brother. We met once at a BATSS function."

Did Violet have a brother named Stan? Grace couldn't remember. "Is Violet okay?"

There was a long pause. "She died ten minutes ago."

Grace's heart pounded painfully, and she fell into a chair. "Oh my God! What happened?"

"I slit her throat with a hunting knife. There's blood everywhere. She couldn't scream for help. She's dead, but her

How to Dance on the Moon 111

eyes are still wide open. She still looks scared."

The words sounded preposterous. Surreal. Untrue. "What's going on? You're lying."

"Do I have your attention now, Grace? That could be you instead of Violet if you aren't careful. Death isn't always seen coming, and if you don't want a visit, don't open the door of your pretty grey house tonight."

Grace pushed the disconnect button on the phone's handset. Her shaking hands made it difficult to push the right numbers on the phone, but after several attempts, Grace succeeded in reaching her friend. Violet assured her she was alive, drinking a Tab, and did not have a brother named Stan.

"It didn't sound like George this time," Grace said, pacing the kitchen floor. "Who else knows us both, Violet? And knows I live in a gray house?"

"Do you think George disguised his voice?"

"Everything was different, though. Not just the voice, but the words he used and how he spoke."

"What did the caller ID say?"

"The number was blocked. I'm freaking out. I can't handle having two different people doing this to me now. Should I call the police?"

"Yes, but what can they do they haven't already done? Do you want me to come and sit with you?"

"No, it's too late," Grace said, calming. "I'll call Biscuit. He's close. He won't mind."

"That's a good idea. And try not to worry. Only in campfire stories do bad things happen after scary phone calls. Lock your doors and put a funny movie in the VCR until Biscuit can get there. I'll have my cousin tell George the police have tapped your line. If it's him, maybe that will stop him."

After thanking Violet, Grace phoned Biscuit. His answering machine kicked in, and she remembered he had the night shift that week. She tried to watch television, but couldn't get her nerves to settle. She went to the living room window and

Laura Ginter 112

peeked outside. Although the summer sun had not set, the trees' shadows on the vacant lots surrounding her house were thick. A man could be out there watching her, and she wouldn't be able to see him.

Her nervousness escalated into panic. She wondered who she could call. A white paper rose resting on the table near the front door caught her eye. She picked it up and saw the phone number scrawled on the bottom. Grace picked up the phone. She knew Biscuit might not be happy, but Biscuit wasn't there to help her. Twenty minutes later, Blake was standing at her front door, holding a real white rose, petals in full bloom.

"I was hoping you'd call," he said and handed her the rose. "I've been saving this for my new friend."

Grace beamed.

15.

Grace plugged one end of the telephone cord into the computer and the other into the phone jack. She switched on the power to the CPU. The monitor remained dark, and she bristled and smacked it. The doorbell rang. Grace hurried to the door and greeted Violet with a hug. "Thanks for coming."

Violet waved a hand in front of her face. "September is not supposed to be this hot." She went to the kitchen and took a water glass from the cabinet.

Grace took the glass from Violet, filled it with water and handed it back. "I am desperate! I can't even get my computer to turn on. How will I figure out this internet thing?"

"Why do you want the internet, anyway? I hear it's only good for watching porn."

"Loretta wants me to use it to connect with fundraisers and

How to Dance on the Moon 113

grantors. I'm trying it at home first." Together they stared at the computer.

Violet sipped at her water. "Loretta shouldn't expect you to do this at home. The internet is expensive, and ties up your telephone."

"George won't be able to call me then, will he?"

Violet shook her head. "Grace, it's been two months since your date with George. My brother says it's not him making those calls. George is a decent guy, and he was over you five minutes after you turned him down for a second date. He has a new girlfriend he adores, and they are moving to Sacramento together. It's someone else harassing you."

"Okay, then, I'll name the guy the Breather." Grace pushed the computer's power switch off and moved the phone cord from one slot on the CPU to a different one. "Let's see what happens now." Grace flipped a switch and the women stared at the computer's screen. "Nothing."

"Don't you have to sign up with some company to get internet?" Violet asked.

"Mosaic, it's called. But I think you must get on the internet first to sign up for it."

"I see. You can't get on the internet without signing up for service, but you can't sign up for service until you get on the internet." Violet shook her head. "And isn't Mosaic a modem?"

"What's a modem?"

"It's the thingy that converts your phone line to the internet. Maybe the phone company can tell you if you need one."

Grace snorted. "Oh yeah, the same phone company that told me to change my phone number to stop the Breather, then published it?"

"I sense sarcasm," Violet said. They stared at the blank computer screen. "So what does the internet connect to, exactly?"

Grace shrugged. "That's what I want to find out, if I can ever get it to work."

"You need more help than I can give you. Technical and psychological, both."

"Probably," said Grace. "But from where?"

"Maybe the guy Loretta uses," answered Violet, glancing at the back of the equipment. "The television part is not plugged in to that big box."

"Do you think that's the problem?"

Violet gave Grace a smug look. "You don't need the internet at home, Grace. It's a fad. I'm never going to get it. If I want to enjoy some porn, I'll get a boyfriend. Let's quit staring at this screen." Violet finished her water and set the glass on the counter. "Is there something else I can help with since I've solved your internet problem?"

"Besides helping me pick a place for us to eat?"

"Where's Jennie?"

Grace opened her refrigerator and pulled out two beers. "Spending the night at her friend Lucy's house. I'm alone tonight."

"And Blake?"

Grace opened the beers and handed one to Violet. "I didn't invite him over. And since you asked, I do have something else you can help me with."

"Let me guess. Blake?" asked Violet. Grace nodded. "How long have you two been friends now? Two months? And you still don't think he's a little weird?"

"He's helped me."

Violet drank from her beer bottle. "Helped you how?"

"He's made the Breather easier to deal with. It's pretty awful to know some pervert has your phone number, and even if you change it, he finds your new one, and how many times can I change my phone number?"

"A thousand?"

"Violet, you know that's not realistic. I've done everything

How to Dance on the Moon 115

I can to stop this guy, and nothing works. Blake helped me pick out an alarm system and now, if the Breather calls, at least I know he can't get in my house. I feel much safer. But if I do get scared, Blake will come over."

"Did you ever hear from that Stan guy again?"

"No! That was the worst. Thank God it only happened once! I am still trying to figure out who would do that to me."

"Are you keeping your log of Breather calls, like the police said?"

"Yes, but the trap the phone company put on my line hasn't turned up a single phone call that didn't come from a phone booth." Grace shook her head. "But Blake helps me with more than just the Breather calls. The other day he changed some bulbs I couldn't reach, and he unclogged my sink. Saved me a plumbing bill. He's a gentleman and we have fun. I hadn't realized how crusty and stale I had become, living just to work at BATSS and to be Jennie's mother. I'm laughing and playing again."

"Sounds like you like him more than a little."

"He's so stinking cute, I was starting to!" Grace moaned. "But spare me the lecture. I know I have to keep things in check. Dating would be too hard right now. And he understands. So we're just friends who help each other out. He brings me security and helps me with the house. I bring him companionship and spaghetti dinners."

"I sense a 'but'. . ."

"But, he used to come over just when I asked him, but now it seems like he's over every night. He's trying to dominate my time, and push me into decisions that go against my better judgment. Once, I caught him checking my caller ID. He said he wanted to see if I got calls from men. I can't ignore his behavior anymore. This friendship is becoming too much work."

"Must it be all or nothing? Can't you rein him in?"

Grace shook her head. "It's gone too far to go backwards like that."

Laura Ginter   116

Violet shrugged. "Appears obvious, then. It's a dead end relationship. You've made it clear you don't want to date, but he's trying to control you anyway. There are red flags all over the place, and you have to watch out for Jennie."

"He loves Jennie. He's always been sweet to her. It's hard to know what to do when someone is both helpful and difficult at the same time, like Blake is. But I think I made a mistake letting him get too close. This one snuck up on me and now I need to fix it."

"Grace, you are a strong woman. What you have had to endure alone, while raising a child would have broken a lot of people. Now you have some creep trying to steal your sense of safety, and before Blake, you had nobody to help you. No husband, no brother or sister, no parent. If you're like me, your toolkit consists of a steak knife, tweezers and a meat pounder. It's no wonder you let this man to charm you and take care of you a little. But your common sense is starting to see the problems here. There are two men trying to control you. The Breather and Blake. Cut loose the one you can. You should thank Blake for his friendship and his support, and send him on his way. Find another way to feel safe and pretty and get your plumbing fixed."

"You're right, Violet."

"Biscuit would love to help you."

"Biscuit would love to help you with what?"

Grace and Violet turned at Blake's interjection. Violet grimaced. "Hi Blake. Grace didn't tell me you were coming over tonight."

"I didn't know he was," said Grace. "How long have you been standing there?"

"I just got here." Blake put his hands in his pockets. "What were you talking about?" He asked the question as if he were inquiring about what television shows she planned to watch.

Violet set down her beer and gave Grace a quick hug. "I think I'll go home. See you at work on Monday."

How to Dance on the Moon 117

Grace walked Violet to the door, and came back to find Blake drinking Violet's beer. "You aren't cutting me loose, are you Grace?"

"No, Blake. But you did a good job sneaking up on me and dispatching Violet.

His eyes focused into the distance. "I don't think you should have Violet come over anymore. She's not the friend you think she is."

"What do you mean? She's my best friend."

"I'd hate to make you choose between her and me."

Grace stared at Blake in disbelief, and his face broke into a grin. "Lighten up. I'm kidding. Someday, you'll get my humor." Blake glanced around the room. "Where's Jennie?"

"I was just going to walk down and get her at Lucy's," Grace lied, suddenly needing to be away from Blake. "She's feeling sick. You should probably not hang here tonight." She turned toward the door, but Blake blocked her way. "Can we have an hour first?"

16.

When Grace arrived home after work, the kitchen smelled like cooked beef and onions. She lifted the slow cooker's lid and stirred the boiling stew with a wooden spoon. Jennie pulled a chair next to Grace and stood on it. "I'm so hungry, I could eat like a pig!" she said, clutching her stomach.

"We'll eat as soon as Blake gets here." Grace wondered if Jennie would fuss over Blake's invitation to dinner, but the little girl said nothing. Grace pulled a bag of frozen peas from the freezer and added some to the pot.

Jennie pulled her finger through a gravy drip on the counter and licked it. "Mommy, have you ever known a pig?"

Laura Ginter 118

Grace chuckled. "That's a funny question, but yes, sort of. Piggy Penserton in second grade."

Jennie giggled. "Piggy Pants-are-down? What a silly name! Why did they call him Piggy? Did he ever pull his pants down?"

"He was called Piggy because he would snort in class behind the teacher's back for a nickel. I don't remember if he ever pulled down his pants, but I wouldn't be surprised if he did."

"Did he snort like this?" Jennie sucked air noisily through her mouth.

"No, more like this." Grace bellowed a loud honk that startled them both. Jennie laughed, and Grace laughed with her as she pulled dinner rolls from the refrigerator.

Jennie pushed her nose in with her finger. "Did he talk like a pig, too?"

"How does a pig talk?" asked Grace, expecting more snorts. But Jennie surprised her with her answer.

"The one who talks to me at Tiny Tots sounds like this." Jennie lowered her voice. "Hello, Jennie."

"There is a talking pig toy at the daycare?"

"It's not a toy. It's a real pig. He lives under a bush by the playground."

"Does he play with you? Does he push you on the swings?" Grace asked, playing along.

"No, he's a pig. How could he push me on the swings? His name is Wally. He wants to meet you."

Before Grace could answer, Blake came through the front door and staggered into the kitchen, making loud, painful moans. "I'm so hungry I could eat a child," he said, wiggling his fingers in front of Jennie's face. Jennie giggled and poked his stomach.

Grace tossed the dinner rolls onto a cookie sheet and into the oven. As she pulled silverware from the drawer, Blake lifted Jennie off the chair. He danced with her through the house, singing a silly song about a careless monkey eaten by an

How to Dance on the Moon 119

alligator. Jennie's laughter came from deep in her belly.

Grace set down the silverware and clapped her hands to the rhythm of Blake's voice. "Sing for me too, okay?" Blake carried Jennie back into the kitchen and set her on the counter. He reached for Grace's hand and swept his arm around her waist, pulling her close to his chest. His MadCrush cologne brought out his natural musky scent, and never failed to make her head swim. He held her hand, and they swayed in quiet harmony. He sang a slow song, crooning in her ear in perfect pitch as she fell into the dance's rhythm. Their movements became a ballet that erased everything from her mind.

His stubbly chin rubbed against her forehead. He gripped her hand and caressed her waist. She knew it was wrong, but she found herself enjoying a moment of romantic desire. The illusion of being with a handsome, loving, Blake. The Blake she first met.

"Would you miss me if I ever went away?" Blake asked.

"Of course I would." Grace closed her eyes.

Blake slipped into a new song. Grace continued to move her body with his, adjusting to the new rhythm. He tightened his grip around her waist and pulled her closer, clamping onto her hand. He squeezed her fingers together, and she wiggled them to loosen his. His grasp tightened, and his voice grew louder.

"Blake, you're hurting me." Blake relaxed his grip on her waist, but he did not lessen his hold on her hand. Her hand began to throb. "Ouch!" she cried, both in pain and as a final warning.

"Mommy!" Jenny called out.

Blake sang on, ignoring the alarm in Grace's voice.

"Blake! Let go!" Grace pulled her free hand from Blake's neck and wedged it between their chests, pushing him far enough away to reach his hand and pry it open. Blake released her and flashed his broadest, sexiest grin. Before Grace could shake the blood back into her hand, he grabbed her again and

Laura Ginter 120

tried to spin her around. He had another song in his repertoire for the evening, and he seemed determined to sing it.

"I'm the best you will know, I'll never let you go, I'm all that you need, don't make my heart bleed, I'm the best you can do, if you leave me I'll find you."

She stumbled, and he squeezed her hand when he pulled her back up, crushing her knuckles. She screeched and strained to get free, but he pulled her into his body, preventing her from moving away from him. He swung her around too fast, and Grace became dizzy. He pulled her close again.

"Blake, the rolls are burning."

"I'm the best you will know."

"Mommy, smoke!"

"Blake, let me go!"

He stopped singing and whispered to her, "If you leave me I'll find you!"

Grace pulled her foot back and kicked Blake solidly in the shin. He gasped and released her. The smell of burning bread filled the kitchen. Grace shook her damaged hand as she opened the oven with the other, releasing a rolling smoke ball and setting off the smoke detector. "Blake, open the front door!" she yelled. She grabbed a potholder, pulled the cookie sheet from the oven and dumped the smoldering black lumps that had been the dinner rolls into the sink. The alarm quieted after she waved her potholder at it. She turned to Blake angrily, massaging her hand. "Look what you did. What were you thinking?"

Blake's face darkened, and his eyes grew wide. He raised his fist in the air over Grace's head, and she recoiled. As though a switch had been thrown, his expression changed instantly from anger to fear. He looked at his hovering hand and lowered it, taking a step back. "Grace, I am sorry. I didn't mean to scare you. I would never hurt you."

Grace's face burned. "Get out!"

Before Grace could say more, Blake crossed the room and

How to Dance on the Moon 121

hurried out the front door, slamming it shut behind him.

"Mommy?"

Grace turned to Jennie, who was still sitting on the counter. Her daughter's tears caused Grace to grasp the true depth of the damage done by Blake's angry gesture. She hugged Jennie and kissed her repeatedly on the cheek. "I'm sorry that happened, Jennie."

"He scared me. He shouldn't get so mad. And he danced too tight to you."

Grace wiped Jennie's tears and lifted her off the counter, then opened the kitchen window to release more of the burnt, smoky smell. She ran water over the smoldering rolls in the sink and ground them in the garbage disposal. Jennie watched, her expression hard, her lips downturned. Grace bent down to her daughter. "Talk to me, Jennie. What are you thinking?"

"I am thinking I don't like Blake any more."

Grace took Jennie's hands and held them. "I am thinking I don't either."

****

They ate their dinner silently, and after Jennie's bath, they read a book together. When Jennie fell asleep, Grace put a video in her VCR and settled in on her den sofa. She and Blake had been planning to watch the Cheer's finale she had taped, but now she would be watching it alone.

Her eyes followed the action on the screen, but she couldn't keep her mind from reliving the evening's drama. She shivered every time she thought about it. But was she overreacting? In fairness to Blake, she had danced provocatively with him. It embarrassed her now to think about it, but she had let him inside her emotions, and he had seized on the opportunity to create intimacy. She must have confused him when she pushed him away. And she had kicked him hard. But he had hurt her, and he hadn't let her go when she demanded it, and had scared her with his hand raised in anger. And he had done it in front of Jennie.

Grace might have allowed him leeway, if the evening's events had been an isolated instance. But he had become dominating, and, if she were to be honest, intimidating. Still, she didn't want to deal with George alone. And Violet was wrong. George was the person calling her. If she had to choose between living with the calls and keeping Blake around, wasn't Blake the lesser of two evils?

Grace remembered her mother trying to cover a purple bruise on her upper arm and saying, "Sometimes women get caught in the crossfire." She shook her head to erase the picture. No. Her mother was wrong. Women should never be in the crossfire, and Grace wasn't going to be like her mother. She would not be anyone's victim. Blake had to go before he hurt her and before he hurt Jennie. They weren't safe with him anymore. She had to cut him loose. Violet was right about that. She could find other ways to deal with George.

The doorbell chimed. Startled, Grace slipped into the living room and peeked through the window, then crossed the room and opened the door. Biscuit slid past her and pushed the door shut behind him.

"Biscuit!" Grace gave the man a quick hug. "You scared me, ringing my doorbell this late."

"I'm sorry," Biscuit said, "but I saw your light on and hoped you were still up."

"This is a dead end street. You did not just drive by my house."

Biscuit raised an eyebrow and frowned. "Can we sit out back so I can have a smoke?" Grace turned off the television and led Biscuit out to the backyard patio before fetching him the ashtray and a beer she knew he'd appreciate. He thanked her and lit up as she sat in the chair next to his, imagining how much more attractive he'd be without a cigarette in his hand. "It's a beautiful night, isn't it?"

How to Dance on the Moon 123

Grace took a deep breath. "Even the air smells warm."

"How is Jennie?" Biscuit asked. "I haven't seen her in awhile. Bet she's getting big."

"I just learned she has an imaginary friend at Tiny Tots Day Care." Grace said. "A talking pig, of all things."

"Don't imaginary friends mean an active imagination?"

"Or stress." Grace remembered her Teen-a Doll. "I had imaginary friends when I was about her age. I guess it's no big deal."

Biscuit took a drag off his cigarette and exhaled slowly. "What about the phone calls?"

Grace shrugged in response. "So what's up with you?"

With a nervous twitch, Biscuit flicked his cigarette ash into the ashtray. "I've been having problems with Loretta ever since we broke up."

Grace's eyebrows rose. "You broke up? When?"

"About a month ago. You didn't know?"

"I noticed I hadn't seen you in weeks, but Loretta hasn't said a word. What happened?"

Biscuit smashed his cigarette butt in the ashtray and lit another. "She's a great gal in many ways. Smart. But she's demanding. And expensive. And difficult. Sometimes the way she talked to me bothered me, like I was a naughty child. You know the drill better than anyone."

"I have my struggles with her."

Biscuit exhaled, and took another drag on his cigarette. "I wouldn't have said anything except I figured you knew."

"You came by to talk about your breakup?"

"No. Maybe I shouldn't tell you the rest."

"Tell me."

Biscuit took a deep breath before continuing. "She's following me in a BATSS van. I see it all the time, day and night."

"She's using a company van to stalk you?" Grace asked, appalled. "Really?"

"The white one. Tonight, I went to a tavern to watch the game, and she was there in the van when I left."

Grace sat taller in her chair and shook her head. "Does she know you see her?"

"Yes, but she never does anything. Just stares at me from the van. I don't want to approach her. It might be what she's hoping for. But if I report her to the police, she could lose her job. Could you talk to her?"

Grace shrugged. "Maybe I can find a way to make her see how bad it would look if the Board found out about this, without letting on how I know what she's doing. Yeah, should be easy!"

Biscuit missed the sarcasm. "Thank you, Grace. I knew you would help."

Grace frowned. "You don't think Loretta followed you here, do you?"

A black shadow cut through the moonlight and darkened Biscuit's face. "No. I watched. I lost her."

"Because if Loretta saw your car here and thought you and I were dating, she wouldn't fire me. She'd kill me. And it wouldn't be instant death. It would be death by torture."

Biscuit laughed and smashed the rest of his cigarette into the ashtray. "I don't know why she is acting like this. She's a good person, deep down."

Grace took Biscuit's hand in hers. "I'll do whatever I can."

"Saving Grace, that's you! Always helping everyone."

Grace blushed and released Biscuit's hand. "No, Biscuit, I'm just me. Just-Grace-All-Alone."

Biscuit stood up, taking Grace in his arms. "Another reason to get her out of my life."

Grace let him hug her, and she relaxed in his grasp.

"It's a beautiful moon up there. You can see the old man." Biscuit swayed slightly as he held her.

"It's actually a rabbit who dances on the moon to spin it." Grace twisted to look up at the sky behind her. Her breasts

How to Dance on the Moon 125

rubbed across Biscuit's body a little too firmly, in a way Blake would have misread as an invitation, but Blake wasn't holding her. Just Biscuit. She turned back and saw Biscuit staring at her with a mixed expression of pleasure and sadness. "I'd better go," Biscuit said. They went back through the house and out the front door.

"I taped the Cheers finale," Grace said. "Do you want to stay and watch it? Blake was going to, but he had to go."

"I wish. Early shift tomorrow." Biscuit started to light another cigarette but stopped. He raised an eyebrow. "Blake from the golf course?" Grace nodded. "You two are friends?" There was annoyance in his tone.

Grace bristled. "Blake is a good friend. Or he was."

"Grace, why would you hang around with a married man?"

"I wouldn't," Grace said, crossing her arms. "He's never been married."

"Her name is Amanda and she's in the Navy, stationed in Japan, and she has about a month left before she is discharged. He talks about her all the time at the club."

Grace's stomach felt suddenly sick. "Why didn't you tell me?"

"I didn't know you two had become friends."

Grace walked Biscuit to his car. "Well, that's the end of Blake. It was going to be over anyway. I feel stupid."

"Don't worry, Grace. Smart women can be been fooled by shady men. You were just friends, right?"

"Yes, just friends."

"Then no harm. When I see Blake, do you want me to tell him to leave you alone?"

"No," Grace said. "I'll deal with him."

Biscuit gave Grace a peck on the cheek, and she watched him back out of the driveway and drive down the street. A car parked by a vacant lot pulled out behind him without headlights, and it struck Grace as odd, and worrisome. But the car was too small to be the BATSS van, and she had enough

Laura Ginter   126

troubles without imagining more.

Grace went back inside, turned on Cheers and pulled her feet up under her legs on the sofa. She tried to watch the show, but Biscuit's bomb had thrown her mind into frenzy. Blake was married. And he had lied to her and she hadn't caught it. It made her feel foolish, but it also made her decision to expel Blake from her life easier. She felt unsettled, though, as if she were opening Pandora's Box, not closing it. The "Cheers" theme song played at the end of the show, and Grace smiled at the irony in the words to the theme song, a song about needing friends to help you though life's tough spots.

The telephone rang. Grace grumbled, rose from her chair and went into the kitchen. The Caller ID read "blocked". She let the answering machine take the call. The Breather exhaled slowly twice. "That guy Biscuit has soiled you, hasn't he?" he asked with uncharacteristic clarity. "He was with you tonight. I saw him. I'll kill him if he comes back."

Grace lifted the handset and pushed the off button. She went to her phone log and noted the time and location listed on the caller I.D. She would not let the violent words scare her. But her hand shook, realizing it had to have been the Breather who had pulled out behind Biscuit in the car. He was no longer just using the phone to harass her. He had become a stalker. Like Loretta. But how did the Breather know who Biscuit was? The phone rang again. Again, the caller ID read 'blocked'. Grace lifted the handset to her ear, anger overcoming sense. "Get out of my life!"

"Hello Grace. This is Stan Bean. Violet's brother. Remember me?" Grace was shocked into silence by the voice she had heard just once before but whose words had terrified her more than the Breather ever had. He continued, "That last call? He's not kidding. Biscuit could get his throat slit, too, like you, if he gets too close."

Grace dropped the phone onto its base. The Breather knew Biscuit, and Stan Bean knew both Blake and Biscuit. What

How to Dance on the Moon 127

was happening? Who were these people? Her hands shook with rage. She was done with these jerks calling her. And she didn't care if Violet thought George was involved or not. He had to be the Breather. Tomorrow, she would have Violet get George's phone number and address and insist the police do something to protect her against George and whoever Stan Bean was.

She went through the house, turning on lights, checking the doors, windows, and the alarm, then fell back onto the sofa. Thank God for the alarm. She would be depending on it more than ever, since Blake wouldn't be there for her anymore.

17.

The next day Grace went to work with a sore throat. By noon, her sniffles and aches were bad enough to make her seek out Violet and ask her to replace her at a middle school open house that night. She also told Violet about the latest calls from the Breather and Stan Bean, but left out the awkward tidbit that Blake was married. She wanted to talk to Blake first. Violet said she would attend the open house, and she would help Grace get whatever information she needed about George to prove his innocence or guilt, definitively. Either outcome would be a step toward ending Grace's problem.

The house alarm did not sound its warning beep when Grace opened the front door, and her stomach fluttered. Had she forgotten to set the alarm? She entered with small, cautious steps and glanced into the living room. Blake was sitting in an armchair, holding a glass of wine.

Grace put her hand over her heart. "You scared me! How did you get in? Where's your car?"

"I used the outside key. How was your day?"

Laura Ginter 128

"Stressful," she answered, dropping onto a chair across from him. "What are you doing here? I told you I had an open house tonight."

"Then why aren't you there? Where is Jennie?"

"I'm sick. Jennie is at Lucy's. I have to get her." She looked up at him, and he held out the wine glass for her to take. "You know I don't drink around Jennie. And you can't turn off my alarm and come into my house whenever you feel like it."

Blake set the wine on the table beside him. "I didn't turn off the alarm. I don't know the code. You must not have set it." Blake crossed the room. He placed his hands on each side of her neck and began to massage her shoulders. "Poor Grace. You had a bad day?"

Grace shook his hands off. "I have a cold, and Loretta yelled at me for missing a deadline I didn't know about. And I had to bail on the open house." Grace pulled a phlegmy tissue from her slacks' pocket. "Really, Blake. Why are you here?"

"I want to apologize," Blake said, "for last night. What I did was inexcusable." He came around to hug her, and she sneezed. "Grace!" He swiped at his face. "Are you trying to get me sick, too?"

"We need to talk, Blake, but I can't tonight. Maybe you should go home."

He rubbed Grace's cheek with his thumb and Grace tensed. His face darkened. His cologne was strong enough to penetrate the congestion in her nose. "Okay, I understand. But first, I have a question."

"What?"

Blake pinched Grace's cheek, and she flinched and pushed his hand away. "Did I hurt you? I'm sorry." He went to the table next to his chair and grasped two photographs sitting next to the wine glass. He held them up. "Why do you have pictures of Biscuit with his arm around you?"

The unnatural calmness in Blake's voice set off an alarm in Grace's head. She glanced at the picture. "Those were in my

How to Dance on the Moon 129

desk in the den."

"Are you seeing him?"

Grace's cheeks burned. "No. We're friends. Loretta wanted me to add the pictures to a publicity packet I'm working on." Grace rubbed her cheek, burning from Blake's pinch, while Blake studied the pictures, his mouth twisted to one side. Did you go through my desk?"

"I was looking for a stamp. Is he cheating on Loretta with you?"

"No!"

Blake narrowed his eyes and snorted.

"Don't act like that," she squeezed the tissue inside her fist. "He can't cheat on Loretta because they broke up, and he can't see anyone without her knowing because she's following him all over town in the BATSS van. And how could I have anyone else in my life when you're here every night?"

Blake dropped the pictures back onto the table. "Why are you being defensive, Grace? What are you hiding?"

"Hiding?"

"Call Biscuit right now while I am standing here. Tell him to stay away. Tell him you are mine."

Grace stared hard at Blake. "What is this? High school? You're married!"

Blake became quiet. After a moment, he asked, "Who said that?"

"Biscuit." She spread her tissue open and blew her nose. "Blake, you lied to me. Did you think I wouldn't find out you had a wife in the navy in Japan? Amanda?"

"Amanda has nothing to do with us. As you point out all the time, you and I aren't dating."

"God, Blake. I can't do this with you anymore."

Blake shook his head and let out a soft snicker. "Amanda and I haven't lived together as man and wife in years. When she gets back we're getting divorced."

"That's your excuse for lying?" Grace sneezed again, then

sighed heavily. "Blake, can't you see we were already getting too involved? Now I find out you are married. It makes things even more awkward and confusing than they already were."

Blake growled. "Awkward? Confusing?" He glared at Grace from under his brows. The fierce set of his jaw frightened her, and she rose from her chair and crossed to the far wall. "All I ever wanted from you was your friendship."

He took several slow steps toward Grace. She felt the wall against her back. He reached her and cupped her ear. "But every night you strut around like a tramp, teasing me, tempting me, draining all my emotions to feed your ego. You've left me frustrated, and now you are tossing me away like that snotty, used tissue in your hand. When Princess gets tired of hanging out with her jester, she sends him away and calls for someone else. Prince Biscuit." He released her and pushed himself away.

Grace rubbed her ear. "What are you talking about?"

"A good person wouldn't do that. A kind person wouldn't do that. What kind of person are you?"

Grace threw her tissue at Blake, hurling it with all the anger boiling inside her. "Right now, I'm a pissed-off person. You're not going to twist this around. I didn't mislead you. The rules were clear between us. And, oh yeah, you're married. It's over for us Blake. We can't be friends. Go home, please. And don't come over ever again. Poor Amanda."

Blake stared at her, his eyes bulging and his jaw clenched. If he were a cartoon, Grace imagined smoke would be coming from his ears. "You know why I really came tonight?" he asked, spitting his words at her. "I thought you were bringing Biscuit home with you, and I'd catch you two together."

"Just go!" Grace folded her arms around herself and fought back tears. She turned toward the wall and heard him pound the table. Then silence. The quiet stretched out interminably, but Grace resisted the urge to turn around. She sneezed and blew her nose. The front door slammed, and she heard Blake's

How to Dance on the Moon 131

car drive away.

Grace lowered her hands and took a deep breath. She tried to make sense of what had just happened, but it was beyond reason. Stepping over to the table by his chair, she looked for the pictures, but they were gone.

The phone rang. She didn't answer it. No one left a message.

****

The afternoon was balmy and overcast. A thunderstorm was building in clouds trapped west of the Cascade Mountains, and the iron-like smell of ozone warned of its rapid approach. Jennie was playing at Lucy's house. Grace folded laundry while she watched television, and listened to distant rumblings as raindrops began to splatter on the patio. The doorbell rang, and Grace put down the slacks she was folding and went to the door. Through the window, she could see Blake standing on the step, rain splattering his shoulder. She heard the doorknob rattle. "I know you're in there, Grace. Open up. I'm getting soaked."

"You can't come inside."

"Amanda's home. I'm moving to Oregon with her in two days, and I don't want to leave like this."

Grace wavered, and then opened the door, her heart racing. Blake pushed past her, and she followed him into the den. She turned off the television. "When did Amanda get back?" she asked, hoping her voice sounded casual.

Blake stopped pacing and folded his arms. "Three days ago. The night you were sick."

Grace snorted. "Really!" A thunderclap, closer than the others before it, muffled his first words.

". . . going to try to live together again. The movers come tomorrow."

"That soon?"

His eyes widened. "Unless you want me to stay."

Grace's heart beat faster. She tried to keep her hands from shaking. "You need to be with your wife."

"But I would rather be with you. Tell me to stay, and I won't go with Amanda." He covered his face with his hands. "I did lie to you, but I didn't mean to hurt you. Amanda and I haven't had a marriage in a long time."

She was shocked to hear him crying. His anguish seemed heartfelt and pained. "I'm sorry, but we are not supposed to be together, Blake. You were a huge support to me, and we shared a nice interlude during tough times, but you must move on. You must try to make it work with Amanda."

Blake dropped his arms, and the intensity of the anger in his expression made Grace step backward. "I was an interlude to you? An intermission between two acts in a play? I'm in pain here!"

Grace slumped, beaten and exhausted. Her head swam with a numbing gray mist.

The rain quit its patter, and the room became quiet. "Last chance," he said. "I know you want me to stay."

"I don't."

More thunder exploded and the pelting rain returned. Blake pulled a nightgown of Jennie's from the laundry basket and twisted it tightly around his fingers. Darkness clouded his face like a smoke, before his eyes softened again into milky pools. Another thunder clap echoed through the kitchen, but its intensity was fading. The storm was almost over. "I'll still be coming up to Washington occasionally. I'm not finished with school."

Grace's cheeks burned. "Understand this, Blake. You can't come back here. It's time to say goodbye."

The darkness returned to Blake's face. "Your words and your actions say two different things. The more you tell me to go, the more I know you want me to stay. But you've made your decision. I'll make a good life with Amanda. We'll have

How to Dance on the Moon 133

babies and buy a home, and you'll rot away in your pretty suburban fairy tale life." He smirked. "But tell me, Grace, what are you going to do about the Breather without me around to help you? You can't count on Biscuit. He'd run like a scared rabbit if he found out your phone buddy threatened him."

Grace was about to respond, but stopped when the meaning in Blake's words took hold. Fear coursed through her body as though a dam had burst inside her. She turned away so he couldn't see her face. "I'll be okay. I'm getting the police more involved."

"Good luck with that." Before she could react he leaned forward, gave her a quick kiss on the cheek, and he left the house.

Grace fled to the front door, locked it, and reached for her phone to check on Jennie. Lucy's mother assured her Jennie was safe. Grace hung up the phone and hugged herself to control her shaking. She prayed Blake didn't realize he had betrayed himself. She had deliberately not told him about the Breather's call when she had seen him that next night, so how could he know the Breather had threatened Biscuit?

She remembered the dark car that had pulled out behind Biscuit. Had Blake been in that car? Was that why Blake thought she was seeing Biscuit? She tried to think of a time Blake was with her when the Breather had called. Or when Stan Bean called. She couldn't. She had been duped by a manipulator. Spun into a web like a mindless fly sedated with a spider's sugary poison. A handsome, dangerous spider.

A thought occurred to Grace, and a glimmer of hope eased her panic. She lifted the telephone handset to call Violet. Violet had been the only person she had told about the call. Maybe she had mentioned something to Blake? Maybe she also had updated information on George. The phone rang in her hand before she could punch in Violet's number. She checked the caller ID. California. When she said hello, the voice was unfamiliar. "Hi, is this Grace?"

"Yes?"

"This is George Crosby. We had a date a few months ago. I think we should talk."

Grace covered her mouth as her throat filled with burning bile. The voice on the other end did not belong to either the Breather or Stan Bean.

****

The laundry basket sat benignly on the sofa in the den. Grace scooped up the clothes she had folded and tossed them back in the basket. Then she sifted through them, looking for the nightgown Blake had twisted in his anger. The question had now become whether Blake was the Breather, or Stan Bean or both? Was he just an oddball, making harassing phone calls for some weird sick pleasure rush, or was he truly dangerous? A prankster or predator? And how long had he been calling her? The first phone calls had come before she had met him, and she had told him about them at the bar. Obviously, he had used the information to get in her good favor, then to control her.

Grace found the nightgown and tried to flatten it out, but it was ruined. She moaned and wrapped her arms around her waist to steady her nerves. Just because Amanda was home, she could not assume she was safe. In the morning, she would change the locks and her phone number again. Holding up the nightgown, she thought, Stephen would not be happy with me.

****

The next morning, Grace found a jewelry box on her front step containing a bracelet with six ivory roses space evenly around it. Inside the lid was a folded note. She opened it. "*I left some books in your guestroom. I'll be back for them another time.*"

No you won't, Grace thought, and she refolded the note

How to Dance on the Moon   135

and stuffed it inside the box with the bracelet. She looked down her driveway and saw a sparrow in a mangled heap next to her car. From the garage, she took a garden trowel and a grocery sack, scooped up the carcass and dropped it into the sack. She stuck the trowel into a pot of marigolds by her front door and dumped the rest into the trash.

Grace went through her house and put every physical memory of Blake, every note, every small token into a paper bag and tossed it in the trash with the dead bird. During her cleansing, she found the three textbooks in the closet of her guest room where, for a short time, Blake had studied while his apartment was being painted. She started to toss them in the trash too, but instead she put them in a donation box she kept near the water heater. Textbooks were expensive. She worked for a nonprofit and appreciated anything free in a world dominated by donations and grants. They would be valuable to a poor college student, and maybe one decent thing could come from the mistake that had been Blake.

18.

"How long since I made you pan-fried chicken?" Grace asked Jennie as she rinsed pieces of fleshy chicken thighs under the kitchen faucet.

"A long time," Jennie said. "Before even Blake."

Grace shut off the water. "Well, we're making it tonight."

"But Blake's not coming, right? I don't like Blake. He's bad."

Jennie's words filled Grace with sadness and guilt, but she envied Jennie's ability to see most things in black and white, good and bad, like and dislike. "Blake is gone for good."

Laura Ginter 136

Grace dried each thigh before dumping it into a wide, batter-filled bowl. After stirring everything together, she placed her first four pieces in the frying pan. Jennie pulled a chair up to the stove and tried to wiggle closer to the burner, but Grace gently pushed her back. "The oil spits, honey. I don't want you to get burned." She arranged the chicken pieces in the pan with tongs, making sure none overlapped.

"I saw him today," Jennie said. "In his car."

Grace dropped the thigh, and she gasped when oil spattered and stung her wrist. "Blake? Are you sure? Where?"

"He drove by at recess. He waved at me."

"Did you wave back?"

"No." The chicken sizzled in the pan. She turned the largest chicken thigh.

"Jennie, he is never allowed back in our house. You must tell me if you see him again."

"I will, Mommy. That chicken smells yummy!"

Grace pulled the thighs from the pan and onto a cooling rack. She pulled the French fries from the oven and a salad from the refrigerator. "Do you want ketchup with your fries?"

"No. Ketchup looks too much like blood!" Grace laughed as she served the food. But she found the whole conversation with Jennie disturbing.

****

At bedtime, Jennie asked if she could sleep with Grace, and Grace said yes. After Jennie was asleep, Grace pulled out a book to read.

The phone rang. Grace lifted the handset tentatively. "Hello?"

"Hello Grace. This is Stan Bean calling. Violet's brother."

Grace glanced down at her daughter lying next to her. She spoke in a whisper. "I changed this number. How did you get it?"

How to Dance on the Moon 137

"Just wanted to tell you to expect company." A click and the dial tone's drone announced the call's end.

Grace put the phone back in its base and hurried downstairs to make sure she had locked all the doors and windows and had set the alarm. She still kept a key outside, but she didn't dare leave the house to retrieve it. However, she was certain no one could find it in its new hiding place under a rock on the far end of the vacant lot next door.

She returned to bed, and eventually slept, although fitfully. She dreamt of the Wailing Witch, a creature whose story she had learned as a child. In her dream, the Wailing Witch drooled red, sludgy seaweed as she spewed a child's arm from her mouth, and then she started to beep.

Grace opened her eyes and calmed herself by taking deep breaths. As the nightmare's grip on her subsided, her eyes focused on a figure between her and the window, backlit by moonlight. A colorless, fluid shadow grew larger until it was over her. A hand appeared from the shadow. MadCrush cologne permeated the air. Grace screeched and pushed the hand away.

"Mommy!"

The shadow hunched over and fled from the room. Grace reached for her daughter and hugged her protectively. "You're safe, Jennie!"

"I smell Blake."

"Stay still." Grace rose from her bed, shut the bedroom door and locked it. She wedged the chair from her vanity between the doorknob and the floor.

"Mommy, are you okay?"

Grace turned back to Jennie. The little girl's eyes were dark circles, shrouded with pinched-up stress. Grace blinked back tears and went to her daughter. "Of course I am!" She wrapped her arms around her little girl's slender, fragile frame. "Blake is not here."

"But he was! I smelled him."

Laura Ginter

Grace combed her fingers through Jennie's hair, pulling her bangs from her forehead to look into her daughter's eyes. Jennie resembled a female version of Stephen but mirrored Grace's personality. Grace often used this commonality to gauge Jennie's emotions. She stroked her daughter's head, noting that the mirror worked two ways. Jennie's eyes reflected Grace's anxieties. "I am going to call the police. I'm going to call my friend Biscuit, too."

Grace pulled Jennie onto her lap while she made the calls, and then wrapped her arms around her daughter. But Jennie's warm skin could not calm her.

"Why did you put the chair by the door?" Jennie asked.

"A chair will keep Blake away until the police get here."

"Will it help keep the gun away?"

Grace looked down at her daughter. "What gun?"

"Wally said Blake has a gun."

"Wally the pig?" A stand of hair had fallen into Jennie's face, and Grace swept it away. "Blake hates guns. I promise he doesn't have one."

"Mommy, do you want me to stay awake until the police get here?"

"Whatever makes you feel better." Grace clenched her eyes to disperse the tears trying to spring from her eyes.

Ten minutes later, she heard Biscuit call out to her. Grace untangled herself from her daughter's arms and legs, threw on a robe, moved the chair from the door and carried Jennie downstairs. Biscuit had found the front door open, and a house key and one white rose were on the step. He handed the items to Grace. "How did he get in?" he asked.

Grace put the key in her robe pocket and brought the rose into the house. "He must have found the key outside. He must know the alarm code."

Together they waited for the police.

19.

The next morning, Grace brought Blake's white rose to Loretta. Loretta thanked Grace and tucked its stem into a vase Grace had given her for her birthday. "I need to take a couple of hours off this morning," Grace said. Loretta gestured for Grace to shut the door, and she lit a cigarette.

Loretta could have been attractive if she didn't try so hard to be fashionable. Her hair framed her head in an even two-inch thickness, and she had structured the styling to such detail, she could have numbered the hairs to locate any that fell out of place. Her makeup outlined narrow eyes and thin lips, like a child's paint-by-numbers picture. Despite these rough edges, she managed to accentuate her cheekbones and highlight her skin tone in a way that gave her balance, and softened what otherwise would have been a face of squares and triangles.

"What's going on?" Loretta asked.

Grace didn't want to tell Loretta she was going to the court house for a restraining order against Blake. "Jennie has a doctor appointment," she said instead, and hoped her face didn't betray her lie.

"Is Jennie sick?"

Grace shrugged, avoiding a direct answer.

Loretta stared at Grace for a long moment. "Just be back in time for our principals' meeting this afternoon." Without giving Grace a chance to respond, Loretta launched into a monologue about BATSS' poor representation at a neighborhood PTA function held the previous night. It took all Grace's willpower to focus on Loretta's lecture. She wondered bitterly if Loretta was still stalking Biscuit.

When Loretta ran out of complaints, she dismissed Grace by asking her to send a volunteer to her office. Grace nodded, tagged a volunteer, and returned to her desk. She called Biscuit, who had offered to take her to the courthouse, and told him she was ready to go. They arranged to meet at the back door of the building, near the employee parking lot. She clicked off her computer, reached for her purse and sweater and left her office.

A hallway with vending machines and a couple of tables with chairs led to the back door of the building. The door was propped open. Biscuit was not yet there. A flickering light from a vending machine drew Grace's gaze. She approached the machine and pulled a dollar from her purse. She set her purse and sweater on a chair. Because she was preoccupied with her selection, or maybe because she had spent thirty years ignoring shadows, Grace failed to notice the huddled figure lurking behind the back door.

Grace scanned the selections, and chose a peppermint patty, remembering that Biscuit liked them. She flattened the dollar bill against the machine, and when she reached up to feed her money into the payment slot, a strong tug on her arm caused her to stumble and drop her dollar.

"Eating candy will make you fat." Blake's casual tone contradicted the twisted sneer on his face. Before Grace could react, he pulled her away from the vending machine and toward a door in the hall she had never noticed before. She started to scream, but he covered her mouth and twisted her head sideways. Grace struggled, but she could not break free from his grip. Once inside, he kicked the heavy door shut behind him with his foot.

A single bulb in the ceiling emitted a dim light, creating distorted and dark shadows around electrical boxes lining the walls, and wires and cables cutting into the ceiling. The hum from a failing transformer filled the cramped room. Blake snarled. "You can scream now." He pushed Grace around to face a shelf on which sat two photographs. "Look who's here."

She strained to see in the poor light. They were the photographs of her and Biscuit that Blake had taken from her house. Blake's grip tightened painfully. "Let me go." She swung at him with her free hand. He knocked her arm down

How to Dance on the Moon								141

and shook her hard. "Blake, stop! You're hurting me!"

"Too bad Biscuit's not married. A married man is safe. You can use him, then crush him like a bug, and he can't do anything about it."

"Let me go, Blake. We can talk in my office."

Blake shoved her against the wall. A stabbing pain shot through her upper arm when she fell against an exposed valve. Blake grabbed her shoulders and pushed her to the floor. Her head hit the concrete. Blake knelt and grasped her again by the shoulders. Grace twisted and tried to slug him, but his grip was strong and constraining, and she could not muster any impetus to make a solid strike.

Blake dropped on top of her, pinning her to the floor, and covered her mouth with one hand, pushing the other into her chest. When Grace stopped struggling he asked, "Will you be still if I take my hand away?"

Grace nodded, and Blake removed his hand from her mouth. He sat up and pulled her next to him. Her head and arm throbbed. When she spoke, her voice sounded thin and pitchy. "You're the Breather."

Blake chuckled. "Interesting theory." His eyes narrowed. "I saw Biscuit at your house last night. I saw him kiss you."

"Biscuit kissed my cheek. You are upset, Blake, but we can still make everything right between us."

"You think that's what I want?" Blake chuckled again. "No, I just want my textbooks. You took them from the guest room."

"Why didn't you take them before you moved? Or just ask for them last night?"

"I didn't want Jennie dragged into our little problem. Where are they?"

"I threw them out," Grace said.

"It would be very bad for you if you did."

"They are here, upstairs in my office."

Blake smirked. "You do have them." Grace began to sob, and Blake used his thumb to wipe her tears. "Stop making such

Laura Ginter 142

a fuss. Maybe you'll feel better if I tell you it's over between me and Amanda."

"What do you mean?"

"Amanda's been cheating on me. I hid in a closet and caught her with her boyfriend. Amanda threw a clock at me, and If I'd had a gun I would have killed her." He told his story evenly, dispassionately, as though he were reporting a change in temperature on the weather channel. Grace scrutinized Blake's expression while she absorbed the fact that Blake had hidden in a closet to spy on his wife and had wanted to kill her. "Can I go now?" she asked.

Blake bent closer to her face and grasped her chin, cradling it. "I could make you love me."

Grace seized what could be an opportunity to appeal to him. "I do love you, Blake. If you let me go, I'll do anything you want. I'll be your girlfriend, and you can be my boyfriend."

Blake snorted and pulled back. "Stupid girl. I don't want you, now that Biscuit has had you. But I could make so you can't want anyone else. Maybe throw you in the trunk of my car. I could get a gun and blow Biscuit's head off, and make you watch him die with his blood splattered all over your face. Then we could find a big fat tree and drive into it."

Grace shuddered at the reference to her husband's death. Tears of pain and helpless terror splashed down her face. What if Blake wasn't just talking? What if he had hidden a weapon in the room? A hammer or a cord for her neck? Or the gun Jennie had seen in her dream? Maybe he did intend to kill them both in some perverted form of revenge. A murder-suicide? She closed her eyes and pulled her legs up, curling into a ball, holding her injured arm with one hand, and clutching her head with the other. Her mind separated from her body. Her need to defend herself shut down. She sank into a sludgy dark pit and hid inside herself, refusing to think or feel, waiting for what would happen next.

"Look at me." Blake said.

How to Dance on the Moon 143

Grace turned her head. Blake stood and took the pictures from the shelf. "Have my books ready for me the next time I come to the house." He opened the door to the room and flipped off the light switch. The door closed, and the room went black.

Grace heard a muffled thump. She rose to her knees and felt her way to the door, stepping cautiously through the void. Standing, she pushed on the door handle, but it wouldn't turn. She felt around the wall for the light switch but couldn't find it. Panic overcame her, and she screamed and pounded on the door until a muffled voice called to her that help was coming. When the door opened, a shadow blocked the light. Grace fell into Biscuit's arms.

20.

The volunteer at the reception desk looked up with a horrified expression when Grace stumbled in with Biscuit. Grace limped down the hallway until her knee buckled and she sank to the floor. When the tears started, she could not stop them. Her sobs were loud and wet, and her effort to control her crying made her throat hitch. Violet handed Grace a tissue. "Are you okay?" She rubbed Grace's shoulder and Grace flinched. Seeing the bruise on Grace's arm, Violet pulled away. "What happened?"

"Everyone get in here," Loretta bellowed. Grace blew her nose and took several deep breaths to control her tears. Biscuit helped her to her feet and guided her into Loretta's office. Violet followed them inside.

"What the hell is going on?" Loretta sounded more annoyed than concerned, as if Grace were unaware that she was creating problems for everyone else.

Biscuit crossed his arms. "Blake trapped her in the electrical room."

Loretta looked confused. "I thought you and Blake were best buddies."

Grace shook her head, and recounted the events leading to her ambush that morning, but omitted Biscuit's involvement. Loretta listened intently, occasionally shaking her head, and when Grace finished, she blew a lung-full of cigarette smoke toward the ceiling. "How did Blake get into your house last night?"

"He found my outside key, and I guess he knew the alarm code."

"Don't you have a warning beep on your alarm?"

"I was asleep. The beeps became part of my dream." Grace looked at the white rose, sitting primly in Loretta's vase. "And Stan Bean has my new phone number. The police think a volunteer might have given it out."

"Do you want me to interrogate the volunteers?"

What Grace wanted was sympathy, caring and reassuring words, but one look at Loretta's stiff posture and she knew that wasn't going to happen. "I need a restraining order. That's where I was going this morning."

Biscuit rubbed his chin. "We'll file another police report when you get your order."

Grace saw that Loretta was studying her, her brows squeezed together. "I'd like to speak to Grace in private if you two don't mind."

Biscuit patted Grace's shoulder as he and Violet left, shutting the office door behind them. Loretta pulled Grace's white rose from the vase and sniffed it. "So you lied to me about the doctor appointment. If I had known the truth, I would have sent someone to walk you to your car, and you could have prevented this."

"I'm sorry Loretta."

"The damage is done. What matters now is fixing this ugly

How to Dance on the Moon 145

situation you're in. Blake is out of control, and frankly, I'm not sure a Restraining Order will be enough to protect you."

"But that's what it's for."

"He still has to be served, and you may not be able to find him."

"A process server could find him."

"What if Blake ignores the order? Why haven't you changed your code on your security system?"

"I didn't think he knew it."

"Well obviously he does. Change it. It won't stop him, but it might slow him down. And leaving a key outside? That's just stupid. Don't do that anymore." Loretta sniffed the rose again and flung it into her wastebasket. "Biscuit seemed worried about you." Her eyes narrowed. "It sounds like he is planning to take you to get the order."

"I think so." Grace was overwhelmed with sadness and embarrassment. "I'm so sorry about this, Loretta."

"Why? For lying? For having your boyfriend disrupt our office? Or for stealing mine?"

Grace couldn't imagine what she could say that wouldn't sound pitiful. She watched Loretta light a cigarette. "You've had a bad couple days, and you look pretty beat up. Take the rest of the day off. Get your Restraining Order and file your report so the police can go after Blake. You may go."

Grace limped to the ladies' room and caught sight of herself in the full length mirror. Her blouse's tear-stained shoulders made her look as though she had been in a rain storm without a coat. Her hair was ratted, and her eyes were swollen into slits. She rinsed her face, and brushed her hair with her fingers. Her arm throbbed from slamming into the valve. Her head also ached.

Violet was waiting for Grace outside the ladies' room. "I'm okay, Violet," Grace said, dismissing her friend. She returned to her office and found someone had placed her purse and sweater on her desk. She called her security company and her

Laura Ginter 146

locksmith, and then turned off the light and left the room.

Loretta was standing in the hall with a male volunteer. "Mike will walk you to your car." She lowered her eyes and looked at Grace through her lashes, in a way Grace had seen her do when she was angry, but never before at her. "Your problem isn't just about you anymore. You've made this about us all. You have put this office at risk."

Grace had no words to defend herself. "I have to go now." She turned away and exited from the BATSS offices, Mike following her. When she reached the hall where an hour earlier Blake had ambushed her, she thought Biscuit might be there waiting for her, but he wasn't. She limped through the door that lead to the parking lot, peering around to make sure Blake wasn't hiding somewhere, poised to pounce on her again.

When she reached her car, she had to use both hands to control her shaking to unlock the door. Once inside she relocked the doors, waved to Mike, and glanced at her watch. Eleven o'clock. She had time to get to the courthouse and complete the legal paperwork and get home to meet the locksmith who had agreed to meet her that afternoon. She turned the key in the ignition. A rap on her window startled her. She gasped, and looked up to see Biscuit staring in at her. She rolled down her window. "I thought you left."

"I had to call the station. I'll follow you in my car."

Grace put her hand to her chest to slow her heart.

****

Grace pulled a beer from the refrigerator and handed it to Biscuit. "I'm not changing my phone number again. It won't stop him."

The doorbell announced the locksmith's arrival. Biscuit took a hefty swallow of his beer and set down the can. "We can talk about that later. That's my cue to get to work."

While Biscuit assisted the locksmith, Grace busied herself

How to Dance on the Moon 147

with kitchen chores. The light was flashing on the answering machine, and the anxiety of not knowing who had left messages overcame her reluctance to find out. With a deep breath, she approached the machine. Two messages were waiting for her. She pushed the play button. The first was from Aunt Bootie. "Hi Gracie. Haven't heard from you. Is Jennie still getting out of school early tomorrow? Did you get the afternoon off? Are we still going shopping? I need new clothes! Call me back."

Grace smirked, thinking Loretta would not be giving her time off to go shopping. Maybe Aunt Bootie could pick up Jennie at Tiny Tots, and the two could go. Jennie would love it.

The answering machine moved to the next message. The voice said, "Hello, Grace. This is Stan Bean, Violet's brother. You have a problem. Blake wants his books but he can't have them. Don't ditch them either. He's coming back for them, and if they aren't there, he'll be very mad. Have you ever seen Jennie bleed?"

Grace's vision spun, and she became dizzy. She hit the erase button, pressing it repeatedly, pounding on it, raging with frustration. Little screams escaped from her throat.

Biscuit came into the kitchen and grasped Grace's hands. "What's wrong?" Grace repeated Stan Bean's message. "Jennie and I can't stay here. I haven't changed the alarm code yet." Short, tight sobs escaped from her throat, and Biscuit grabbed her shoulders and forced her around to face him. "Grace, I'm not going to let Blake hurt you. You and Jennie can come home with me tonight, and we'll figure out what to do. Where is Jennie?"

"At Tiny Tots."

"Get your toothbrushes and whatever else you need." Biscuit shook his head. "No, let's just leave now."

"What about the books?"

"We'll sort out the book problem later." Biscuit pushed her out of the house, locked the door with a new key from the

Laura Ginter 148

locksmith, and led her to his car.

****

The next morning, Biscuit and Grace drove Jennie to school before heading back to the house. The security company's salesman was waiting for her. Biscuit checked the house over and gave Grace her new keys before leaving, promising to come back that evening. They had decided to take Blake's books to the police station after work. Until then, they would have to stay in the garage. The salesman changed Grace's security code, and she bought outdoor motion sensing lights and a video camera. The salesman said the installers would be there by three o'clock. It appeared Grace would be home early after all.

After the salesman left, Grace hurriedly changed her clothes. She located her purse and keys, threw on a jacket, and when she left her house, she wedged a scrap of paper between the door and the jamb, a habit she had begun after Blake surprised her in her living room the night she had been sick. She hurried to her car, and was surprised to find the door unlocked. After peering into the back seat, Grace scooted in behind the steering wheel and locked herself in. A pile of little white papers on the seat caught her eye. Spreading them out, she saw pieces of her face, along with Biscuit's. She scraped the picture scraps into her hand and dropped them into the ashtray. She shivered knowing, without a doubt, it was a message. Blake was out there watching her.

Surrounded by forested empty lots, she wondered where he was hiding. She whipped her head toward the sound of crunching leaves on the side of her house, but she saw nothing. The sound returned, closer. A shadow crossed in front of a large fir. A tree branch crashed to the ground. A squirrel darted across the driveway. Saplings swayed without a breeze. Squawking birds flew in circles, spooked by an unseen threat.

How to Dance on the Moon 149

She heard a twig snap behind the car. Fear coursed up into her throat, and she whimpered. She started the car engine and put the gears into reverse. The car bounced and scratched and made the terrible metallic scraping noise. But she couldn't stop the car. When she reached the road, she gassed it.

****

Grace called Loretta from the gas station and told her what had happened. "Do you think Blake flattened your tire?" Loretta asked. Grace said yes, and heard Loretta suck on her cigarette. "I'm worried about you Grace. How are you holding up?"

The question surprised Grace. Loretta was asking sincerely about her well-being. "I'm doing my best," was Grace's cautious reply. "I rekeyed my locks and upgraded my security. And I have the restraining order ready to be served."

"You think you've thought of everything?" Grace hoped the question was rhetorical and did not respond. Loretta took another drag from her cigarette. "I spoke with the board president this morning. He's not happy."

"I'll talk to him," Grace said. "I'll tell him the steps I've taken to fix this."

Loretta blew into the receiver. "And Blake called me, too. Late last night, at my home."

Grace frowned. "Why would he call you?"

"I asked him that. He was polite. He said he wanted to clear up a misunderstanding between you about some books, and thought I could talk to you on his behalf. I asked him what he had planned to accomplish by pulling you into the electrical closet."

Grace pulled on a strand of hair. "What did he say?"

"He said you went in there willingly, so you both could talk privately, and things got out of hand. He denied making threatening phone calls to your house."

Grace's frustration exploded. "He's lying. He's not a polite young man clearing up a misunderstanding. He's a narcissistic monster!"

"I know that, Grace. The man is obsessed and dangerous." Loretta paused to take another drag on her cigarette. "But Blake also told me some unflattering things he had heard about me. Have you ever talked to Blake about me and Biscuit?"

Grace glanced down at the floor. Had she told Blake about Loretta stalking Biscuit? She couldn't remember, but her embarrassment at the possibility made her wish she could hang up and crawl into a deep, deep hole. She realized Loretta's earlier compassion was a trick to get her to drop her defenses. Her job was in serious jeopardy, and could depend on how she answered this question. "Blake is a master manipulator. He's shooting from the hip and he's hoping for a bulls-eye. He wants to anger you to hurt me."

Loretta took a long drag and blew out the smoke with a loud puff. "This all has to stop, Grace. Our non-profit is an outreach program that nurtures the minds and bodies of young people. When this type of problem comes to the office, it puts our entire mission at risk. You are going on administrative leave until this is resolved."

"What?"

"Take two weeks. Get healthy, and get your problems resolved. Violet can fill in until you come back. You will remain on the payroll, but you'll use your vacation time."

Grace closed her eyes, letting Loretta's words sink in. "Should I come in today?"

"No." Loretta paused, and then said. "I care about you, Grace, and your daughter. I also fear for you both. Don't let the steps you've taken give you a false sense of security. I agree. Blake will stop. But not because you have a restraining order, or new locks or an upgraded alarm or he gets therapy from some shrink. He will stop when he goes to jail or finds a new Grace."

How to Dance on the Moon   151

Grace cringed. Her head hurt, and her throat was dry. "You are wrong, Loretta."

"I'm not. And if you don't fix this situation, you risk losing more than two weeks of work and a tire." The phone call ended.

Grace shuffled back to her seat in the garage waiting room. Administrative leave. Loretta may as well have slapped her across the face. But she still had a job. And as hard as it was to admit, Loretta was right. Blake was not finished with her. She imagined how Jennie must have felt to see Blake drive by her school. Yes, Loretta was right. She was still at risk, and she had much to lose.

21.

It was one o'clock before the tire repair was finished, and Grace turned her car toward Tiny Tots. She had forgotten to cancel her shopping plans with Aunt Bootie, and she made a note to phone her aunt when she got home to apologize with the standard "busy mom" excuse.

Grace entered the day care and glanced around for her daughter. She spotted Mrs. Fish, the administrator in the preschool room, and Mrs. Fish looked confused when Grace asked her about Jennie. Jennie hadn't come that afternoon, Mrs. Fish said. When she wasn't on the bus, Mrs. Fish had called the school. The secretary had said a man calling himself Biscuit had brought in a note saying Jennie was to take the bus to her home instead of to daycare. "They tried to call you," Mrs. Fish said, "but Jennie told the secretary she was going shopping with your aunt and was sure you had forgotten to give her the note. The secretary let her go home."

Nausea backed up into Grace's throat, and she gagged.

Mrs. Fish's words faded as she imagined Jennie getting off the school bus. Jennie walking up the street to the house alone. Blake pulling Jennie into the house and slamming the door shut behind her. Grace fled the building. Mrs. Fish yelled something to her, but Grace didn't stop to listen.

****

Grace saw the paper scrap she had wedged in her front door jamb on the ground. She braced her shaking hand to maneuver the house key into the door's lock. There was no click when she turned the key. The door was unlocked. With a hand pressed to her chest, Grace opened the door. The warning beep of the alarm did not sound. A puff of air slapped her face. Its dank and malignant chill validated the fact made clear by the unlocked door and silent alarm. Blake had found a way inside the house again. Was Jennie inside with him?

A sudden rage surged inside Grace, and her crippling fear was gone. How dare he do this to her and Jennie? How dare he use Jennie to control her, and make her feel scared and weak? How dare he frighten Jennie? Or hurt her? The urge to rush into the house overwhelmed her, but she fought it. If she ran inside in a frantic panic without a plan, he could easily overpower her. She had to be smart and approach the situation with a level head. The only advantage she would have was if she could surprise him. Instead of handing herself over to Blake, she could sneak in, and gain precious seconds to call the police, something she should have done at Tiny Tots. Then she could find Jennie.

Grace lingered on the step, listening for a clue to help her pinpoint Blake's or Jennie's location, but the house was silent, as though a black hole inside was sucking away all sound. A glint of light to her left drew her eye. The garden trowel used to scoop up the dead bird was sticking up from the pot of marigolds. She bent over and pulled it free, wiping the soil

How to Dance on the Moon 153

from its tip with her finger. She glanced down the road to see if anyone would hear her if she screamed out for help, but she saw no one. With a deep breath, she stepped purposefully and silently inside her home.

Grace whimpered, her angry courage slipping away like a wisp of fluff. She peered to her left, into the empty living room, and felt oddly disconnected, as though seeing the room through a stranger's eyes. Her home did not provide the protected embrace of a sanctuary as it should. Too many closed doors, shuttered closets and dark corners stood between her and any sense of protection, as if all the house was working together to shield *him* and protect *him* instead of her. He had corrupted everything. Would she ever feel safe in her own home again?

Grace glanced back over her shoulder at the open doorway and her escape route. *No.* She took another deep breath. *I have to do this. I can do this. One step at a time.* She glanced up the staircase in front of her before taking four steps down the hall. She stopped beside the powder room. The door was slightly ajar. Easing it open with her foot, the light from the hallway spilled inside the empty room. She tiptoed to the kitchen and spotted the phone on the counter. She lunged for it, and put the handset to her ear. There was no dial tone.

Grace stifled a whimper and went back to the entryway. She peered up the staircase again. *Where are you hiding, Snake? What have you done with my daughter?* She gripped the spade more firmly, and began her ascent, avoiding a spot on the third stair that creaked.

When her gaze reached the same height as the landing, Grace paused. Jennie's bedroom was in front of her. The door was open, and the room was undisturbed. By tilting her head, Grace could see that nothing was under the bed. The closet was too full of clothes and toys to hide an intruder. *Where were they*? Could Blake have left before she got home? Could he have Jennie somewhere else? *Where the hell was her daughter?*

Grace continued up the stairs. Her bedroom was to the left, and the guestroom to the right. There was another phone in her bedroom. She tiptoed down the hall and stopped in front of her bedroom door. It was open enough for her to see a wedge of the room. The closed draperies fluttered from a breeze coming through a window. A cold draft brushed across her hot skin, soothing her like a damp cloth on a fever. The room was dark, but appeared to be undisturbed. She leaned sideways to peer into the gap between the door and the jamb to see what was not visible from the doorway.

A flicker of movement, more intuited than seen, made her jump back. She raised the trowel higher. The draperies made the shadows shift on the wall. Grace again approached the door. She sniffed and caught a whiff of a sweetly rancid odor that made her think of spoiled meat. She stepped forward, sucked in her breath, and pushed on the door.

With a heavy thump, the door stopped abruptly before hitting the wall, and swung back toward her. Blake leaped from behind it. A scream erupted from deep inside her lungs. He grabbed her arm, forcing her to drop the trowel, and he shoved her toward the bed. His eyes bulged, and his mouth was a twisted grimace.

Grace shrieked, and kicked to get away from him. He flipped her down on the bed savagely, snapping her head backward. Dropping on top of her, he disabled her with his weight. She could not stop screaming, even with his hand clasped over her mouth. She heard him tell her to shut up, but she could not understand anything else he said. As she twisted to get out from under him, she saw his eyes glaring down at her. His free arm stretched across the bed, and he pushed a pillow over her face

22.

A warm, prickly sensation crept through Grace's body, and an intense pressure filled her head while the pillow continued to cut off her air. When Blake lifted the pillow off her face, she sucked in several deep, raspy breaths and coughed. He was on her, pinning her down. She was too dizzy and weak to push him away. Her face was now under his armpit. She recognized the rotten meat smell from earlier was stale MadCrush cologne mixed with sweat. "Are you going to scream?" he asked.

Grace shook her head. She wheezed when she tried to speak. Blake chuckled. "Wonder how I keep finding your keys, or getting past your security? You never asked me what I did in the military." He placed his face against hers on the mattress, pulled her house key from his pocket and pushed it inside her bra.

"Where is Jennie?"

"I don't know. She should have been here by now. Where is your boyfriend?"

"Who?"

Blake brought his face close to hers, his stale breath assaulting her nose. "I thought Biscuit would come with you."

"Blake, stop it!"

Blake's face darkened and twisted into a caricature of barely contained rage. He grabbed her hair and yanked it. "Did you ever love me?"

"Don't hurt me!"

He released her hair. "Where are my books?"

"In the garage."

Blake stood and pulled her up by the arm to her feet. "Show me." He pushed Grace through the doorway, and she stumbled on the stairs. They passed through the den and into the garage, and Grace pointed to the corner where she had stacked them. Blake pulled her with him to the corner.

A door slammed outside, and the static of a police radio

sputtered. She heard Aunt Bootie call out for her, and then Jennie. Blake shoved Grace away from him and picked up his books. He hefted them, as if checking their weight.

"We're in here!" Grace screamed out. Blake gave Grace a little salute and went back inside the house, Grace presumed to slip out the back door. Grace hurried over to the garage door and opened it.

****

Grace examined the business card, her third in three days. The key Blake had dropped down her bra was on the counter. Aunt Bootie was speaking with the two policemen at the front door. Jennie sidled up next to her mother, clutching a beige teddy bear the policeman had given her. "I'm sorry, Mommy. This is my fault."

Grace knelt and hugged her daughter. "Jennie! This is not your fault. Your teacher told you to come home. You did what you were told."

"I could have saved you."

"You didn't need to save me. I'm fine. Blake didn't hurt me."

"But Wally says I have to help you make Blake go away."

"Wally, the pretend pig?"

"He's not pretend," Jennie said.

"Jennie, Wally wouldn't want you to protect me. He would want you to be safe. You were smart going home with Lucy's mom."

"I didn't want to. Mrs. Tynan saw me get off the bus and she wouldn't let me walk home. She tried to call you."

"And I saw her sitting on Ann Tynan's front steps. I thought we were going shopping." Aunt Bootie crossed the room and stood by Grace. "The policeman said Mrs. Fish at Tiny Tots called them."

"I was so scared," Grace said, "I didn't think before rushing

How to Dance on the Moon 157

home. And then my phone didn't work here."

"The police also said Blake cut the phone line and then the power to the alarm. He used a key he found outside to get in. And you just change your locks yesterday? Why did you put a key outside?"

Grace flinched and looked down. "Stephen always insisted on it. His father used to lock him out of the house when he didn't want him around, and he hated it. I promised him Jennie would always have a way inside."

"Grace, your efforts to honor Stephen have become misdirected. Don't leave any more keys outside. Ever."

"I won't. Please don't be angry at me."

"I'm not angry. But why didn't you tell me all this was happening to you?"

"I'm sorry, Aunt Bootie. I thought you'd worry." Grace looked into her aunt's face, and her heart broke at the depth of hurt and sadness in her eyes.

"You and Jennie are staying with me until we can sort this out."

Through the open front door, Grace saw the security company's van pull into the driveway. "Can you take Jennie out of here now? She's so upset. I'll come as soon as the installers finish. I won't be alone."

Bootie reached out to give Grace a hug, but Grace stepped backwards. "I can't have you read me right now."

"I wasn't doing that, Grace," said Bootie.

Grace led Bootie and Jennie to the car and watched them leave. She returned to her kitchen, set the officer's business card with the others and reached for her aspirin bottle. Her face ached, her head throbbed, and her arm was still sore. She swallowed three pills and climbed the stairs to her bedroom. The bed covers were on the floor. The sight made her feel sick, and her composure began to slip through her grasp like a greasy glass about to shatter. She looked at her reflection in her dresser mirror and rubbed her bruised arm. "I refuse to let

Laura Ginter   158

this beat me," she said aloud. "I am going to hold it together. For Jennie. For Stephen."

An installer came to her bedroom door. "Excuse me Mrs. Abram. The telephone company can't fix the phone line until morning. We will have to finish tomorrow. Do you have a place to go?"

"My aunt's. Can you stay long enough for me to pack a bag?"

"We have another half hour of work."

Grace looked at her watch. Fifteen minutes before five. She thanked the installer, shut her door and pulled a suitcase from the closet. When she tossed it onto her bed, a tan rectangular object, half buried by the bedspread, caught her eye. She bent over and picked up a wallet. Inside she found a driver's license and a ten-dollar bill. She pulled out the license. Blake's face smiled back at her. A folded newspaper clipping had been wedged behind the license inside the wallet. A chill ran through her. She removed the clipping, set the wallet on her bed, and unfolded the little piece of paper.

It was dated August 11, 1992. It was over a year old. The headline read **Two Found Fatally Shot in Home**. Below the headline was the picture of an attractive blonde woman, who looked to be in her twenties. The next words blurred when Grace read them.

On Sunday evening, Amanda Morton was found by her husband, Blake Morton, dead in her home. She had sustained a gunshot wound to the head. Also found dead was Conrad Wilson. . .

Grace stopped reading and replaced the clipping. She dropped the wallet inside the front pocket of her suitcase. After packing clothes for herself and Jennie, she carried the bag down to the kitchen. She slipped on her coat, and when she left her house she waved to the installers waiting in the van to leave.

The shadows were deepening around the trees, but she did

How to Dance on the Moon 159

not sense Blake's presence. A storm had begun to spew rain, and chilling gusts of wind were swirling dead leaves into piles of debris. Grace pulled her suitcase to the car, but paused before opening the door. Heavy wintery raindrops began to smack her on the head and shoulders. Each icy droplet felt like a punishing rebuke for letting her life spin so badly out of control. She toyed with the idea of standing in the storm, arms outstretched, allowing herself to be drenched by the rain. Washing away her sins like a rite of baptism. But the installers wanted to leave, and she didn't have time to waste on wistful metaphors. She waved to the men, and buckled herself into her car.

Part 3

How to Dance on the Moon

Bootie 1948

23.

No one knew the exact age of Henry Kurz's cousin Theo, but speculation put her somewhere between thirty-five and fifty. Her lemony hair, long legs and ample bosom gave her the potential beauty of her older cousin Madeline, but cigarettes, gin and social excesses had creased the fabric of her face into a harder edge.

Theodora Mae Rawson was the third and youngest child of Alexander Hamilton Rawson's brother, Wilber, and his socialite wife, Isadora Rawson. At a young age, Theo learned from her mother that self-pampering, flirting and entertaining were legitimate life pursuits for girls of her social standing, as long as discretion and restraint were maintained. But she yearned for the freedom from discipline her older brothers enjoyed, and she indulged her flamboyant and reckless spirit. Seeing trouble ahead for his daughter, Alexander sent her to a boarding school specializing in wealthy but difficult girls. She reacted to her exile by running away repeatedly until her father brought her back home for good.

When Theo turned seventeen, she began sneaking from

How to Dance on the Moon 161

the house with the cook's son. When Wilber discovered this, he was enraged and banished her from the house, cutting off all financial support, hoping hard life lessons would tame her. But Theo's mother made sure her daughter's bank account always had ample funds to sustain her independence. Theo never looked back.

After her mother died, and Theo lost her source of funds, she went to her brothers, now the Savings and Loan managing partners. Father had been dead for five years and she was entitled to an inheritance. To pacify her, the brothers agreed to give her a monthly stipend. When she complained the amount was too small, they told her to get a husband, and ended all discussion on the subject.

Theo didn't want to marry. She enjoyed her freedom too much to trade it in for responsibility, even if a marriage could bring her security. But after years of carefree affluence, she was now always running out of money. She fell in with a crowd who shared her taste for luxury and disdain for accountability. Her new friends taught her creative ways to keep her lifestyle with her more limited means.

After Aunt Theo moved into the lake house with the children, she returned to the bank and insisted her brothers cover the household expenses from the Rawson Trust. She was pleased to learn a trust already existed. It had been accumulating funds for four years with monthly stipends much greater than hers. The brothers would not allow Theo direct access to the money, but agreed to pay all the bills, and to raise her personal stipend if she did not move the children from their home. Aunt Theo found the arrangement suitable. She also found a way to siphon some of the children's money into her own account by padding the grocery bill.

****

When the news spread that the court had appointed Theo

Laura Ginter 162

to be the Kurz children's guardian, neighbors worried the children would suffer more calamities. With Theo they would receive little guidance or discipline. The older boys would run wild. And worse, the girls would emulate their aunt's disreputable behavior. But the state assumed Theo's female chromosomes gave her an innate ability to be a caretaker, even to traumatized children whose parents were criminals and were often on the newspaper's front page. There were no classes, no texts, and no counseling, and if a social worker ever visited the family, no one remembered it.

The Kurz youngsters defied all the doomsday predictions. Except for a tendency by the boys to skip school, the children behaved well, replied politely to any inquiries about their family, and stayed inconspicuous, keeping their business to themselves. In time, the community adjusted to their notoriety. And when new scandals replaced old ones, people stopped giving them any particular notice.

In the early days, denial over the seriousness of their situation came easily to the children. They missed their parents, but they believed the court would clear Mother and Father of all charges, and they would come home rested and happy, as though they had been on a trip to the Poconos.

Aunt Theo let the children do whatever they wanted, as long as they allowed her the same courtesy, which suited everyone just fine. In the meantime, Aunt Theo made the household's mood playful. She shared her make-up with the girls, told raunchy jokes to the boys, and taught them all how to play poker. In the beginning, the family even had outings. Fancy dinners in Plymouth and a weekend trip to Stowe, Vermont.

Aunt Theo went out most evenings to visit friends, and sometimes she stayed out all night. She would come home bent and droopy-eyed, her aura a mossy gray. Occasionally she would sleep all day, and if the children left her alone, she would dispense pennies and bubble gum from her purse when she

How to Dance on the Moon 163

woke up. The older boys looked forward to her parties. Like squirrels to acorns, they foraged for unattended packs of Chesterfields and gin bottles and smuggled them to the island. The children would stifle amused giggles as a tired Aunt Theo searched for her missing cigarettes and wondered aloud how her friends could drink so much liquor in one night.

Then the lawyers requested a postponement of the Kurz trials until late spring, and Beulah Kurz was transferred to the state hospital. The children had to face the fact their parents would be gone for a long time. The holiday atmosphere degenerated into lethargic apathy. An unhealthy pattern of neglect crept into the children's lives, and the house became a place filled with despair and depression, wrapped in a festive but grimy wrapper.

Bernice tried to keep up with the housework, but dirty clutter overtook every room. Dishes were washed as needed. The sheets on the beds were never changed, and the bathroom smelled like the mildewed towels tossed in the corner. Mrs. Kennedy watched Ike during the school day, but even with that much help, Bernice could not do all the cooking and shopping and stay ahead of the growing mess in the house. Her skin itched from eczema and her cheeks now stuck out from her face like stones on concrete. She rarely had the chance to spend time with Mickey Kennedy, and feared losing him to a prettier girl who didn't have six children depending on her.

Clark was struggling, too, and his unhappiness was festering. He and Woody stopped going to school at all, preferring to row out to Putnam's Island to make campfires, read comic books, and smoke cigarettes.

Bootie tried to stay cheerful, but she was slipping into her own dark and gloomy chasm. Only she knew for certain her parents were guilty, and she suffered with a picture of an eternally parentless household. But she kept it to herself.

As autumn slipped into winter, it became clear to the older children their new life was unsustainable. But Aunt Theo

Laura Ginter 164

seemed unfazed by the chaos and dirt creeping higher up the walls. She lived like a butterfly within a battle zone, fluttering aimlessly between parties, social clubs, and clothes stores. And if the unscheduled visit from two school district representatives dropping by to discuss "a concerning situation" forced Aunt Theo to take notice of the children's desperate situation, it was not enough to motivate her to change.

****

Bootie heard knocking on the door as she finished making a Spam sandwich for Ike. "Eat this," she said, holding out the sandwich for her brother.

Ike stamped his foot and buried his hands under his shirt. "No. I hate Spam. Where's Neese?"

"She went to see Mickey." Bootie pulled Ike's hand out and forced the sandwich into his hand. "Eat it!" Ike flung it to the floor. Insistent knocking at the door stopped her from smacking her brother's hand. She scowled. "Pick it up and eat it," she said and left the kitchen.

Bootie crossed the living room and opened the door. Her eyes widened at the sight of Woody's schoolteacher, Miss Belcher, with a man Bootie did not recognize. She couldn't have been more surprised if President Truman himself had been standing in the doorway. Miss Belcher's purse hung from the crook of her arm. She wore two braids, each twisted and pinned around her ears, resembling thick, black earmuffs. Nested between the braids on the top of her head was a banana-shaped green hat that pointed down to her long, narrow nose. A red feather poked out from the hat's side. Mrs. Belcher's eyes were angry, as they always were. It matched the mood of the aura that constantly wrapped her in an orange cocoon.

The man standing beside her was round, white and bald. A baseball with arms and legs. Bootie did not recognize him. He

How to Dance on the Moon

seemed squirmy in his gray, wool suit, as if his under drawers were crawling up his behind and he itched to pull them out. His aura had no color, and his eyes were empty of character.

Bootie stared at Mrs. Belcher with both confusion and awe, and barely heard when the woman asked her if Miss Theodora Rawson was available for a conference. Without taking her eyes off the teacher, Bootie hollered for Aunt Theo.

Miss Belcher covered her ears and clicked her tongue. "Don't holler, Beulah. Invite us in and then go find your aunt."

"Sorry ma'am." Bootie gestured for the visitors to step inside, before leaving to locate Aunt Theo. She found her aunt in the bathroom bleaching her nicotine-stained teeth with baking soda and told her about the guests. When Aunt Theo came to the door, her smile sparkled with bright white speckles of powder.

"How may I help you?" Aunt Theo asked, pleasantly.

"I am Miss Belcher," said the teacher. "And this is Mr. Wickner."

"Yes, I'm Mr. Wickner," the baseball-man repeated.

"We are here to speak to you about Woodrow and Clark."

"Yes, Woodrow and Clark." Mr. Wickner said, his bald head bobbing like a baby chick.

"I am Woodrow's teacher, and Mr. Wickner is the county's Administrator of Education." Miss Belcher nodded toward her companion. Aunt Theo invited them to join her in the living room, and, in keeping with her social upbringing, hardly noticed when the crone-faced woman sucked in her breath and shielded her nose.

Aunt Theo gestured to her guests to sit, and lowered herself into a chair as Mrs. Belcher and Mr. Wickner sat across from her on the couch.

"Would either of you like coffee or tea? Or if you are hungry, I could have Bootie make you something to eat."

Mrs. Belcher looked down at a plate of dried baked beans balancing on the coffee table's edge, next to an apple core and glass of soured milk.

"How about a cigarette?" Aunt Theo asked. "Do you smoke? Bootie!"

"I'm right here, Aunt Theo."

"Oh!" Aunt Theo looked both startled and pleased. "Bootie, could you find my cigarettes, and make tea for our guests?"

"No tea, thank you," interrupted Miss Belcher. "Although, Beulah, you may remove those dishes."

Bootie collected the plate, glass and apple core and raced into the kitchen, passing Ike lying on the floor next to the Spam from his sandwich. She dropped the pile by the sink, flashed her brother an angry look, and returned to her place next to her aunt's chair.

Aunt Theo had folded her hands in her lap. "So, what good news brings you here today?" Bootie knew a visit from school officials never meant good news. Didn't Aunt Theo know Woody and Clark had not been to school in weeks?

Miss Belcher sniffed. "Before we begin, could we open a window?"

"Yes, fresh air would be nice," Wickner agreed.

Bootie ran to the window next to Miss Belcher and pushed up on the sash. A breeze rustled the curtains and cooled her face. Aunt Theo shifted in her chair. "What can I do for you two?"

"Miss Rawson, are Clark and Woodrow ill?" asked Miss Belcher.

"Tell us, are the boys ill?" parroted Mr. Wickner.

"Absolutely not!" Theo said. "They are healthy, strapping young boys."

"Do you know where they are right now? We would like to speak with them."

"Yes, do you know where the boys are right now?"

Aunt Theo looked around the room. "I believe they are in school."

How to Dance on the Moon 167

Miss Belcher huffed. "They are not in school."

"No, they are not in school." Mr. Wickner knitted his brows.

Aunt Theo turned to look at Bootie by the window, who glanced at the clock on the table and shook her head. Aunt Theo laughed nervously. "Well, of course not. Silly me. School would be over by now." She motioned for Bootie to approach and gave her an odd, strained smile as both Miss Belcher and Mr. Wickner leaned forward.

"Do you know where your brothers are?" The smile widened into a squinty-eyed grimace. Clearly, Aunt Theo had no idea what was happening, but expected Bootie to fix whatever was wrong.

"Not for sure, ma'am." Bootie shrugged. "Maybe the island?"

"You don't keep a close watch on the boys?" sniffed Mrs. Belcher. "Are you aware that neither Clark nor Woodrow has been to school for two weeks?"

"No, not for two weeks," echoed Mr. Wickner.

"Oh sweet mother! Really?"

"It's true, and, knowing the circumstances of their, ah, situation, we were concerned."

"Yes, we were concerned, about their situation, that is."

"Well, I must admit, I had no idea!" Aunt Theo's eyes narrowed. "I must thank you for bringing this to my attention. I assumed Bernice was driving them to school every day. How diligently you monitor your students." She batted her eyes at Mr. Wickner. "I do not know where they are at this immediate moment, so I cannot get them for you. However, I will speak to them both and to Bernice, too, and they will be back to school first thing in the morning."

"There is no school, tomorrow, Miss Rawson," said Miss Belcher.

"There's no school tomorrow?" Aunt Theo looked at Bootie again.

Bootie shook her head. "Tomorrow is Saturday, Aunt Theo. No school until Monday."

"Then first thing Monday." Aunt Theo turned again to Mr. Wickner and tilted her head. "What a nice tie you are wearing, Mr. Wickner."

Miss Belcher cleared her throat, and Aunt Theo returned her gaze to the crotchety school marm. "We were supposed to bring the truant officer into this, but we convinced the school board to make allowances."

"Yes, we made allowances," said Mr. Wickner, with a flushed face.

Aunt Theo's eyes widened. Her aura changed from sunny yellow to dusky orange. "Their 'situation' as you call it, has been hard on the boys. And, well, boys will be boys." Aunt Theo's eyelids fluttered again, and she patted at her hair. "Isn't that right, Mr. Wickner? Boys will be boys?"

Mr. Wickner cleared his throat and pulled at his collar. "No, Miss Rawson. Boys cannot be allowed to be boys."

"Is that true?" Aunt Theo lowered her arm. "Boys cannot be boys?" Aunt Theo stood. "If we are finished, I must be getting back to my chores."

Miss Belcher raised her palm. "Please, if we could have one more minute."

Aunt Theo sat back in her chair.

"Miss Rawson, you are an unmarried woman. When you agreed to become guardian to these children, did you realize how much you were taking on?"

"They are my cousin's children, and I am all they have while their parents are engaged elsewhere. It's temporary. My cousin will be home soon."

"How are you paying for their expenses?"

Aunt Theo's eye twitched, and her aura darkened again. "I don't see what these questions have to do with the boys missing school."

"We want to make sure you have the support you need.

How to Dance on the Moon 169

Financial and otherwise. Being the legal guardian of these children brings responsibilities."

Oh dear, thought Bootie, and she stared hard at Aunt Theo, now standing again. "I know my responsibilities."

"Please," said Miss Belcher. With the authority that came naturally to her, she signaled with her finger for Aunt Theo to sit back down. Aunt Theo slowly lowered herself into her chair, her aura clouding like an approaching storm. "Raising children is hard work. Even more so without the help of a husband. The sacrifices and commitments are enormous. No one would fault you if you decided this guardianship was more work than you could handle. The school district could arrange for someone to come by and help you. We could also suggest the court find another guardian if you want." Miss Belcher opened her palms and stretched them outward. "Maybe someone better equipped to meet the children's needs."

Aunt Theo's anger sat on her cheeks, like two red strawberries. "Do you have this conversation with widows?"

Miss Belcher put her hands back in her lap, sniffed the air another time and wrinkled her nose. "We're not trying to offend you, Miss Rawson. We want to help you. Clark and Woodrow will be in school on Monday?"

Aunt Theo stood, and before the couple could stop her again, she crossed the room to the front door. "I will make sure you see the boys. Now, if you'll excuse me, I must get back to my responsibilities."

Miss Belcher and Mr. Wickner rose from their chairs as Ike entered the living room. He walked up to Bootie with Spam squished between his fingers. "I hate Spam!" he yelled, and flung the mangled meat to the floor.

Bootie bent to scrape up the Spam, and she dropped it into an ashtray. Miss Belcher glanced at Mr. Wickner and raised one eyebrow before turning to Aunt Theo. "Thank you for your time, Miss Rawson. We knew you would want to know about the boys' absenteeism. And, again, we want you to know you have our support with whatever decisions you may make regarding your future with the children."

"You have our support, Miss Rawson," said Mr. Wickner.

Aunt Theo shut the door as soon as the couple had stepped outside. "What a nasty woman!" Aunt Theo snorted. "And she had the nerve to imply I couldn't raise you children. She had that fat little man on a short leash, didn't she? And that ugly hat! Is she that rude to the children in her class? No wonder the boys don't want to go to school."

Bootie snorted. "Clark's teacher Miss Snively is much worse. She farts in class and tries to blame it on the boys."

Aunt Theo laughed, her anger forgotten with a wave of her hand, and she scurried back to the bathroom. Ike disappeared into the kitchen, but Bootie chose to follow her aunt rather than chase after Ike. Aunt Theo, standing at the sink, clenched her jaw and pulled back her lips to expose her teeth.

"Aunt Theo, can we get a maid?"

"Absolutely not."

"Why not? Our house is disgusting. Miss Belcher made us open a window, it stunk so bad. Isn't it your job to keep it clean?"

Aunt Theo closed her mouth and sucked her teeth as she studied Bootie through the mirror. "I am doing my job when I tell you baking soda whitens even the dullest smile. You children must learn how to take care of yourselves. When the house gets dirty enough, you will start cleaning it on your own. Besides, do you want a stranger coming into the house and snooping into our business?"

Aunt Theo picked up a soap bar, wet it, and lathered her face, making small circles over her skin with her fingertips. She splashed herself with water. "Hand me a towel, will you, Bootie?" Bootie complied, and Aunt Theo dried her face. Without makeup, Aunt Theo looked both older and more childlike. A gentler, more innocent version of herself.

One by one, Aunt Theo removed every powder and cream

How to Dance on the Moon 171

in her cosmetics bag and applied each one to a different section of skin. When she finished, Aunt Theo gave herself an admiring primp in the mirror, and caught Bootie's eye one last time in the reflection. "Is there something else?"

"No ma'am." Bootie backed out of the bathroom and went to find Ike. He was crying in the kitchen. "What is the matter, Ike?"

"I'm hungry. I want Neese!"

"I'll make you a different sandwich." Bootie took a peanut butter jar from the pantry. Aunt Theo came in, dressed in a ruffled pink and yellow dress with a matching, wide brimmed hat. She floated in a sea of rose-scented eau de cologne. "I'll be out late tonight," she said in her sweetest voice. "Bootie, find your brothers and tell them to go back to school. We don't want that horrible woman back here, do we?" Aunt Theo patted Bootie's head before leaving the room as quickly as she had entered. The front door banged shut.

****

When Bootie told Bernice about Miss Belcher's visit Bernice's face flushed with anger. "Enough!" she announced. "I can't stand this anymore. The house is filthy. Everyone is half-starved. Clark and Woody look like homeless boys. Bootie, is Aunt Theo going out tonight?"

"Yes. She said late," said Bootie. As both girls knew, late was often code for overnight.

"Good. Find the boys. If they are on the island, use the bell to get them back. I will get Sellie, Scooter and Baby Ike, and we'll all meet on the sleeping porch. I can't snap my fingers and make everything right again, but I can bring order to this family."

Bootie's heart swelled with hope Bernice could make things better, and she went to round up her brothers and sisters.

Laura Ginter 172

"I can't do everything around here by myself," Bernice said when the children were assembled. "You all have to share in the work. This meeting is to get us organized."

Woody grumbled, but Clark shushed him. "She's right. The house is disgusting."

Bernice nodded toward her brother. "I have made a list of chores we need do on a regular basis. Sellie, you will be this meeting's secretary. Here is the list." Bernice handed Sellie a paper and pencil. "Sellie will read each chore on the list, and I want someone to volunteer to do it. If nobody volunteers, I will assign it."

Woody crossed his arms at his chest. "Who made you boss?" he snarled.

Bernice looked down at her brother and narrowed her eyes. "I did."

Woody's squinted back at her. "If Mother and Father were here you'd be in trouble."

Scooter said, "Shut up, Woody. Mother and Father aren't here. So just shut up."

"Listen, everybody," said Bernice, raising her voice. "Sellie will read the list. Go on, Sellie."

Sellie regarded the paper in her hand and read the first item. "Meals."

"I will share the cooking with Bootie and Sellie," said Bernice. "We will make a schedule between us. What's next?"

"Washing dishes."

"Any volunteers?" When Bernice's eyes scanned the room, Bootie glanced down at her feet. "Nobody? Then I'll do them on Sundays, Clark and Woody will do them on Tuesdays, Thursdays, and Fridays. Sellie and Bootie will do them the other days."

This time Clark objected. "Hey! Boys don't do dishes."

"They do now! Next on the list, please?"

"Clothes."

"Mrs. Chew will let us bring our clothes to her laundry on

How to Dance on the Moon 173

Mondays and Wednesdays. Bootie, you will collect the clothes, and we will take them in before school."

Scooter raised his hand. "Do you have anything I can do?"

Bernice grinned, "Yes! Scooter, you can do your exercises every day without someone telling you to, and you can collect the mail and sort out the bills for the bank. If you hear anything else you want to do, speak up."

Woody jumped from his chair and swung his arm toward Bernice as though she were a fly he wanted to swat. "This is shit. I'm not doing it."

"You have to, Woody," Bernice said. "Did you know Miss Belcher was here with a school official?"

"So what?"

"So you and Clark both must go back to school every day. If you don't, they will not let Aunt Theo be our guardian, and they will split us up. She may not be great at taking care of us, but at least we are together. Besides, Mother and Father would be upset if they knew you weren't going to school."

"Do you think we'll get to see Mother and Father soon?" asked Sellie.

Bernice bit her lip. "I don't know." Scooter put his hands around his head and leaned over to hide the tears everyone saw anyway. Bernice added, "We must be patient. Once the court gives us permission, we'll see them. Meanwhile, we must take care of this house, for Mother and Father's sake."

Scooter still had his hands over his face. Bootie slid closer to him and put her arm around his shoulders. The anguish from his thin frame rolled up her arm and squeezed her chest. On the surface, he appeared to be dealing with their parents' absence as well as any of them, but it was just a brave face. He was old enough to understand the situation, but too young and fragile to know how to cope. Bootie's heart ached for her little brother, trapped in braces, trapped in the limitations that restricted him more than anyone else, trapped in a house with no parents, trapped with no outlets for expressing his pain.

"I agree with Bernice," Bootie said. "We must do this for Mother and Father." Bootie thrust her free hand, palm down, into the circle's center.

"For Mother and Father." Sellie placed hers on Bootie's, followed by Clark and Bernice. Scooter took his hands off his face and placed one on Bernice's. Even Ike put his hand onto the pile and giggled. "For Mama."

Only Woody held out. "I'm not making any deals," he said. "I hate you, Bernice," and ran out the door and thumped down the steps. The darkness quickly obscured him, but the sound of his feet pounding the walkway over the marsh made it clear he was heading to the lake.

With Woody's demons weighing on him, Bootie couldn't keep her own stream of dark thoughts from gurgling to the surface. As much as she tried to wear a happy face, she, too, was in a hate-filled state. She hated the emptiness of a home without parents, she hated her smelly clothes, she hated eating bad food, and she hated Aunt Theo for leaving them alone so much, and for not getting a maid and for expecting her to make the boys go to school. She hated Woody for walking out when Bernice was working hard to keep them together. She hated Bernice for trying to fix everything when she could fix nothing. She hated being different from other people, knowing secrets, seeing invisible colors, and she hated the haunts who were visiting with more frequency at night. But mostly she hated how she had known about her parents' secret for a long time and had done nothing to stop them and save the family from being in this terrible place.

Bernice ended the morose silence. "Well, if Woody's too upset to participate," she said, "then we'll let him be, for now. Sellie, continue with the list."

The children finished splitting the chores among themselves, keeping Woody on the list as a dishwasher, errand runner, and trash burner, a chore they all agreed he would enjoy. They also pledged to scrub the house until every room

How to Dance on the Moon 175

was as clean as if Mother were directing the effort herself. Even if they woke Aunt Theo, if Aunt Theo came home.

Again, the six children thrust a hand into a circle and piled them together in a pledge to work together. A shallow spring of hope sprung from Bootie's heart, and the darkness that had awakened during the meeting went back into its cave. Even if Bernice's plan didn't work perfectly, things would be better.

Woody came home and picked up his clothes in a conciliatory gesture toward the new regime, and Bootie crawled into bed that night, comforted that someone was in control again. The next day the children worked together and scrubbed the house. Bernice rewarded them all by cooking a pizza pie for supper.

Bootie and Grace 1993

24.

Bootie was sitting at a table with Jennie when Grace walked into the tearoom, pulling her suitcase behind her. Her hair was plastered to her head in a wet ponytail and her coat shimmered with reflected rainwater. Bloodshot, puffy eyes seemed too small in her round, full face. She pulled her lips into a tight grimace she tried to pass off as a smile. "Auntie, I'm here."

Bootie stood and approached Grace. "Put your suitcase over there and give me your coat."

Grace handed her coat to her aunt, set her bag on the floor and pulled out Jennie's pajamas. "We may have to stay a few nights."

"You will stay until you are safe. Do you want a towel for your hair?"

Grace fell into a chair next to Jennie. "No, I'm fine."

Jennie giggled. "Aunt Bootie made me tuna sandwiches cut like stars. They were yummy!"

Grace handed Jennie her pajamas. "I know it's early, Jennie, but I need you to get ready for bed. You can change in the kitchen." Jennie scooted off the chair, and skipped to the kitchen.

"Are you going to tell me what's been going on and why you haven't told me anything before now?" Bootie asked.

Grace set her jaw and looked toward the kitchen. A sapphire light emanated from around her somber face. Bootie waited for Grace to respond. A ticking clock in the kitchen marked the uncomfortable silence. Finally, Grace shook her head. "After Jennie goes to bed."

Bootie reached over to pat Grace on the hand, but Grace pulled away, and Bootie caught a defiant flicker in her niece's tired eyes.

"Auntie! Stop trying to read me!"

"Okay, that time I was trying to read you." Grace flashed a genuine smile for the first time all day. She stretched up and gave Bootie a quick kiss on the cheek. "There. Read that!"

Grace did not intend for the kiss to give Bootie any information, but she felt a sharp, painful pinprick on her cheek, like a bee sting. Bootie refrained from massaging the spot on her face. Jennie came back dressed in her pajamas and sat in the chair next to her mother.

"Have you eaten, Grace?" Bootie asked. "I can whip you up a sandwich, too."

"Thanks Auntie. Just tea. But I'll get it."

"No, let me spoil you tonight. Would you like dessert, Jennie?"

"I want a chocolate T Rex!" Jennie growled and clawed the air.

How to Dance on the Moon 177

"She's been bugging me to take her to see Jurassic Park," Grace said.

"I don't have any T Rexes. Something else?"

"How about, hmm, cherry pie and chocolate ice cream!"

Bootie laughed. "How did you know I had cherry pie and chocolate ice cream? Is it okay, Grace?"

"She can have whatever she wants. I think I'll have pie and ice cream, too, if you have enough."

Bootie went to the kitchen, set a teapot on the stove. She filled a water pitcher for Grace and poured a glass of milk for Jennie. As she went about her tasks, she tried to remember all she could about Blake. She hadn't liked him. His handshake had created a vision of black energy, spinning in every direction at a million miles an hour. He had radiated a muddy aura, like swamp water, with fiery streaks shooting out from his chest. He had reminded her of the raccoons who lived in the barn when she was a child, friendly-looking and cute, but dangerous with their sharp claws and teeth. Fanning the spark in this man, Bootie had feared, would be playing with fire. But somehow, she had missed the signs that he would victimize Grace.

The memory of the confusing vision she had received a few months back, about Grace, popped into her mind and pricked her conscience. Why had she not taken the signs of trouble more seriously?

Bootie put two thick cherry pie pieces on plates and warmed them the microwave. Then she covered the lattice crusts with ice cream and topped them with whipped cream dollops and a dusting of cinnamon. When the kettle whistled, Bootie assembled a tray and brought out the food and drinks. Grace and Jennie were studying the cover of a ragged two-year-old gardening magazine. Grace startled when Bootie set the tray on the table.

"You are tense!" Grace slid the magazine aside to make room for Bootie to set down the plates.

Grace lifted her fork. "The pie smells yummy. Eat, Jennie."

Grace broke off a small piece of crust and dipped it in the soft ice cream, before swirling it in her mouth.

Bootie watched her niece eat. She has never looked more like her mother, Bootie thought, but unlike Sellie, Grace did little to enhance her appearance, choosing to wear loose-fitting clothes and little makeup. Probably to distance herself from her mother's flamboyance. But Grace couldn't hide her beauty, passed to her through the Rawson genes. And although Jennie resembled Stephen more, she was developing her mother's loveliness.

Grace, are you taking time off from work?" Bootie asked.

Jennie started to say something, but Grace gave her a stern look that hushed her. "Finish your pie, then I'm taking you upstairs to watch television. Aunt Bootie and I want to talk."

Jennie scooted off her chair. "I'm done, Mommy. See you in the morning, Aunt Bootie!"

Bootie hugged Jennie, and cleared the dishes while Grace took Jennie upstairs to settle her in. When Grace returned Bootie said, "It's not like you to be short with Jennie."

Grace sat. "Loretta put me on administrative leave for two weeks."

"Why?" Bootie asked, surprised.

"She thinks I'm dating Biscuit and her stupid jealousy is making everything that's already horrible even worse." Grace's eyes flashed with anger. "Loretta is the most arrogant, self-absorbed person I've ever met. I hate her."

"This has to be more complicated than who's dating who."

"This is unfair. I miss my husband. I miss Stephen." Caught by surprise at Grace's wistful outburst, Bootie didn't know what to say. Grace closed her eyes and rubbed them. "Auntie, my life is a total mess."

"Are you ready to fill in the blanks for me?"

"I think so." Grace rose from her chair, went to her suitcase and pulled out Blake's wallet. She returned to the table and handed the wallet to her aunt. "Let's start with this,"

How to Dance on the Moon 179

she said. Bootie opened the wallet and saw Blake's license. "Look behind the license," Grace prompted. Bootie did so and found the newspaper clipping. She took it out, unfolded it and read it. "Oh my God, Grace."

Grace folded her hands in her lap and began the story of her relationship with Blake, most of which Bootie already knew.

25.

Bootie rose to switch on the lights. Grace drank from her water glass but her eyes were unfocused, her skin pale, and her shoulders slumped, as though the effort of telling her story had deadened something inside her. She seemed too weak to be able to deal with the horrors she had described. Her aura was the deepest blue. "Should we check on Jennie?"

"She's fine. She understands."

Bootie lifted the water pitcher and refilled Grace's glass while Grace clenched and unclenched her hands. "Have you had enough for one day?"

"But you must have questions."

Bootie returned to her seat and rubbed her hand over Blake's wallet. "He lied about Amanda. Do you think school was another lie?"

"He seemed to be going to classes." Grace looked up at Bootie expectantly. "Do you think this could all be over since he has his books now?"

Bootie shook her head. It wasn't going to be that simple. "I just wish I could figure out why he wanted them so badly." She looked at Grace. A light flickered across her niece's face, the reflection of a car's headlight outside. "You had a strong vision when Blake held the pillow over your face. Tell me about it."

"You mean about Buster?" Grace asked. "Do I want to know how you knew about him?"

Bootie raised her eyebrows and smiled.

Grace closed her eyes, reaching into her memory. "When Blake cut off my air with the pillow a face emerged from the darkness. I didn't recognize the face at first, but when it came into focus, I saw it was Buster Tyler, a friend from grade school. When we were nine years old, his brother suffocated him with a pillow. I wondered if seeing his face so clearly meant I was dying." She opened her eyes. Dewy tears filled them. "Do you know if people from your past come to help you die?"

Bootie straightened. "No. I've had visions of death, but I've never seen what happens to a person when he dies."

"I sat next to Buster in the fourth grade. He was nice for a boy. The day Buster was murdered he had come to school in his Cub Scout uniform. His troop was having a Christmas party, and Buster had brought in his gift, wrapped up in red paper with gold reindeers. It sat on the shelf above the coat rack all day as a temptation, and a reminder that our own Christmas party was just a few days away. At the end of the day, we put our chairs up on our desks, and I teased Buster about his crew cut. He told me if he got a stupid present at the party he would rewrap it and give it to me."

Grace smiled at the memory before continuing. "But while Buster was at Cub Scouts, his older brother, a Marine they thought was in Vietnam, strolled into his family home without telling anyone he was coming, and for no known reason strangled his mother. The police believed Buster walked in on his brother, and before he could run away, his brother grabbed him, carried him to his bedroom and held a pillow on his face until he died." Grace looked away. "In my vision, Buster showed me his present from the party had been a G.I. Joe."

Grace paused to sip her water. "When I was young, I used to put a pillow over my face and try to hold my breath, to understand how Buster felt to die that way. But I could always

How to Dance on the Moon 181

remove the pillow when it became uncomfortable. Then, when it was *my* life and death struggle, suffocation wasn't how I imagined at all. In real life, having no control over your breathing sets off a panic that fills your mind like a balloon blowing up too big for its space and it can't be popped. Buster came to calm me. To help me die or help me live, I don't know."

"Your gift called on Buster to save you."

The little color in Grace's face darkened. "I don't have your gift, Aunt Bootie. No matter how much you think I do, it's not there." Grace put her elbows on the table and lowered her head between her hands.

Bootie let Grace stay in her own thoughts for a long time before pulling her back. "Is there more to this than you've told me?" she asked, gently. "Something you might be afraid to talk about? Because you can tell me anything. I'd never judge you."

Fresh tears filled Grace's eyes. "Blake became the best friend I ever had, besides Stephen. He brought me back to life after Stephen's death left me feeling dead, too. And he made me feel protected. Even without the horrible phone calls, it's hard to be out there with a child and with no one to help you ward off the demons. I am not a superhero." Grace covered her face as her tears fell. "I am just me."

Bootie tried to touch Grace's arm, but Grace pulled it away.

"Gracie, relax," Bootie said, frustrated. "I'm not trying to get a vision from you."

"But Auntie, it was all a lie. He stole the little sense of security I had, along with my time, my sleep, my daughter's safety, my sanity, and maybe my job. I hate him for hurting me and scaring me. I hate him most for turning me into a foolish woman, who can't tell the difference between a good person and a bad one, just like my mother. And I believe with everything inside me he killed Amanda and that man."

Bootie sat silently until Grace's tears slowed. "At least he has his books," Grace said. "Let's hope it's over. Because if it isn't, I don't know what else can I do I haven't done. I don't know how I will protect Jennie."

Bootie tilted her head and glanced sideways at Grace. "I have a good friend who is a psychologist, Janet Fleming. She's usually booked far in advance, but if I gave her a call and explained how serious your situation was, I bet she would squeeze us in tomorrow during lunch or after hours, and we could get professional advice."

Grace put her head back between her hands. "Okay."

Bootie reached for the water pitcher and noticed a brown lump under the table. She leaned forward for a closer look. "Oh my gosh! Mrs. Wallaby!" Bootie scooped up the little cottontail, and she rolled onto her side in Bootie's arms. Bootie stroked her fur.

"Is she okay?" asked Grace.

"I don't know. She's very still." The rabbit's paw twitched in her arms and Bootie's anxiety eased. "I'll take her into the kitchen and see if I can get her to drink some water." Bootie waved a hand in Grace's direction. "Go upstairs and get some rest. We'll talk more in the morning."

"Thanks Auntie. I will in a minute. I want to call Biscuit, and Mrs. Fish to thank her. I think I have her home phone number. See you tomorrow." Bootie paused, but Grace smiled and waved her off. "I'm okay."

Bootie carried Mrs. Wallaby into the kitchen. She placed the rabbit in the dog bed she had bought for her and kept in the corner. Next to the bed, she set a bowl of water. Bootie sat on her knees and stroked the rabbit's fur. Mrs. Wallaby nuzzled Bootie's hand.

Bootie thought about her sister, Sellie, who should have been the one there, supporting Grace. But Sellie had lived through so much grief at such a young age her heart had never learned to love her own child in a traditional way. And Bootie knew Grace so much better than Sellie did. Only Bootie could

How to Dance on the Moon

understand how strong Grace's gift was, and how it still lived inside her, even if it was buried.

It was a paradox of the gift, that those with it rarely saw it in someone else, but Bootie had known the truth about little Grace when she had spoken about a troll and a snake living in her closet. Her monsters had been strikingly more intrusive and powerful than Bootie's monkey-beast. And Buster, the young boy in Grace's story, had to have come from Grace's gift. It was a lucky miracle Grace had been able to contain her gift. It might have been how she survived it.

It was clear that, sadly, Sellie couldn't help Grace right now the way Bootie could. But Bootie had missed the signs Grace was in trouble, even after having a warning vision. Bootie hadn't seen much of Grace, and Grace had not come to her for help, but that was no excuse. Grace had already paid a steep price for Bootie's inattention. Hopefully it wasn't too late to keep her niece from going into her own dark place when she realized how much battle still lay ahead.

Bootie scratched Mrs. Wallaby between the ears. The rabbit raised herself upright and looked at Bootie before nuzzling her leg. Bootie allowed the bunny's soft fur to comfort her. She appreciated how everyone could see Mrs. Wallaby, unlike some of her childhood pets.

****

Exhausted, Grace rose from the table, and after she made her calls she went upstairs to check on Jennie. Her daughter had fallen asleep in the bed they would be sharing while they stayed with Aunt Bootie. In the bathroom, Grace removed her clothes and examined her arm. The bruise had darkened to a greenish black, but the yellow edges showed it was healing.

Grace stepped into the shower and let the hot water steam away her thoughts. She shut down all the emotions that would have stirred in her relentlessly if she had not learned how to separate herself from them. She was becoming skilled at numbing herself, and she had developed a new compulsion for cleanliness, when though scrubbing her body could make her problems wash away. She scrubbed her skin with her washcloth until she was sore. She rubbed her thighs the hardest.

26.

Bootie was encouraged by how much better Grace looked the next morning. Her eyes were clearer, as though a fog had lifted, and her body, clenched last night, seemed more relaxed. Refusing Bootie's offer of tea, Grace made coffee, buttered a blueberry muffin for Jennie's breakfast, and helped herself to a buttermilk-currant scone. Grace drove Jennie to school while Bootie went about her routine for preparing the tearoom to open. When Erline arrived, Bootie asked her to call Faye into work, and at one o'clock, Bootie drove Grace to her appointment with Janet Fleming.

Soft music and the scent of Jasmine incense greeted Bootie and Grace when they entered Janet's office. A receptionist in a headscarf gestured for them to have a seat. Framed posters with inspirational messages and comforting pictures covered the walls. Women's magazines and a book entitled *Divorce Is Not Death* sat on the table. A nine-inch tall Buddha grinned at the waiting room guests from the receptionist's desk.

Soon Janet appeared and greeted Bootie with a warm hug before leading the two women to her office. She was dressed in a floor-length blue dress and sandals. Hoop earrings skimmed her shoulders. Her office was an extension of her lobby, with more framed posters, original artwork, two deep cushioned sofas, an upholstered armchair, floor pillows and a

How to Dance on the Moon   185

large tissue box. Under a window was a narrow shelf with a candle and a vase and various small objects, including a wallet-size photo, a comb and a handkerchief. Janet noticed Bootie studying the display. "That is a project from my women's group," she said. "I asked everyone to bring in an object that represented something troubling in their life and place it on the shelf. Grace, thinking about what you've been going through, what would you add?"

Grace thought for a moment. "My keychain with my picture of Jennie."

"Jennie is your daughter. Bootie told me it took you a long time to have a child."

"Over ten years. It was a difficult time. I had given up hope I would ever get pregnant."

"She's precious to you."

Grace's eyes filled with tears. "She is everything to me. She's all I have left of Stephen."

"I understand your mother lives on the east coast and your father is deceased. Where are Jennie's paternal grandparents?"

"Gil is not worthy of his granddaughter. Stephen's mother Vicky has been living on an Israeli kibbutz since 1970. We see her a week a year in the winter."

Janet smiled. "Why would you add your keychain with Jennie's picture to the shelf?"

"It was the first thing of mine Blake touched."

"Interesting. With the right key, you could lock Blake from your life. Or, you are locked in a frightening prison, and you can't find the key that will let you out." Janet placed her hand on the shelf. "Subconscious symbolisms or irrelevant metaphors?"

Bootie leaned forward. "You think people experience subconscious symbolism a lot?"

Janet nodded. "And irrelevant metaphor. That's what we're working on in our women's group. Tell me, Grace. Did you go to counseling after your husband died?"

"Briefly. I didn't like it."

"The right therapist can help you if you stick with it."

Grace lowered her eyes. "I do appreciate you taking time from your lunch hour to see me."

Janet gestured for the women to sit on a sofa, and she lowered herself onto the armchair. "Someday I want to hear your story first hand, but from what your aunt told me last night, the immediate priority is your safety. If we discuss your stalker's psychology, what may be going on in his head, it will help you choose the best strategy to protect yourself."

"I'm hoping he just wanted his textbooks back," Grace interjected. "He has them now."

Janet reached for Grace's hand and gave it a gentle squeeze. "I doubt Blake's motives have ever been about his books. Stalking is a crime of passion and obsession. Although stalkers come in many shapes and sizes, psychologists categorize them by common behaviors and psychological disorders. And the threat they pose to their targets varies extensively.

"A stalker tends to be male, and a loner with delusional and narcissistic disorders. From what your aunt has told me, yours most closely resembles a dangerous version of the rejected suitor type. He wants an intimate, loving relationship, and he believes his target is in love with him as much as he is in love with his target. Any interaction or response, even a negative one, can encourage him. He also can believe he deserves to be loved by his target because he is so deeply invested in stalking her. He can think his target is playing hard to get. Every obstacle thrown in his way encourages him to try harder to prove his love. For example, enhancing your security goaded him, and he found ways around it. The rejected suitor is often unresponsive to restraining orders because he views them as challenges he must overcome. He doesn't believe his behavior is stalking. Often, he thinks of himself as the victim."

How to Dance on the Moon

Grace smirked.

Janet shrugged. "I know. Hard to believe. The rejected suitor also uses tactics to intimidate and control women. Having control over a woman makes him feel as though he is in a relationship with her. Blake has been trying to control you since he met you. He has used the phone calls to scare you so he can rescue you. Have you seen other behavior like this while you were friends?"

"He would check my caller ID. He went through my things when I wasn't home."

Janet nodded. "Fits the pattern. There is also research suggesting a stalker is aroused by the chase. Certain neurons in the brain light up when he is in hunting mode, and it acts like a drug. What's alarming for me, though, is that Blake's personality disorder seems to encompass more severe psychosis. He has injured you. And he lied to you about his wife's violent death. What do you think? Did he kill her? Or did her death cause him to be the way he is now?"

"He killed her."

"Physical danger can come into play when he recognizes he is being rejected, or when his target enters into another relationship. Make sure the Seattle police know his wife and her friend were murdered in Oregon. It might motivate them to take another look at him. But as for protecting yourself, you must expand your safety plan. Can you move from your house for awhile? Go somewhere away from there?"

"I can stay with my aunt."

Janet turned to Bootie. "Does he know where you live?"

"He came to the tearoom once, but I don't think he'd follow her there."

"I wouldn't depend on that." Janet said. "Grace, try never to be alone. That's when he's most likely to come after you. Always let someone know where you are or where you are going and when you expect to return. Change your routine. Shop at different stores. Go to work at different hours."

"Jennie needs to go to school. I can't change the school's schedule."

"Maybe change her school. Or home-school her. At least ask the principal about your options. Also, keep a record of everything Blake does. Every phone call and every sighting, and report it all to the police. If you ever see him, cause a ruckus. Scream, kick, pound on your car horn. And take a class on self-defense, in case he does come at you again."

"Will all this stop him? Will it make it end?"

For the first time, Janet seemed to lose confidence in her words. "Sometimes stalkers are caught and go to jail. Sometimes they find a new person to focus on. Sometimes they go silent, turning up months or years later. But they all stop at some point, one way or another."

Grace looked frightened. "But what if he doesn't? He could kill me, like he killed Amanda!"

Joyce squeezed Grace's hand again. "We don't know that he killed Amanda. And the police will get him eventually. Until then, be vigilant."

****

After the session, Bootie drove Grace back to the tearoom, and they shared a pot of tea. Grace's hand shook as she lifted her cup, spilling tea on the table. "Look at me, Auntie. I'm a mess. I can't do all those things Janet said. And how does she know Blake will stop someday?"

"She had good advice on ways to protect yourself, if you follow her suggestions."

Grace interrupted. "The police already told me most of what she said. Seriously. I can only see one thing I can do that would be effective."

Bootie laughed aloud. "You are not getting a handgun. You, of all people, know how I feel about guns."

"Blake probably already has a gun, if he killed his wife and

How to Dance on the Moon 189

that guy."

"You'd shoot yourself by accident or Blake would take it away from you and use it to shoot you."

"I will take lessons, and I'll use the gun just in an emergency, but I'm tired of being a victim."

Bootie saw the determination in Grace's eyes and knew there would be no changing her mind. "Uncle Ike is a hunter. If you"re determined to take this dangerous course, then go to New Hampshire. He can teach you to shoot. And you can rest while you are there, and maybe get perspective."

"But Jennie is in school."

"She'll survive a week or two away."

Grace hesitated. "Okay, I'll do it if you think Uncle Ike will help me."

"You could visit your mother, too."

Grace shrugged. "Visit Mother? If she's around. If she'll see me."

Bootie's shoulders relaxed. "I'll call my travel agent friend and have her get you on a flight."

"But I don't want Uncle Ike to know what's going on."

"He won't question a single mother wanting to learn how to protect herself. But for the record, I still hate the idea of you having a gun."

****

Grace's life had turned into a cesspool of stress, but it washed away at the homestead on the shore of the blue, shimmery lake. The closest Grace ever came to being continuously happy was at the lake house in New Hampshire. Her mother had brought her there often to escape her own unpleasant adult realities. Now, Grace and Jennie basked in the herbal New England air, rich and thick with the autumnal aromas of wet leaves and pine needles.

The house on the lake cleansed her spirit like balsam soap

for the soul. Warm and cozy, it smelled of burning wood and cider. The sparkles dancing on the lake water became pinpricks, releasing the poison from inside her. At each day's end, Grace and Jennie snuggled under quilts her grandmother had made for her aunts and uncles when they were children, and Grace listened contentedly to her sleeping daughter breathe to the rhythms of her dreams. It soothed her like a salve.

Together they visited Aunt Theo in the nursing home. Aunt Theo hugged the little girl enthusiastically, and when they returned to the lake house, Jennie told Grace that Aunt Theo had a special sadness inside her.

"Why do you think that?" asked Grace.

"She thinks she killed Clark Kent," said Jennie. "Is that Superman?"

"Oh Jennie, your imagination is crazy. I promise Aunt Theo did not kill Superman." Grace rubbed her daughter's cheek and made her smile.

With distance, Blake's grip on Grace slipped away. As soon as her second day at the lake, she had stopped worrying Blake would pop out at her from behind a tree. By the fourth day, she could listen to a ringing phone without having a panic attack. The bruise on her arm faded. A new vitality filled Grace, and she embraced the return of her depleted energy. But she did not confide in anyone about her troubles.

Grace excelled at her lessons. Besides having basic target practice, she learned loading, unloading, defending the gun and how to shoot while moving and at close quarters. Her biggest challenge was conquering the fear of killing someone, but she imagined Blake threatening Jennie, and knew she could pull the trigger.

By her trip's end, Grace believed she could fix all she had done wrong with Blake, with Jennie, and with Loretta. She recognized how she had allowed Blake to evolve from a friend to a monster, and had empowered him to abuse her. With the

How to Dance on the Moon 191

Restraining Order and the gun for defense, she could strip his power, and render him harmless. She could make him go away. She could reclaim her life. Stephen would be proud, she thought. It was time to go home.

27.

Bootie flipped the tearoom's CLOSED sign and ordered a pizza for delivery from a pizzeria on the beach. She brought out from the kitchen a glass of Chablis and a diet cola, and set the cola in front of Grace before sitting across from her. "Having any jet lag?"

Grace took a sip of her cola. "A little. But Jennie was excited to get back to school."

"Your Uncle Ike told me you had a good visit, and your lessons went well."

"The lake house looks like a Bed and Breakfast. I showed him that picture we took of you at Jennie's open house. He said your hair is too dark, and you should stop wearing so much green. It makes you look like a frog."

Bootie chuckled. "Better than a tomato. I'm sticking to black these days."

"Does it bother you Uncle Ike says you look like a frog?" asked Grace.

"No, I'm glad he's comfortable enough to speak his mind. Did you see your mother?"

"I called her. She was leaving for London. She yelled at me for not giving her any notice I was coming." Grace gestured at the wine glass and wrinkled her nose. "Is that stuff from a box? It smells sweet."

"Are you insulting my wine?" Bootie sniffed dramatically.

"Your Uncle Eddie would have liked it."

"Uncle Eddie?" Grace raised her eyebrows. "What made you think of him?"

Bootie looked away. "Uncle Ike told me you two talked about him. It made me miss him."

"I know how that feels." Grace said.

Bootie sipped her wine. "It does get better, you know."

"That's what people say." Grace smiled. "Uncle Ike said you married Uncle Eddie after only knowing him seven days. I never knew that."

Bootie tilted her head, picturing her husband's face. "Eddie was handsome and tall and sweet, and he intrigued me because I couldn't see inside him. Like he had kryptonite around his psychic transmitters. Not many people can surprise me, but Eddie could. I was lonely, and he was, too, and we had a lot in common. I think that was why he asked me to marry him. We were married eleven years before he died."

"Did you tell him about your gift?"

"Of course. It made him uncomfortable so we pretended it wasn't there. I never shared anything with him that came from my gift."

"Uncle Ike said you were told he died in a helicopter crash, but you didn't believe it."

"Not at first. The only vision I ever had of Eddie came after that crash and it showed him alive. It made me doubt the official story."

"Didn't that upset you? Didn't it make you want to find out the truth?"

Bootie sat back and folded her arms across her chest. "I was going to look for him, but changed my mind. I'm at peace with it all now. It was a long time ago."

Grace arched her brow. "Not that long ago. And I can tell by your posture you are not at all at peace with it. What if Uncle Eddie were still alive today? He could need you. If I had your gift, I would never stop looking for the truth after having a

How to Dance on the Moon 193

vision. I'd still be looking."

"It's complicated, Grace."

The door to the tearoom opened, and a college age youth came in with a blue vinyl pizza carrier. Bootie stood. "That was fast. You can bring that over here, please." The young man crossed the room and set the carrier in front of Grace. As he removed the pizza, his hand grazed Bootie's arm. "How much do I owe you, Gavin?" Bootie reached for her purse.

"Eight dollars." The young man said. "How did you know my name was Gavin?"

Oops, though Bootie. She gave him a ten-dollar bill and told him to keep the change. When their fingers touched, Bootie felt a light but pleasant tingle and looked up at the boy's face. He had bright eyes and fiery hair that spiked like a child's drawing of a lit torch. "Your mother has eaten here. Mary."

Gavin grinned. "I know. I look like her."

"It's the hair. Are you the son who's going to Seattle University? "

"Does she talk about me?" Bootie hoped so. Gavin put the bill in the envelope. "Thanks for the tip. I'll tell my mother you remembered her. She loves your food."

"Thank you, Gavin."

When Gavin left, Grace asked Bootie, "Little slip up there, Aunt Bootie? And he's a bit young for you, don't you think?"

Bootie locked the front door. "Oh really? Too young for me?"

Grace squinted, accusingly. "What's going on?"

"I ordered half cheese and half pepperoni. Which do you prefer?"

"Pepperoni!"

Bootie dished pizza onto each plate. "It's a treat to eat something besides tearoom food. You'll love this pizza."

"You're not eating pepperoni?"

"No," Bootie mumbled through her food. "It's not on my diet." She swallowed. "You would think, with all the running around I do around here, I'd be as skinny as Mrs. Wallaby's carrots. How much walking would you guess I do in a day?"

"I don't know. A mile or so."

"That's all?" Bootie frowned. "Do you think my rear end is getting bigger?"

Grace smirked. "You mean Bootie's got booty?"

"I hate how my name is now a synonym for buttocks."

"Seriously, no one thinks of you like that." Grace's eyes focused over Bootie's shoulder. "Look Auntie, here comes Mrs. Wallaby." Bootie's bunny hopped along the wall, working her way toward the two women. "She looks better."

"Did you let her in?" Bootie asked.

"Nope. She must have got in by herself," Grace said, and added. "Do you think she was once someone's pet? She doesn't seem feral."

"She showed up in my garden about a year ago, on the day I lost the rabbit's foot I'd had since a child. I had always kept my rabbit's foot in my dresser, but that day it was gone, and when I went through the trashcan in the garden searching for it, Mrs. Wallaby thumped up behind me." Bootie broke off some pizza crust and popped it in her mouth. "Has there been any word from Blake?"

"None from Blake, the Breather or Stan Bean. Biscuit's been checking my messages and my security tapes."

"And what about the restraining order?"

"The processor served Blake and told him the police will arrest him if he comes near me. I hope that's true."

"So what's your plan?"

"To go to the store, pick up my gun, buy a gun safe for my bedroom, and then go home."

"Don't get the gun, Grace. With all your security equipment, you shouldn't need it."

"I promise it will be okay." Grace's expression brightened. "There is good news! Loretta wants to see me in the morning. If all goes well, I'll be back at work tomorrow. And I spoke to

How to Dance on the Moon 195

Jennie's teacher when I dropped her off at school this morning. There will be no more changes made to Jennie's schedule without talking to me and only me. No calls, better security, the restraining order has been served, I have my job back and Jennie safe at school. The worst is behind me, I think."

"But promise me, if you sense any trouble, you will call the police. Don't rely on a gun."

"I promise. And I promise you're going to have trouble getting that red pizza sauce drip off your shirt." Bootie pulled back to look down at her blouse. Grace giggled, and Bootie rolled her eyes and swiped at the drip with her finger. "Auntie, what was going on with that Gavin boy?"

"Remember I told you about Polly whose father died a few months ago?"

"Yes, I think so."

"When she was here with Erline's granddaughter Ashley, I saw a vision of a boy she was going to start dating."

"Was it Gavin?"

"Yep. And I just saw she's going to marry him."

"You saw the future?"

"No. I saw the cord that connects them."

Grace smiled. "Are you going to introduce them?"

"I don't know. I hate to interfere. I might make a mess of things."

"But maybe you are meant to bring them together."

"Maybe. I'll think about it."

Grace picked up her cola and Bootie followed her lead with her wine. "Here's to Polly and Gavin. If somebody's going to have a happy marriage, I hope it's them."

"And here's to you, Gracie. Here's to a normal life."

"Thank you, Auntie," said Grace. "That's all I want."

Bootie 1949

28.

With the introduction of personal responsibility, regular meals and a clean house, life settled into a healthier routine for the Kurz children, until love entered Aunt Theo's life in the form of a thick-lipped, droopy-eyed grifter named Harley Boggs.

Harley and Aunt Theo were about the same height, although Harley was thinner by twenty pounds and younger by several years. His aura was most often a toxic blend of milky browns. Everything else about him was black, except for his bleached clamshell complexion. He had black hair, black eyes, steeply arched black brows, and a black mustache so bushy it looked like a black baby squirrel had nested between his nose and his lip. His mustache hung down both sides of his mouth, and sometimes he would twirl the ends with his fingers, twisting them knitting needle thin. He always wore black slacks with a black shirt and black jacket. His jacket had once been elegant, but now it frayed at the cuffs, and the pockets bulged in the middle from carrying cigarettes, matches, a gin flask, a deck of cards and a money clip with no money. He wore black shoes, but unlike his suit, his shoes were polished and looked new. His little black bolo tie completed the illusion of an exotic vampire who had fallen on hard times. Or a comic book villain. Both would also apply to his personality.

He smelled like whiskey, tobacco and mildew. His hands were large for his size, with skin that flaked around the palms and fingers. And he used big words. Bootie suspected he invented some of them to sound educated.

Harley came to the house almost every night in his 1929 black Rolls Royce that, like him, was a remnant of tattered glamour from a past age. It sputtered and blew out smoke, and the passenger door never closed completely. On Sundays, he

How to Dance on the Moon 197

came to the house early and stayed the whole day. He would still be there when Bootie went to bed, and sometimes he would be drinking coffee in the kitchen when she got up for school. He never had any money, not that he ever needed any. He had a flair for talking Aunt Theo out of hers.

The children, who Harley referred to as fleas and fleaettes, bristled at the shameful way he would grab whatever flesh on Aunt Theo he could reach, while she playfully slapped his hands away and scolded him for fondling her in front of the children. They tried to ignore Harley's rudeness to their aunt, but when she wasn't looking, he would leer at Bernice with shifty eyes and tug on his mustache. If Bernice strayed within earshot, he would tell her she was pretty and scratch at his black pants. He was a snake, hungry for dinner, hoping to sucker an unsuspecting mouse. Bernice, who was not at all like a mouse, managed to stay far from his reach. She often used Clark as a shield. Harley especially enjoyed picking on Clark. Clark was Harley's target if anything displeased him.

The children didn't understand why their aunt liked Harley, with his bad manners and tattered old clothes, and they were suspicious of his intentions. Yet Aunt Theo seemed to enjoy his company and be unconcerned about any unscrupulous motives. So the children tried to adapt because they loved their Aunt Theo, and they needed her to stay together as a family. Harley became the newest family secret in a growing list. He was silently endured to prevent anyone from questioning what happened at the Kurz house.

Bootie had her own concerns about Harley. She often spotted a haunt hovering behind him. A black hole with one pinprick of light that shined through its belly and slipped in and out of the form of a small person. Why would Harley host such an odd haunt? It broke her rules to use her gift to learn secrets about people, but she was tempted to use it on Harley. If she could expose him for a liar or a gold digger, or something even worse, she could convince Aunt Theo to send him on his way.

By chance one night, Bootie found herself sitting beside Harley at the dinner table. As he shoveled a spoonful of peas into his mouth, she poked the sleeve of his shirt with her finger. A poof of red smoke erupted from the spot where she touched him, and an electric spark scorched her fingertip. She jerked her hand away and blew on the smoky, black burn left on her skin. Harley squinted at her, licked the peas off his lips, and sniggered. "Hey fleaette, don't you be poking me like that unless you mean it."

Bootie did not need Harley's warning. Her charred fingertip insured she would never touch him again. But she had seen an explosive fuse lit inside him, and she was even more determined to figure him out. If she could not use her gift, she would use more traditional methods to find what fueled that flame.

The following morning, Aunt Theo asked Bootie for help finding a missing cigarette pack. Although Bootie knew Woody had snitched it the previous night, Bootie joined her aunt in the search, taking the opportunity to ask questions about Harley.

"How come a fancy Boston girl like you would spend time with a skunk bear like him?" Bootie asked, wedging her arm between the back of the sofa and the cushion. "You're so sophisticated. He's like a bum who stole the clothes from a thrift store mannequin to make people think he's rich."

"Harley is a bit flamboyant," Aunt Theo said. But he has an interesting edge to him. Don't you think so?"

Bootie shrugged. "Even skunk bears can be interesting, I guess."

"You should work on your tact, Bootie," said Aunt Theo, on her hands and knees and peering under the coffee table.

"His mustache is ugly. And how did he get such a big black mole on his face?"

"It's not a mole, it's a birthmark."

"There's a hair growing out of it. He's got hairs growing out of everything on his face."

How to Dance on the Moon 199

"All men have facial hair. Someday you'll like it."

Bootie grew indignant. "No, I won't. I want to pluck that mole hair. Doesn't he know how stupid it looks?"

"I've never noticed a hair growing out of his birthmark."

"And he's always scavenging through the chair cushions for money. Like a skunk bear would."

Aunt Theo chuckled, and sitting up, mussed Bootie's hair. "Oh sweet mother! You have now called Harley a skunk bear three times. Do you even know what a skunk bear is?"

Bootie rolled her eyes, dramatically. "All right then, he looks like Cinder, Mr. Crowley's Doberman." Bootie plopped onto the sofa, tired of looking for cigarettes they would never find. "I hate how he calls us all fleas and fleaettes. Like we're no better than bloodsucking insects.

"Bootie, why are you being hard on him? You haven't given him a chance. He's a good man, and he likes you children."

Bootie almost told Aunt Theo how everyone thought he was vulgar, and they hated the way he picked on Clark and stared at Bernice, like he saw her naked. "He's not good enough for you. You should be romancing movie stars, like Cary Grant or Red Sox players like Ted Williams. Clark would love you to romance Ted Williams."

"Believe me. I would romance Ted Williams if I could." Aunt Theo waved her hands and stood up. "I can't imagine what happened to those cigarettes. Harley will be here soon. He'll have some. Thanks for helping me look Bootie. You can run along."

"Okay, but I still don't get why you like Harley."

Bootie began to raise herself upright, but Aunt Theo latched onto Bootie's arm and looked into her eyes, her face taut and her mouth pinched. "Bootie, I'm going to be honest with you," she said. "Yes, Harley is flashy, and he makes his money by playing cards and pulling a con now and then, but there are things you are too young to understand. I'm over forty years old now. There aren't many men out there who will romance a woman with seven kids. I don't want to be alone, Bootie."

"You're not alone. You have us."

Aunt Theo released Bootie's arm. "I'm sad you think so poorly of Harley because he wants to be part of the family, and I want that too. You should try and get to know him better. See his good qualities."

Bootie was about to argue the point, but a vision of her aunt hiding her own doubts about Harley's character stopped her. Bootie also saw Aunt Theo with a badly broken heart.

"You can do better, Aunt Theo."

"No, I can't, but thank you for believing that."

Bootie rose to her feet. Her need to get away from her aunt pressed inside her stomach. "I have to use the bathroom," she said, and as she scampered from the room, she heard Aunt Theo call out to her. "Let me know if you find my cigarettes."

****

Bootie had seen Sellie and Woody heading down the walkway to the beach. Bootie threw on her coat and hurried to catch up with them. She found them climbing into the boat. She clambered in with them and told them what she had learned from Aunt Theo. "That awful man can't move in here," said Sellie, her words spilling out from her mouth in steamy puffs. "He's a phony and a cheat. He smells bad, and he is mean to Clark! What happens if he is here when Mother and Father come back? They'll hate him, and they'll be mad at Aunt Theo, and we'll never see her again."

"I know, I know," agreed Woody. "He has to go away. We need a plan to get rid of him."

A wooden plank from the walkway behind the children creaked, and the children sprang around to see Harley making his way down the path. "Speak of the devil and he'll appear,"

How to Dance on the Moon 201

whispered Sellie. "Do you think he heard us?"

When Harley reached the beach, he twisted his lips into an awkward grin and gave a quick little wave. "Hey! Why are you fleas progestering so visibly? Your faces look like meeces trapped by a cat. Did I catch you doing something provocative?"

The children scrambled out of the rowboat, and Woody was the first to speak. "We aren't doing anything wrong."

Harley snorted. "When a flea says he's not doing anything wrong, it usually means he is."

Bootie examined his aura for any sense of maliciousness behind Harley's sudden appearance. He wore a black wool coat over his black suit. Despite the early hour, cigarette and alcohol odors already polluted the air around him, but he had no shadowy haunt trailing him, and Bootie sensed no threat in his motives. "He's at the Kennedy's with Aiden. What do you want, Harley?" Bootie asked.

"Theo tells me she spoke with one of you fleas, and she thinks we need to spend proficient and profitable time together, so we can learn to be robust friends." Harley's grin skewered into a smirk. "How's that sound?"

Woody shrugged. "If we have to."

Sellie turned and glared at her brother. Harley smoothed his mustache down over his top lip. "Son, go obtain your eldest brother's whereabouts, and when you do, convelate to the porch. Go on now."

"What are we going to do?" asked Woody.

"Do what you're told, son." Harley sneered at the girls as he stroked his mustache again. "Just the male fleas allowed this time. I'll have to proclivitate a way to become better acquainted with you fleaettes another time. A way that won't procure me any trouble." Harley's laugh made Bootie cringe. "I am fond of pretty girls." He reached over to Sellie, and, pinching his fingers together, pretended to lift up her coat hem as if he were helping himself to a peak at what was underneath.

"Yes, I do like pretty girls!" Harley turned and went back up the boardwalk to the house.

"I hate him," Sellie said, spitting the words at Harley's back. "He is a pigman."

"A skunk bear," Bootie replied, emphatically. "Woody, I don't want you and Clark left alone with Harley. There's a slow burn in that man ready to burst into flames."

"Don't worry," said Woody. "If he tries anything, I'll smack him around."

Bootie didn't argue, but she knew she had to shield her brothers from Harley's fire. Whatever activity Harley had in mind, she would have to find a way to be included.

****

Bootie waited for Woody and Clark to appear at the porch door, and joined them when they took seats at the pine table with Harley. Harley said, "The fire's hot, boys. Take off your coats. You'll be setting a spell." Woody and Clark pulled their arms from the sleeves of their jackets.

Harley eyed Bootie. "Not supposed to be entertaining the fleaettes," he said, but didn't ask her to leave. He displayed his large teeth in a broad smile. "When Theo challenged me to find a way to entertain you and educate you about the ways of the world, I thought to myself, this may be difficult, seeing how I have skills of a highly specialized nature. But perhaps even you fleas," Harley nodded to Bootie, "and fleaette can learn something from me to ensure you'll always have a spetulation of money in your pocket."

"Like you, Harley?" Clark asked.

Harley seemed to miss the sarcasm. He reached inside his jacket pocket and pulled out his deck of cards. "This, fleas and fleaette, is the entertainment portion of our show." He laid the cards on the table. "Watch closely." He put hands on top of the card deck, and with a twirling motion, raised his right hand up

How to Dance on the Moon   203

and pointed it toward the ceiling. In his hand was an ace of spades. "Wow!" said Woody. Can you do that again?" He repeated the motion with his left hand and displayed an ace of hearts.

Clark shook his head. "That's nothing but a flimflam man's chicanery."

Harley laughed. "That's a big word for you, son. And if you promise to keep the secret, I'll show you how you can use this trick to your prodigious benefit. Now for the educational component of our show." Harley placed the aces on the table and reached his hand in his pocket again, pulled out a pistol and set it on the table. Bootie gasped. "I'm going to teach you fleas about weaponry."

"Why do you have a gun?" Clark asked. His tone was casual, as if he were asking Harley why he had a handkerchief.

"The proper nomenclature for this weapon is Luger," Harley said. He stroked the barrel. "It can shoot eight bullets without having to be reloaded. This isn't like your old cap gun the Feds got. I obtained this killer through personal heroism and fortitude during the war."

Woody's eyes opened wide. "You were in the war?"

"There's much you don't know about me, son."

"Did you kill a German? Is that how you got the gun?" Clark hit Woody on the arm. "Ow! I was just asking!"

"If truth be exemplerated, I did shoot a Jerry. He wasn't going to relegate his gun. I had to extinguish his life before he did the same to me."

"Wow! Clark! Did you hear that?"

Clark's eyes narrowed. "Are you old enough to have fought in the war?"

Harley snarled at Clark. "Are you calling me a prestidigitator, Son?"

"No, just a liar."

"We'll see who's what around here, soon," said Harley, and surprisingly, he let the matter drop.

"Why do you even have a gun?" asked Bootie, repeating Clark's question.

Harley answered slowly, his inflection curiously switching from a gentlemanly drawl to a mountain man twang. "Because I've been to prison, and I ain't never going back."

"Can I hold it?" Woody asked.

Harley lifted the pistol and placed it into Woody's hand with the muzzle pointing out. "It isn't loaded, but you should practice holding it properly." Harley's voice was back to normal. Woody cradled the gun as a woman would someone else's baby, and scrutinized the gun, before replacing it on the table.

Harley turned to Clark. "You can hold it too, if you promise not to run away with it."

Clark crossed his arms over his chest.

"Do you ever shoot it?" asked Woody.

"As a matter of fact, that's what we're doing today. Follicitating out to that island and practicing on birds and, if we're lucky, a raccoon or two.

"We don't shoot raccoons," said Clark

"Yes we do. Raccoons are useless, dirty critters, meaner than a woman who's caught her husband with a hooker. They need to be killed."

Bootie pushed on Clark's arm. "What's a hooker?"

"Never mind, Bootie," said Clark. "My father doesn't want us to kill raccoons, Harley, and that's the end of it."

"It's true," Woody added. "He once spit in Mr. Kennedy's eye for shooting a raccoon."

Harley laughed so hard, tears spilled down his cheeks. "Your father didn't spit in Mr. Kennedy's eye, and if he did, it wasn't over a raccoon."

"He did too!" Woody's voice grew stronger and more excited. "Then Mr. Kennedy threw a lit cigar at my father, and it caught him on the neck and burned him. He's got a scar. Now they hate each other."

Clark motioned for Woody to be quiet. He turned to face

How to Dance on the Moon 205

Harley, who was still trying to control his laughter. "You can't shoot the raccoons. I'm watching out for them until Father comes home."

"Well guess what?" Harley picked up the pistol and swung it around. "I already got rid of the big one. Dumped his body in the woods. He was your father's favorite. He was wearing his watch and bending over for cigarettes."

Clark leapt at Harley, arms swinging. Harley's gun hand flinched, and he dropped the gun as he tried to pin down Clark's hands.

Woody scrambled from his chair and pushed Clark away. "When my father comes home he's gonna whoop you, Harley, and kick you out of here!"

"Son, it's about time somebody told you the truth. Your father ain't coming home." Harley picked up the pistol and aimed it at the ceiling. The mountain man twang came back. "And I ain't going anywhere. From now on, I'm the only father you'll know. You fleas have a nice little trust fund your Aunt Theo manages, and there's plenty in there to take care of everybody. And if anyone tries to say anything to stop that from happening," Harley let the pistol's muzzle drop until it pointed at Clark, "then I'll have to shut them up."

Clark, Woody and Bootie did not move as Harley stood and put the pistol and the card deck back in his pocket. Looking at Clark, he said, "Son, you are the biggest idiot I've ever met. Someday you'll rile someone and then you'll learn how to be a real man the hard way." Harley turned to Woody. "And you and your father will be together again soon, when you, too, become a guest of the state. But right now, I think I'll go to your little island without you and do more target practice. Class dismissed."

Harley turned his back on the three children and strode out the porch door, shadowed by the haunt Bootie had seen follow him many times before. Woody took off his shoe and aimed it at Harley, but Clark grabbed his arm. "No, Woody."

"I hate him," said Woody. "We have to stop him."

Clark clenched and unclenched his fists. Bootie couldn't miss the angry red aura spitting out from around him like flames. "Not while he's mad and he has that gun in his pocket."

"But he's trying to scare us into not telling Aunt Theo what he's up to," cried Woody. "We have to get him good! We must tell her!"

"We must ignore him," Clark said, with an eerie, disembodied calm that defied the red rage in his aura. "Aunt Theo won't listen to us. But someday soon, she will see through his scheme and make him leave. Or Father will fix him when he gets home." Clark picked up his coat. "I'm going to go help Aiden with the horses. I'll probably stay over."

Bootie reached out to stop Clark. She wanted to tell him what Aunt Theo had said about Harley moving in, but when she touched his arm, images flashed behind her eyes with their own independent energy, swirling without focus, without direction. Of all the pictures, blurred in confusing lights and disconnected faces, one image formed clearly, and one fact emerged. One black fact. If she did not prevent it, Harley would do something terrible to Clark, and it would involve Harley's Luger.

"What do you want, Bootie?" Clark asked. She stared into her brother's blue eyes, and watched them fade to white as the life in his eyes drained away. Instead of answering, she ran from the kitchen to the porch.

Harley was hurrying down the wooden planks covering the marsh, his gun in hand, the haunt still trailing him. Bootie tried to think of a way to get Harley's gun from him. She tried to summon her gift for help, but no vision would come.

Then, an idea took hold in her head, not seen in a vision, but spoken in an unheard voice, and it rapidly fleshed out. A scheme that would get Harley to go away and never come back. Then the gun wouldn't matter, because this was the perfect plan. She would need help from Woody and Sellie, but the three of them could handle it alone. Bernice and Clark would

How to Dance on the Moon   207

not have to be involved. It wouldn't be easy, but they could do it. They had to do it.

****

After dinner, Bootie, Woody and Sellie huddled in the attic to work out the plan's details. They discussed strategies until they believed they had covered all contingencies.

"When do we do it?" asked Sellie.

"The next time Harley spends the night," answered Bootie. "Tomorrow, if we can."

Woody's eyes grew wide. "Tomorrow?"

"What are we doing tomorrow?" The three conspirators jerked upright at the sound of Clark's voice. Nobody had heard him coming, even though the stairs creaked as if they were going to split whenever anyone climbed them.

"I thought you were going to stay at Aiden's tonight." Woody said.

"He got sick, so I came home," Clark said. "What are we doing tomorrow?" Nobody spoke. "Never mind," said Clark, shuffling to his bed on the attic's far side. "Have your little secrets. I'm going to read." He thumped down on his mattress, stretched his arm to the floor and picked up his favorite book, a musty binder of fables from around the world he had found in the old barn. The children sat quietly, listening to the radio music coming up from the living room.

"Clark?" Sellie pulled her legs to her chest and clasped them. "Can you tell us a story?"

Clark looked surprised. "Tonight? I'm kind of tired."

"Please?" Sellie pleaded.

"We could use one," Woody said, adding, "It would cheer us all up."

Clark looked at Bootie. "Do you want to hear a story, too?"

She nodded. "Always."

"Let me think for a minute." Clark placed his book beside

him on the bed. "I know a story that can tell you how to dance on the moon. It's about a rabbit named Sellie that belonged to Bootie the pirate princess."

"Yeah!' Sellie beamed. "A story about me!" She bounced from her bed and into Clark's and snuggled into him. He put his arm around her shoulders. "Go ahead, Clark, tell the story." Woody and Bootie crawled under their own covers as Clark began.

29.

How to Dance on the Moon

When Princess Bootie was a little girl, before the pirates came to her village and kidnapped her father, she raised beautiful rabbits with the softest fur in the kingdom. Princess Bootie kept them in a big rabbit hutch, and played with them, and fed them, and promised when they died of old, old age, they would still live on because their fur would be used to keep children and old women warm in winter. This pleased the rabbits, because it gave them a purpose to live, and a way to die with dignity. And although people didn't know it, Princess Bootie's rabbits loved to dance. At night, when nobody could see them, they danced and danced and danced, especially when the moon was full.

One day, an old fat hare limped into the rabbit house, looking for food. The rabbits asked him where he had come from and if he was lost. The old hare laughed and shared a story about an angel who had come to him in his warren in the middle of the night and had told him about a secret way he could dance on the moon forever and never die. The old hare asked the angel what a rabbit had to do to dance on the moon.

The Angel said it required the greatest kind of bravery, then she disappeared, and the old fat hare had been on a journey ever since, to find the angel, and convince her to share the secret. He lifted his leg to show them his paw was missing. "I have done every brave thing I can think of. I have even had my foot cut off and given to a king, but that was not enough. Cutting off my foot just made me weak and sick. And who can dance with just one foot?"

The rabbits prepared a feast of carrots, lettuce and dandelions for the old fat hare, and after the meal he thanked them and said goodbye and went on his way. The rabbits talked and talked about what the old fat hare had told them. They liked it that Princess Bootie made their fur live after they were gone, but wasn't it better to not to be separated from their fur at all?

One young rabbit, named Sellie Rabbit, had listened intently to all the chatter, and secretly decided she wasn't going to just talk about learning the secret of how to dance on the moon. She would go on her own quest. In the middle of the night, after silently bidding goodbye to all her cousins (for all the rabbits in the rabbit hutch were related to each other,) she slipped away, not knowing if she would ever return.

Almost immediately, she stumbled upon a hungry fox, and found herself hopping for her life. This is not brave, she thought, to run like a scared rabbit. But what do I do? She hopped far ahead of the fox, and came to a big oak tree. There, little Sellie came up with an ingenious plan. She circled the tree many times to leave rabbit tracks around it. Then she jumped into a blackberry bush to hide. When the hungry fox got to the tree and found the tracks, he thought the rabbit had hopped up into the tree. He tried to leap into its branches but fell backwards and broke his leg. Off he stumbled through the woods, and Sellie Rabbit came out from the blackberry bush. Well the fox didn't get me, she thought, picking thorns from her fur, but I am scratched and sore, and I have not found the secret to dancing forever. Bravery with cunning is not the secret.

Sellie Rabbit continued on her journey, and soon became hungry herself. She saw an old man sitting on a rock outside a garden. He had a basket full of cabbage beside him. Sellie Rabbit crept behind the old man, and used all her strength to throw a rock onto his foot. The man tried to stand, but his foot was broken and he fell. Sellie took a cabbage and ran away. Once she felt safe, she bit into the cabbage, but it wasn't a cabbage at all. It was a poisonous kale. Sellie Rabbit threw it away after eating one bite and held her stomach. It ached from the poison. Well, attacking the old man for his food wasn't the secret, either. I'm scratched and sore, and now I'm sick. Bravery with strength is not the secret to living forever.

Sellie Rabbit hopped along, sadly, and was about to give up her quest and go home, when she encountered a young girl crying by the roadside. The girl had not yet learned animals cannot talk. "Hello little rabbit," she said. "I wish you were a potato, for I have not eaten in a week. Or a blanket, for I am cold." I am hungry and cold, too, thought Sellie Rabbit. The child motioned for Sellie to follow her, and they left the road and entered the woods.

The child approached a campfire, roaring within a clearing of maple trees. "I am so hungry, little rabbit, I will die if I do not eat." Sellie Rabbit felt her heart break for the child, then fill with love for all the child could someday be, if she did not die. What good is my own life, thought Sellie. I am injured and sick, and I have not found the secret to living forever, and I don't think I ever will. Since I must die someday anyway, why not do so now and have some good come of it? She can eat my meat and warm herself as my fur sustains the fire." Sellie Rabbit closed her eyes and pictured her cousins in the rabbit hutch in Princess Bootie's kingdom. Then she took a deep breath and jumped into the fire. But as soon as her paws felt the flames' heat, the fire turned to mist.

Sellie looked for the little girl, but she, too, was gone, and in

How to Dance on the Moon   211

her place was a beautiful angel. "Sellie Rabbit, you have done a brave and wonderful thing." *The angel lifted Sellie and put her into a basket that had magically appeared where the fire had been and was attached to a thousand balloons. Little Sellie floated into the sky, going higher and higher until she reached the moon. She landed in the middle of a colorful garden that seemed to stretch forever in every direction. The angel was already there, waiting for her.* "This is your new home," *the angel said.* "You will live here forever because bravery with sacrifice is the greatest form of bravery, because sacrifice is the greatest form of love. And brave love is what you must experience to dance on the moon. Your story will be retold for everyone to hear. And you will dance to make the moon spin. It will change every night and everyone will be continually reminded of your special gift."

The angel spread her wings and disappeared, and Sellie Rabbit did dance happily forever and ever and ever after, on the moon. And if you look at the moon when it's full, you can see her outline as clear as the nose on my face.

"That was beautiful, Clark," Sellie said, dreamily.

Clark said, "I'm not finished yet, Sellie."

The angel was true to her word, and spread the news throughout the world about Sellie Rabbit's great love and sacrifice, and the courage it took, and the little rabbit became a legend. This is the poem still shared today among the rabbits when they look up at their cousin, Sellie Rabbit, on the moon.

Dancing Rabbit on the moon,
I'll come to you in my balloon,
When I have paid the highest price
When I have bravely sacrificed
And loved someone enough to give
All I have, then I will live
With Dancing Rabbit on the moon,
I hope to dance beside you soon.

"I want to be brave," Bootie said, twirling her hair with her

Laura Ginter 212

fingers. "Not just act bravely. I want to know how to dance on the moon forever because I am brave and my bravery is pure."

"I don't know, Bootie," said Sellie. "It's hard to be brave. It takes courage."

Woody snorted. "Angels and princesses and rabbits. Couldn't a zombie have eaten the rabbits? Clark, are you ever going back to school?"

Clark looked startled by the sudden change in conversation. "I don't know. Why?"

"Everybody is being nice, and nobody says anything about, well, you know. They all keep asking about you."

Bootie added, "Clark, if you don't go, they might send the truant officer next time, and then they might take you away."

A slight lip-curl pulled at Clark's mouth. "I've been thinking about going back to school. Maybe tomorrow. It's boring around here without Woody to punch."

Woody's face splashed a wide grin. Clark leapt from his bed like a mountain lion, landing on Woody, and sending the girls scurrying across the attic away from the jostling. The boys wrestled in the harmless and spirited way that brothers do. Bootie laughed at their lively roughhousing. How long had it been since she had seen Clark smile? Not since Josephine Kennedy's birthday party.

"Stop!"

At the abrupt command, both boys jumped from the bed. Bootie and Sellie also stood at seeing Harley in the doorway. He turned his head toward each startled face, staring into their eyes one at a time. "Go to bed! Theo and I can't hear the radio for all the prodigious thumping coming from here." Bootie winced from the smoke and alcohol stench spewing from his mouth. She looked away, and when she looked back, Harley had disappeared as abruptly as he had arrived.

"What a pigman," said Sellie.

"It's late anyway," Clark said. He clunked each sister on the head, before returning to his bed. Bootie slipped under her

How to Dance on the Moon 213

covers and watched Woody and Sellie do the same. The three children passed a silent signal among themselves, confirming their commitment to carry out their plan the next time Harley stayed over night.

30.

"Where are Sellie and Woody?" Bernice asked Bootie. "They've been gone all afternoon." Bernice took her pot roast out from the oven. She had become an accomplished cook, and the children had lost their gaunt, orphaned look.

"We're here," Sellie said, rushing into the kitchen. "Bernice that smells yummy!"

"Well you two don't smell yummy at all. In fact, you stink. You both go wash up before dinner." Sellie gave Bootie a long, serious look, before disappearing into the bathroom.

Bootie, Sellie and Woody ate together and watched Harley finish off two helpings of beef and a tumbler of whiskey. He lifted his napkin and dabbed at his mustache, struggling to keep his eyes open. The three accomplices exchanged glances.

"Mr. Kennedy called today, Aunt Theo," Bootie said, with a concerned edge in her voice. "He wanted to know who had been shooting a gun over here. He sounded mad."

Harley burped. "Why would Mr. Kennedy be mad? He should appreciate the annihilation of the raccoons he so despises."

Bootie shook her head. "He sounded pretty bent up. He said shots also came from the island. His kids play there, and he was going to tell Sheriff O'Brien if he found out who did it."

"He isn't going to notify Sheriff O'Brien of anything."

"He asked if it was you, Harley."

Harley's face flushed, and he waved a finger at Bootie. His

Laura Ginter 214

peculiar twang slipped into his speech. "Mr. Kennedy ain't gonna call no police about my activities. He don't even know me."

"Are you sure?" asked Sellie. "You know him."

Aunt Theo ended the conversation by giving Harley another whiskey tumbler.

After dinner, Bernice worked on homework, while Sellie bathed Baby Ike and Bootie and Clark washed the dishes. The children listened to Abbott and Costello until Bernice put Baby Ike to bed. The older children switched to gin rummy, playing while Harley snored contentedly. Scooter fell asleep on the floor, and Bernice carried the little boy to bed and did not return. A short time later, Harley woke long enough to haul himself into Aunt Theo's room. Bootie and Sellie went to the attic, leaving Woody downstairs. Bootie dozed until Woody pulled on her arm.

"Everyone's asleep," he whispered. "It's time."

Bootie rubbed her eyes, and tried to shake off her drowsiness. Sellie was doing the same. Together, the three conspirators tiptoed down the attic stairs. With the silent focus of experienced burglars that may have come naturally to them, they went about their assignments.

Bootie stood outside Aunt Theo's door, and heard Harley snoring. She reached for the doorknob, but an unexpected twinge of doubt stopped her. "Sellie, I didn't think about what would happen if Harley wakes up before I can get to his clothes."

"Quiet!" Sellie blurted in a strained whisper. "Follow the plan and we'll be rid of the nasty pigman forever."

Bootie took a deep breath and grasped the doorknob. The metal felt like ice on her palm, and the cold threaded through her body. She shivered. Her eyesight blurred, and a vision swam in her head. Many pictures flashed through her mind, but a picture of a naked Harley pointing the Luger at her was the only one clear enough to recognize.

How to Dance on the Moon   215

"Hurry!" whispered Sellie.

The vision cleared. Bootie tried to open the door, but her hand froze again. She could not twist the knob, and she looked helplessly at her sister. "I think we're making a mistake."

Sellie pushed Bootie aside, opened the door and tiptoed into the room, returning with Harley's black frayed, smoky clothes and his shoes. She dumped them into Bootie's arms and joined Woody by the open front door. The two slipped into the night together, leaving the door ajar.

Bootie dropped Harley's clothes onto the couch and set the shoes on the floor. A bang only she could hear made her recoil, and smoke rose from Harley's shoes. Bootie now understood she had made a dangerous miscalculation. She had foolishly dismissed her vision's warning about finding the gun in favor of this doomed plan. Now she had to stop it. Woody and Sellie would be mad at her, but she could not help that.

Woody came through the door first. Bootie went to him, but he slid past her and sped up the attic stairs to his bed.

Sellie came in behind Woody, and Bootie latched onto her arm. "We can't do this," Bootie whispered. "It's not going to work unless we have the gun."

"We don't need the gun," Sellie said.

"Yes, we do! Listen to me!"

Sellie broke free from Bootie's grip. "No. We're doing this." She rushed to Aunt Theo's bedroom door. "Aunt Theo!" Sellie put a panicky edge in her voice and banged on the door. "Wake up! There's a fire up the hill! Please wake up!"

Her aunt's bedroom door opened. Aunt Theo peered out, as Harley yelled, "What's going on?"

"There's a fire!" Sellie repeated. "I think it's Harley's Rolls!"

Aunt Theo cinched her robe and scurried into the living room. She peered through the open front door. An orange light flickered across her face. "Oh, my sweet mother! Harley! Your Rolls IS on fire!"

"My Rolls?" Harley's sleep-thickened voice bellowed from the bedroom. "Let me out! Where's my pants? Where's my clothes? My Rolls! Where's my clothes? Theo!"

Aunt Theo flitted back and forth between her bedroom and the front door. "Oh my sweet mother!" The living room filled with children, awakened by the commotion.

"Bootie, call the fire department," Aunt Theo screeched. Harley ran naked from Aunt Theo's room and bolted outside. The children shrieked. Harley's white rump flapped as he fled through the door into the frigid night air. Aunt Theo followed him out.

"This isn't going to work!" Bootie said to Sellie, who waved Bootie off with a flick of her wrist.

"It's working perfectly." Sellie leaned into Bootie to say something else, but stopped when Harley screamed.

Aunt Theo ran back into the house. "Oh my dear, dear, dear sweet mother! Did one of you do this? Answer me!" She scurried into her bedroom, only to return a moment later. "Where are Harley's clothes?"

No one answered. Aunt Theo flapped her hands in the air and fled back into her bedroom. Woody slipped through the door and disappeared into the darkness. Aunt Theo reemerged carrying Harley's wool coat. She had not yet stepped off the front step when a blast like a cannon reverberated through the night.

Aunt Theo screeched and put a hand to her heart, then rushed outside. Bootie hurried after her. Everyone followed except Ike and Scooter. Ike was hiding behind his brother, clutching his braces.

When Bootie reached the top of the driveway, she saw the mechanics of their plan had worked flawlessly. Two fires near the Rolls roared, one to the side and one in front. From the distance and the night's darkness, the Rolls did look trapped in a fireball. The explosion had thrown horseshit from Kennedy's stables, spread over the ground by Sellie and Woody, along

How to Dance on the Moon   217

with mud and sticky leaves, all over Harley's exposed skin. Harley let out another loud wail. Aunt Theo reached Harley and covered him with his coat while Woody and Clark extinguished the fires.

"Look Harley," said Sellie. "There's a paper stuck on your windshield."

Harley swiped the paper off his car, grabbed Aunt Theo's arm and pulled her back with him to the house. Everyone followed. Harley did not bother to clean himself before going inside, and fecal smears marked his footprints in the living room.

Bernice fetched a bath towel for Aunt Theo. The children gathered in the living room. The house smelled badly, and Bootie covered her nose. Harley handed the note to Aunt Theo. "Read this."

"What?"

"READ THIS!"

Aunt Theo read the words aloud. "I know what you did and so does Sheriff O'Brien. Leave town or you will go back to jail."

"Read it again!"

"I KNOW WHAT YOU DID AND SO DOES SHERIFF O'BRIEN."

Harley took the paper from Aunt Theo. He balled it into one hand. Red-faced, he eyed each child in turn. "Who wrote this?" Anger dripped from every word.

"I bet it was Mr. Kennedy," said Sellie. "He was mad about someone shooting a gun on the island."

"Mr. Kennedy didn't write this. Mr. Kennedy didn't throw no firecracker at me, or cover the yard in shit. It was one of you fleas. Theo, go see if my keys are in my car."

Aunt Theo ran out the door.

"Where are my clothes?"

"Are those them?" Clark pointed to the heap on the couch.

Harley looked to where Clark pointed, then, nostrils flaring, arms shaking, he approached the boy. "How did you know where my clothes were?" Harley snarled at Clark.

Clark furrowed his brow and crossed his arms over his chest. I saw them there."

"How come you're dressed?"

"I mostly sleep in my clothes," Clark answered. "Why? Do you think I did this?"

Harley gave Clark a hard sucker-punch in the stomach. Clark doubled over and gasped for breath. He lifted his eyes and glared into Harley's face, the intensity of his hatred matching the man's. Still hunched over he repeated himself. "Do you think I did this?"

Harley's coat was draped over his shoulders and hanging open to expose fecal-spotted flesh down the length of his body. Muddy debris fell to the floor around his feet. He reached into his pocket, pulled out the Luger, and pointed it at Clark.

Aunt Theo reentered the house, wiping her feet across the towel now laid out on the floor. "Here are your keys." She saw the gun in Harley's hand, aimed at Clark. "Harley, please, put down the gun! Clark, did you do this?"

Clark stood tall and looked at all his brothers and sisters, who were watching the drama in silent shock. Woody was standing in a corner next to Sellie. "No, Aunt Theo," he said, shaking his head. "I swear, Clark didn't do it."

"I swear, too," said Sellie.

Bootie took a step toward Harley. "Leave Clark alone. He didn't do it!"

Clark put his hand up to silence Bootie. "Harley, look at you standing there, exposing your privates to the girls. You are a disgusting, shameless con man using my aunt to get her money. You know what? I did do it. I did it and the only thing that went wrong is that shit didn't fill your mouth to make you shut up. So shoot me if you want, you pervert. Shoot me now!"

Harley cocked the gun. Clark balled his hands into fists and squeezed his eyes shut. The gunshot reverberated through the house. Aunt Theo screamed. Bootie fell to the floor and rolled

How to Dance on the Moon 219

into a ball. After several silent seconds, she uncurled enough to look toward the wall and see her brother still standing. She peeked at the front door, and saw Harley drop the gun into his coat pocket. "You know what, son? You are not worth going back to prison over. I don't want to meet your father there. But I hope you enjoyed my joke as much as I enjoyed yours."

Clark opened his eyes, and Bootie stood and slid over to him. The bullet had made a hole in the wall, and dust was spreading out around him, like a smoky aura. She held her arms out to Harley. "Clark didn't do this, Harley. I'm trying to tell you I did! Be mad at me."

"Sissy girl," Harley hissed. "You're not smart enough to do this. You're a gutless jellyfish. A scared little bunny rabbit. Run away, sissy girl. Save yourself. I know the truth."

Clark stared hard at Harley. "You are disgusting." He turned toward Aunt Theo. "You, too." Clark turned back to face his brothers and sisters. "If Aunt Theo can't see it, I can. We don't need her to stay together. I'm going to get you all away from here. I promise." Before anybody could react, he raced out the front door. Only Bootie saw Harley's black haunt with the one lit hole follow Clark out, aping his strides.

Aunt Theo pushed past Harley and screeched into the darkness. "Clark, come back! You don't have a coat!"

Harley reached over to Theo and twisted her arm behind her back. She let out a pained yelp. He turned her toward him and gave her a loud slap across the face. She stared at him, stunned.

"That was for allowing this to happen," he said.

Aunt Theo touched her cheek with one hand, and when Harley released her, he took his keys from her hand. She reached for him, and he shoved her with his foot. She fell against the wall. Harley grabbed his clothes and shoes, and was out the door.

Aunt Theo staggered into her bedroom and slammed the door. No one moved or spoke. When Aunt Theo reemerged, she was dressed. Her purse dangled from her arm. "I must go find him!" she proclaimed, and she, too, disappeared into the night.

Woody ran to the door. "I'll fix this."

"No," said Bernice. "Too many people running around out there already."

"God damn it!" he yelled, and began to cry.

Bootie's stomach convulsed and she gagged, tasting sour vomit. She crossed through the kitchen and shut herself in the bathroom. This was her fault. How could she have believed her stupid plan would work? Her vision had warned her to find the gun but she hadn't. She had made no allowance for failure, and now Harley was in a rage, and Clark was gone. Where would Clark go? What if Harley came back? What if Clark didn't?

Bootie started to gag again, her fear backing up in her throat like acid. As she held her stomach, poised over the commode, she wondered who Aunt Theo worried about more, and who did she go to find? Clark or Harley?

****

Neither Clark nor Aunt Theo came back that night. The Matlows called about the explosion, making sure everything was okay, but no one else did. The children were used to Aunt Theo's absences, but they were frantic about Clark. When he didn't come home the next day, they asked Aiden Kennedy and Clark's other friends if they had seen him, but no one had. Woody and Bootie rowed over to Putnam's Island, breaking through the thin ice shelf covering the lake, even though the boat had not moved in days. They found nothing.

On the second day, Woody showed the children Clark's empty dresser drawer. "And his baseball cards aren't here," he added. "The tin is gone. That means he's been here!" Bootie wanted to believe what Woody believed, but she wondered why Clark would sneak into the house, take his things and leave

How to Dance on the Moon   221

again.

Aunt Theo came home in the evening of the second day, her arm in a sling and her left eye blackened. She told the children Harley was not returning, and with a smirk announced he looked plenty worse than she did. When they told her Clark was still gone, she called Sheriff O'Brien to report him missing, and cried for two days straight, heartbroken and swearing if she had known Clark had not come home she would not have stayed away. No one asked her why she hadn't phoned to check on him. Every day Aunt Theo promised the children the sheriff would find him. She swore on her life that, from now on, she would be a better guardian.

The townspeople expressed sympathy for the missing boy's family and sheriff's department did a perfunctory search for him, but Clark was a habitual truant who came from a disgraced family and no one was surprised when he could not be found. However, four days after Clark ran away, Aiden Kennedy did not come home from school. Now, with two boys missing and one a Kennedy, the sheriff held a county-wide search and offered a reward for any information. The sheriff's department looked for the boys until Mr. Kennedy, in his grief, called off the search, declaring that the best friends had probably run away together.

****

Three weeks later, late at night, Clark appeared at the foot of Bootie's bed. She had been tossing restlessly under the sheets, trying to ignore the lights zipping around her head and the haunt that had taken shape in an attic corner. It had been there since Clark had disappeared. She opened her eyes when she heard her brother call her name. Bootie sprang forward to hug him, but her arms went through him as if she were hugging mist. Clark grinned at her, and brushed at a curl that had fallen onto his forehead.

"Bootie, I know you've been worried about me, but don't

be."

Bootie glanced at Woody and Sellie, both sleeping soundly. All but one sparkle above her bed had disappeared, and it continued to dance between her and her brother.

"Are you. . ." she couldn't say the word she was thinking.

He chuckled. "I'm not dead."

"Then why can't I touch you?"

Clark looked puzzled. "I don't know." He leaned toward her. "I needed to talk to you, so I wished myself here. I knew you would be able to see me. You're good at that."

"Are you sure you're all right?"

Clark frowned. "Why do you keep asking me that? I have to tell you, though. Your plan to get rid of Harley was dumb. Woody could have burned down the whole house with those old fireworks. Then where would we all be?"

"The little kids think the Wailing Witch got you and Aiden both. Are you with Aiden?"

"Don't ask me about Aiden."

"When you are coming home?"

"I don't know when. But I'm doing good. I saw Ted Williams play at Fenway Park."

"But it's winter."

"He's the greatest ballplayer ever. I'm going to be like him someday. You watch. I'm going to hit a million home runs for the Red Sox."

Bootie pointed to a long red scratch on Clark's cheek. "What's that?"

"What's what?"

"What's that mark on your cheek?"

Clark rubbed his hand across both sides of his face. "I don't know. I can't feel it."

Clark leaned on the bed's footboard. The fairy sparkle lit on his belt buckle. "I also came to tell you some news."

"News about what?" Bootie asked.

"Mother died three days ago. Aunt Theo is afraid to tell

How to Dance on the Moon 223

everyone because you are all worried about me, which now you know you don't have to be."

Bootie's breath caught in her throat. "What happened to Mother?"

"I don't know. But I've seen her, and she's okay. She wanted me to come here and tell you to get Aunt Theo to open up about it. She also wants you to know she's sorry she didn't get to talk to you more about your secret before she died. But she knows you'll always do right by it. And she's happy she's not in the hospital anymore. Will you tell everyone she's happy and is doing good? And me too?"

"I will."

"Tell Woody to stay away from Harley. He'll be coming for him next."

"No! Clark! Harley's gone for good! You can come home! Please! We need you home! I should have gotten that gun from Harley. If I'd been braver, if I had stood up better to Harley, you'd still be living here."

"Brave like the rabbit in the story who jumped in the fire?

"Yes."

"Bootie, I know for a fact you will someday dance on the moon."

She reached for him again, but he was gone.

Sobs convulsed in Bootie's throat when she tried to hide the sound of her crying. She buried her head under her covers and cried so hard, her jaw muscles ached from trying to be quiet. And before she went to sleep, she cried until she dried up all the anger and sadness inside her.

The next morning, Bootie sat on her bed, her eyes swollen, and rubbed her rabbit's foot. "Please, God," she said. "Don't let Mother be dead, and bring Clark home. I will go to church every day for the rest of my life. I'll become a nun. Just bring Mother, Father and Clark home." She rubbed her rabbit's foot and prayed all morning.

Bootie told no one about seeing Clark. In the afternoon,

she found the courage to ask Aunt Theo about Mother, and Aunt Theo burst into tears.

Another month passed, and Clark did not come home. The fairy sparkles went away, but the haunt stayed in the attic's corner for two more weeks until it dissolved into the night. On an early spring morning, Bootie rowed out to the Wailing Witch and flung her rabbit's foot at the big, scary rock. It was back under her pillow that night.

Bootie and Grace 1993

31.

On her first day home, Grace had a lackluster but promising meeting with Loretta and the rest of the day passed without incident. Even so, Grace found herself slipping back into her defensive posture. Again, a ringing phone sent a jolt through her chest. She couldn't enter a room without visually searching it, or open her car door without peeking around the tires and into the back seat. Apprehension and vigilant positioning dominated her life and stole her ability to do anything but exist in the moment, or to think of anything but the terror of an unexpected encounter with Blake. She never took off her protective armor, always alert for a sneak attack by the enemy.

A second uneventful day went by, and a third and fourth. Five days passed without any word from Blake, and a sixth, and a seventh. Slowly, one Blake-free day at a time, one normal phone call at a time, the knot in her stomach started to unwind.

On the ninth day, after finishing dinner, Grace rinsed the dirty dinner plates and placed them in the dishwasher while

How to Dance on the Moon 225

Jennie watched television. After pouring soap into the dispenser, she closed the dishwasher door and pushed the start button. The familiar whoosh of water assured her the cleaning cycle had started.

Grace sat and nibbled on a half-eaten cookie Jennie had left on the table, thinking about how her view of the world had skewered from what it had been before Blake. How his violent intrusions had altered her values. He had hijacked her days, and pirated her time and energy, and she had lost her gauge by which she could judge which decisions were important, which activities should have priority, and how to construct a daily routine that was not about avoiding harm. But she was getting healthy again, and hoped nine quiet days, added to the time spent in New Hampshire, meant the peace would last, and she could start to rebuild her life.

On the eleventh day, after a trip to the supermarket with Jennie, Grace took advantage of the quiet Sunday afternoon to sit at her desk and brainstorm ideas for the project Loretta had assigned to her, finding ways to bring more disabled children into BATSS programs. Grace pulled paper from her desk and scratched out her thoughts, enthusiastic about the opportunities the new project brought.

The sound of the doorbell pierced the quiet. Grace flinched and clenched her fists. After two calming breaths, she went into the living room and peered out the window. It was Biscuit, wearing black sweat pants and a Led Zeppelin tee shirt. Grace squealed and ran to open the door. "Biscuit! Hello!"

"Hey, kid. I was on my bike cruising around and thought I'd come by and check on you. How've you been doing?"

Grace locked the door after Biscuit came inside. "Great. Counting my time in New Hampshire, I haven't heard a peep from you-know-who in almost three weeks."

"That's good news. Do you have any beer?"

Biscuit followed Grace into the kitchen. She opened the refrigerator, pulled out an Olympia beer and handed it to him.

"Do you want an ashtray?"

"No, kid. I quit."

Grace looked up into Biscuit's face, expecting him to cap his joke with a punch line, but he just grinned at her, twisted open the beer and took a long gulp.

"Well that's good news, too."

"Yeah, I figured out how hard it would be to find a pretty new girlfriend if I smoked. I am interviewing, by the way. Do you want to apply?"

Grace snatched his beer bottle and dangled it in front of him. "You can't have this. You are too funny when you've been drinking." Biscuit made a dodging motion, and grabbed his beer away from her when she turned. Grace giggled and pushed the bottom of the bottle up toward his mouth when he tried to take a sip, making the beer splash his chin.

The phone rang. Grace shivered and gripped a kitchen chair.

"Whoa, Grace. It's only the phone!"

She checked the caller ID, and gave Biscuit a thumbs up before lifting the handset.

"I haven't heard from you, lately," Aunt Bootie said. "I assume that's good."

"It is good. I smell pot pies. Is that your lunch special today?"

"Yes, Grace, as a matter of fact, it is. Be careful, your gift is showing."

"I don't have the gift, Aunt Bootie. Let it go. So, what's up?"

"No Breather phone calls? No Stan Bean? No visits?"

"I was telling Biscuit. Not a word. I am cautiously optimistic my problems might be over."

"Your friend Biscuit is there?"

"Come over and we'll all have a beer."

"I wish. How is Jennie?"

"Great. She's watching a movie in my bedroom."

How to Dance on the Moon 227

"You're busy. I'll let you go. I called for another reason, but I forgot what it was. Oh well, it must have been a lie."

Grace laughed, and hung up the phone. Before her hand was off the handset, the phone rang again. Grace picked it up.

"Did you remember what you forgot?"

"Hello Grace. This is Stan Bean, Violet's brother." The voice was a punch in the stomach. She glanced at Biscuit, and shook her head. He gestured for her to keep talking, and ran to the stairs, climbing them two at a time.

"Who did you say this was?"

"Blake left a gift for you. Find it, then get out of the house."

She heard a dial tone in her ear. Biscuit returned to the kitchen and took the handset still in Grace's hand, placing it back in its cradle. "It was Stan Bean. Did you hear him?"

Biscuit shook his head. "All I heard was a dial tone."

"He told me I had to find something Blake left in the house and then we needed to leave."

Biscuit wrapped his arms around Grace's shoulders. "You're shaking. Don't be scared by this jerk. Be angry!"

Grace pulled away. "I AM angry! It had been almost three weeks, Biscuit. This isn't fair!"

"Mommy?"

Grace hadn't heard Jennie come into the kitchen. She was frowning. "Jennie, what is it?"

"The movie ended, and when I went in my room, my closet door was broken. Everything inside is moved around."

Grace looked at Biscuit. "Do you want me to go look?" he asked.

"No, it needs to be me. You won't know if something's wrong. Stay with Jennie. And stay close."

Grace hurried to the staircase and paused to calm herself before climbing the stairs. In Jennie's bedroom, a closet door hung loose, as though it had fallen off its track. She crept toward it and peered inside. Blake's face stared back at her.

Laura Ginter 228

Grace shrieked and jerked backwards. She took a deep breath and reached into the closet, removing the eight by ten photograph of Blake's face taped to the wall. She folded it, pushed it into her pocket, and left the room.

Jennie and Biscuit were waiting for her at the foot of the stairs. "Was something in there?" asked Jennie.

Grace squatted in front of her daughter. "Because you are a big girl, Jennie, I'm going to tell you the truth. Someone was in our house today, I think when we were at the store."

Jennie's gaze shifted back and forth between her mother and Biscuit. "Blake?"

"I think so. But we are going to call the police and wait outside in the car until they get here." Grace stood and pulled the picture from her pocket and showed it to Biscuit. "This was taped inside Jennie's closet. Look at the smug expression."

Biscuit shook his head. "Did you set your alarm when you went to the store?"

"Yes!" Grace set Blake's photo on the counter and lifted her daughter into her arms. A motion sensor lit up outside her kitchen window. A shadowy shift, as vague and foggy as a whiff of smoke, slipped past the window. "Someone is out there!" Grace whispered.

Jennie dug her face into Grace's shoulder. "Stop it, Mommy! You're scaring me!"

Biscuit crossed the room and went to the front door. "There's no one here. I'll check outside. Call 911."

"Don't leave me and Jennie!" Grace balanced her daughter in her arms and reached for the phone. They heard a thump in the backyard. Grace squealed and stood on her toes to look outside the window. Another thump, this time in the den. She turned toward the sound. Blake charged toward her, his eyes bulging. Grace screamed for help and pulled Jennie tighter into her chest. Biscuit came back around the corner and lunged across the short distance separating Blake from Grace and Jennie. He grabbed Blake by the neck and pushed him to the

How to Dance on the Moon 229

carpet.

"Don't look, Jennie!" With shaking hands, Grace punched 911 and shrieked for help. She couldn't hear the operator's questions. Frightening grunts and growls came from the den. Biscuit was strong, but Blake was like a bull, and Grace feared Biscuit couldn't hold him for long.

A siren approached from a distance, and grew in volume until it reached the house. Grace dropped the phone and surrounded Jennie with her body. She closed her eyes as the sound of the men's fighting intensified. A bang on the front door made Grace scream. Two uniformed men charged into the house with guns drawn, followed by four more. Police bellowed violent-sounding threats amid much stomping and rumbling, but within a minute, the house quieted to conversational tones interrupted by an occasional radio beep.

Grace straightened and opened her eyes, still clutching onto Jennie. The police were milling around, their guns put away. She heard one officer speak into a crackling radio. "Yes, it's secured." Another officer took her by the arm. "We have the intruder restrained."

Grace scanned the room, looking for Blake, and didn't see him. "Where is he?" she asked.

"On the floor over there, leaning against the wall."

Grace looked to where the officer pointed. Blood ran from Biscuit's nose, staining his shirt, and he had been handcuffed.

"Mommy?" Jennie stared at Grace with large, frightened eyes. "Is Mr. Biscuit okay?"

"Yes, Jennie." Grace rocked her daughter back and forth, unable to put her down. "It's over."

32.

Bootie pulled in next to a police cruiser parked in Grace's driveway. She scrambled from her car and hurried into the house. Grace was in the den. An officer was speaking to her, and she was leaning against the wall, frowning. Bootie waved to her, and she crossed the room and surprised Bootie with a hug. Pictures of the afternoon's ordeal exploded in Bootie's head, and when she stepped away from her niece, she stumbled. A muscular man with silver hair grabbed her arm to keep her from falling. "Are you okay?"

Bootie tried to look cheerful. "Yes. You must be Biscuit. Nice to meet you, finally."

"Not the way I had hoped, but glad to meet you too."

"Grace is lucky you were here!" She turned to her niece. "How did he get in?"

"Through the slider in the den." Grace combed her fingers through her bangs. "When Jennie and I were at the market he broke the glass. The drapes covered it. He put tin foil over the sensor, and crawled through the house to get past the motion detectors. He knew where they were mounted. He taped his picture in Jennie's closet while we were out, to scare us I suppose. The irony of all this is that every time he has broken in, he has expected to see Biscuit. This time I don't think he did."

"I had a good hold on him," Biscuit said, "but he kicked me in the putzes. I lost my grip, and he punched me in the nose."

"Did he steal anything?" Bootie asked.

"I had set his picture on the counter, and I think he grabbed it before he ran out. Nothing else. And I haven't told you this. Stan Bean called to warn me Blake was coming five minutes before it happened. "

"That makes no sense, if Blake is Stan Bean."

"I don't think Blake is Stan Bean," Grace said. "Which means someone is paying very close attention to me. Jennie is

How to Dance on the Moon 231

in the living room with a female officer. Can you sit with her, Auntie? She's scared, too."

Bootie went to Jennie, and told the policewoman she would stay with the girl. "Are you all right, Jennie?"

Jennie clutched a red teddy bear. "I'm okay."

"Pretty bear."

"The lady policeman gave it to me for being brave. This is my second bear. Every time Blake comes in our house I get a new one."

Bootie rubbed the little girl's back, but no pictures came through to help Bootie gauge her emotions. Her walls are up, thought Bootie.

"This is my fault you know," Jennie said. She looked up at Bootie. "Like the last time. I didn't protect Mommy like I was supposed to."

The memory of Scooter on the day her parents were arrested flashed before her eyes. *White-eye William Shipburner should have protected us from the bad pirate, but I didn't. I couldn't. This is all my fault.*

"This is not your fault, Jennie. It isn't your job to protect your mother. She loves you and would never want anything bad to happen to you or to her."

Jennie pulled her bear to her chest. Bootie looked up and saw Grace and the officers congregating at the front door. An officer handed Grace a card.

After the police left, Bootie, Grace and Biscuit stood and looked at each other. No one could think of anything to say. Although Biscuit had rinsed his face, blood covered Robert Plant's forehead on his tee shirt. "Do you want a ride home, Biscuit?" Bootie asked, ending the silence. "You can put your bike in the garage."

Biscuit nodded. "Thank you."

"Should I take my car?" Grace asked. "I have to work tomorrow."

"You shouldn't drive. I'll bring you back in the morning."

Jennie pulled on her mother's sleeve. "Can we go now?"

"Soon as I get my gun," Grace said and turned toward the stairs, but Biscuit blocked her way. "You have a gun? Since when?"

"Since I got back from the lake. My Uncle Ike taught me how to shoot."

"You were in New Hampshire a week. After five or six lessons, you think you can handle a gun? Bad idea, Grace, on so many levels. Where is it?"

"In a safe in my bedroom."

"Get it and give to me, before you shoot yourself."

"No! You can lose that macho attitude. I'm not giving you my gun! I need it."

Biscuit's gray aura deepened.   "And how helpful was it to you today?"

"Mommy, let's go!"

"Biscuit! Get out of my way!"

"Mrs. Baxter, tell Grace to get rid of the gun. It's useless in the safe and dangerous out."

Bootie looked back and forth between Grace and Biscuit. "Any chance Blake knows about the gun?" Grace shook her head. "Leave it here. I don't want a gun in the tearoom."

"Okay, but I'm not giving it to Biscuit."

Biscuit glowered. "What are you thinking? You have a six-year-old!"

"Blake is getting crazier and more violent every time he shows up. I have to protect my family. I'm not going to shoot myself!"

"Enough!" Bootie glared at the fighting couple and they drew back. "Let's go."

The four made a multifarious group, walking to the car, and once everyone was strapped in, Bootie pulled out of the driveway and took off down the street. As Biscuit and Grace tried to cheer Jennie, Bootie noticed a white van parked on the roadside. A blue and green circle emblazoned the passenger

How to Dance on the Moon 233

door.

****

During the drive to Seattle, Bootie followed the stream of red taillights cutting a path through the darkened night, and she wrestled with her concerns for Grace. It was a good sign that Grace let Bootie touch her. It showed Grace trusted her, and that was vital if Bootie was to help her.

She crossed Lake Washington and drove onto the freeway that bisected Seattle. The city's fluorescence shined around them, aglow and alive with a sophisticated and purposeful energy. The Space Needle projected a light beam of a giant flashlight into a murky sky. Even the water in the harbor was illuminated, and the houseboats floated on Lake Union in tranquil repose. Jennie slept in the back seat. Bootie stole a peek at her niece, whose eyes were closed in either sleep, or, more likely, in an attempt to escape to a less stressful place. Bootie didn't disturb her. Their conversation could wait.

Beyond the city lights and to the east, Bootie spotted the full moon. It reminded her of the story Clark had told the night before he disappeared — a folk story modified to suit his audience and his imagination - about the little rabbit who attained immortality with her selfless act, her image forever engraved on the moonscape. The memory of the story added to Bootie's own depressed mood. She was beginning to understand that she herself might have to jump into the fire to save Grace. But could she? The words to Clark's poem coursed through her head, part memory, and part vision. *Dancing Rabbit on the moon, I might be up there with you soon.*

****

The next morning, Bootie, Grace and Jennie left early to take Jennie to school and Grace to her car. Two hours later,

Laura Ginter 234

while chopping onions for the tuna fish salad special, Bootie heard someone enter the kitchen. She turned to see Grace holding a large cardboard box.

"Loretta placed me on administrative leave without pay. That's management talk for firing me." Grace set the box on the counter. A cardboard folder protruded from the top, along with a sweater and a picture of Jennie. "Do you have anything for a headache?"

Bootie set her knife on the counter and reached into a cabinet for an aspirin bottle. Bobby, who had been dicing tomatoes, wiped his hands on his apron and patted Grace on the shoulder. "Tough morning, Grace?" he asked.

"You might say that."

Bootie flicked two aspirins into Grace's hand and poured her a glass of water.

Erline strolled in, a box of pastries in her hands. "Good morning, everyone. Have you seen that black sky? The beach will be empty. I'm going to tell Faye to stay home." She removed her coat and hung it on a hook in the back hallway outside the kitchen door. "Hi, Grace. Dear, you've been crying!"

"Loretta fired me." Grace mumbled the words as she tried to swallow her aspirin. Erline glanced at Bootie.

"We haven't had time to talk," Bootie added.

"Bobby," Erline said. "How is the prep work coming?"

"Just the salad dressing left."

Erline studied Grace's face again, and said, "Bootie, why don't you and Grace clip what's left of the dahlias before this storm hits. I'll finish the tuna. Bobby and I can handle things for a bit. We'll let Faye come in, as planned."

"We won't need Faye. Grace can help us today. Don't take off your coat yet, Grace."

Bootie led her niece outside through the garden door. "Sit on the bench until your head feels better." Bootie shivered. "Erline's right. It's going to be a nasty storm."

How to Dance on the Moon

"I'm sorry, Auntie. I've been such a pain in the. . ."

"Buttocks? Don't bring up buttocks! You know I have walked three times this week and my slacks aren't any looser. Do you think I could have a thyroid problem?"

Bootie was happy to see a smile creep onto Grace's face. "You know it takes more than three walks to make a difference. Why don't you join a gym?"

"Join a gym and have men see me in a leotard? I don't think so."

"Women don't wear leotards anymore. Shorts and a tee-shirt would be fine. You could join a women's gym."

Bootie picked up a pair of clippers off a ledge by the door and worked her way to the garden's far end. The wind rattled a ceramic chime hanging on the holly tree, and the air smelled wet and electric. She inspected her overgrown, tired plants. The cold nights had triggered the change of seasons, and autumn was sucking the garden back into the ground. The leggy basil had wilted, and her tomato plants were black stalks dotted with inedible green balls. The weakened geraniums were still struggling along like a last place baseball team in the ninth inning of the season's final game, but even in Seattle where winter came late, killing frost would soon overpower even the most stubborn survivors.

"Can you watch for Mrs. Wallaby?" Bootie asked Grace. She worked her way over to a yellow dahlia bush. "I'm going to dig up these bulbs and split them soon. Do you want any?"

"If you tell me how to plant them. I'd love to dig a garden with Jennie."

"Dahlias are easy. Stick them in the ground sometime before spring, mix in fertilizer, and voila! Dahlias!" Bootie reached in to another bush and clipped a pink Starburst. "So what happened?"

Grace rubbed her temples. "Loretta has decided my personal problems are too disruptive for the office."

Bootie spotted two more blooms deep inside the dahlia.

Laura Ginter 236

She stretched forward, wove her hands through the stems and snipped them. "Do you think it has anything to do with the BATSS van being parked on your street when we left last night?"

"You saw the BATSS van? How do you know?"

"I didn't, until I saw the folder in your box. It has a sticker matching the emblem on the van's door."

"Loretta!" Grace rubbed her eyes. "That's why I got fired."

"You think Loretta was in the van?"

"Yes. She's been stalking Biscuit. See the irony? Like Janet said, stalkers come in all shapes and sizes."

"You are sure it was Loretta?"

"Biscuit sees her everywhere, and she doesn't try to hide from him. She would have been furious seeing him at my house with all the police cars. I'll never get my job back."

Bootie straightened and turned to her niece, searching for reassuring words, but Grace interrupted her before she could speak. "There's something else."

"Blake?"

"Stan Bean."

"What did he say?"

"That Blake wants to see me again."

"Did you report the call to the police?"

"Yes, but they acted pretty blasé."

"You tell them every time you get a call."

Grace glanced up at Bootie. "The alarm company is moving the sensors around in my house this afternoon. They're getting the window fixed for me, too. They said they don't need me there. They know my house pretty well. Biscuit is getting a system, too."

Bootie brought the dahlia blooms to the bench and handed them to Grace. "Only five flowers, but we will make do."

A rustling across the pathway drew the women's attention. "Mrs. Wallaby! Grace, could you get some lettuce from the kitchen?"

How to Dance on the Moon 237

Grace set the flowers down and disappeared into the building. She returned with a large lettuce leaf and handed it to Bootie. Bootie placed a piece of the leaf on the ground six inches from her feet. Mrs. Wallaby stuck her head out from under a blackberry bush and sniffed the air, her nose twitching rapidly.

"Come on, Mrs. Wallaby. Let's get you inside." A large raindrop plopped on Bootie's head. Within moments, drenching water bombs were pelting the walkway. Mrs. Wallaby darted back under the bush. Bootie searched the bushes as rain dripped down her face.

"Auntie, you are getting soaked!"

"Okay, I give up," Bootie said. "Mrs. Wallaby will have to take care of herself."

The wind scattered the cut flowers across the bench. Grace scooped them up and ran into the building. Bootie came in behind her. "I'm going to put on dry clothes," said Bootie. "Can you help me in the tearoom today?"

"I'll help you every day, Auntie."

****

Four days passed before Grace and Bootie went to check on the house. The alarm beeped when Grace opened the front door, and she punched in the code to disarm it. The light on the answering machine in the kitchen was flickering. Grace approached the machine. She glanced up at her aunt. "It says I have three new messages."

Bootie asked, "What does the caller ID say?"

"Blocked, local and blocked." Grace pushed machine's play button.

The first message started. "You have won a trip to Las Vegas."

"Yeah, right." Grace pushed the erase button.

The next message was for Jennie. "This is Lucy Tynan. Can

Laura Ginter 238

Jennie could come over and play today? Thank you."

Grace took a deep breath. "Last call."

The last message clicked on. Bootie heard long, deep breaths that built in intensity and volume. The only word she understood was "Grace". The click of a hang-up indicated the call's end.

Grace stared at the phone, and Bootie could see her despair in her deep violet aura. "He's violated the order, Grace. Call the police."

"It won't do any good." Grace's defeated look seemed permanently frozen on her face.

"Call them."

Grace shrugged. She turned away from Bootie and stared into the sink.

"Can you change your phone number?" Bootie asked.

"Again? Why? He won't let that stop him." Grace turned to face Bootie. Grace's eyes and nose were wet and red, and Bootie could see the strain was becoming too much for her niece. "How can he do this to me? What can I do to make him stop?"

"I don't know, Grace. I don't know what you can do." Bootie reached up to rub her niece's shoulder, and her thoughts turned dark. A vision pummeled her of Mother dying in an insane asylum, Father dying in prison, Grace's tear-stained face. For the first time, Bootie worried Grace might not survive her stalker. *Dancing rabbit on the moon. . .*

How to Dance on the Moon 239

Bootie 1954

33.

During the weeks leading up to her eighteenth birthday, Bootie Kurz reflected on the best way to observe her transition into legal maturity. Her birthday coincided with the last day of high school. To celebrate two such significant milestones with cake and candles seemed childish, and Bootie had no boyfriend to treat her to a movie or dinner, so she decided to do the most adult thing she could think of. Visit her father in prison.

Bootie had not seen her father since his arrest when she was twelve. Aunt Theo had refused to go to the jail or the prison, and no one else had ever volunteered to take the children. Bernice and Woody had talked about going, but it had just been talk. Now, Bootie was old enough to go herself, and there were no more excuses for waiting until tomorrow to face her responsibility. It was time to do the right thing. To do the adult thing. Bootie chose to skip her last day of school and drive to the New Hampshire State Prison for Men, in Concord.

When the day arrived, she borrowed the old Chevy Suburban and chose a slow, rural road. She had begun to question her decision, and hoped the extra time would strengthen her resolve and help her prepare for the reunion. But as she navigated her way toward the state capital, she grew more uneasy with each passing mile. By the time she arrived at the prison parking lot, anxiety had so overcome her, she had to bribe herself from the car with the promise of an ice cream cone when the visit was over. She hoped Father would be pleased to see her. She pasted a cool, ambiguous expression on her face and joined the line of visitors waiting to enter the prison.

The prison was in the midst of major construction, and the guards were using the exercise yard for visitations one hour a day. The visitors' door would not open for fifteen minutes, and the queue was long, filled mostly with women who had brought children.

Bootie imagined herself with Aunt Theo and her brothers and sisters, standing in that same line, clinging to each other with brave faces. Aunt Theo would have been sharing the details of their drama to all who would listen while she dabbed her eyes with a handkerchief. She might even have brought a boyfriend along to help ease her distress. The children would have had to revisit the trauma that had led them there, picking at the scabs that had formed over their wounds. And Bootie could imagine Father's pain if Clark wasn't with them. It would have been disastrous.

Although the air was warm, Bootie pulled her sweater more tightly around her body. She was surprised to see so many visitors. It had never occurred to her so many people would care about criminals. Curious, she glanced down the line of women and children and promptly rejected any similarity between their circumstances and hers. These people were here to see inmates who were dangerous men from bad families, with violent and abusive histories. Years of hardship and loneliness would be these women's reward for love and loyalty. They were pitiable. She wasn't one of them. Her father was different.

Father didn't deserve this life. He had been a professional man. He had been a Harvard man. And a caring man. A father. She remembered how much he enjoyed feeding his raccoons, and listening to the radio during dinner. She searched for more memories to reinforce her belief in the quality of his character, but she couldn't find any. The truth was, her father was an imprisoned outlaw, and her gifted, beautiful mother, with the gift of second sight, had died in a mental hospital. Parents were supposed to protect and love their children, but her parents had, in essence, turned their children into orphans. Worse than orphans. Pariahs. The objects of pity.

When everything was still new and raw, Bootie's sadness

How to Dance on the Moon 241

and guilt over her parents' arrest had weighed on her like a boulder she was destined to carry forever on her shoulders. She had lacked the skills and resources to learn how to forgive herself and make peace with her loss, so she had created an imaginary world where she could escape. Where her parents still loved her, where the prison had freed her father and the hospital had found her mother alive, and they were home again. Where they were a real family again, blending in with everyone else again. Where they were happy.

The illusion lived in the corner of her mind like a haunt in the attic, and it was a comforting friend whenever the pain attacked. But as she grew older, the illusion lost its power to comfort her, although she could still call on it as needed. Now, as Bootie stood in line, the barbed wire surrounding the New Hampshire State Prison for Men's courtyard unceremoniously sliced away the last tiny remnants of her illusion. The remaining reality was naked, frigid, heartless and blindingly bright. She took her place in line and thought, happy birthday to me.

The doors opened, and the line crept forward. Bootie's knees weakened, and she felt woozy. A litany of questions cycled through her thoughts like teasers at the end of a soap opera. Would Father look different? Would he recognize her? Would he be mad at her? Would he refuse to see her? That particular idea hadn't occurred to her before. Bootie shook her head. If her anxious thoughts didn't stop their relentless spinning, she might panic and dash back to the car. She searched for a distraction.

A lilac bush was the focal point of the tired landscape near the entry door. One late-blooming purple cluster remained among its dried sisters. Bootie remembered how every spring, Mother picked lilacs from bushes near the road to fill the house with their perfume, calling the fragrance "sugar for the nose". Bootie wished she could pluck that last lilac by the prison door and bring it in with her, as a link to her own world while trying

Laura Ginter 242

to relate to her father's.

A tap on her shoulder interrupted her thoughts. "Excuse me," said a voice, thick with Midwestern twang. Startled, Bootie adjusted her focus onto the woman standing before her. She was taller than Bootie by a head, and looked to be about ten years older. Gaunt and feathery as a fern, she had skin so translucent, veins streaked through her face and hands. She wore a pleated blue skirt and a faded, calico print smock. Her shoes were institutional white. She might have been a hospital clerk. The wispy woman fidgeted with the handle of her small cloth purse and smiled at Bootie with stretched lips, trying to hide a missing a front tooth. "What's yours in here for?"

"I'm sorry," said Bootie. What do you mean?"

"Your husband? Or is it your boyfriend? What's he in here for?"

The woman's rudeness startled Bootie at first, but after thinking about it, she supposed it was a common question under the circumstances. "Burglary," Bootie replied. "And it's my father."

"Oh." The woman nodded with tacit understanding as though they shared a secret. "My husband's here because he shot a senator during a speech against Communism."

Surprised, Bootie studied the woman with a new interest. She knew the story, more infamous than her parents' case. This woman's husband, whose name Bootie couldn't remember, had mistaken a little-known New Hampshire state senator for Joseph McCarthy and had shot him. "I heard about him," Bootie said.

The woman nodded her head. "Everyone has. Makes it hard to get an appeal. But you probably already know that. I haven't seen you here before. What's your name?"

"Bootie."

"I'm Coral Dickford. Delighted to meet you, Bootie."

Frank Dickford. That was the man's name. "Nice to meet you, too," Bootie responded politely. Coral reached into her

How to Dance on the Moon 243

purse and rifled through it until she found a hankie, and used it to wipe her nose.

A sudden empathy filled Bootie, and she tried to think of something friendly to say to Coral. "This is my first time coming. Is the line always this long?"

"Line's always long before Father's Day."

"It's Father's Day this weekend? I guess I hadn't thought about that."

"Well, your daddy's not home so you wouldn't think about that." Coral patted Bootie on the arm with the dirty hankie, as though they were equals. She was lumping them together as two women with one heart. Co-conspirators in the crime of loving a man in prison. Coral hoped they could become friends. Bootie pursed her lips and turned her head away. Coral continued with her story, oblivious to Bootie's terse displeasure.

"He's just got eight years left in his sentence," Coral said, her eyes focusing into the distance. "And less with good behavior. When he gets out, we're moving to Cuba. There's lots of jobs there for men like my Frank, and nice beaches too. And warm weather all the time."

"Well, good luck, Coral. I wish you well."

Bootie bent over and adjusted her stockings. When she straightened back up, Coral had started a conversation with the woman standing in front of her, who had a baby nestled into her hip. "What's yours in for?" the young mother asked Coral. Bootie returned her attention to the lilac bush, toward which the line was moving. She focused on the flower, keeping her mind clear of thoughts until she reached the prison entry.

****

After signing in at the visitors' desk, Bootie received a badge on a lanyard, and she draped it over her neck. She followed the other visitors to the exercise yard and looked for her father. He sat at a vacant metal table between the prison wall and a basketball court. She couldn't believe how much he had changed. He seemed old and small. He still wore his hair combed straight back from his forehead, and only his temples had grayed, but his red hair wasn't shiny from pomade the way Bootie remembered. She watched him scan the crowd for her.

Bootie called out to him. Her voice drew his eye, and he waved her over. She crossed the yard to his table and sat across from him before he could reach out to her. "Hello Father," she said. "It's me, Bootie."

He shielded his eyes with his hand and squinted. "I know who it is. Move out of the sun so I can see you."

Bootie moved to the far end of his side of the bench. His eyes were glazed and dull, almost as though he were sleepwalking. His aura was a colorless shadow. "How are you, Father?"

"Not too bad. Had a hard day at work yesterday," he answered. "How's your mother?"

Bootie winced. Was Father joking? He had to know Mother had been dead for over five years. She studied his face and understood without any help from her gift that Father wasn't all there with her. He was living in an imaginary safe house, where his wife was alive and he was a respected family man who held a job in a big building in Concord. He was escaping the same way Bootie had, but unlike her, he was living in his safe house all the time. Her empathy for him made her eyes fill with tears. She blinked them back, and decided not to burden him with too much truth.

"I'm sure Mother would want me to say hello for her."

"I hear Theo is staying with you. A wild one she is. Keep an eye on her. Do you have a cigarette?"

"No."

"Too bad. I could use a cigarette. Maybe you could send a box or two?"

Bootie did not recollect ever seeing her father smoke. She

How to Dance on the Moon   245

had forgotten much about who he was. "If they'll let me," she replied.

"Why wouldn't they let you?" Father asked. Bootie didn't know. Neither spoke for an uncomfortably long time. So much life had happened since they had last seen each other, and Bootie could find no clear starting point for a conversation. How could she talk about herself? How could she summarize the changes and growth in a girl between the ages of twelve and eighteen? Likewise, how could he explain prison?

Father scratched his scalp briskly with both hands and broke the silence. His tone was an angry, anxious jumble. "How come nobody writes or comes by? I'm not dead, you know."

"I'll be better from now on, I promise."

"All these years and not one visitor. Not one. Are you mad at me?" he asked suddenly. "For having to leave you all?"

The questions startled Bootie. Feeling anger toward her parents had never occurred to her. She had only been upset with herself, faulting herself for not intervening when she could have. Maybe she had anger she had never looked at directly.

Memories flooded back of the clipped whispers that surrounded her whenever she went to town with Bernice the first year after the arrest, after the police and FBI and reporters had taken their turns with the Kurz children, and then dropped them for the next big story. She remembered how their neighbors and teachers had held them at arm's length, as though a pox had infected them. People had regarded them as peculiar – as curious objects. Like folkloric changelings, they were seen as incomplete. Missing parts. It made living a normal life impossible, and the children's lives painful beyond words.

Bootie had never thought about her father experiencing struggles similar to her own, or being ill-equipped to deal with those struggles. The children had recovered to various degrees. But he was so destroyed, he had to live in an imaginary world

Laura Ginter 246

just to survive. How could she be angry with him the way he was? He was her father. "No, Father. No one is angry."

"All I was doing was trying to earn a living. You forgive me for letting them get me?"

"We forgive you. We love you. I love you."

Henry Kurz scratched his nose, and Bootie looked up at the sky. "Pleasant day. I'm glad summer is almost here." Again, a wall of silence settled between them, and Bootie searched for something else to say.

"How is everybody doing?" Father suddenly asked. "You know. All the boys? And Bernice and Sellie?"

Finally, the questions she had known he would ask and had been dreading. She could imagine how starved he was for news from home, but she hadn't wanted to say anything to him. Things weren't good. But maybe a few censored family stories were gifts she could give him, more valuable than even cigarettes. "Ike is getting tall!" Bootie said, smiling. "He is nine years old and smarter than all of us." (That was true). "Scooter is strong, but still needs braces to walk." (That was also true, but what Bootie didn't say was how Scooter now spent more time in his wheelchair than on his feet.)

Henry Kurz shook his head. "We should never have lived in that damned city. You all got sick there, but the poor little guy was the only one to get the polio bad. Best thing we ever did was move to the lake. How about the others? How about Sellie?"

"Sellie is almost seventeen and very helpful around the house. She's beautiful." (Sellie truly was beautiful, slim and statuesque, and a pregnant high school dropout.) "Our Woodrow is nineteen and is thinking about joining the army." (Woody had busted a Maslow boy's jaw in a fight, and the judge was forcing him to choose between going to jail and going into the military.) "Bernice is twenty-two, and has been married for three years. Her baby, little Patty is two years old now."

"Who did Bernice marry?"

How to Dance on the Moon   247

Bootie paused, and then said. "Mickey Kennedy."

Henry's face darkened. "She married a Kennedy?" He scowled and spit into the dirt. "I hate that family. Patrick Kennedy killed my coons and laughed about it. I can't believe my little Bernice would marry a Kennedy."

Bootie ignored her father's outburst. "She and Mickey moved to Massachusetts. He has a good job, and they are happy." That was all true. She changed the subject before her father could ask her about Clark. "How are you doing, Father?"

"Pretty good. Pretty good. We got a new cook. Food's not as bad as it used to be. I'm the equipment manager for the baseball team. Make sure you tell Clark that." He spoke about prison life as if he was at summer camp. "I'm making furniture in the wood shop. They sell our pieces in a store in town across from the mill. Pretty good looking furniture. You should take a look."

"How will I know if I see something you made?"

"I make mostly stools. Look for the stools."

"I'll look for the stools."

Father and daughter strained through another thirty minutes of talk about furniture making. A buzzer sounded, announcing the end of visiting hour. When he rose to leave, she said, "Father, it's my birthday today."

"How old are you, fourteen? Fifteen?"

"I'm eighteen."

He squinted at her again, studying her the same way he had when he first saw her. "Well, happy birthday. Are you going to see your mother today, too?"

Bootie gave him a slight, noncommittal nod.

"Tell her to wait for me." He forced his lips into a twisted smile.

"I will, Father." They stood up, and he put out his hand. She reached over and shook it. A dull pain shot up her arm, but no pictures. He turned and walked away.

Relief washed over Bootie. It was over, and the first visit

Laura Ginter 248

had been a success. Now she could visit him again without fear, and, unless something unexpected happened, she would go to the prison regularly. She wondered when the next time would be, but emptied the thought from her mind, in case her gift had the inclination to tell her.

Walking briskly toward the exit gate, Bootie noticed a man approaching from the side. She sped up to stay in front of him. "Hello, there," he called out. She glanced over her shoulder and was surprised to see he was speaking to her. "You walk fast for such a short thing," he said. Bootie stifled a smirk, and slowed to let him catch up. She barely came to his shoulder and had to look up to see his face, which was youthful despite creases around his eyes and mouth. She sensed no threat, but had no idea what he could want.

"Can I help you?" she asked him. Her words sounded terser than she intended.

"Thought you might want an escort. There are a lot of criminals around here."

This time, Bootie chuckled aloud, but she wasn't in the mood to indulge someone's need to feel chivalrous. "No, thank you." She swooshed him off with her hand as if she often waved off men who sought her attentions. She quickened her pace, but he kept up with her.

"So, who are you visiting today?" he asked.

"Why do you ask?" she answered testily.

"I suppose it's your father. Or else you are married to a much older man. I saw you together in the yard."

"He is my father," she said. "He stole money from banks. There. You would have gotten around to asking why he was here, so I've told you. I've learned it's the official conversation opener." This time, her flippancy was intentional. She normally wasn't unsociable, but today was her birthday and she was not having fun. She wanted ice cream more than the company of a stranger, even if he did make her laugh.

"I'm glad he wasn't your husband," the man continued,

How to Dance on the Moon 249

undeterred. You're too pretty to be married to an old prison cock."

Bootie giggled again. She had never heard the term prison cock. She contemplated telling him thanks but no thanks, but he had gone to all the effort to catch up with her, and he was cute in a brotherly way. And funny. "What's yours in here for?' Bootie asked, softening her tone. "Your father, too, I assume. Or brother?"

"Yes, my father. He murdered my mother."

Bootie stopped and looked up at him again. This man had mentioned the circumstances that put his father in prison as if he were describing his father's career as a plumber. She studied him more carefully.

He wore his hair trimmed short around the sides, but longer on the top, where an erratic lock of hair drooped onto his forehead. His eyes were purple-blue color of the lilac flower at the prison entrance, a color she had never seen before in a person's eyes. They were wide set and framed with long eyelashes that softened his hard-lined face. His lips were pink and plump. She looked away. It seemed inappropriate to be noticing how handsome he was in the middle of a prison yard. She fought the urge to ask, but surrendered to her curiosity. "Your father killed your mother?"

"They called it a crime of passion. He stabbed her and her boyfriend, too. On Valentine's Day. Will you have coffee with me?"

He held his hands out. His sleeves were rolled to his elbows, and she couldn't help but notice how muscular his arms were. She swished her own arms in front of her face and walked faster.

"Are you married?" he asked, keeping pace with her.

"No. Do I look married?"

"I'm sorry," he said, "I don't get to meet many pretty women here. So, how about that coffee?"

"I don't drink coffee," she answered. "Though I did

Laura Ginter 250

promise myself an ice cream cone."

"Okay, ice cream!"

She rolled her eyes. "Fine. As long as murderers don't run in your family." The words popped out without forethought, and she regretted them immediately. It was as insensitive as a person could be, and she turned to him to apologize. But he just laughed and fell into step beside her, and Bootie allowed herself to enjoy the moment just a little bit. She didn't know why she had agreed to let him buy her an ice cream cone, but agreeing felt like the right thing to do. Something about his eyes reminded her of someone, but she couldn't place who.

The bold, violet-eyed man took her arm to lead her through the gate, and Bootie's breath caught in her throat at the electricity in his touch. She took the opportunity to steal a vision from him. To her surprise, she saw nothing. No aura, no pictures, not even a swirl of shadow. That disarmed her more than his eyes or his smile or his forwardness. "I can't leave with you until I at least know your name," she said.

"I want to know your name, too. See, we already have something in common." He laughed again. "My name is Eddie. Eddie Baxter."

Bootie found his laugh oddly comforting, and the morning stress dissolved like morning fog before a sunny day. And no man had ever called her pretty before. This will be interesting, she though. Happy birthday to me. Happy birthday to me, after all.

34.

After leaving the New Hampshire State Prison for Men, Bootie and Eddie found a Woolworth's and sat at the soda fountain. But instead of ice cream cones, they shared

How to Dance on the Moon   251

milkshakes and burgers. When they finished, they strolled until they found a duck pond. They sat on a bench and watched an elderly woman toss cereal from a box into the pond. The ducks darted about and thrust their beaks in the water to scoop up each flake. Bootie learned Eddie was a second lieutenant in the army, on leave before his assignment to Fort Rucker in Alabama for nine weeks, and then South Korea for a year. And his father did stab his mother and her lover, fourteen and twenty-two times respectively.

Eddie was six years older than Bootie, had no siblings, and had been living on his own since his father's arrest when he was fourteen. He had slipped through the welfare system's cracks by telling his school's social worker he had moved in with his grandmother. Because he looked older than fourteen, or because the landlord didn't care, he was able to rent a one-room apartment with a hot plate and icebox and he avoided discovery by those who might want to help him.

He stayed in school, working at a grocery store, and at eighteen, he enrolled in the University of New Hampshire, which he paid for with his grocery wages. During his senior year, he crashed his bike into the Army recruitment center to avoid hitting a dog. He tumbled against a wall and looked up to see a poster of a B17 soaring over mountains larger and more rugged than those in New Hampshire. Dazzled, he entered and signed the enlistment paperwork.

The Army accepted Eddie into officer candidate school, and from there he went to a special school to learn how to fly H-13 Sioux helicopters. Now, after two years, he was a second lieutenant with fourteen days until he had to report to Fort Rucker, where he would complete his aviation training before starting his tour in South Korea. On the day he met Bootie, he was at the prison to say goodbye to his father.

Bootie asked him why he would maintain a relationship with the man who killed his mother. Eddie shrugged, saying what his father had done was heinous, but he was his father.

Bootie tried to understand how Eddie could be glib about how his parents had derailed his life with their actions, but Eddie seemed to shrug everything off. Even though his reaction seemed oddly impassive, Bootie refused to judge him by it. She had her own way of looking at things others wouldn't understand if they had not experienced what she had. Wouldn't the same be true for him?

Impending darkness forced Bootie and Eddie to look for a restaurant. Eddie ordered cake for Bootie, and sang Happy Birthday and followed it up with the only other song he remembered his mother singing to him, Itsy Bitsy Spider. He twisted his fingers to project a climbing and stumbling bug drowning in rain. He asked Bootie what her favorite song was. She thought for a moment, and said "Mister Me and Missus You." Eddie grinned and sang.

"*Mister me and Missus you, with you I will stay, to you I'll be true. Though our lives will go by our love will never die, it will always be you and me, a love song for two, Mister me, Missus you.*"

Bootie's heart never beat so fast.

When Eddie invited Bootie to stay with him at his friend's house, she telephoned Sellie and told her she would not be home that night. Bootie made the same call the next night, and the night after. Then she told Sellie she would be gone another ten days.

"Ten days? Aunt Theo is getting tired of us borrowing her car," Sellie said. "And Ike says you promised to help him switch out beds on the sleeping porch. Bootie, what's going on?"

"I'm getting married!" Bootie gushed.

****

After the blood tests, the signatures on the dotted lines and the three-day waiting period, Bootie and Eddie said their I dos and shared a long kiss. They spent their honeymoon at a

How to Dance on the Moon 253

small hotel at Hampton Beach, where Bootie told Eddie about her gift. It pleased her when Eddie reacted as though she had just told him she liked chocolate, and put more importance on the new clothes he bought her. They whirled to the rhythm of their ballroom dance for as long as time would let them.

When the day arrived for Eddie to leave, they drove back to Concord, where Eddie was to catch a train. "Come with me," he said. "You are an officer's wife now. You can live on base, and be with other wives."

Bootie looked at her wedding ring. "I'm Ike's mother now, and Scooter needs help with his legs. You'll be in training. I wouldn't see you anyway."

Eddie set his duffle bag on the platform, pulled out his wallet and handed Bootie five twenty-dollar bills, the most money Bootie had ever held in her hand at one time. "If you won't come now, come in September, when training is over. If you don't show up, I'll go AWOL to get you, and you can visit me in prison, too."

Bootie's eyes misted, and she dabbed them with the sleeve of her new sweater.

He looked down at her, and with a gentle sweep of his hand, he lifted her chin and kissed her, pushing on her lips softly, sweetly, holding the kiss long enough for them to each taste the other for one last time. "Happy birthday, Mrs. Baxter," he added. He hoisted his duffle bag over his shoulder, stepped up into the train and was gone. She stared at the last spot she saw him, until his shadow faded from view, and then watched until the train disappeared behind a hill.

Bootie's chest was so heavy she believed her ribs were caving in on her heart. She had left to take a day trip to see her father in prison, and she was going home two weeks later with a wedding ring but without a husband. During the war, she had seen pictures of women sending their soldier husbands to war with kisses, tears and perfume-drenched handkerchiefs. Now she was one of those women. She had never before known romantic love. Now she understood what it meant to die of a broken heart. She sat in her car until she flushed out all her tears and untangled her emotions enough to drive home.

As Bootie pulled into her driveway, the familiarity of her home made her short time with Eddie suddenly seem like a dream, and the grim reality of her situation hit her. She was eighteen years old plus almost two weeks, married before she had ever had a date, with a husband at an Alabama military base. She had known Eddie for a very short time, and now he was going to be a thousand miles away for nine weeks and overseas for a year.

Her impulsive decision to marry someone she had known for a few days may have seemed romantic in the moment, but now it seemed impractical and absurd. She tried to picture Eddie, but thin clouds were already forming around her memories and obscuring his face. This morning, she had believed she knew him better than she knew anyone else, and now she feared she didn't know him at all.

Bootie slumped in her seat. Would he be there for her in September? And how could she go to him? She had responsibilities to her family. It would be impossible to leave. Her breath caught in her throat. She despaired her marriage was unsustainable, and already failing.

She spotted Scooter and Ike in the window and straightened. They waved to her, and Ike ran outside to greet her, a wide grin on his face. Bootie tried to present the image of a happy bride, but she knew the first dance with Eddie was over. Was it also her last?

For two weeks, she had been a starry-eyed Cinderella whose prince had swept her around the palace floor with both her glass slippers snug on her feet. But the ball had ended, and her glass slipper had fallen off. With shaken confidence, Bootie visualized her rabbit's foot and mentally stroked it, praying Eddie would want to retrieve that slipper in September.

How to Dance on the Moon 255

****

The days passed with the tedious rhythm of a long, dry Sunday sermon. Eddie wrote her twice a week and phoned every Sunday. She composed several letters back to him, editing and rewriting them until they were the perfect blend of happy news and wistful anticipation of the future. It was bliss. It was torture. She didn't know she could be elated and miserable at the same time. She drifted through her days, doing her chores without any thought to what she was doing. But as her trip to Alabama approached, her nerves made her jittery, knowing she would be with him soon, and they would be making permanent plans, or pulling the plug.

Inevitably, the day for Bootie to leave for Alabama arrived. Train ticket in hand, she left New England for the first time in her life to be with a husband she hardly knew, and she would have a day and a half on a train to dwell on what that meant. When Bootie arrived in Alabama and Eddie greeted her at the train station with flowers, chocolates, and a deep passionate kiss, Bootie's heart filled with joy, thrilled to know her weeks of anxiety turned out to be just an insecure girl's misgivings.

This time, when Eddie's leave ended, they said their goodbyes without words. Neither could say anything to the other to make parting hurt less. Their reunion had brought more than romance. Now she and Eddie had intimacy. They had history. They had a deeper friendship. And she had something else she had not had before. She had confidence.

They stood on the train station platform, Eddie, starched and polished in his dress uniform, and Bootie in a new lavender dress. Bootie tried to memorize everything about Eddie. The freckles on his cheeks, his eyelashes framing his eyes, the wedding ring that allowed her to claim him. She wanted to be able to close her eyes and touch him with her mind. This time the memories would have to last a year.

As the train approached, he wrapped her in his arms. The

wind whipped her skirt around her knees. She was afraid to let him go because when he stepped away, the moment would end and he'd be gone. If the last separation was almost unbearable, this one would surely kill her. South Korea was dangerous, especially for helicopter pilots. What if the war started again? He could be shot down, or captured, or worse. One last time Bootie searched inside herself for a vision. She had to know he would be safe and come back to her. There were no pictures to calm her fears, and she cursed her gift for not being there for her the one time she genuinely needed it.

The train doors opened. She stepped aboard, and he passed her case to her. After she settled into her seat, she looked out the window. Eddie rocked on his feet, his arms folded across his chest. He spotted her and blew her a kiss. She smiled and made a motion to catch it, and the train started down the track. She watched him at the window until the train turned into a tunnel.

35.

While one is waiting for time to run its course, life brings change. New surroundings, people and experiences replace the old. And as Bootie awaited Eddie's return from Korea, the changes that occurred around her helped to move time faster toward her reunion with her husband.

Bernice became pregnant with her second child and bought a bigger house in the Boston suburbs. Her trips to the lake house slowed in direct proportion to the size of her belly.

Sellie moved from the house and married, not the boy who had made her pregnant, but the policeman who had rushed her to the hospital with a severe stomach bug that turned out to be

How to Dance on the Moon 257

morning sickness. His name was Donald "Dinny" Summers, and it was love at first sight for poor Dinny. He promised the seventeen-year-old beauty a new television if she would marry him. His offer was too good to turn down.

Sellie gave birth to a baby girl, but the infant died before she could take three breaths. Sellie was inconsolable and wouldn't speak to anyone for weeks. Dinny doted on her with compassion more profound than Bootie had ever witnessed in another human being. The family was thankful Sellie married Dinny and not the high school tomcat.

Woody decided to join the Navy and left for Hawaii. Scooter became weaker, Ike smarter, Aunt Theo fatter. Bootie moved into the second bedroom when Scooter moved onto the sleeping porch with Ike. A new raccoon made a home in the barn and gave birth to twin kits but left soon after. They would be the last raccoons ever to live in the barn.

The apple trees blossomed and made fruit, and Ike helped Bootie pick the tree clean in October. She cooked, juiced and canned the apples as her mother had taught her. The leaves sprouted on the maples and oaks, fluttered in the summer breezes, and fell to earth before winter, forming a crunchy carpet of red, amber, coppery orange and brown.

Bootie became thinner and more stoic. She visited her father in Concord every other week, bringing with her cigarettes and whichever sibling was home, and she introduced herself to Eddie's father, adding him to her schedule. She spent her free time at the lake's edge, reliving the past and dreaming about the future.

****

Eddie's service in Korea brought him commendations and a promotion to first lieutenant, and when his overseas duty ended, he went to New Hampshire. He and Bootie had a joyous, feverish reunion in Concord, before driving to the lake house where Bootie introduced him to her family. The chaos and camaraderie of the big family overwhelmed Eddie. He had never had brothers or sisters. He told Bootie he had trouble feeling sorry for her, now that he saw the life she had come from.

When they were alone, Sellie mentioned to Bootie how much Eddie resembled Clark. They had the same shape eyes, the same cowlicks and curls, and the same physical build. Bootie had never noticed the similarities between her husband and her brother, but instead of brooding over her sister's comment, she ignored it.

Eddie's next assignment was to Fort Sill in Oklahoma. It was time for Bootie to leave her family and the house on the lake. As much as she wanted to be with her husband and start her real life, and as hard as the sacrifices had been during their year apart, she was conflicted. Ike, who was now nine years old, still needed a parent more reliable than Aunt Theo. Scooter was moving to Boston to take a job at the same bank that had employed his father, twenty years earlier. He had found a boarding house in the city that catered to the needs of the disabled. Sellie was trying to make a life with Dinny, but still mourned her baby's death. Woody was locked into the Navy for three more years, and Bernice had her own family now in Massachusetts.

Bootie saw no solution to her problem. Heartsick, she cried to her older sister. "What do I do?"

"Ike needs a family," Bernice said. "But Bootie, you deserve happiness. You have carried the brunt of the responsibility for years, now. I will talk to Mickey about having Ike live with us."

"But you're going to have another baby."

"Ike could be helpful around the house." Bernice said. "Will Aunt Theo stay after you leave? We don't want the house to be empty, in case we hear from Clark."

"I'm sure she will," said Bootie, "but I'll check. Thank you,

How to Dance on the Moon 259

Bernice. You have saved my marriage."

Bootie heard the smile through the phone. "You are a lucky girl, Bootie Kurz Baxter."

Ike did move in with Bernice, and Scooter moved to Boston. Aunt Theo, with her usual dramatic flair, agreed to do everyone a big favor and stay at the lake house. So, in love, in lust, and in awe of the grand adventure awaiting her, Bootie packed all the clothing she could fit in her father's old leather suitcase, taping her rabbit's foot securely inside, and moved to Oklahoma. She was nineteen years old, a married woman for over a year who had not lived with her husband as man and wife for more than three weeks, and she was ready to start her life.

****

For six years, Bootie and Eddie moved from base to base. Each transfer brought new friends, new experiences, and, paradoxically, more stability for Bootie. She made many friends who entertained her with stories of lifestyles Bootie had never imagined. She censored what she told people about herself, not wanting anyone to know about her gift or that her parents were the infamous New Hampshire burglars whose deeds still made the newspaper occasionally. She worked as a waitress, and for the first time in her life, she had her own money.

But while Bootie lived the perfect life as the perfect wife, she missed the signs Eddie didn't share her enthusiasm for marriage. Her gift had always told her everything she needed to know about someone, and she had never learned to read body language. And she did not recognize how the childhood scars that had brought her and Eddie together were splitting them apart.

The marriages both Bootie and Eddie had been exposed to as children had been maladjusted, and theirs didn't grow roots. Bootie's life with a large family had taught her that being alone was a precious gift. Yet she sought Eddie out and followed him everywhere he went around the house, clinging to his words and needing his reassurances. Eddie believed being alone was a curse, yet her constant attention smothered him. The harder she tried to please him, the more he pulled away.

Bootie believed the perfect marriage was about being cheerful all the time. When Eddie was sullen or temperamental, she would attribute his unpleasant mood to overwork. He was under stress, and her job was to relieve it.

With all her cheerleading and noble intentions, it did not occur to her he could be unhappy with her. But she bluntly and brutally learned of his dissatisfaction when, one night at dinner, Eddie told Bootie he was leaving the next day for a two-year tour in West Germany, and she wasn't going with him.

At first, Bootie didn't think she heard him correctly. When he confirmed he was going alone, she argued that the Army allowed wives to go to West Germany with their husbands. Why couldn't she go? He sat her on the sofa, held her hands, and told her he believed the break would be good for them.

"It is cruel of you to tell me now, the day before you are leaving," Bootie said, numb with shock. "How long have you known? Don't you love me anymore?"

"There's no reason to leave the base," he replied. "I will come back when I've finished my tour."

He packed his bag the next day, while she watched in stunned silence. "I'll write," he said, and skimmed her cheek with a kiss. Bootie still could not believe he could walk away from her so suddenly, and with such coldness. But the vacant hollowness in his expression when he said goodbye forced her to face the truth. He had stopped loving her.

At that moment, she hated Eddie. Why had there been no sign he felt this way? Maybe he was heartless, and maybe she couldn't see inside someone with no heart. Someone incapable of real feelings. After all, here was a man who was undisturbed over his father murdering his mother.

How to Dance on the Moon 261

Bootie wanted to claw his face and slap him and beat the cruelty out of him, but instead, she watched him walk out the door. He was gone. Again, her life had changed direction unexpectedly and dramatically and in minutes. As it had when her parents went away. As it had when Harley pulled a gun on Clark. A caustic wind blew through her heart and scorched all her old scars, causing them to bleed into her newest wound.

****

Bootie didn't stay on base, choosing instead to move back to the lake house. Only Aunt Theo lived there now, and Bootie had nothing to distract her from her broken heart. She relived every moment of her last days with Eddie, looking for clues as to what had happened to make him want to leave her. Eddie wrote to her, but his letters were irregular and impersonal, filled with vague references to "classified" activities. Even so, she scoured them for double meanings and hints of regret about leaving her behind, wanting to find a sign, some hope it was not over between them. That he still loved her.

She dealt with her depression by filling her days repeating old habits, trying to find comfort in the familiar, like a sick child who wraps herself a ratty but beloved old blanket. She cooked and cleaned and sat by the water. She spent more time visiting her father, who looked frailer with each visit. She did not realize his health was failing, beaten down by his own long battles with depression, guilt, anger and loneliness.

Bootie and Grace 1993

36.

Bootie was resting in her bedroom after a busy lunch when Grace knocked on her door.

"My house alarm went off." Grace was trembling. "The police want to meet me there. Will you go with me?"

Bootie rose from her bed. "Blake?"

"I think so. I'll call Biscuit. If he's not working he'll want to be there, too."

"Is Jennie at Tiny Tots?"

Grace nodded. "They can keep her until six." Grace rubbed her forehead. "I'm sorry to put you through this, Aunt Bootie."

"Don't apologize. Maybe we can finally stop this jerk."

****

When Grace and Bootie arrived at the house, Biscuit's car was in the driveway next to a patrol car. The lights were on throughout the house, made to look brighter by an overcast sky. Bootie opened the front door and the women hurried down the hall to the kitchen. Biscuit was sitting at the table with two policemen. Strain lined his face. The blond officer had been to the house before, and Bootie guessed he had recognized Biscuit and had let him inside.

Bootie and Grace removed their coats. "What's happening?" Grace asked.

"A door was forced open on the side of the garage," answered the blond officer. "He did a lot of damage in a short time."

"We also found a dead bird on the counter," Biscuit said. He gestured toward the officer. "We searched the house. He's

How to Dance on the Moon 263

not here. But he trashed the bedroom. Not sure if he was looking for something or if he was just angry. Grace, you should check the safe for your gun."

Grace ran upstairs, and returned shortly after. "It's there."

"I've called in a physical description and his automobile ID to the station," said the officer. "There is a bulletin out, and there will be an extra patrol in your neighborhood. Hopefully he's still around." The policeman held out a card for Grace. "Here's your case number. We will contact you if we find him."

Grace took the card and thanked the officer. When he left, Grace asked Biscuit why he thought Blake didn't disarm the alarm, as he had before. "Do you think he tried? Do you think he'll come back tonight?"

Biscuit shrugged. "I have no idea."

Grace put out her hand to Bootie. "What do you think Aunt Bootie? Will he come back?"

Bootie glanced at Biscuit and discretely took Grace's hand. She received no specific pictures, just a vague uneasiness. "We should assume he's close and still wants something from you."

Grace slumped. Her face was gray, her eyes sunken, her lips turned inward, and she moved lethargically, as if mud had replaced all her blood. And most frightening, her darkened aura was deepening to black.

"One day at a time, remember?" Bootie said, releasing Grace's hand. "And you might get lucky this time. The police could find him."

They all left together. Biscuit went home, and Bootie and Grace went to Tiny Tots. Jennie stiffened when she saw her mother. "Blake is back, isn't he?"

"The police are looking for him."

Jennie let out a pained squeal. Grace hugged her daughter and looked at Bootie with worried eyes.

****

Laura Ginter   264

The ride to the tearoom was quiet. Once back, they had a light dinner, and Jennie cried when Grace sent her to bed. "Don't leave me alone! Come hug me to sleep."

"Okay, Jennie."

Jennie grabbed onto Bootie's forearm and pulled on it. "You come too!"

"Of course!" Bootie buried her face in the little girl's neck and smacked her with rapid little kisses, and Jennie rewarded her with a burst of giggles.

Once Jennie was asleep, Grace slipped from the bed and joined Bootie in her apartment living room.

"We must work out a strategy to keep you safe," Bootie added. "And Grace, you must think hard about what's best for Jennie. Certainly not living like this."

"I know," said Grace. "I keep trying to do the right things to stop Blake, but every time I punch he punches harder. Grace bit her lip. "I've been fighting it, but with Stephen gone, and me jobless, maybe it's time to move back to Marblehead. Try to work things out with my mother."

Bootie placed her hand on Grace's shoulder, but before she could comfort her, a prickling ran down her spine and her eyesight blurred. She saw a vision of Blake holding a stack of heavy books. He was paging through the top one. His face grew larger until she could only see his eyes. Bootie's vision returned to normal, and Grace was looking at her with a worried expression.

"Aunt Bootie, you left me there for a minute."

Bootie tried to make sense of what she saw. "I think Blake is still looking for you Grace, and his obsession with his books is more complicated than we think." Grace shivered, and Bootie reached across to her and hugged her. "We're all exhausted," Bootie said, standing. "Let's call it a night. We'll give the police a chance to find him, and work on a plan in the morning."

Grace slumped in her seat. "Wait. I want to talk to you."

Bootie straightened. "What's the matter?"

How to Dance on the Moon 265

Grace took a deep breath. She gestured toward the bedroom. "I must talk quietly." She rubbed her hands together vigorously. "You asked me once if I had told you the whole story about me and Blake. I had said yes, but you knew I wasn't being truthful. You figured out my secret. I know you did."

Bootie's heart filled with sorrow for Grace, but also with gladness. Grace was sharing what was more painful to her than all her bruises. "Because you let me touch you."

"I need to trust you."

"Talk to me."

Grace rubbed her temples. "One night, early in our friendship, Blake and I were cuddling, and we got caught up in the moment. We slipped, like two teenagers. Then it happened again. And again."

"And now you feel like you betrayed Stephen."

Grace nodded. "Do you have any tissues?"

Bootie rose and went to the bathroom for a box of tissues. Grace pulled one from the box and blew her nose. "It happened only one more time, during an argument. He berated me for not letting him come over one night, and I placated him. On top of the horrible guilt, it made me feel sick that I used sex to control him. He must have sensed my feelings because he became even more dominating. Thinking back, the Breather calls began again after they had stopped for a while." Grace started to cry. She took another tissue and dabbed at her eyes. "This is humiliating."

"Hush." Bootie said. "I'm not judging you. Sex is a powerful force. It seemed unrealistic he would stalk you because he enjoyed your beef stew."

A raspy chuckle slipped out through Grace's sniffles. "Don't make me laugh," she said. "I'm not finished." Grace's sobs grew more intense, but Bootie resisted the urge to rush to her, knowing Grace had to release the emotion. When Grace's crying slowed, she said, "Remember the time I came home and found Blake in my bedroom?"

"Yes."

"When he threw me down on the bed and covered my face with the pillow, I thought I would die. When I could breathe again, I realized Blake had unzipped my pants. I was terrified." Grace sobbed. "I was dizzy, and my chest and head hurt, and I had to make a decision to try to push him off or to let it happen."

"So you let it happen."

"I thought he would be pacified, and leave without hurting me even more. Any issues that came from it I could deal with later. I shut down my feelings and waited for it to be over. It was a poor choice. I should have fought him."

"Was it the only time?"

"Yes. He started to inside the electrical room, but stopped."

"Grace, you were raped. You must tell the police!"

"But I didn't fight him. I let it happen."

"You need to understand what happened to you. I could get you in to see Janet again."

"Auntie, I don't need a psychologist. I need Blake to go away, so I can forget it happened. What I did was terrible, and it's caused all this trouble."

"Listen, Grace. Blake isn't harassing you because you were intimate. He's sick. I'm no expert, but I suspect the best way you could have protected yourself was not to fight. I'm going to help you through this."

"Thank you, Auntie. I love you so much."

"I love you too. Now go to bed. If Jennie wakes up she'll be upset if you aren't there."

"You need sleep, too."

"Don't worry about me."

Grace dabbed her eyes with the tissue balled in her hand, and after hugging Bootie, went to her room. Bootie sat alone for another ten minutes.

How to Dance on the Moon 267

****

Grace found Jennie curled into a kittenish ball in the bed. She locked the door behind her, put on pajamas, and crawled in beside her daughter, sinking into the mattress's soft spots. If the police didn't find Blake, the confrontation they had avoided that night surely would come the next day, and she needed her rest. But even with the warmth coming from her little girl, she dozed fitfully, slipping in and out of slumber, confusing dreams with reality. When she slipped into deep sleep, she dreamed about her father.

She is in her pajamas, walking down a two-lane road. Maple trees with garnet leaves line one side of the road, and on the other side is a harvested cornfield littered with drying stalks. Despite the signs of autumn, the air has a summer balminess that makes her skin feel warm and damp. A sliver-thin moon and flecks of stars provided the only light in the sky. However, everything around her is lit well enough to see easily down the road. Without warning, the road ends at the edge of the lake near the Kurz family home in New Hampshire. She looks up and sees a rabbit sitting on the slim arc of the moon, blowing kisses down at her.

One kiss swoops toward her, like a lightening bug dancing in the dark. As it touches her cheek, a hot, bitter wind whisks her from the road and carries her away through the darkness. She is gently placed inside the first house she remembers living in, the house where she was Just-Grace-All-Alone. People she doesn't know fill the living room, and sitting in a rocking chair is her father, who is home on a visit, taking a break from death. She runs to him, but can't get close because many people are around him, competing for his attention. "Daddy!" she calls out.

"Grace, I'm here!" her father answers. She hasn't heard his voice in thirty years, but she knows it is his. He is speaking to her. To her! Even with all the people trying to get his attention,

Laura Ginter 268

he has chosen to speak to her.

"Daddy! I've missed you so much!"

"I've missed you too. Why don't you go to bed and I'll come in to say goodnight after my meetings."

Grace doesn't want to leave. She is not confident he will come to her. He is dead, and she doesn't know what the rules are for dead people who are allowed a visit with their families. Still, she wants desperately to please him. She goes to bed and waits.

Soon, she sees a shadow in her room. "Daddy?" She calls out hopefully, but it isn't her father. It is the troll from her childhood who lived in her closet. Now it is at the foot of her bed. As she watches, the shadow dissolves and re-forms into Blake.

"Mommy, hug me to sleep," he says.

Grace jerked awake. She forced her eyes open and lifted herself on one elbow to peer into the darkness. Someone was there. The troll? No, a person. Her father? No. Her eyes adjusted to the darkness. A shadow was at the foot of her bed. "Auntie?"

The shadow slid next to her. She smelled MadCrush cologne.

37.

Blake pushed down on Grace with his body and clamped on her throat before she could scream. Jennie tensed under the covers but kept her eyes tightly closed. Blake slipped a thick strap behind Grace's neck and released her long enough to put both ends in one hand. He pushed down on her chest with his free hand. With Jennie awake next to her, Grace could not

How to Dance on the Moon

269

show fear. She lay still, trying to slow her spastic breathing. "I don't want to hurt you," Blake said, whispering. She wanted to turn away from his stale breath, but forced herself to face him. Sweat glistened on his forehead, and his words sounded thick and sticky. "Please don't make me hurt you."

"How did you get in here?" Grace whispered as she inched her hand over to Jennie's.

Blake put his lips up to Grace's ear. "Tell me, Grace. Do you remember when I used to sing to you? And you promised you would love me always?"

Jennie's hand twitched and Grace squeezed it. "Please, let me go, Blake."

A shadow darkened Blake's face. "Do you love me, Grace?"

"Don't ask me that."

"Do you think I am a threat to you?"

Grace didn't respond, and Blake shook his head and closed his eyes. The anguish in his face confounded her. He twisted his hand, and the belt tightened around her neck. "This is sick. I've been waiting hours to see you." He laughed softly. "I could easily make it so I never see you again." Blake moved closer to her face. "Should I do that, Grace? Should I end the misery?"

Blake pulled on the belt, lifting Grace's head up to his and kissed her on the mouth. She felt a sudden stab of pain on her bottom lip and twisted her head away. She tasted blood. He released the belt, made an L with his thumb and forefinger, and flicked his wrist to simulate shooting a gun. Without another word, he rose from the bed, opened the bedroom door, and slipped into the darkness. Grace saw him cut through the parking lot through the window, and rose from the bed to wake Aunt Bootie.

****

"Really, Grace, I don't understand why you didn't scream. I could have called the police. We could have caught him."

Laura Ginter 270

"Jennie was awake in bed next to me. Should I have risked Blake hurting her?" Grace put pressure on the tissue pressed against her bleeding lip. "He bit me. He drew blood. Don't imply I wasn't doing whatever I could to protect my daughter."

Jennie squeezed herself against her mother. "Mommy, you're scaring me more."

"Grace, comfort your daughter," Bootie said. "I'll get you ice for that lip after I call the police."

****

The officer took statements and walked through the house. He found a soda can and an empty cookie box in the attic, and a hairpin stuck in the lock on Grace's bedroom door. After giving Grace another case number and the usual reassurances, he left.

Jennie had fallen asleep on the sofa. Neither Grace nor Bootie could sleep, so Bootie cooked eggs and bacon in her apartment kitchen. Grace said she couldn't eat, and the cooked food smell made Bootie's stomach queasy. She tossed it all in the trash.

At five o'clock, the women were watching an old movie on television. A knock sounded on the tearoom door. Grace whimpered. Bootie descended the stairs to the tearoom and answered the door. Grace eased her way down the stairs to see the officer who had been there two hours earlier. Bootie and the officer spoke for several minutes. When the door closed, Bootie returned to the living room. "They found him," Bootie said.

"Where?" Grace asked

"Sleeping under the bleachers at the sports field about a half mile from here," Bootie replied. "They also found his car at an impound lot. It looked like it had been abandoned." Neither woman spoke for several minutes.

"What happens now?" Grace asked.

Bootie sat and leaned on her forearms. "He was

How to Dance on the Moon 271

incoherent and didn't know his name. He had no wallet and no identification. But he did have a business card in his pocket with a psychiatrist's name. They called the psychiatrist, and after some discussion, they decided to put him in the hospital for observation. He will be there at least seventy-two hours."

"They didn't arrest him? I have four complaints filed!"

"The policeman thinks assault and battery charges will be filed against him, along with restraining order violations, but you must file another report tomorrow, and give them time to review your complaints."

"So what's next?"

"They said they'd call you later this morning with the details."

"Blake was faking it," said Grace. "He pretended to be crazy so they wouldn't arrest him."

"The police are professionals," Bootie said. "All that matters is they have him. It means we are safe for now."

They disappeared into their own thoughts, and the room became quiet. Bootie stood and stretched. "I'm going back to bed for a bit," she said. "You should call Biscuit. He'd want to know. He's been worried about you and Jennie."

"I don't want to wake him."

"He won't mind. He's very much in love with you Grace," Bootie said. "I saw the truth when he grabbed my arm."

"I know."

"How do you feel about him?"

"I'm not sure. He's been amazing. Literally a life saver. But there are too many complications in my life right now. It seems absurd to think about dating when I don't know how to have a day that doesn't involve being afraid. Plus this fat lip may change his feelings."

"I doubt it," said Bootie, and Grace twisted her lips into a crooked, swollen smile.

****

The next morning, Jennie awoke sullen and withdrawn. Grace kept her home from school. A policeman called Grace to inform her Blake's doctor had extended his hospital stay to a fourteen-day involuntary commitment. They would keep her informed regarding his arrest status. Grace and Jennie went home.

Grace called Loretta with the news about Blake and asked about her job. Loretta said she had filled Grace's position, but Grace was free to apply for a different job. A hollow pain of defeat settled in her heart. Whether it was jealousy, or gossip or spite that motivated Loretta, Grace knew now, for certain, Loretta would never let Grace return to work. Later, Violet called to reassure Grace she was doing her best to get Loretta to reconsider her position. Violet is such a good friend, thought Grace.

As the days passed, Grace marked each one off on her calendar, with the 14th day circled in red.

Bootie 1961

38.

On her twenty-fifth birthday, Bootie made the drive to Concord to see her father. She no longer had the elitist attitude she had borne on her eighteenth birthday toward the others in the queue. Now she talked to the other visitors in line, listening to their stories and sympathizing with their challenges. She was, in fact, one of them. One of the people in the line at the prison, no better, no worse.

How to Dance on the Moon 273

This was a chillier trip than the one she had made on her birthday seven years earlier, and the line was shorter. The lilac tree was still there, thicker and taller, but its flowers had dried on their stems. The blossoms were shrunken carcasses of what they had been two weeks earlier. She moved forward until she reached the check-in desk. A guard she did not recognize asked who she was there to visit, and she gave him her father's name. He asked for her name and relationship, had her sign in, and then requested she stand aside. That had never happened before, and Bootie hesitated. The guard saw her quizzical look, and informed her Henry Kurz was a patient in the medical clinic. She needed to wait for an escort to take her to see him.

An orderly wearing scrubs and carrying an oversized key ring came through a different door and called her name. When she approached, he instructed her to follow him. She walked behind him down a hall, into a part of the prison she had never been to. Bright fluorescent lights lit the hall. She saw no windows.

They passed through a locked metal door, and entered a sterile, oppressively warm steel-colored corridor with eight beds, four backed up against each wall. Patients lay in three beds, surrounded by hospital equipment. A room with a large window was at the far end, and a nurse studied her from behind the glass.

The orderly pointed to a bed with an old man lying in it. She recognized him by his red hair. He slept face up, a blanket tucked under his arms, with an IV tube draining into his hand. She could not find a chair, and wasn't sure if she should ask for one. "Father," she said, tentatively. When he did not respond, Bootie raised her arm to get the orderly's attention. "What's wrong with him?" she asked. "Is he unconscious or just asleep?"

"He collapsed this morning in his cell. The doctor hasn't seen him yet. But it's probably alcohol poisoning."

The orderly's diagnosis confused Bootie. "Alcohol

Laura Ginter 274

poisoning? How would he get alcohol poisoning?"

"He needs to sleep it off," the attendant said.

Bootie looked back at her father. More than ever, she couldn't reconcile this fragile, feeble man with the father who lived in her memories. But with sudden clarity, she understood she was done trying, and a door shut in her mind with a thud. It was pointless to look back any more. It was time to accept things for what they were. She thought about Eddie. Was it time to shut that door, too?

Bootie decided not to wake her father. She would return when he was feeling better. After all, the orderly, trained in the medical sciences that he was, had assured her that her father "needed to sleep it off". She asked the orderly to let her out, and she returned to the front desk where she signed out and exited to her car.

Three days later the phone call came from the prison doctor saying Henry Kurz had died. She took the news stoically. With all she had been going through with Eddie, her feeling had been deserting her like the rats off a sinking ship, and she was unable to absorb any more pain. Happy birthday again, Mrs. Baxter, she thought to herself, and dialed Bernice's phone number.

****

It was the first gathering of the six children in over five years. Bernice, who came with her husband Mickey, brought Ike, Scooter, and her two children, Patty and Theodore. The Navy granted Woody a leave, and he came alone. Sellie was pregnant again and had come up from her new home in Marblehead with her husband Dinny in tow. The pain from losing her first baby still hung like smoke in the air around them, and Dinny fussed over her like a midwife, refusing to give her a cigarette, making her sit on pillows.

They held the funeral at the Episcopal Church and added a

How to Dance on the Moon 275

memorial to their mother to the program. Afterward, the Kurz children gathered at the house to celebrate Beulah and Henry Kurz's lives. Their unique, indelible bond, created from sharing childhoods, secrets, and traumas allowed them to savor the simple pleasure of being together, and the party was cheerful, although Clark's absence created a bittersweet undercurrent.

On Sunday afternoon, as Bernice's family was preparing to leave, Bootie announced a family meeting for the Kurz children only. She asked Mickey and Dinny to take Aunt Theo for a drive up to Squam Lake for an ice cream, and when they left, Bootie situated everyone around an old trunk with rusted hinges, pushed against a wall in the barn.

Woody thumped his fist on the trunk. "This old thing has been here forever."

"This is the trunk where the policeman shot the raccoon when Mother and Father were arrested," replied Bootie. And that's why we are here. I want you all to play Truth or Lie. With me." Confused faces looked back at Bootie, but Woody gave her the thumbs up.

"Okay. Truth or Lie? There's a secret treasure inside here. In the barn."

"Bootie, what's this about?" asked Sellie.

"Play along for a minute. There's a secret treasure inside here. Woody?"

"Okay. I'll say lie."

"That's what you said the last time, too."

Bernice shook her head. "What are you talking about?"

Bootie shook her head. "Do you all remember the night on the island when we caught the Eye-Patch Pirate spying on us?"

"Oh my God!" said Sellie. "That was a horrible night!"

"I don't remember it," said Bernice. "Who's the Eye-Patch Pirate?"

"You weren't there. You were babysitting Ike and moping over Mickey. But me and Clark and Woody and Sellie and Scooter all snuck over to the island when Mother and Father were out one night, and we caught this one-eyed man spying on us, who turned out to be an FBI agent. We were playing Truth or Lie, and when it was my turn, I said 'Truth or lie. There's a secret treasure in the barn.' Woody said 'lie' and told me I had the face of a big fat liar. Sellie, do you remember what you said?"

"I remember everything about that horrid night. I said lie, and so did Clark."

"I said 'truth,'" added Scooter. "I always believed everything you said, Bootie."

Bootie's face flushed with excitement. "We never got through the whole game because Woody got mad, sorry Woody, but you did, and we quit playing. I've called this meeting so we can finish it. So, Bernice and Ike. Truth or Lie? There is a secret treasure hidden here in the barn."

"Truth, I guess," said Ike.

"I still don't understand," said Bernice.

"You'll see in a minute. Woody and Ike, can you push this trunk to the side?"

The brothers tugged at the trunk until the wooden planks beneath it were exposed. Under Bootie's direction, they pulled up the planks, exposing the musty earth underneath. Several earwigs scurried for cover. Bootie handed Woody a shovel and asked him to dig where the trunk had sat. Woody shrugged, and started to dig. About twelve inches down, the shovel clanged on metal. He looked at Bootie and smirked. "Is this what I think it is?"

Bootie nodded. Woody shoveled with renewed enthusiasm. "Ike, come help me." The two brothers worked together to free a metal box from the hole. It had "Laconia Savings Bank" printed on its side. Sweat from the exertion glistened on their foreheads before they succeeded in lifting out. Woody turned to his sister. "You should have the honor."

Bootie's hands were shaking as she flipped open the latch where a lock was meant to secure the box. She tugged, and the

How to Dance on the Moon 277

lid lifted open. Inside were bundles of bills, from ones to hundreds. Bootie lifted out one bundle. Most of the bills looked new. Bootie looked at the astounded faces of her siblings. "There are nine more boxes in there."

Sellie was the first to speak. "The police searched this barn twenty times!"

Ike started to laugh. "You've known all this time, haven't you?"

Bootie nodded again. "I knew when I was twelve that Mother and Father were stealing money, and I knew where they were hiding it. But I was too afraid say anything. I almost told you all that night on the island."

"Why didn't you show this to us sooner?" asked Woody. "I could have used this after the trust went away."

Bernice interjected before Bootie could speak. "Don't everyone get excited, here. This money doesn't belong to us. We must return it."

"Return it to who?" asked Bootie. "The FBI? The bank? The prison system that sent Mother to an insane asylum to die? And like Woody said. We can use it. We can split it between us. We'll even save some for Clark."

"If Clark is still alive," said Sellie. "If Harley didn't. . ."

"Don't say that!" Woody's face turned red. "Clark ran away. He came back and got his stuff, and that means he was alive then, and he still is now. He'll come home when he's ready."

"I'm sorry, Woody," said Sellie. "What about Aunt Theo? Should she get money?"

"She doesn't need it. She has stashed plenty of money away over the years, thanks to our old trust fund. And we can't tell her about this. She isn't always careful about what she says to people."

"But the money's old," argued Bernice. "How can we spend it?"

"The money isn't that old," said Scooter. "And the police

stopped looking for it years ago. You can mix these bills in with newer ones, and deposit a little at a time."

"Bootie, again." Woody shook his head. "Why didn't you tell us sooner?"

"I was protecting Father in case he had a chance of getting a new trial. We don't need to anymore. Does everyone agree we should keep the money?"

Everyone spoke at once, and everyone appeared to agree except for Bernice who shook her head. "It doesn't feel right, Bootie."

"Bernice, you have always been the strong one in the family. You were the one who had to save us all after Mother and Father were arrested. You bore the brunt of the work and the responsibility. It isn't because of Aunt Theo we are here today. It's because of you." Bernice's eyes filled with tears and Bootie took her hand.

"You deserve this money the most. I promise, and believe me, I know these things, nothing bad will happen if we take the money. Nobody will be hurt. And we can put some aside to maintain the house and even some for Clark. We'll make a promise that someone from the family will always live here, and we'll never sell it as long as any of us is alive. We will always leave a light in the living room window for Clark until he comes home again. It will be our refuge. And Aunt Theo can live at the house as long as she wants."

Bootie put her hand upside down into the circle of brothers and sisters, and one at a time, each sibling added theirs to the top. Bernice smiled and put hers on last, forming a complete bond of criminal complicity and familial loyalty.

Woody continued to dig for lock boxes until a screech from Scooter drew the group's attention. Scooter pointed to a space in the wall behind where the trunk had been sitting. Ike reached in and pulled out a white shirt, some blue jeans and a yellow biscuit tin. Ike opened the lid. Inside, baseball cards were stacked in neat piles. Clark's baseball cards. All the Kurz

How to Dance on the Moon 279

children looked at each other. Nobody spoke. Nobody could. Nobody knew what to say.

39.

After her father's funeral, Bootie began to recover from her melancholy over the uncertainty of her marriage. She had not heard from Eddie in weeks, and she realized she didn't care as much. The details of his face and the intimacies of their married life were fading with the ebbing summer heat. She had to leave the past behind and move forward. Eddie was not coming back for her.

It had been a chilly week, but the air had turned warm again. Bootie brought her laundry outside to hang on the clothesline, rather than use the new dryer Aunt Theo had bought. She set the laundry basket on a large flat rock, and pulled out a handful of wooden clothespins from a bag and clipped them across the line. The heat on her face from the sun soothed her. Happiness came easier when the weather was pleasant.

Bootie spun around when she heard her name called out, and had to steady herself against the tree trunk. She stared at the man standing there, demanding more evidence than what her eyes were showing her. That her gift wasn't playing a cruel trick on her. When she had no doubt left in her mind the man was truly Eddie, spiffed and shined in his dress uniform, her body froze, solid and cold as an ice cube. She didn't know what she was supposed to do. Run to him with hugs and kisses, or slap him and demand he leave. So she just stared at him.

He grinned at her sheepishly. "How are you?" he asked. She was acutely aware she was blushing.

"My father died."

"I know. It's why I'm here."

Eddie's reply took Bootie by surprise and added to her discomfort. "A good excuse to take a leave?" she asked, curtly.

Eddie cleared his throat. "I was hoping we could talk." Bootie nodded, turned her back on him, and lifted a blouse from the basket, clipping a sleeve to the line. "Do you want to go get a milkshake and hamburger?" he asked.

"No. We've done that before. It just led to trouble. Whatever you have to say, say it here."

Eddie sidled over to the tree stump and scooted the clothes basket to the side so he could sit. He handed Bootie a pink gingham blouse he had bought for her two birthdays past. She looked at him warily, and took the blouse from him. With shaking hands, she clipped it to the line. He picked up another blouse, and handed it to her. She fumbled with the clothespin again, but managed to get the blouse hung. Soon a rhythm developed between them, and he stood and followed her down the line until the task was completed.

Eddie placed the basket on the ground and led Bootie back to the stump, indicating he wanted her to sit. She complied, bracing herself. She still could not believe he was standing there, so handsome and tall and strong, looking down at her with kindness in his eyes. It was sweetly familiar but at the same time painfully foreign. She knew he wanted to ask her for a divorce. Why else would he come back? And he would steal her chance to end things in her own time and in her own way. It wasn't fair of him.

Eddie took her hands, and enveloped them in his own warm and protective hands. He took a deep breath, and Bootie lowered her head and squeezed her eyes shut. "Is it that hard for you to look at me?" he asked sadly.

"Yes," she replied and, thinking she could salvage some self-respect, decided to say the words first. "I want a divorce."

"Bootie, I must say something."

How to Dance on the Moon   281

"You must leave."

After a pause, Eddie said, "I guess I deserve that. But let me talk. When I'm finished, if you still want a divorce, I will give you one." He cleared his throat again. "I'm nervous. Isn't it funny?" Bootie didn't think it was funny at all, but she opened her eyes and peeked up at him. Eddie clutched her hands tighter. "We didn't know each other when we got married, did we?"

Bootie clenched her teeth. "Obviously."

"I decided to go on this tour without you because I needed to be alone for awhile. I wasn't sure marriage was for me. And the work pressures were making me resent having responsibilities to another person."

"And that would be me?"

"I needed to see if I would be happier on my own. If I was, it would have been wrong to keep you from a better life."

"How thoughtful of you."

"But I have regretted my decision to go to West Germany without you. I know now I love you, Bootie, and I've missed you and I want to be with you. Will you come back to Mannheim with me?"

Bootie pulled her hands free and stood, turning away from him. She would not cry. "Those are the words I have wanted to hear for eighteen months. I've heard them many times in my head, almost exactly as you just spoke them. I have even rehearsed what I would say to you, and all my responses ended with happily-ever-after. But this isn't a fairy tale, Eddie. We aren't a fairy tale."

Bitterness swelled inside her, black and needle sharp. She turned to face him. "You say you love me, and you know now you want to be with me. Did you think your little epiphany would be enough to erase the heartache you have put me through? How arrogant to think you could walk up to me and say you have regrets and think I would leave with you."

"You are right."

Laura Ginter 282

"Why didn't you say these things in your letters? Why didn't you give me any hope if this is how you were feeling? You haven't written in weeks."

"You know my work is classified. I can't always write you. There is still a covert war going on in Europe. Besides, you could tell me to go to hell easier in a letter than in person. So right or wrong, here I am."

"Wrong. I still want a divorce. You should take me up on it before I change my mind."

"Bootie." He spoke her name as though she were an unreasonable child.

"Don't patronize me."

"I don't mean to patronize you, and I don't want a divorce, and I don't think you do, either. I'm sorry I left you behind and I was so cold. Forgive me?" He paused, and took her hand.

"Mister me and Missus you, with you I will stay, to you I'll be true. Though our lives will go by our love will never die, it will always be you and me, a love song for two, Mister me, Missus you. I have six more months in Mannheim. Please come."

Bootie had never wished more than at that moment to see inside Eddie's heart. How could she go back to him, open herself up to him again until she knew if his words were sincere? How did she know he wasn't just bored or lonely, and saw her as an easy fix? She could not survive him tossing her aside again. She looked into her husband's eyes. He was right. She did not want a divorce. Bootie put her hand to her chest. "How long are you here for?"

"A week."

"You have seven days to convince me to go."

A grin splashed across Eddie's face. "Thank you. I've done it before, I can do it again."

Bootie ultimately agreed to move to Germany with Eddie, and at twenty-five, she began her second marriage to her husband. Bruised and wary, she clung to the flimsy olive branch Eddie extended to her, and committed to working with

How to Dance on the Moon 283

him to put their troubles behind them and rebuild their life together.

****

Eddie's next tour was at Fort Lewis, in Washington State, and the army promoted him to captain. Bootie took a job waitressing at a hamburger shack just off base. The work was hard, but Bootie enjoyed it, her self-esteem rejuvenated by feeling useful again. Growing up in a large family with no parents had taught Bootie independence and self-sufficiency. Being an Army officer's wife had taught her how to be alone. Now, her job brought her confidence. She had come a long way from the little girl who ate her meals in the pantry.

Bootie's life fell into a relaxed and comfortable rhythm, even though the damage to her marriage hadn't repaired completely. She still loved Eddie but she never trusted his sincerity when he said kind words or showed her affection. She believed he was only masking his ambivalence toward their marriage. For the first time she regretted not having children. Conversely, she was also relieved there were no children to make things more complicated.

Four years into their second marriage, Eddie told Bootie the army had reassigned him to West Germany for another two years. He waited for Bootie's reaction. Bootie interpreted this silence to mean, once again, she was not included in the shipment of household goods. She realized with painful clarity he was slipping away again, like sand through her fingers.

The urge to reverse the slide overwhelmed her. She wanted to demand he take her with him, but when she tried to speak, she froze, fearing rejection. She couldn't bear to hear the words said aloud. Rather than fight for him and lose, she chose not to fight at all. It was better to pretend his going alone was what they both wanted. And hadn't this moment always been inevitable? Eddie was leaving her, and this time, he would be leaving her forever.

She encouraged Eddie to follow the path that led to happiness, and reassured him she would survive fine on her own. No one mentioned divorce, but its shadowy haunt took residence in Bootie's kitchen.

On the day Eddie was to leave, she hugged him and looked at him expectantly, hoping beyond hope that there was still time for him to realize he was making a mistake. That he would say, "I can't go without you. Let's try one more time. I love you. I'll listen more. I'll be a better husband. I'll make you happy." His eyes were sad and sunken, resting deep in his skull. After a long pause, he finally said, "If you want to come, you can."

The desire to grab him and kiss him and ask him to wait while she packed almost overpowered her. But something stopped her. She thought about his words, and realized they weren't the right ones. There was no commitment in them. No words of regret, of love, of desire. It would have been better if he'd said nothing. She replied, "If you want to come back, you can."

"I will."

"No, this time you won't be back." She turned away and let him go.

****

Bootie tucked her tennis shoes into her work bag. She checked her appearance in the mirror and reached for her lipstick in her purse. Six weeks had passed since Eddie had left, and Bootie's melancholy was subsiding. The future was becoming a less scary place. A place where better things awaited her. As much as her New Hampshire roots had tugged her eastward, she had resisted repeating her old habits. It was time to create her individual destiny. She had stayed at Fort Lewis and kept her job at the hamburger shack, taking the time

How to Dance on the Moon   285

she needed to make a thought-out, sensible decision about her future.

She drew the lipstick across her lips and felt an unexpected sense of peace. But as she replaced the cap to her lipstick tube, her eyes blurred, and the room went away, replaced with a black emptiness. Bootie braced against whatever vision she was about to see, but nothing appeared, and her normal sight returned. Bootie knew something dreadful was about to happen.

A knock at the front door interrupted her thoughts, and when Bootie peeked through the window, she saw two men in military dress uniforms were standing with hat in hand. She opened the door. The younger man had the hiccups, but eventually the words came out. He extended an envelope to her and said, "Mrs. Baxter, we regret to inform you. . . "

****

After Eddie's funeral, Bootie made an appointment with a major who had detailed information about Eddie's accident. She examined the major's aura as he recounted the events that led to Eddie's death. *Captain Baxter died during a rescue mission. He was airlifting an ailing American child from West Berlin to a hospital in Mannheim when his helicopter engine stalled. The chopper crashed to the ground in East Germany and burned. Everyone was killed.* The major's aura was milky except around his face where a gloomy gray shadow convinced Bootie he didn't know anything firsthand, and had only said what he had been told to say. She thanked the major, and after meeting with a personnel officer to review her survivor benefits, she went home. It was then she received the only vision of Eddie she would ever have.

In a lonely, reflective moment, she placed his largest Army medal to her cheek. When the medal touched her skin, it warmed her, and pulsed with a heartbeat's rhythm, and Eddie's face appeared. He spoke, but she could not understand his words. However, he was clearly alive.

Bootie played the vision in her mind repeatedly. Maybe she had misread the message. But if she hadn't, and Eddie was alive, why would the military want her, and everyone else too, to believe he had died? Did Eddie want her to think he was dead? They had virtually ended their marriage when he left for West Germany. Did she have the right to interfere at this point? Probably not. Whatever the truth was, and regardless of how much she loved Eddie, she wasn't in a position to take on the military and fight this battle. It was clear she was supposed to have a different life, although she had no idea what that life might be. Her gift never gave her any insights into her own future.

Fort Lewis was now a place of bad memories. It was time to go back to the lake house. It was her sanctuary, her emotional cocoon. She quit her job at the hamburger shack, emptied the bank account, and packed her Chevy station wagon with everything she could fit into it, arranging for the army to ship the rest.

An hour into her trip, road construction detoured Bootie off the freeway. Rain began to pelt her windshield, and it disoriented her. She pulled her Chevy into a parking lot to examine her roadmap. A sunbeam split through the rain and pierced the windshield. She shielded her eyes and reached to pull down the sun visor.

As if emerging magically from the light, a two story brick building with forest green wood siding glued across the front of the first floor came into view. With a blue door, yellow shutters and a prominent FOR SALE sign staring out at her from disproportionately large picture windows, the structure seemed too tall for its base and had the illusion of a tilt toward the left. Its inspiration seemed to come from a toddler's preschool drawing rather than a thought-out architectural design.

The optimistic freshness of a new blue awning appeared

How to Dance on the Moon 287

incongruous with the rest of the timeworn exterior, but it improved the building's street appeal. A sign atop a tall post in the parking lot had a working clock that told the correct time, and confidently proclaimed the tenant to be *Luna Park Tea Room.* A rainbow glistened behind it.

Slumped in the doorway, contemplating its knees, sat a handmade scarecrow flanked by fat pumpkins, encouraging guests to enter and escape the autumn rain. Like young, romantic love, Bootie knew at first sight the misshapen, abused and style-confused building was meant to be hers. Her Kansas farmhouse, appearing to her in a glorious burst of clarity when, spinning out from her own personal tornado, her misdirected quest for happiness led her to what would be her own front door. A rosy energy filled her with anticipation. Her journey was over. Bootie left her car and walked to the tearoom entrance. She held her breath and opened the door.

On the first night in her new home, in her pajamas, she christened *Bootie's Tea Room* with a Rainier Beer and created her menu that would not change for thirty years.

Bootie and Grace 1979

40.

On New Years Day, Ike called Bootie with news that sent Bootie straight to the airport for the next flight to Boston. Gil Abram had married another woman.

Bernice met Bootie at Logan Airport and together they drove to the lake house. They kept the conversation light, talking about the tearoom and catching up on Patty's and

Laura Ginter 288

Theodore's latest achievements. When Grace and Ike met them at the front door, Bootie asked, "How is she?"

"The doctor said she'll be okay," Ike said, squeezing Grace's hand, but the medicine that emptied her stomach made her sick. She'll be feeling poorly for a day or so. She won't talk to anyone right now."

"The doctor thinks she was just looking for attention," Grace said. "She got what she was wanted."

"It was a close call," Ike added.

"Has anyone told Aunt Theo?"

"No. She's having trouble adjusting to the retirement home. No one wanted to upset her more."

Bootie removed her coat and gloves, and entered Sellie's bedroom without waiting for an invitation. Her sister was in a chair by the window. She sat like a little girl, her legs curled under and her arms tucked up into her robe's sleeves. Her make-up was on, applied perfectly as usual, but Bootie was struck by the haggardness in her sister's face. Sellie was forty-two years old, and the abuse she had been put through, and had put herself through, radiated from her aura like neon. How could anybody miss the depression hanging on her like a shroud?

Sellie looked up and smiled weakly. "They dragged you all the way out here for me?"

Bootie knelt by her sister's chair and gave her a hug. "I should have come back sooner. You should have told me what was happening."

Sellie smirked. "You didn't see it coming?'

"No, Sellie. How are you feeling?"

"For eleven years Gil's been making promises to me. Dressing me up and showing me off like an expensive necklace, while swearing on his mother's grave he would never get married again. But everyone knows a man won't marry a woman he's lived with first. And look at me now. I'm ugly! I'm old and ugly!" Her face exploded into bitter tears, and Bootie

How to Dance on the Moon 289

did her best to hold her. "Sellie. You are still the most beautiful women I've ever known. Maybe this is good. You'll finally be able to move forward. There is a whole world out there for you to enjoy.

Sellie's gaze hardened. "How would you know, Bootie? Have you ever been reeled in, over and over by some jackass, just to be continually thrown back, like a stinky old jellyfish hooked by mistake?"

Bootie bristled. She did know how it felt to have the man you love desert you, but she tried to see herself through her sister's eyes. Sellie didn't know she and Eddie had separated a second time before his death. And Bootie had never been a victim of a man's temper as Sellie had. "Sellie, I do know how it feels to lose a husband, like you did with Dinny."

Sellie's expression softened. "Dinny, the perfect man. Why did he have to get leukemia? I'd be happy with him, I know it. Why do these things happen to me, Bootie?"

Grace knocked at the door and stepped inside the room. "Mom, Stephen is here."

Sellie exploded. "Tell him to leave now! I never want him in this house again. And I forbid you to see him again, Grace. I'm your mother and this time you will do as I say."

Grace stiffened. Bootie tried to massage Sellie's shoulder, but Sellie pulled away. "Tell him!" she shouted, and Grace fled the room.

Bootie said, "Sellie, that was harsh. This isn't Stephen's fault. Don't blame him. He came to see you because he's worried about you. Don't do this to your daughter. Remember when Father forbid Bernice to see Mickey? What if she had done what he said? We wouldn't have Patty and Theodore."

"I don't care. I can't have that boy near me. And don't you ever compare me to Father again." Sellie went to her bed and curled into a ball under her covers. Please leave me alone."

Bernice was waiting for Bootie when she left the room. "Are Woody and Scooter coming?" Bootie asked.

Bernice grinned. "Scooter will kill you if you call him Scooter."

"Okay, Woody and William?"

"Woody took emergency leave and he's picking William up on his way here. I told William not to come, but he said his new chair makes it easier to travel. The worst is behind us now, but we must help Sellie get through the next week or so."

"We're worried about Gracie, too," said Ike, joining the conversation. "She's been fighting with her mother a lot, and she and Stephen are so close. I think she's going to bail on us."

"What do you mean, bail on us."

"We think she's going to leave home," said Bernice. "And if she does, she won't be back. She's had it with her mother."

"But Grace abandoning Sellie would be the worst thing that could happen to Sellie right now. Can we stop her?"

"Grace is eighteen," said Ike. "We have to let her go. And I would understand."

"Don't say that, Ike. You cannot make it okay for her to leave. I must talk to her. Where is she?"

"She's in the kitchen with Stephen," said Bernice.

Bootie found Grace making coffee. Grace gestured to Stephen. "Aunt Bootie, we want to talk to you. Do you want coffee?"

Bootie shook her head.

Grace poured out two cups and handed one to Stephen. "We have a secret, and you can't tell anyone." Grace said. "We are going to Connecticut to get married this weekend. We've been planning this for a month. Before all this happened. And we're not going to let Mom's bad behavior stop us."

"Now that you are here, we want you to come with us," said Stephen. "Will you?"

Bootie could not hide her shock. "This weekend? This is the worst possible time, Gracie. Your mother needs you. Don't you care anything about her?"

"I care about the woman in there, but she's never been my

How to Dance on the Moon 291

mother. I've been more of a mother to her."

"She's done the best she can."

"But can't you see through her game? She's trying to control me with all these dramatics. And you, too."

"You almost lost your mother yesterday. You think this is a game for her?"

"Yes. And by getting married I'm showing her I'm not playing."

"Do you agree, Stephen?" Stephen nodded. "You two cannot get married. You are only eighteen. You aren't ready."

Grace's eyes grew wide. "How can you say that? You got married when you were eighteen. And Stephen is nineteen."

Bootie's anger made it difficult to keep her hands from shaking. "But I was an adult, and you are still a child. I did something you still must do before I can consider you an adult. When my father was in prison, I went to see him, and I told him I loved him and I forgave him for what he did to our family. I grew up that day. You must show some compassion and tell your mother you love her, too."

Bootie's voice trembled. "Your mother lost her parents when she was eleven years old. She witnessed men abusing her aunt. She watched her brother almost get killed, and mourned him when he disappeared without a trace. She lost a baby when she was younger than you. Then she lost the one man in her life who genuinely loved her. Now she has been deserted again. All us Kurz children went through hell growing up, but we all made it through to the other side except for your mother. You think she's trying to control you? She doesn't even know how to control herself. She may be beautiful, but she is damaged, and you have to find compassion in your heart. If you can't, then I have to say you are not ready to be an adult. Forget about getting married."

Grace rose from the table, her cheeks red. "Don't you dare ask me to forgive my mother." Bootie slammed her hand on the table and Grace ran from the room with Stephen behind

Laura Ginter 292

her.

Bernice came into the kitchen. "I heard that," she said, gently. "Are you all right?"

Bootie threw her arms into the air. "What is wrong with that girl? Her mother almost died yesterday."

"Woody and William are here. We thought we'd all go to Sellie together."

Bootie took a deep breath and looked at her sister. "Should I try to get Grace to join us?"

Bernice shook her head. "Let Grace think about what you said for a bit."

Bernice and Bootie went to the living room and Bootie greeted her brothers. Ike knocked on Sellie's door, and they all went inside. Sellie was still lying on the bed, facing the door with her eyes closed. "Sellie?" said William, maneuvering his wheelchair to her side. "Woody and I are here, and we want to say. . ." His voice broke and he stopped.

Ike picked up where William left off. "We want to say we hope you feel better."

Bernice said, "We love you Sellie, and whatever you need us to do, we'll do it."

Bootie swiped at a tear on her cheek. "I know where Bernice hides her Seventeen magazines if you want one." Sellie opened one eye and frowned.

Woody said, "She doesn't want a stupid girl magazine, Bootie. She wants my Dick Tracey comics. She sneaks them when she thinks I'm not looking."

Ike said, "I don't know anything about that stuff. I just know Sellie makes better Spam sandwiches than Bootie does."

Bootie put her hands on her hips. "Sellie puts jelly on hers so you'll eat them while she sneaks out to smoke cigarettes."

Sellie groaned. "Stop it! You guys are annoying."

William said, "William White-Eye Shipburner here. You're right. These smelly old pirates don't deserve a princess like you. If you want me to make anyone walk the plank, you let me

How to Dance on the Moon 293

know, Sellie, and I'll run 'em off!"

Sellie rolled onto her back and opened her eyes. "Run them all off, White-Eye!" Sellie smirked. "Except Bernice. I need her to fix my hair."

Woody said. "Why bother. Can't fix ugly."

Sellie sat up, pulled her pillow from behind her head and threw it at Woody. "Shut up Bratman. Can't fix stupid, either." She smiled.

"Hey you guys," said Bernice. "I'm in charge here. Let's all be nice to each other, just for today." Bernice put her hand upside down into the center of the siblings. "For Sellie."

One by one, each brother and sister added a hand. Sellie put hers on last, forming a complete stack. "To the Kurz kids," said Bootie.

The bedroom door opened, and Grace peeked in. "Can I come in?"

Sellie looked at her daughter. "Can we speak privately please?"

The siblings looked at each other. "Of course," said Bootie.

"Can Aunt Bootie stay?" asked Grace.

Sellie nodded, and the room emptied of all but Bootie, Grace and Sellie. Sellie's eyes narrowed. "What do you want, Grace?"

Grace stood, clutching her elbows. "I want to tell you, Mother; I love you, and hope you feel better."

Sellie showed no emotion. "Is Stephen still here?"

"No. He left."

"Are you going to see him again?"

Grace looked at Bootie. "I want to marry him."

Bootie gasped. "Grace, not now!"

Sellie waved her hand in the air. "It's okay, Bootie. Grace, I love you, too. More than you will ever know or believe. You are my baby girl. I want you to follow your heart. Don't worry that someday it will explode on you. It is your destiny as a member of this family. I guarantee it. Now go, please."

Laura Ginter 294

Grace reached down and put her arms around her mother. Sellie did not hug her daughter back, but she did grasp her hand and squeeze it.

Bootie and Grace 1993

41.

By the fifth day of Blake's hospital stay, a pleasant routine had returned to Grace's life. Jennie was at home after school every day, and they were painting her bedroom pink. Grace had pulled out her resume and was reading the want ads. Biscuit had stopped in twice with Chinese food, and it amused Grace to watch his uncharacteristically adolescent awkwardness when he was around her.

Grace called the hospital every day for an update on Blake's progress. On day number five, she still did not know what would happen when the hospital discharged him, but she had nine more days until it became an issue. Dealing with her problems with Blake was not part of a normal day. Normal was all she could handle right now.

Grace was pulling eggs from the refrigerator when the telephone rang. "How are you girls doing?" Aunt Bootie asked.

"There's no school, and Jennie's friend Lucy came over to play. It's the first time in weeks."

"I'm happy for you both," said Bootie.

"How's your lunch crowd today?" Grace asked her aunt.

"Busy for eleven thirty, but Faye is here." Aunt Bootie paused, then added, "Do you have a minute?"

"What's wrong?" Grace asked, not sure she wanted to

How to Dance on the Moon 295

know.

"I've been thinking about Blake and his books."

The subject of Aunt Bootie's concern took Grace by surprise. "What about them?"

"If Blake shot and killed two people, at some point he had a gun. And he would have disposed of it or hidden it. Have you ever had a vision of Blake with a gun?"

"No, Aunt Bootie, I don't have visions. What does all this have to do with Blake's books?"

"What if he had hidden the gun inside a book? Cut out the pages and put the gun inside? People hide things in books all the time. It's a cliché. And what if he had hidden that book in your house? It would explain why he obsessed about getting his books back after you sent him away."

"Which means if he has his books, he has his gun? But none of this matters if Blake's going to jail."

"How do you know he's going to jail?" Aunt Bootie's tone was mistrustful. "And if he does, what if he makes bail?"

Grace took a breath to calm her nerves. "Is your gift telling you something?"

"It's telling me not to dismiss this gun issue. If he retrieved his gun but didn't have it when the police found him, he must have hidden it again."

"In Oregon somewhere?"

"I don't think he would bring a murder weapon back into Oregon. Does he have other friends in the area?"

"No. He didn't live here long."

"Then your house is probably the only place he could safely hide it. And if the gun is there, it means he'll be back. And what if Jennie stumbles across it?"

"I don't know. There are a lot of what-ifs in this story."

"But it's not a lot of what-ifs. I've seen pictures."

Grace could sense her aunt pacing the floor. "Pictures in a vision?"

"He's a ticking time bomb."

Goosebumps rose on Grace's arms. "You are right."

Bootie continued. "When I was a child, I had a powerful vision warning me to find a hidden gun. But I didn't, and that gun was the catalyst for my brother Clark running away. I never saw Clark again. I have had the same type of vision about Blake."

"Where do you think he would hide it?"

"I would look outside around the house, first, where he could get to it easily. I want to come help you look for it. I might find it quicker than you can. And maybe I'll see that there isn't a gun at all. But I doubt that."

"Okay. Your insights would be helpful."

"I'll come after lunch."

"Auntie?"

"Yes, dear?"

"Thank you. And can you bring those dahlia bulbs if they're ready? Jennie and I dug a garden for them in the back yard. I could use about six or eight."

"Of course. It's too early to plant them, but you can store them."

"What would I do without you?"

"I wish I had a snappy answer to that question."

Grace hung up the phone and went to check on Jennie and Ann, who were playing dolls in Jennie's bedroom. All was quiet, and Grace closed the bedroom door, replaying her aunt's words in her mind. When Aunt Bootie had a feeling about something, it was best to take it seriously. And she was right. Blake was insane. His hospitalization had instilled in Grace a false sense of security, and she had not followed up with the police on what would happen to Blake in just a few days. She still hesitated when she turned a corner in a supermarket aisle, walked to her car, or entered her house. What if Blake didn't go to jail? She and Jennie would have to move to a place where he couldn't find them. Live in a self-imposed exile. Would they be safe even then?

How to Dance on the Moon 297

Grace went to her pile of case numbers stacked on the kitchen counter, and spread them. Seeing them helped her remember she was living with an illusion that had to stop. Lunch could wait. She pulled out the card with most current case number, and phoned the policeman whose name was on the card, leaving a message for him to call her back. Then Grace did something most people never do in their lives. She began to search her home for a murderer's gun.

****

Bootie held the phone in her hand, listening to the dial tone. Anxiety coursed through her blood and spread like an oil slick. Ignoring prescient warnings were mistakes that could kill a person. When she set the phone in its cradle, a new vision punched its way into her head.

Pictures formed and moved around in a disjointed rhythm. Her family, living and dead. Mother and Father, Grace, Eddie, Aunt Theo and Clark, Agent Chandler, the snarly, perverse face of Harley. The faces expanded and contracted, blurring before clearing into three-dimensional clarity. They cycled repeatedly, and swirled and blended. The whirlwind of images whipped around faster, coalescing into one single picture that torpedoed free from the chaos as all the rest blew away. She saw Blake in Grace's kitchen, holding Harley's luger, the barrel smoking.

Bootie dropped into the nearest chair, the dread in her stomach weighing her down like an anchor. She was stunned, and confused by the images, but one fact had emerged, clear and bold. If there had been any doubt before, there was none now. If they didn't find Blake's gun, he would use it on Grace. Bootie was not going to ignore *this* warning. She had failed to save Clark, but she would not fail to save Grace.

Bootie stood and retrieved her coat and purse, and found Erline in the kitchen with Faye. Erline took one look at her friend's face and whisked her out the front door. "Go," Erline

Laura Ginter 298

said. "We'll be fine."

Bootie opened the door and lobbed her purse over to the passenger seat, looking back toward her tearoom. Through the window, she could see the garden lights twinkling on her silk Ficus tree, illuminating the adjacent relics. Her heart swelled as she observed her creation from a detached distance, seeing the tearoom as a visitor would.

Erline was standing at a table, laughing with customers as she picked up their dirty plates and balanced them on her forearm. Bootie loved Erline. She could not have managed the tearoom without Erline. She could not have managed her life's special challenges without Erline. A bittersweet nostalgia overwhelmed her, but instead of soothing her, it made her weary. Abruptly, she turned away from the building and got into her car. The past was the past. It was time to get the gun and save Grace.

****

At the same moment, Grace was searching the shrubbery that framed her house, working her way from the back yard to the front. Like a dog scratching for an old bone, she looked for soft dirt where someone might have buried something.

A shadow fell beside her, and Grace looked up to see Jennie. "Where's Ann?"

"She left."

"I hope she didn't walk home by herself."

"Her mom met her on the way. I made her scared."

She took her daughter's hand, and they sat together on the grass. "How did you scare her?"

"I told her I smelled Blake."

Grace touched her little girl's hand. "Blake's in the hospital, Jennie. He's with doctors."

Jennie looked into her mother's eyes. "I don't think so. And Aunt Bootie is right. Blake has a gun."

How to Dance on the Moon 299

"Jennie! It's impolite to listen in on other people's phone calls."

"I saw it, Mommy. I saw the gun."

Grace grabbed Jennie by the arms. "For real this time?"

"In my head. It's real."

A shadow darkened the window in the garage door, and was gone. Jennie pointed and shrieked. "It's Blake! He's here! He's in the garage!"

Grace turned to look, then reached for her daughter and wrapped her in her arms to stop her from shaking. "No, Jennie. A cloud moved in front of the sun. Blake is in the hospital. He's not here. We are safe."

"Really? You know it?"

"Yes, I know it. I called the hospital this morning." She stroked Jennie's hair until the little girl relaxed. She decided the search for the gun could wait until Aunt Bootie arrived. "Are you hungry?" she asked her daughter. "Let's boil eggs. I'll teach you how to make egg salad."

Jennie looked up at her mother and nodded. Together they stood, and Grace led her daughter into the kitchen. She pulled a chair next to the stove for Jennie to stand on, and took an egg carton from the refrigerator, unaware her panicked Aunt Bootie was now racing to reach Grace. She had seen another vision.

****

Grace filled a pot with water and set it on the stove. Once the water began to boil, she allowed Jennie to drop eggs into the pot with a large spoon and set the timer. Jennie brought playing cards down from her room, and they played a game of Old Maid. Before they could start a second game, the buzzer sounded. Grace scooped up the cards and handed them to Jennie. "Put these back in your bedroom, okay?" she said, and Jennie ran from the kitchen.

Grace stepped back to the stove and removed the cooked eggs. The phone rang. The handset was beside the stove and she picked it up.

"Hello, Grace."

"No!" Grace screamed into the phone. A cool breeze brushed her arms.

"This is Stan Bean. Turn around."

Grace whipped around and her breath caught in her throat. Blake took a step toward her. A sour, sweaty sheen covered his face, as streaky and red as an infected wound. His eyes were glassy, and he was slumped like an old man. He looked thirty years older than when she had first met him. His overcoat hung on his frame. He stared at her blankly, his hands hanging at his side.

"Honey, I'm home." He came closer, stopping at the far end of the kitchen counter. "Why is your door unlocked? That's not safe."

Grace pushed the buttons on the handset for 911, but Blake yanked the phone base from the jack and threw it behind him. It split apart when it hit the floor. Grace dropped the handset. "You can't be here."

"Where is Jennie?"

Jennie stepped into the hallway from the living room entry and stood behind Blake.

"Jennie went down to Ann's house. She saw you, and she is calling 911!" Grace shooed Jennie with her hand. Jennie stared at her mother with large, unblinking eyes and shook her head.

Blake looked confused. "No, she didn't. I just got here."

Grace shooed Jennie again. "Go!"

"Why would I go?" Blake asked. "What are you looking at?" He glanced over his shoulder as Jennie disappeared back into the living room.

"Leave now or I am going to go to the big bedroom, lock the door, call 911, and hide under the bed," Grace said loudly.

How to Dance on the Moon   301

"What the hell are you talking about?" Blake asked, scowling. "Aren't you happy to see me?"

"Why aren't you in the hospital?"

"I didn't like it there. I decided to come home. Can you make me lunch?"

"I have a restraining order against you. I've filed police reports."

Blake straightened. His eyes focused on Grace's. His mouth curled into a snarl. "You know what? I should have a restraining order against you. You are the bad person, here. Not me." He took two more steps toward her. If he reached out he could touch her. "Leave my house!" he said. "Go on! Get out of here! You are evil!"

"Please, Blake."

Blake glanced around the kitchen. "They took my car. I don't know where it is. I have no home, no money, my things are gone. They said they are going to arrest me. Why would they do that? Do you know why they would do that? Amanda are you listening? You dug a beautiful garden outside. Let's plant it after lunch."

Blake took another step toward her. Grace wondered if Jennie had gone to Grace's room and called the police. She remembered the pan of scalding water left over from the cooked eggs, and she grasped the handle. Blake chuckled. "What are you going to do? Hit me with a pot?"

"Not if you leave."

"But I have presents for you." Blake reached in his pocket, pulled out a paper folded in quarters. He opened it and showed Grace the picture he had taped inside Jennie's closet. He reached in his other pocket and pulled out a white paper rose. He stretched out his hands for her to take her gifts.

"I don't want them."

"Okay," He dropped them on the floor. Grace adjusted her hand on the pot handle. "You have your presents, now. Let's go plant a garden." He reached for Grace as she heaved the pot at him with both hands. Burning water spilled onto her arm. Blake yelped as water hit his face. He hurled himself past her to the sink and splashed water from the faucet onto his skin. Grace tried to run, but she slipped and fell. She latched onto a cabinet and pulled herself up, but she slipped again. Her knee slammed against the floor. Blake lifted her and pulled her to him. She pelted him on the face, aiming for his burns. Blake shrieked and released her. He held his face.

Grace latched onto a chair for balance, taking care not to fall. Blake was now behind her. She charged toward the stairs, hoping to get to her room and find Jennie inside calling the police, but stopped abruptly. Jennie was squatting next to the sofa in the living room. If Blake took four steps, he would see her.

"Grace! Don't move!" Blake's voice grew louder. "We must plant our garden."

Grace turned to face him, trying to slow her breathing, trying not to look at Jennie. Blake pulled a handgun from his coat pocket. Her breath caught in her throat. "Please," she pleaded, trembling, "put that away. You're hurt. Let me call an ambulance."

Blake took a step toward her "We'll have pretty, blonde and red-headed roses. A treasure chest of roses. Let's go look, Amanda." Blake took another step toward Grace. "Let's look at the hole."

She moved closer to him to prevent him from getting any closer to the living room entryway. She peeked quickly to the side, and didn't see Jennie.

"Let's go outside, Amanda."

Grace forced a smile. Her voice cracked. "Okay. That sounds nice. You show me the garden. I'll follow you."

He glanced over Grace's shoulder. "Look who's here!" Grace panicked and turned to see if Jennie had come up behind her. Blake's gunstock swept toward the back of her head.

How to Dance on the Moon 303

****

Bootie threw her car into park and rushed to Grace's open front door. She called out for Grace, then Jennie. There was no response. She stepped inside and saw the broken telephone base. Making her way into the kitchen, she slipped on the wet floor as she assimilated the mayhem around her. Activity outside the window drew her eye, and a fluttery gasp escaped from her throat. Grace was lying face down in a dirt pit. A tall, thin man with a gun stood over her. He didn't resemble the man she had met, but she knew it was Blake. His face was a grotesque mask of scarlet and white, like raw meat and bone. Grace moved her arm and rolled her head to the side. Where was Jennie?

Blake turned and looked toward the house, and Bootie ducked to the side. When she peeked out again, he was speaking to Grace, but Bootie couldn't make out his words. Blake aimed the gun at Grace, who rolled over and clutched her head. Blake dropped his arm. He aimed the gun at Grace again.

Instinctively, Bootie grabbed the phone receiver and started to dial 911, but remembered the base was smashed open on the floor. She recalled Grace had an extension in her bedroom, and she turned toward the stairs, but a vision stopped her. A shape spun into the haunt of someone she had not seen in forty-five years. Bootie put her hand over her heart.

Mother looked young. And more beautiful than Bootie remembered. She had on a pink flowered dress under a white apron. Bootie whimpered. How she had missed her mother! How lonely her life had been without her. Tears filled her eyes. Mother held out a knife, as though Bootie was to take it from her. "Bootie, please. There's no time." Her mother's bright light threw the rest of the room into shadow, but when Bootie reached out to her there was nothing there. Mother's light

Laura Ginter 304

dimmed. Her words repeated in Bootie's mind. "There's no time."

"Where is Jennie?" Bootie asked the fading apparition. There wasn't a response. Her mother was gone.

Bootie swiped at her tears and hurriedly searched Grace's kitchen drawers for a knife, removing the largest she could find. She ran from the house to the back yard. Blake had his back to her. She shielded the knife under her arm. "Drop the gun, Blake."

Blake twisted with remarkable swiftness. He turned the gun on Bootie, and she saw her knife would be useless. He could kill her before she could take two steps. From the corner of her eye, she saw Grace pull her legs up under her. Police sirens were blaring in the distance. Bootie latched on to her unexpected opportunity. "The police are coming," she said. "Put the gun down."

Blake smirked. "Are you Amanda's mother? You're too late. I'm taking her with me."

As he pointed the gun back at Grace, ribbons of blackness wound around Bootie, binding her like a rope and blinding her. Through the blackness came Clark. "Hurry, Bootie!" he said. Bootie's heart pounded as though it would burst from her chest. She tried to push through the blackness and touch her brother, but stopped. Harley was behind him. Harley lifted his arm. He was holding the Luger. Harley put the gun to Clark's head and pulled the trigger. Bootie tasted blood. Clark and Harley splintered into sparkly shards and fell to the ground like rain.

Bootie's eyes cleared, and she was facing Blake again. He was still pointing the gun at Grace. He turned his head back toward Bootie, and grinned broadly, but it wasn't Blake's face mocking her. It was Harley Boggs. His wicked grin scorned her. "Sissy girl," he said to her. "You're a gutless jellyfish. A scared little bunny rabbit. Run away, Sissy girl. Save yourself."

Bootie's head swelled with red rage. A rage that came

How to Dance on the Moon 305

from a lifetime of loneliness and relentless guilt and repressed anger. Of shadowy haunts and nightmarish visions and isolation. She charged at Blake and plunged the knife into his arm. His mouth fell open. He dropped the gun and Bootie kicked it away. Blake stared at the knife. Blood dripped down his arm. Bootie took a step toward Grace, but Blake blocked her path. He looked at her, as though he were really seeing her for the first time and his face tightened. He snarled and pulled the knife from his arm. The sirens continued to grow louder. Blake brandished the knife in the air and stepped toward Bootie, looming larger and larger over her.

A small, brown rabbit hopped onto the grass and twitched its white tail. A shot rang out. Then another, more muted gunshot. The knife fell to the ground as Blake grappled Bootie. Blood spurted from his nose and mouth, and he grinned with the arrogant pleasure of someone who had beaten a hated rival. Over his shoulder Bootie saw Grace standing beside the pit, her legs spread, arms outstretched with Blake's gun held in both hands. Jennie was there too, standing to her mother's side, also with a gun in her hand. Jennie dropped her gun on the grass. Police cars screeched into the driveway.

Bootie's eyes clouded, and her vision faded. She and Blake fell to the ground together in a twisted embrace. She saw blood and then black.

42.

Grace watched in horror as Jennie dropped the gun. Blake and Aunt Bootie toppled into a twisted pile of arms and legs. Police circled the scene with guns drawn. An officer rushed to Jennie and lifted her into his arms. Grace flung Blake's gun into the garden bed, and she tried to run to her aunt, but her knee,

Laura Ginter 306

throbbing with pain, gave out, and she fell beside the policeman who was separating Bootie from Blake.

Aunt Bootie groaned. Blood and white chunks of skull were splattered over her hair and face, as well as the lawn. Grace looked to see Blake, blood dripping from his eyes, nose and mouth. Along with the coppery odor of the blood, she smelled urine. Grace's throat tightened, and she gagged. A policeman pulled her back. The yard spun and disappeared.

When Grace came to, she was stretched out on the grass. Someone was cradling her head as a medic took her pulse. She heard someone say, "Not all gunshot wounds to the head will kill you. He was lucky."

"She's awake," said the medic. "Hi, there."

Grace tilted her head up to look at the medic. "Where's my daughter?" Her heart raced as the medic helped her sit. "Where's Jennie? Where's my little girl? I need to see her!"

Biscuit appeared at Grace's side. "She's safe. She's in the house with a police woman."

"Ow! My head!"

"Sorry," said the medic. "We need to clean this gash."

"Biscuit?"

He squatted beside her and took her hand. "They don't want Jennie out here until they have removed the body."

"Who called you?"

"No one. I called you. Jennie answered, from your bedroom I think, and told me Blake was here."

"She did?" Everything that had happened after Blake walked into her house was muddled in Grace's mind. But one fact was clear. Blake was dead! He had dropped his gun and she had shot him. But Jennie had shot him, too. "Biscuit, don't let the police talk to Jennie. Don't let them take her away. Tell them I shot Blake." The yard started spinning again.

"Be still," said the medic. "You might have a concussion."

"Where's Aunt Bootie?"

"I'm here, Grace." Aunt Bootie lowered herself on to the

How to Dance on the Moon 307

ground beside her. The blood had been rinsed from her face, but some was still in her hair. Her right hand hung limp at her side.

"You're hurt!"

Bootie nodded. "Stabbing people is harder than it looks."

"You stabbed Blake? I didn't even know you were here until I saw you fall. You could have been shot!"

"But I wasn't shot."

The policeman came back into Grace's view. "Ambulances are coming."

Grace tried to stand, but the medic pulled her back. "Please be still."

"No!" Grace protested. She looked up into Biscuit's eyes. "I must see Jennie with my own eyes. I need to see she's not hurt. And I need to know where she found that gun before the police talk to her."

"They've talked to her," Biscuit said. "It was your gun. From your safe."

Biscuit's words shocked Grace. "That's impossible."

"It's true, Grace," Bootie said. "But her shot missed Blake. She didn't hit him."

A shadow fell over Grace. She looked up to see Jennie staring at her, a cobalt blue teddy bear tucked into her side. Grace grabbed her daughter by the arms and hugged her to her chest. "You're okay! Thank God! They let you out of the house?"

"I pretended to go to the bathroom." Jennie pulled herself free of her mother's grasp and stood over her. "Mommy, I saved you with our gun."

Grace clutched her daughter's hand. "How did you get the gun out of a locked safe?"

"I closed my eyes and turned the knob to the secret numbers. Left-right-left."

"How did you know the numbers?"

"Wally told them to me. Wally said I had to shoot Blake so

Laura Ginter 308

he wouldn't shoot you. He was mad because Blake came four times before I made him dead."

"Wally? The pig in the bushes at Tiny Tots told you to do it?"

"Yes. Wally said Blake was scary bad."

A shiver coursed through Bootie's body. Dear God. Jennie had the gift! A policeman took Bootie by the elbow. "Can you answer some questions?" Bootie nodded, and the policeman led her back into the house. His pager beeped as he pulled up a chair in the kitchen for her. He glanced at his pager and said, "I will be right back."

Bootie nodded. Her heart ached, thinking about Jennie. The little girl had opened Grace's safe by following the directions of a pig living in the bushes at the daycare. Mother could open safes. And Wally the pig sounded too much like Grace's closet troll and her own monkey-beast to be a coincidence. A wet piece of paper was sticking out from under her shoe, and Bootie bent to pick it up. When she looked at it, Blake's cocky smirk and wide-set cat eyes looked back at her. His expression matched the one he wore when he died. It was a look of smug success. She dropped it back on the floor.

The phone began to ring. Bootie glanced over at the broken receiver across the room. She rose and stepped over to the counter to the handset. It was flashing. She lifted it and put it to her ear.

"Hello, Aunt Bootie. This is Stan Bean." The voice was slow and monotonic with a funny accent. "You know who I am, don't you? I am your niece, I am your mother, I am your grandmother. Blake is dead, and we all wear his blood instead of Grace's. You all did good, so I'm going away, for now. Watch over Jennie. Teach her all about me."

43.

Lunch was over, and Bootie had talked Erline into a walk along Alki beach. Erline glanced over at Bootie, hustling along at a steady clip, arms swinging. "I'm proud of you," Erline said. "You've been talking about walking, and here you are doing it."

"Three days last week and now today. I'm feeling positively virtuous! Goodbye fat-butt."

The air was chilled by a brisk sea breeze, and they both had started their walk with warm jackets, but Bootie now wore hers tied around her waist. She enjoyed looking at the glittery Seattle skyline to the left, and the million dollar condominiums with the weathered beach houses squeezed between on her right.

Erline nudged Bootie. "So are you ready to talk about what happened?"

Bootie smiled at her friend. "You're just itching to know if I had a vision when Blake died."

Erline looked hurt. "No! I'm worried about you. You have never touched someone at the moment he died. It could have gone badly."

Bootie snorted. "Well, I did learn something. I learned dying hurts, the way you would imagine a lightening bolt hurts. Then there's nothing. No regrets, no joy. No God, no friend to greet you at a light of a tunnel. No graceful transition into another universe or dimension. No Elvis. No answers."

"It was someone else's death. Sounds like at the time of passing, you got cut from the process."

Bootie kicked a rock in her path. "But what if there's nothing? I thought death moved us through to God. I've always seen my gift as a long, thick rope that connects this world to His world, and I have spent my life dealing with what I thought slipped up and down that rope between those worlds. The visions, the shadows, the fairy sparkles, the nasty séance spirits. Sometimes, when I was little, I would stare into the eyes of a haunt, and I would search for God in its needy, twisted face, wondering if it was doing the same to me. And I prayed for my parents to stop stealing, for Harley Boggs to go away, for my brother Scooter to lose his crutches, for Eddie to love me again. All those prayers were answered in ways that made everything worse. I was angry at Him for a long time."

Erline slowed her pace. "I don't think God minds if you are angry with Him if it gets you where you need to be. He gave you a gift that has forced you to forge a lonely path without any roadmaps."

"But that's my point. What if my gift is not from God? What if it comes from someone else or some other place? It shows itself in the most grotesque ways, monkey beasts and troll and snakes. And terrible things happen. It has always felt more like a curse than a blessing. One of my grandmothers was accused of being a witch. My mother died in a prison psychiatric ward. Stan Bean was a nightmare for Grace, and I have suffered with loss all my life. Do you think my gift could come from evil?"

Erline shook her head. "No, Bootie! Your gift is not evil. It comes from God, and His gift to you is incredible. He gave it to you because He has special plans for you. He wants you to do great things. He has set a high bar for you, but He knows you can handle it, that you'll figure it out."

"Then what do you think He wants me to figure out?"

"Among other things, how to forgive yourself, and love yourself."

"Seriously? You think forgiveness and love is what all this is about?"

"Seriously!"

"You should write greeting cards."

"Bootie, be nice. Swing your arms harder, if you want to make your walk count for something."

"I look silly enough swinging them this much. I'm too fat."

"Bootie, don't be so hard on yourself. Let's change the

How to Dance on the Moon   311

subject. How is Grace?"

"Grace doesn't believe she created Stan Bean, but she accepts Jennie's gift, and knows I can help her with it. Maybe I can lessen Jennie's struggle and spare her some unhappiness. Maybe she'll be the one to do great things. Otherwise, Grace is working through everything. She has started counseling with Janet. That will help."

"So Grace is moving forward. Can you?"

Bootie snorted. "How? By forgiving and loving myself?"

"By walking faster so you don't miss your appointment."

Bootie glanced at her watch. "Yikes!"

Erline laughed and lengthened her stride. Bootie swung her arms jauntily to keep up.

****

Back at the tearoom, the women set their jackets on a chair near the hostess stand and entered the kitchen. "Bobby, why are you still here?" asked Bootie.

"I'm cleaning the cooler. Have a good walk?"

"Yes," said Erline, "and I'm ready for some tea. What about you, Bootie?"

"No tea for me." Bootie said, and snatched a chocolate muffin off the dessert tray.

Erline rolled her eyes. "Bootie! What about fat-butt?"

"I exercised! It's okay to eat now!"

Erline took the muffin from Bootie and pushed her toward the stairs. "Go change. It's almost five. I'll make tea and guard your muffin."

Bootie climbed the stairs to her apartment and pulled slacks and a sweater from her dresser. She went to the window to draw the shade. Movement in the corner drew her eye. A shadow had wedged itself between the wall and her nightstand. In no mood for a creepy little haunt, she flicked her wrist at it, but instead of vanishing, it began to shrink in size. A

Laura Ginter 312

recognizable shape emerged.

"Mrs. Wallaby! How did you get in here?" Bootie changed clothes, and then tucked Mrs. Wallaby under her arm and took her downstairs to the kitchen. Bobby took the rabbit and promised to feed her before he left.

Bootie found Erline in the dining room with a cup of tea and the chocolate muffin. She sat across from her friend, picked off a corner of the muffin and popped it into her mouth. "I hate my gift."

"Now why?"

"The other day I told Grace about my vision of Eddie being alive after I was told he had died. She challenged my decision not to look for him, and that forced me to revisit all the old questions that stopped me from having a good night's sleep for years."

"What questions?" Erline asked.

"Did I let Eddie down? Could he still be alive? Could he still need me?"

Erline patted Bootie's arm. "You did the right thing at the time."

"But is always doing the right thing, the right thing to do?" Bootie popped more muffin in her mouth.

Erline smirked. "When are you going to start looking for him?"

"Not today. I have something else to do."

The bell on the front door jingled. "My appointment," said Bootie. The women rose and crossed the room to greet Ashley and Polly with enthusiastic hugs.

"Miss Bootie invited me and Polly to dinner," said Ashley to her grandmother as she removed her coat. "She said she'd read our tea leaves."

Erline turned to Bootie and frowned. "You've started reading tea leaves?"

Bootie waved Erline off. "All good psychotics should be able to do at least that." She led the girls to the garden window

How to Dance on the Moon   313

table. "I'll get your tea. Dinner will be here soon. Something I know you will enjoy."

As if on cue, the bell on the front door jingled again. In came a young man with red hair pointing in every direction, carrying a large blue vinyl pizza carrier. He grinned at Bootie. "Hello, Mrs. Baxter!"

Bootie took him by the elbow and led him across the room. "Gavin, set the pizza here, please. These are my friends Ashley and Polly. Girls, this is Gavin."

Ashley smiled politely, but Polly's cheeks flushed like two plums as she giggled and stole a glance at Gavin from under her eyelashes. "You look familiar," said Polly. Her voice was dulcet and high-pitched. "Do I know you from school?"

"You're in Smith's Intro to Psych class. You sit next to the kid who wears the red scarf and always argues about his quiz scores."

Gavin removed the pizza from the carrier, and the three began chatting among themselves, their conversation taking a turn into topics foreign to Bootie and Erline. Polly's hand brushed across Gavin's elbow.

Erline walked over to Bootie and put her arm around her shoulders. "That's the boy you saw in your vision of Polly, isn't it? The boy she's going to marry. Tell me. Will they live happily ever after?"

Bootie sighed, then smiled. "You know, we Kurz's don't have much experience with happily-ever-after, but I believe they will do better than most."

Bootie and Erline returned to their own table. Gavin wouldn't be able to stay long, and for Bootie's plan to work, he and the two girls needed time apart from the nosy grandma and her old friend with the bulbous rear end.

As Bootie broke off another piece of muffin, a sudden gloominess overcame her. The last few weeks had been difficult. If having a deranged murderer stalking Grace wasn't bad enough, she had been forced to relive some dreadful

Laura Ginter 314

memories, and question her gift's true nature. Yet, despite her low spirits, she had achieved something great. By saving Grace, she had thrown herself into the fire and proved her bravery. Had she learned how to dance on the moon? She didn't think so. Was Erline right? Did she still have to learn to love herself? To forgive herself? Bootie sighed. Maybe she just needed to be easier on herself. How many times had Erline told her to do just that?

"You're so quiet," Erline said. "Are you okay?"

Bootie shrugged. "Should we check on Mrs. Wallaby?"

Erline studied Bootie quizzically. "Tell me Bootie, how do you think Mrs. Wallaby can jump four feet in the air to the top of the prep table without anyone ever seeing her do it?"

Bootie thought about that. "I don't know."

"Why hasn't the clock on the signpost outside ever stopped? And why does your teapot glow for no reason?"

Bootie shrugged. "If I was a person who needed a logical explanation for everything, I would have really gone insane."

Erline looked up at the yellow teapot, sitting on the shelf across the room. "Bootie, I've never seen you take your teapot off that shelf."

"It makes me sad to touch it."

"Sad, because your mother gave it to you?"

"No, sad because the teapot itself is sad. Looking at it gives me all the pleasure I need. Did you know I have a lock of Clark's hair in there?"

"You told me. Have you ever received a vision of Clark from the hair in the teapot?"

"No, but I have seen other things, hard to understand but unpleasant."

Erline grabbed Bootie's hand and squeezed it affectionately. "You don't see as much if you only see what you can understand. Isn't it better to see as much as you can of life's juicy little quirks?"

Bootie shrugged. "And speaking of juice, I think I will have

How to Dance on the Moon 315

some tea. Would you like some more?"

"No, let's open a box of Chablis."

Bootie smiled in spite of herself. Erline always knew how to cheer her up.

The End

Made in the USA
San Bernardino, CA
13 October 2016